FAEWOLF

by
D. M. Atkins
and
Chris Taylor

Circlet Press, Inc.
Cambridge, MA

Faewolf
by D. M. Atkins and Chris Taylor
Published by Circlet Press, Inc.

Copyright © 2009 by D. M. Atkins and Chris Taylor
Cover art © 2009 by Ponderosa

ISBN 978-1-885865-67-0

Circlet Press has specialized in erotic science fiction since 1992. Traditionally printed books, ebooks, and print on demand editions of many other Circlet Press erotic science fiction titles can be pur-chased through fine bookstores, online retailers, and through the Circlet Press website at www.circlet.com.

For a printed catalog, academic reading copies, or other informa-tion, please write to us at

Circlet Press
39 Hurlbut Street
Cambridge, MA 02138

To my beloved husbands, Troy and Lon.
Your love continues to inspire me every day.

DMA

Prologue

Saoi was a lone wolf.

Humans seemed to think that was sexy. It implied independence and daring and all kinds of alluring things to them.

That wasn't the way the wolves saw it. His elders had taught him that a lone wolf was barely still a wolf. Without a mate, his pack, and the clan, a wolf would soon forget what it meant to be a wolf.

To be a wolf was to be a creature of not just field and forest, but of kin and family. Each wolf was devoted to the others of his pack. Hunting together was a combination of different strengths and efforts, with some wolves tracking, some faster and hounding, and other, stronger wolves breaking bones and making the kill. A lone wolf could kill only the smallest and weakest of prey. A lone wolf usually went hungry. A pack could feed and then return to rest in warm groups of fur and body heat in dens that had been used for generations. A lone wolf huddled under brambles, subject to the whims of weather. A pack was full of play and games-affectionate nips, games of tag, wrestling and rolling around. It was a family with pups who squealed and climbed over everyone in the pack, making life feel lighter and warmer. In the pack, every scent had an origin and a name-the smell and taste and sight of every member was intimately known, immediately recognized.

If tragedy struck and a wolf lost his pack—these days that usually meant to the guns of humans—then he sought out a new one.

Either he joined an existing one, even if it meant a loss in status, or he found a mate and started a new one. Only when there was no other choice did a wolf remain alone. It was said that if a wolf was alone too long, he stopped being a wolf; that he lost his way, dying in spirit if not in the flesh.

Saoi had done the unthinkable. He had left his pack. Not to find a mate, but to find an answer. The clans were dying. Each year packs grew smaller; the litters produced fewer pups and there was more strife among them. He'd left his own pack to save this race-to find a solution to the slow death of the Faewolves.

There were often times, though, when Saoi believed his elders were right. He ran all night in the dark woods that were bright with scents and sound, large paws digging into the earth at the thrill of chasing deer. He reveled in the pungent smell of blood, the feel of fur and flesh ripping under his teeth and the taste of fresh wild meat as he gulped it down. He sniffed and marked his boundaries with his own pungent scent. Saoi did everything he could to remember the things that made him a wolf. Yet, it wasn't enough. Loneliness was eating him up inside, starving him as surely and slowly as a lack of meat. Sometimes when he woke alone and cold, he lay whimpering in his den like a wounded pup, wishing for the comfort of another-aching for the touch of a muzzle against his own, for the languid feeling of sleeping between other warm bodies, limbs all tangled up and nose nestled in the scruff of a pack-mate. Saoi was desperate for the sounds and smells and feelings of belonging.

He'd learned to blend in, to act like the humans, but he wasn't one of them. He had to keep his distance to keep his secret. He knew what he'd been taught. How the humans would hunt them down and slaughter them all if they knew. And, in the time he'd spent among them, he had seen no reason to doubt that. It didn't stop the longing he felt, however, when he saw groups of them together, touching in ways that reminded him of the comfort of a pack. It ate away at part of him every time he had to force himself to hold back, to not touch or get too close.

6

Chapter One

Kiya White Cloud sighed tiredly and tossed his waist-length, dark brown hair back over his shoulder, before beginning the climb up the concrete stairs to the third floor of the five story building. His dorm room was in the last apartment building, at the top of the hill of the college, bordering the redwood forest. His suitcase dragging behind him, Kiya listened absently to the smacking sounds it made as it clunked up each stair.

The plane trip back from South Dakota to California had gone a little easier than the first time, since he now knew what to expect. He was getting used to the transition between Deadwood and the university. For that, Kiya was grateful. After getting off of the plane, he picked up his things from the baggage claim area and took an airport shuttle over the mountain to Santa Cruz. It dropped him in the downtown area, on the Pacific Garden Mall, and from there he'd had to take a bus up to campus and to College Ten where his room was. It was a long trip and by the time he was among the redwood trees on campus, he was worn out.

Kiya reached his floor and the wheels of his suitcase clicked as he made his way along the corridor toward his dorm room.

"Don't you look edible?" a male voice purred.

Kiya froze and looked up to find Ted, Kiya's recently ex-boyfriend, leaning against a nearby doorway, smiling over at him. Ted was tall, blond and muscular with the kind of dominant attitude that Kiya found hot. Unfortunately, Ted was an asshole.

"Fuck, Ted, what are you doing here?"

"Waiting for you, baby," Ted drawled, pushing off of the door jam and reaching a hand for Kiya. He flashed him his winning smile.

Kiya took a step back, shaking his hair out of his face. "Why?" Kiya asked. He had broken up with Ted just before leaving for Spring Break. Seeing the man again was one of the things that Kiya had been dreading.

Ted stepped closer. "Don't be that way," he chided, reaching to stroke Kiya's hair.

"Why are you here?" Kiya demanded, leaning away from his hand, heart speeding up in confusion and anger. "You know what I told you before."

Ted didn't flinch but leaned in, cupping Kiya's cheek with his hand. "I've missed you, and I know you miss me too," he insisted.

Kiya flinched. Did Ted actually think that he could change his mind like that? Well, apparently he did, and really, it wasn't all that surprising. Ted always thought he could persuade him to do anything, and Kiya didn't even realize what he was doing until after they had broken up. None of that mattered now, Kiya didn't want to hear anything Ted had to say. He wouldn't go back to him. Not this time. "I don't miss you, actually," Kiya insisted, backing up again and finding himself up against the metal railing. "We're not together anymore, Ted."

"Aww, I know you weren't serious about that," Ted chided. "Everyone knows we belong together." He gave Kiya a playful grin that had usually worked to get Kiya to relent when they had argued.

"If we belonged together, you would've stopped when I said to, and you would have listened to me about using a condom," Kiya argued, flushing with embarrassment and anger at the memory.

"You're still sore about that?" Ted asked with a tone that was incredulous. He moved after Kiya again, taking the Kiya's hand. "And we both know that you enjoyed it."

"That's not the point!" Kiya exclaimed, yanking his hand away. "I told you to stop, and you didn't. Doesn't matter whether or not you think I liked it."

"Now how was I supposed to know you were serious with your cock all hard and that beautiful ass wriggling," Ted protested. "You can't blame me for not being able to keep my hands off you. It's not my fault that you make me lose control, Kiya."

"Just go away," Kiya demanded, crossing his arms over his chest. Ted just didn't seem to get it. It had nothing to do with the way his body reacted. It was the way Ted treated him. "Now."

Ted clucked his tongue. "I suppose I should give you a few more days to calm down," he said, shaking his head and then fixing his eyes on Kiya's. "You belong to me, baby; I'm not giving up on us."

"Too bad. I already have," Kiya said quietly, refusing to give in. He wanted to be brave, to stand up for himself this time. "Now go."

Ted shook his head again, moving toward the stairs. "See you soon, my pretty boy," he insisted, and then he was gone.

Kiya leaned against the rail for another moment, trying to calm down, but then hurried to the apartment, deciding not to risk Ted coming back. Kiya wondered why he seemed to be a magnet for bad guys, and his plan this year was to stop that once and for all. He was going to start looking for guys that had a decent personality as well and not just base everything on how good they were in bed or how gorgeous they were. No more men who just wanted Kiya for his looks. Kiya sighed again. Ted was officially the worst mistake he had made here so far.

No one was in the front room, but since there was already a pizza box on the coffee table, Kiya figured someone else was home. At least he hoped the pizza box was recent. There were four other people who lived in his two-bedroom apartment with him, including his roommate, James Miller, which was just fine with Kiya, because that meant it wasn't as crowded as a regular dorm but he still had people to hang out with. And there were seldom long lines for the bathroom. Actually, he had to admit that he was probably the only guy in the apartment that took more than ten minutes in there, it seemed.

Kiya made his way to his bedroom, noticing that the door was closed, which might have meant that James was in. He wasn't even sure if his roommate had gone home over the break or not. But if he had, it was still early on Sunday and not all the students had gotten back just yet. As he thought of this, he walked up to the door and began pushing it open, only to gasp and freeze in the doorway.

James was lying in bed-naked. Even worse, sitting atop him was a red-headed girl-also naked. The two of them were making particularly obscene sounds as she bounced, obviously having the time of her life. Now, Kiya had seen James naked more than once and, yes, he was good looking with his almost always styled brown hair and light blue eyes. If it had not been for his attitude and, well, obvious heterosexuality, Kiya would have flirted with him every chance he got. But now, no, now wasn't a good time, and he did not want to see the naked girl on top of him. Not that he hadn't seen women naked before, it just wasn't something he particularly enjoyed looking at.

"Fuck, James!" Kiya yelled, turning away quickly, but the image was already burned into his mind. Unfortunately.

"Key, what are you doing back?" James asked, as if he was in the middle of a television show instead of sex. The girl squeaked and grabbed the blanket.

"It's, uh, the end of vacation, you jerk," Kiya replied, his back to them. He couldn't stand that James was taking this so lightly, like it was nothing! He also hated it when he called him Key. Kiya was a short enough name, it didn't need a nickname.

"Can you come back later, Key?" James asked, still cheerful.

"I seem to have no fucking choice. And don't call me Key!" Kiya hissed, stepping back out and slamming the door closed behind him. He huffed and set his suitcase down next to the door. "What a great start to the new quarter," he muttered.

From the sounds that came drifting out, James and the girl had gone back to whatever it was they had been doing before the interruption.

The door to the other room opened and Joe came out. "Hey, Kiya. What's up?"

Kiya looked up and, despite being annoyed at James, smiled a little. "Hey, Joey," he said. "How was your spring break?"

Joseph Swartz, more affectionately known as Joey, was one of Kiya's first friends when he moved to the campus. He was nice, very easy to talk to, good looking, and he didn't piss Kiya off. That made him good enough in Kiya's mind. He had kind of hoped that they would have been roommates, but Joey shared the triple room with Derrick and Miguel. "I stayed here and got to spend every day surfing," Joe said, grinning and flopping onto the sofa beside Kiya.

"Sounds like fun. Weren't you going to teach me?" Kiya asked, raising an eyebrow as he made a point of shifting closer. Technically he had heard that Joey was straight, as were most of the guys he knew, but he couldn't help flirting just a little. It came naturally.

"Sure, any time," Joey said "How was your trip home?"

And of course, just like always, Joey seemed to not notice Kiya's advances. Either he really didn't notice, or he just ignored them. "It was great," Kiya told him, smiling. "Missed my parents more than I thought I would. And it was wonderful getting to see my brother and sister and my grandparents."

Joe gave him one of those looks that implied Kiya spoke a different language. "Visiting my parents wouldn't be my idea of a fun spring break."

"Not the only difference between you and me," Kiya laughed, glad to have this distraction while he waited for James to finish. "Hey, you wouldn't happen to know when that girl came here?"

"Thursday," Joey huffed and rolled his eyes.

"And they've been in the room ever since?" Kiya sighed, glancing down at his watch.

"I wish. They come out for food and television," Joe answered.

"Well, now that I'm back, things will obviously change. I'll give them another five minutes, tops." Yes, he had been kicked out of the room once before so that James could 'take care' of himself. He timed it, of course. Kiya was not going to put up with this shit. No, he was going to give James hell for the rest of the quarter, and he'd do it with a smile on his face.

Joe gave him a look. "Do that and you are my hero," he answered.

Kiya waved it off. "I'll let him have his fun for now," he said. "For now."

Joe huffed with a nod, picked up the TV remote and turned it on.

∾

Kiya had to rush the next morning to get to his biology class in time to grab a seat in the front row. The mammoth building was like a huge concrete set of building blocks-set in the middle of the woods. But at least it wasn't far from his dorms. Kiya trudged up the stairs to the lecture hall entrance, which was at the back of the large slanted room. He made his way down another set of stairs to the front of the hall. Dropping his back-pack onto the chair next to him, he started to pull his books out just as the professor began speaking. Kiya tried not to show how grumpy he was about being up so early for a nine o'clock class, but he was failing, slouching in his chair with a frown as he took notes. He glanced up from his notebook when the professor began to introduce the graduate students who would be work-ing with the class.

"Your teaching assistants this term will be Rachael Burrows, Darren Turner and Brian Fenwick," Professor Steinhart was explaining and then going through the instructions of how to sign up for specific sections.

When Kiya looked at the TAs, he felt a frisson of unexpected pleasure. His attention was riveted on Brian Fenwick. Brian looked to be in his mid-twenties, and was probably six feet tall. He had short red-brown hair, a slightly tanned complexion and looked lean and muscular, filling out the button-down work blue shirt and 501 jeans in a way that made them look oddly more fashionable than the designer jeans and t-shirts most students wore. He wasn't just attractive, he had an intensity that captured Kiya's attention. The man shifted under the attention of the students, head turned a bit to the side. He had a physical presence that made Kiya want to reach out and touch him.

The teaching assistants, including Fenwick, went to take their seats at the other end of the front row and the professor began his lecture. Kiya couldn't take his eyes off of Brian, willing the man to look at him now. Kiya knew about the rule prohibiting teachers from dating students, but that didn't stop him from looking. And he was frustrated that the man didn't seem to notice him at all. Fenwick glanced his direction several times but didn't look directly at Kiya.

The professor talked about the syllabus and what they should expect in the class. It actually didn't sound as difficult as Kiya had thought it would be. He'd just have to keep up with his notes and read the book. But he had to admit that he wasn't giving the instructor up front his complete attention as he angled his body in his attempts to see more of one particular T.A.

With more than a hundred students all trying to sign up for sections, Kiya had to struggle just to get to the wall with the sign-up sheets on them. Once he finally reached the wall, two of Brian's sections were filled out, completely full. The last one was close to being filled up, and Kiya quickly went about writing his name down, restraining himself from writing more-like his phone number. It was only when he stepped back that he realized the time of the section, making him curse under his breath. Friday, at nine in the morning again! Friday was to be Kiya's day off; a day he was looking forward to just sleeping in. He glanced back at Fenwick thinking that he had better be worth it.

Fenwick was sitting at a table at the front of the room surrounded by half a dozen other students, apparently answering questions. Kiya couldn't help notice the way some of the girls were looking at the gorgeous man. Which only annoyed him further. That was it-he wasn't going to wait until Friday to meet Brian. He pulled his book bag up onto his shoulder and went back to the table, carefully pushing his way through the other students so that he was directly in front of the TA. He ignored the sounds of discontent, holding his hand out for Brian to shake.

"Professor Fenwick, I'm Kiya White Cloud, and I'm looking forward to taking your section," he said, making sure to give him a brilliant smile.

Brian looked startled and some of the other students snickered. But the man took Kiya's hand. "Just call me Brian. I'm not a professor, just a graduate student." He smiled and Kiya could see his eyes were brown, a kind of light brown that almost made them look golden-like dark amber. Brian's own glance into Kiya's eyes was brief and then he quickly looked away, his face appearing flushed.

Kiya could almost get lost in those eyes, thinking that Brian looked even better up close. So maybe sacrificing his day off would be worth it. "Brian," he repeated, nodding as his hand tightened around the man's slightly. "I'll have to remember that."

Brian gave Kiya's hand a little squeeze as he let go. "You had a question?"

"Ah, no, just wanted to tell you that I'm looking forward to Friday now," Kiya said, unable to think of a quick question. Usually he was able to come up with something cool to say under any circumstances, but apparently not today. Brian gave him an odd glance but didn't say anything as several other students began asking the teaching assistant questions about the field trip aspects of the sections.

Kiya stayed around to listen to that, thinking that he really would enjoy the class and not only because of the teacher. Going on trips in the woods around the school? Now that would be fun, and much better than going alone. He learned from the discussion with a couple of students that Brian was an experienced hiker and climber, though he would be "keeping it light" for the sections.

Kiya didn't think that he'd have to take it lightly, but he supposed the rest of the class couldn't say the same. He had had enough practice at home; he'd walked a lot, went both hiking and horse-back riding. Sometimes he went with his father to the Black Hills, and sometimes he went alone. Maybe he'd tell Brian about that on Friday. Then they could go hiking ... just the two of them. He could imagine them stopping in the middle of woods for a little "rest and relaxation." Yeah, sure. He'd probably push him down on the grassy ground and suck Brian off until he was screaming his name. He smirked at the thought, probably being too optimistic, but it was fun to imagine.

While Kiya was daydreaming about being alone with Brian, the man slung his backpack onto his shoulder and explained to the milling students that he needed to go. The next class was about to start anyway, so it was time to leave. Kiya snapped out of his daydream and moved to leave the room, clutching his books to his chest. He had a small break before his next class, sociology, so he headed back to his dorm room.

When Kiya got back to the apartment, James wasn't there. Nor, luckily, was his new girlfriend, but their were clothes strewn all over the floor of the room. It didn't bother Kiya, since they weren't his clothes. If James didn't bug him so much, he might have picked them up for him and put them on the other guy's bed, but yeah, not going to happen. He set his books down on his desk and kicked his shoes off, pulling his hair up into a pony-tail before he went through his drawer to pull out his bag of hard candy. He always had to have one, so his mother made sure to send him off with at least one full bag. He looked through it for a moment and then pulled out a cherry flavored lollipop, pulling the wrapper off and moving back to lie down on his bed as he popped it in his mouth.

He let his thoughts stray to the memory of Brian when his cell phone chirped. He had downloaded a ring-tone that sounded like a bird. He pulled it out of his pocket and flipped it open. "Hi," he said around the candy in his mouth.

"Hi, baby," Ted said.

Kiya groaned, pulling the lollipop out of his mouth. "No," he said.

"Come on, sweet thing," Ted insisted. "I'm right outside. Let's go to lunch."

"Leave me alone," Kiya pleaded and snapped the phone shut. He didn't know how much clearer he could be with Ted. Kiya popped the lollipop back into his mouth, finding it comforting as he lay back again.

⌒

The rest of the week was a typical first week of classes. With only ten weeks in the quarter, things started quicker than most schools and Kiya already had too much homework. Even so, he was actually kind of bored with most of his classes. Except, of course, for biology class, where he couldn't take his eyes off that hot TA.

Ted called Kiya's cell phone over and over again, but Kiya never answered. He didn't even listen to the messages, just deleted them. He nearly called his mom to complain about it, but the last thing he wanted was for her to be worried about him. She was worried enough with him being so far away.

Finally Friday, the day Kiya had been looking forward to the most. He woke up early that morning and was showered and dressed long before the other students that lived with him were even awake. He even did his hair, which took him nearly an hour to comb out and play with until it was straight and gleaming. He usually did it at most once a week, but today was particularly special.

Kiya made it to the new classroom early and took a seat in the front. Now all he had to do was wait for Fenwick.

Chapter Two

Brian Fenwick looked and acted the part of the diligent graduate student. It wasn't all an act. He worked extremely hard to keep up with his studies, research and teaching responsibilities. The trouble was that he had less time to do that in than most other young men his age. Because he wasn't a man. And he couldn't let himself forget that.

Where his fellow students probably spent their free time going to visit family or at the beach or out partying, Brian had divided his time between his work and the woods. He'd ventured far up the Santa Cruz Mountains, following the forest. This was only his second year in Santa Cruz and there was a lot of forest to explore. He had to keep most of the exploration to those hours after the sun went down, when he would be less likely to be seen. It didn't hinder him. His night vision was better than a human's and his other senses, hearing and smell in particular, were far beyond what humans could reach.

Sometimes he would hunt. Saoi, as he was known in his pack, couldn't kill too many animals in such a high population area, but he could follow their trails, the scent leading him on, stalking them quietly as he drew closer and then, when they finally got wind of him, his heart pumped exhilaration as he gave chase. He took in lungfuls of air as he dodged around trees and through brush in pursuit of prey. He thrilled at the intensity of the sensation when his teeth sunk through fur and into flesh, the pounding of the life's blood of the animal as it spurted down his throat, soaking his muzzle in warmth. Hunting helped keep his instincts sharp and it was the most relaxing thing Saoi knew. Deer in the area weren't the challenge that a moose or caribou would be, though. The only other real predator they had in Santa Cruz was the occasional mountain lion. Cars killed more of them than animals. Without a wolf pack to weed out the weak, the deer in his area were stupid and slow. Yet, hunting them still fed some of his needs.

Sometimes, when Saoi went far enough from his own den, he would allow himself the luxury of howling. He would take long full breaths and let the sound fill him, rising into the night air. It was inevitably mournful. Nothing was sadder than a solitary wolf howl. Humans probably thought it was simply another human playing around. Yet, doing it allowed a part of him to be more fully alive, to be a wolf again. And no matter how many times he reminded himself that there were no other wolves in the area, he was always listening, longing to hear an answering call.

Over the week of spring break, Saoi had gone nearly four days and nights without returning to human form. He'd slept in makeshift burrows in the day, digging holes under tree roots or into the sides of hills to curl into the sheltering earth. When night fell, he ran again. He knew the wavering heat image and unique scent of every kind of animal and plant in the redwoods.

Besides the danger of getting caught, he also had to remember that he was Brian Fenwick. Saoi didn't care about schedules or homework. As a wolf, he felt the natural rhythms of night and day, of seasons and weather. But to live as Brian, he had to remember things like calendars and clocks, to return to his den in time to prepare for the upcoming school term. After four days of immersion in his true form, Saoi reluctantly transformed himself and washed away all the wonderful scents of the woods.

Brian emerged again, sitting in a chair, turning on his computer and logging in to check email and voice messages. Professor Steinhart had scheduled a teaching assistants meeting for that Sunday and Brian needed to have his lesson guides for the field trips ready by then. With a long sigh, Brian pulled out the books and set to work.

❧

Monday morning had brought a surprise for Brian. He was,

thankfully, prepared for the class he was assisting and eager to begin working with students. He had made the proposal that he teach a very hands-on version of the sections, one that included actual field trips. Students could opt for other sections, but his would be geared towards those who wanted to get out and explore ecosystems on campus and at the beach. It was something he was very excited about.

Brian was gratified that his idea was greeted well, not only by Professor Steinhart, but by many of the students. What he hadn't really counted on was the reaction to his physical presence that a number of the young women, and one young man in particular, would have. Human flirting wasn't something Brian was very good at understanding, and certainly not something he did. He'd been away from his own kind a long time and it was tempting, but he didn't feel that he could safely get involved with a human, let alone a student.

Wolves were very direct and physical about their attentions. Humans had complicated rules that Brian still didn't understand very well. And one of those rules, he did know, was that a teaching assistant couldn't be involved with students in the class he taught. Brian tried very hard to follow the human rules. He didn't want the trouble that breaking them would bring, nor did he know when or how they could be broken without incurring punishment. So he did his best to ignore the advances directed his way.

One of the difficulties about it was that he could smell arousal in others. It was one of the stranger aspects of humans for him that they couldn't. He supposed they used flirting to find out what he knew just by inhaling-who was or was not interested. That made it a challenge for him to be suddenly surrounded by a group of people who were talking about his class but whose smells told him they wanted to touch him. And even more startling was that one of them was a beautiful young man.

When Brian had looked up into those green eyes, he had felt something in him falter. The wolf was awake. Brian barely suppressed a sharp intake of air as he struggled internally to push the wolf back without betraying who he really was. Usually, he was able to suppress that part of himself when at school. Yet there he was, palm sliding against the smooth skin of the young man's hand and those eyes meeting his and it was like Saoi was suddenly alert, trying to meet the challenge and pushing at his skin. Brian could feel the curiosity, the sudden want, the matching arousal as the wolf focused his attention on the scents fairly rolling off of the young man in waves of desire. The danger weaving in and out of the moment as the wolf locked in on the student and pushed harder was a wave of heat startling the teaching assistant. Brian withdrew his hand as quickly as he dared and tried to remember to speak. He managed, but it has been an effort.

Again, Wednesday morning, Brian could feel the boy's eyes on him and he tried to keep his face firmly turned away. It would not help to look at what he could not have. He needed to remember his work and his rules. He stole a few glances but thought he had managed to disguise his interest. The real test, he knew, would be the section Kiya had signed up for on Friday. He hoped the boy would realize it was impossible and let it go. Most students knew their teachers couldn't get involved with them. He hoped Kiya would realize this and back off. Or, at least, part of him did.

༄

Brian had gone early to the seminar room set aside for sections that Friday morning, and was startled to find any student already there, let alone Kiya. Suddenly tense and aroused, Brian tried to control his reactions. The very smell of the young man was a distraction, awakening parts of himself he did not bring to the human world. Brian knew he would need to remain alert and strong during this class.

"Uh, hi. Well, you're early," he said, going to the front of the room and setting his notes on the desk.

"Yes, I woke up early. I hope you don't mind," Kiya replied, leaning his cheek on his hand and smiling. Kiya greedily took in the sight of Brian, thinking he was even more gorgeous than he remembered.

Brian frowned. The young man's smile was dazzling. Brian looked down, forcing himself to try to ignore the way Kiya's gaze felt like a touch. He focused on his notes, turning and writing instructions on the white board.

Kiya drank in the sight of those long lean legs and that firm ass in tight jeans. "So, is this your first time teaching?" he asked, wanting to start a conversation before anyone else came in.

"No," Brian answered shortly, resisting the urge to turn around and look again. The hair on the back of his neck prickled. He was relieved when several more students arrived and he could turn his attention to them.

Kiya pouted slightly at the bland reply. "Damn," he murmured, beginning to worry that Brian just wasn't interested in him. For all Kiya knew, maybe Brian was married, even though he didn't see a ring. Or he was straight. Kiya made a face at that.

Brian waited until a couple minutes after start time and then began taking attendance. He couldn't help but let his eyes rest on Kiya when he called out the student's name. Kiya's high cheekbones and full lips might have been feminine on a woman, but Kiya gave them a strikingly masculine beauty. Yet, it wasn't just the physical attraction that affected Brian; there seemed to be something lurking behind those green eyes that called to him and to the wolf. It took a lot of effort not to let his gaze linger, and he was startled when he found himself wondering how that long brown hair would feel if he were to touch it, to run his hands through it.

"Here," Kiya answered with a grin. Now he was getting something ... finally. Not so straight or married after all, he thought. He leaned back in his chair, stretching for effect. He knew he had a great body and he really wanted Brian to get a good look.

"So, I am Brian Fenwick, your instructor for this section. I am a doctoral candidate in Ecology and Evolutionary Biology," he explained. "In addition to the text book, you should also have purchased *The Natural History of Santa Cruz*, a field guide you will be using to help with your lab."

Kiya pulled out his book, managing to keep his eyes on Brian the entire time he spoke. He thought he saw something when Brian looked at him.

"So this," Brian said as he handed a stack of papers to the nearest student, "has your reading assignments, papers and schedule of field trip locations and dates. Next week, we will be taking a hike into the forest in the upper campus. Make sure you have shoes with traction, long pants with socks because there is poison oak, a bottle of water, a pen or pencil and a notebook." Brian went step by step over the schedule, explaining the field trips and then answering questions about the readings and lectures that week. He found himself having to keep a running reminder in his head that teaching assistants could not be involved with their students.

Kiya only looked away to accept the paper from the student next to him, glancing down to look it over. Seemed simple enough, he thought. He looked for the first date that they'd go out and then returned his gaze to Brian, putting his attention back on him. He liked the way Brian took charge, his posture seemed strong and his tone commanding but gentle. Kiya smiled wistfully, imagining other things that voice might say.

Brian had found first sections to be a bit boring, usually just a chance to learn the names of students and go over things. But this time he found himself wishing this one could be that easy. This class was going to test his control. He glanced at Kiya again, a pleasant shiver down his spine when he did. The look in Kiya's eye brought the most inappropriate thoughts to mind and Brian looked quickly away. He would like to have made a run for it right after class, but, as the instructor, he had to stay after to answer questions.

Kiya was already thinking of the first trip. He'd have to be in the front, of course, the closest student to Brian. Now that was something else to look forward to. He smirked when Brian caught his eye, biting into the tip of his thumb. If only the man could read his thoughts. While the other students crowded around Brian, Kiya hung back, waiting for his chance to talk to him.

Finally, the last of the students were leaving but Brian realized, belatedly, that Kiya and he were going to be alone. "Um, Kiya, is it?"

"Yes, Kiya. Kiya White Cloud," he said, gathering up his things and then standing up. "And you're Brian. Not Professor Fenwick. Not yet." He started walking toward Brian's desk as he spoke, keeping the same calm attitude but adding a sway to his hips that he hoped was sexy.

Brian turned his back to Kiya, moving to erase the board and pack up his things. "Did you have a question?" He tried to keep it light, to pretend he couldn't smell the student's arousal-that the smell wasn't making his body tight with his own want.

"Are you married?" Kiya asked, getting straight to the point. Might as well get that question out of the way.

Brian frowned and tried not to think how much he would like to tell Kiya how not married he was. "Kiya, that's not an appropriate question to ask an instructor." Brian frowned, picking up his bag and throwing it over one shoulder. He knew that he needed to get out of there ... now.

"I'm only curious, Brian," Kiya said, blushing. He thought that it was a pretty good guess that Brian wasn't married and probably was attracted to him. "Well then. Since you don't seem to be very talkative today, I guess I'll see you next week. I'll have everything I'll need then. Promise."

Brian tried not to read anything into that statement but the look Kiya gave him didn't help. "Bye, Kiya," he said, and hurried out of the class, determined to take a cold shower as soon as possible.

Kiya grinned and watched him hurry off, slowly walking out

behind him. "He wants me," he murmured to himself. Kiya was on his way out of the building when he noticed the wall of photos. First a row of names and photos of all the professors, then, below that, the graduate students. Each graduate student had a page with four plastic slots for pictures. Some only had one picture, while others had three or more. Kiya scanned the row until he found the smiling face of Brian Fenwick. There were three pictures. Kiya glanced around to make sure no one was looking before slipping out the nicest one from the pocket and tucking it into his own pocket instead.

Chapter Three

Brian fled the building as soon as he could, the claustrophobic narrow halls making him want to howl with his pent up frustration as he headed for the parking garage nearby. He climbed into his battered white Ford truck and ended up sitting behind the wheel for several minutes, struggling to try to remember how to drive. Maybe if he changed form and went running in the woods, he could let go of these unaccustomed urges. He finally started the truck and headed off campus, turning up the twisting path of Empire Grade. With the forest on both sides, he continued the two miles up until he drove past the llama ranch and finally found the small road, really an unmarked gravel drive, that led back to the cabin he rented. It was a one-room structure with electricity and not much else. He'd rigged a shower outside from a nearby well. It was a cold shower, but it never bothered him. And, at the moment, he thought it might actually help.

Brian threw his bag and keys aside and then stripped as quickly as he could, padding to the back to stand under the frigid spray. His skin felt flushed and the cold was soothing. Finally, shaking water out of his red-brown hair, he shifted into wolf form and headed into the woods. He ran. He ran until he was tired, before making his way back and collapsing onto the pillow covered mattress on the floor of his cabin.

∽

Saoi growled, his haunches rubbing against the back of the boy's thighs as he slid inside him, the tight wet channel making him shudder in pleasure. The boy beneath him whimpered, not in pain, but in obvious enjoyment as he arched up against the wolf atop him, forcing Saoi's prick deeper inside himself. Front paws wrapped around the human's thin waist, Saoi lapped at the smooth damp skin in front of him, beginning to rotate his hips so that he worked himself further inside the boy's slim body.

And then he woke, finding himself humping a pillow. He nearly howled in frustration, the pillow being nowhere near what he needed. He continued his jerky movements for a moment, hoping to find release regardless, but the cloth was scratchy against the moist slick skin of his erection. Saoi threw himself sideways and twisted, nosing his own thick cock where it rose pink and slick from its sheath. He did what he couldn't do in his other form, using his long thick tongue to lap at the swollen shaft while whimpering in pleasure. He couldn't resist imagining it was Kiya's tongue, licking him from root to tip. He licked harder and faster, losing himself in the vision of those plump lips wrapped around the head, sucking him. When his release came, he drank himself, enjoying the taste and the fantasy of Kiya doing it.

When he collapsed back onto the mess of sheets and pillows, he lay there panting. He'd never imagined himself with a human before. His previous sexual experiences had been with his own kind, no matter what their forms at the time. Why was this boy affecting him like this? It was a loss of control Brian couldn't afford. So many things could go wrong with a human. First, there was the basic biology. Humans were fragile. While a Faewolf could heal almost anything short of death, humans could easily be injured by what a wolf might consider normal play. And it was dangerous for him, because he couldn't let humans know about the existence of his kind. He was oath-bound to keep the secret. Despite all this, Saoi couldn't seem to stop thinking about the young man, and it was the memory of the scent of Kiya that clung to him as he drifted off to sleep.

It became the pattern. As Brian, the human form, he could force himself to push away thoughts of Kiya, to focus on his work instead. But the wolf had no such stoicism, reveling in the fantasies of Kiya every night. Saoi wanted the young man with an intensity that was beyond anything he had ever felt before. It was maddening. Each time Brian would chastise himself, telling himself that even if he wasn't Kiya's teacher, a relationship with a human was not only doomed to fail, but very dangerous. Too risky for himself and for his kind.

∽

It was Wednesday night's Queer Coffee House at the campus LGBT center. It was one of the things that Kiya missed while he'd been gone. He hadn't seen his friends, especially Audrey and Jack, since before break, and hadn't even gotten to explain to them about breaking things off with Ted.

The Center was a cool place to hang out. The running joke about UCSC standing for "Uncle Charlie's Summer Camp" was never more appropriate than here. The Center was actually a kind of fancy log cabin on the side of a hill, with a big picture window along one wall. All kinds of groups met there and there were talks and parties. Every Wednesday, Kiya liked to come and hang out with other queer students, which is how he had met Audrey and Jack. There were usually a couple dozen students on any given Wednesday. It was a great way to both meet new people and catch up with friends.

When Kiya arrived, both Audrey and Jack were already ensconced on a sofa with coffee and pastries. They were leaning toward each other, obviously catching up. Audrey grinned and both of them waved.

Kiya was dressed comfortably in a pair of faded jeans and one of his tighter shirts. He had his hair pulled up into a ponytail, but there were a few shorter strands that hung in his face. He grinned back, waving as he made his way over to the two of them. "Hey, you two. How were your vacations?" he asked.

Audrey patted the sofa beside her.

"Saved you a seat; get your coffee and tell us what's up with you." Jack nodded, not answering verbally since he had a mouth full of cookie.

Kiya nodded and headed for the refreshment table, pouring himself a cup of coffee and adding just the right amount of cream and sugar. He grabbed one of the pastries and then sat down next to his friends.

Jack had managed to swallow. "So was how was the trip home?" he asked. Jack had felt that spending spring break in South Dakota instead of Santa Cruz was a weird thing, even if he did know Kiya was close with his family.

"It was great," Kiya replied, taking a sip of his coffee. "It was kind of hard leaving them again to come back here."

"I stayed here. Much more fun than spending spring break back in Fresno," Jack insisted.

"Any place is better than Fresno," Audrey added, and Jack nodded as she continued. "I went back to San Diego, which still feels like a different world than this."

"Yeah, it was different going back to the reservation after staying here for so long. Nice though. Oh, a few things! I'm going to be an uncle," Kiya told them with a grin.

Both of his friends congratulated him, asking for details.

"My brother's wife is pregnant," Kiya said proudly, leaning back in his seat.

"I don't have any brothers or sisters, so I don't get to be an aunt," Audrey sighed. "I love babies."

Kiya and his family were so happy about it because for a while his sister-in-law, Sarah, had thought she wouldn't be able to have a child. She and Kiya's brother, Mapiya, had been trying for several years. "You could have children of your own someday," Kiya told Audrey with a nod. "If you want to go through something like that."

Audrey nodded. "Maybe, if I find the right girl or guy to raise a kid with. I wouldn't want to do it alone."

"Yeah, that wouldn't be easy," Kiya agreed, taking a sip of his coffee. "So, did you guys hear about my break-up?"

Jack nodded as Audrey's eyes widened. "What happened?" she asked.

"I couldn't take it anymore," Kiya said with small shrug. "Ted was too controlling. Like he could do whatever he wanted and I would just let him."

"Yeah," Audrey agreed and Jack nodded again.

"He stopped me outside the Baytree Bookstore on Monday," Jack added.

"For what?" Kiya asked, not wanting his friends getting involved in this.

Jack snorted. "Sean and I were coming out and it felt like he was waiting for us or something." Sean was Jack's boyfriend. "Ted seemed to think you might have a new boyfriend."

"Really? And so what if I got a boyfriend, I am allowed to," Kiya said, rolling his eyes. "Ted keeps calling me, too. Thinks that I just needed time to think about it or whatever. I don't know how long it will take him to get it."

His two friends exchanged a quick look.

"He acts like he owns you, Kiya," Audrey pointed out. "Actually, he's been acting like that for a long time."

"Well, he doesn't. That's why I broke up with him. I don't know why I stayed with him for so long," Kiya said, and then paused, tapping his chin. "No wait, it was the sex. Yeah."

"No one is THAT good, Kiya," Audrey said firmly.

Jack shrugged, apparently thinking that really good sex might have been worth putting up with a lot.

Kiya glanced at Jack. "Hey, Jack agrees with me. It's how I got all A's," Kiya said, smiling a little. "But really, it wasn't just that. He helped me study sometimes." He stopped, not knowing why he was trying to justify why he stayed with Ted.

"That's what they call it when you make that noise?" Jack teased.

Audrey rolled her eyes. "Well, I am glad you broke it off," she assured Kiya. "What finally got you?"

Kiya laughed softly, his cheeks coloring just a little. It wasn't all that apparent though, with his skin color. He looked at Audrey, tucking a bit of his loose hair behind one ear. "Well, he wouldn't use a condom," he explained quietly. "He's older, and I know he wasn't a virgin coming into the relationship ...."

"And you let him go bareback?" Jack asked, clearly shocked.

"No! No, I stopped him. I told him to get one, and he wouldn't listen, so, that was it," Kiya lied quickly, nodding. It hadn't happen that way at all. Ted didn't stop when Kiya had told him to, and he wouldn't get a condom. He forced himself on Kiya despite Kiya's frantic objections. He hated thinking about it, so there was no way he was going to tell Jack and Audrey. Even as Kiya recalled what had happened, he lifted his hand and, without thinking about it, nearly put his thumb into his mouth. It was a habit he'd had since he was a child that reappearedwhen he was stressed or extremely upset. Realizing that his thumb hovered near his lips, Kiya colored more darkly and forced his hand back into his lap.

"Good for you," Audrey said, hugging him then. Jack nodded so vigorously that he nearly spilled his coffee.

Kiya hugged her back, smiling over at Jack. "I mean, it was kind of the last straw," he said as he pulled back.

"Well, I'm glad you didn't let him. Ted creeps me out," Jack agreed.

"He keeps calling me," Kiya sighed, not sure of what to do about that. "It's just annoying me now. I wish he'd leave me alone."

Audrey patted him. "Just be firm and make sure he knows it's over," she assured him.

"I have been," Kiya said, shrugging slightly. He shook his head and took a deep breath, not wanting to talk about Ted anymore. "But enough talk about him! Guess who has the hottest teacher ever, hm? Go on, guess."

Jack laughed and rolled his eyes again.

"Kiya, a teacher?" Audrey asked.

"Teaching assistant, but yeah. He's so fucking gorgeous," Kiya said, looking dreamy at just the thought of Brian. "Now before you say it, I know we're not allowed to date professors and stuff, but he's not really a professor and I can still flirt with him anyway, right?"

"It's not like he can flirt back even if he is interested," Audrey huffed.

"Is he queer?" Jack asked, "Because if he is, then he would be interested. Kiya's too pretty for his own good."

"I asked him if he was married," Kiya said, smirking at Jack's comment. "He didn't give me a straight answer, which told me that he isn't married. And he's obviously restraining himself from looking at me. You should've seen the way he ran out of the room after class. Probably went to jerk off."

"Kiya!" Audrey gasped.

Jack laughed and shook his head. "Not a good idea to tease a man who can't have you," he warned. "So who is he and what does he look like?"

Kiya laughed, grinning at the both of them. "It's fun! His name is Brian Fenwick, he's tall, red-brown hair, and the most beautiful eyes I've ever seen. I mean, they were like-I can't say light brown. More like gold, yeah, gold."

"Golden eyes?" Audrey asked in disbelief, but she was smiling too.

"And his body?" Jack insisted.

"Even though he was probably the only one wearing a button down shirt, it looked good on him. I mean, really good. He's muscular, obviously, but not in the bulky kind of way," Kiya explained, getting an increasingly distant look in his eyes as he spoke. "Tanned skin, too."

"Here we go," Audrey warned. She kept smiling though and they let him babble about Brian for a while before talking about classes and other things. Then it was time to head back to the dorms.

"I'll talk to you guys later," Kiya said to them both, waving before he headed out of the Center. He walked around to the woods where there was a path that led him directly to College Ten. He used to always hang out with Ted along this path, but he didn't want to think about that, because that part of his life was over. He was never going to go back to him, good sex or not.

The nights in Santa Cruz were cool, even in the spring, and the woods were dark. Kiya carried a small flashlight and knew the path well. He reached his building in no time, heading up the stairs to his apartment. He unlocked it and prayed James was either not there or asleep.

James was lying back in his bed, light still on in the room, and reading one of his textbooks.

Kiya sighed, but continued inside, closing and locking the door behind him. He went to his bed and sat down, pulling the hair band out of his hair and then shaking it out. The only good thing about having a hopelessly straight roommate was that James never really looked at him when he did stuff like that.

"So, your boyfriend came by again," James said, not looking up from his homework.

Kiya looked over at him, his eyebrows furrowing as he frowned. "He's not my boyfriend anymore," he told him.

"He's not?" James asked, frowning as well and looking up now. "He's been by here looking for you nearly every day."

"He won't leave me alone," Kiya said, crossing his arms over his chest. "I've broken up with him, and he doesn't seem to realize that I'm serious. If he comes here again, don't let him in or anything. Say I changed dorms or something."

"Just tell him to fuck off," James insisted, shrugging and turning back to his book.

"I have been telling him that. Just-ugh, forget it," Kiya mumbled, taking his shoes off. He looked at James for a moment before he got up, turning away so he could undress and then put on his pajamas.

James paid him no attention at all.

Kiya knew he wouldn't, and it was one of the reasons he did it in the first place. He went to his bag when he was done and pulled out his biology textbook, turning to the right chapter before he settled back on his bed to read. He'd marked his place in the book with the photo he'd stolen of Brian. He couldn't help looking at it, smiling as he thought about the man. Brian was handsome and he looked strong, but it was more than that. Kiya felt a kind of intensity from him that made his skin seem to shiver pleasantly and stirred up a warmth in his belly. When he looked at Brian, he didn't just want sex, though that was certainly high on his list. He wanted to touch, to hold. He imagined those strong arms holding him close and it made Kiya feel safe. Kiya fell asleep atop his book, Brian's photo beside him.

∽

Kiya didn't sleep well that night at all. This was just one more thing that he'd have to learn to adjust to-sleeping alone. He had usually spent most of his nights sleeping at Ted's apartment after they 'studied' together and had become used to having someone else next to him as he slept. He woke up early with a frown on his face and, when he looked, the sun was just rising. James was snoring away on his own bed and Kiya was still desperately tired, but now that he was awake, there was no way he would be able to fall back asleep.

Realizing that for him the night was over, Kiya decided to get up and change, thinking that he could go for a morning jog or do something else to pass the time. But first, he needed a shower. He grabbed his towel and bag of toiletries before heading out to the bathroom, grateful that he wouldn't have to wait for it since no one else seemed to be awake. The apartment was quiet and Kiya savored the early morning peace as he closed the bathroom door behind him and locked it.

Kiya hopped into the shower stall after he undressed, turning the faucet on and standing under the steaming spray of water. Showers were one of the few things that could calm him down and help him not think about the things that worried him so much. Instead he found his thoughts wandering toward new things ... new people that he had met so far. Or rather, one person in particular. Brian.

Just the thought of the handsome teaching assistant sent a spark of arousal through Kiya, reminding him of just how long it had been since he had last had sex. It made him scowl slightly, but he accepted the discomforting reality that he really didn't have much choice right at the particular moment. All he had was his hand. It would have to do for now.

Kiya tilted his head back, letting the water stream down his face and over his neck as he pictured golden eyes and a firm, tanned body standing there next to him in the shower. Bringing his right hand up, he rested it against the cool tiles as his left hand moved over his throat and down his chest rubbing and caressing the warm skin as water ran down his body in rivulets. Kiya's dark hair hung in wet strands down his back, clinging to his body as if to shield him from the steamy vision of Brian watching him with a hungry look in his eyes. The hand on Kiya's chest moved back and forth, teasing each nipple into hardness as the fingers of his other hand tightened reflexively into a fist, still resting against the shower wall but finding nothing to grasp. With his eyes closed against the stinging spray, Kiya seductively smiled at the image of Brian in his head as he let his hand slide further down his glistening torso. The steam swirled in the air creating a fog-like effect and Kiya pictured the handsome teacher stepping closer, reaching out, but not quite touching him.

Pulling his right hand away from the wall, Kiya reached for the soap as he stepped slightly out from under the stream of water and began rubbing the slick bar down his chest, over his flat stomach until he reached the soft, wet hair surrounding his cock. His breath hitched slightly as he caressed the inside of his thigh with one slippery hand and pictured Brian kneeling before him to run his own eager hands over Kiya's trembling body. Kiya dropped the bar of soap just before grasping his now swollen prick and teasing the flesh with skilled fingers. The mental image of Brian began running his own soapy hand up and down Kiya's hard length, squeezing just the way he liked and caressing the head with a slickened thumb. Kiya wondered, briefly, if the real Brian would take things soft and slow or hard and fast. Kiya no longer cared, wanting only to open his eyes and see the other man reaching out with strong hands to take him. Desire pulsated through his body when he pictured himself in the protective embrace of his fantasy.

Kiya felt his heartbeat begin to speed up as he began to pant quietly, ever mindful of those sleeping in nearby rooms. His legs shook slightly when his hand sped up to match the movements of the man in his visions as he whispered, "Brian," into the warm mist. Letting his head slowly fall forward, Kiya pictured Brian reaching around his body to stroke his back lightly before moving further down. Kiya brought his own unoccupied hand snaking around behind him to press one finger lightly against his hole before gently pushing in. As the muscles relaxed slightly, the softly gasping young man moved his finger in and out slowly, lost in images of golden skin and amber eyes. The hand on his cock sped up as Kiya imagined Brian looking up at him with quiet intensity and commanding softly, "Come for me, Kiya." And with a low moan, Kiya did.

Standing under the hot water, Kiya pressed his forehead against the cool tiles as he slowly tried to catch his breath. Once he had himself under control, he finished his shower, washing his hair and his body and hands before turning off the water and getting out. As Kiya ran a dry towel over his water-slicked body, he realized he wouldn't be able to look at Brian without thinking about what he just did. Great.

Chapter Four

Brian waited under a tree at the upper section of the campus. He had given the students directions to meet him there for that weeks' field trip. It was a perfect spring day for the kind of hike he had planned. The lesson today would be about the ecology of the redwood forest itself. Brian tried to keep his mind on his work, even though a part of him was very aware that Kiya was in this section. Of course, Kiya was the first student to show up. Brian couldn't help watching the young man as he moved up the hill toward him. Kiya was dressed in loose jeans and a green t-shirt, his hair down.

"Hey, Brian," Kiya said. It has been easy to be the first one there, since his dorm was right by the meeting spot. And Kiya had wanted a chance to be alone with Brian again. The thought of the last time made Kiya smirk, but he also blushed a little, remembering his new morning ritual of jerking off to thoughts of Brian in the shower. It relieved a lot of stress, he told himself. "So what are we doing today?"

"Hello, Kiya," Brian answered, trying to ignore the way looking at Kiya made heat pool in his belly. Maybe if Kiya didn't wear his silky long hair loose like that. "You might want to put your hair up so it doesn't get caught on branches."

"I'll be fine. Promise I won't walk directly into branches or anything," Kiya said, smiling. Kiya was used to walking around in the woods, but he never got to do it as part of a class before. Kiya loved the woods. He'd received a scholarship for Native American students who had excelled and chosen UCSC in part because of their Legal Studies Program but also because being there reminded him of the Black Hills. "I've had practice, you know," he quipped as he flipped his hair back again.

Brian swallowed hard and tried not to imagine what kind of practice Kiya was talking about, especially when he smiled like that. "Um, good," Brian said, turning his attention to greet the other students as they arrived. The teaching assistant became caught up in instructing arrivals to turn in their assignment for the week and checking to make sure each student had brought bottled water and wore shoes that would work for the hike.

Brian's stammer had made Kiya grin, because even though he hadn't meant it any other way, it was nice to see that he was affecting Brian. "Don't want to know what I meant?" he asked curiously as he moved closer to Brian again.

Brian wanted a lot of things, most of them inappropriate and involving the gorgeous young man. He decided to ignore the question and focused instead on gathering up the papers. Two students hadn't brought water, but Brian had prepared for that, bringing extra. He passed the bottles to the students.

Kiya frowned a little when Brian didn't answer, but shrugged it off, guessing that he'd have another chance to get Brian's attention as the field trip went on. He would definitely put effort into making sure that he had another chance.

Brian gave his students until ten after the hour before leading them up the path and into the cool of the forest. "Now, if you have done the reading, you will know some about the ecology of a redwood forest. Can anyone tell me what part of the ground is thick duff and what it is made of?"

Kiya raised his hand, along with several other students, and was happy when Brian nodded to him to answer. "Isn't it the leaves and branches that build up on the ground over time? And it ends up being good for the soil?"

"Yes," Brian answered, smiling. "And in a natural forest, forest fires sometimes come through and flash burn the duff. The process can actually trigger new growth."

"So the forest can rebuild itself again," Kiya said, nodding and smiling back. "That doesn't mean we shouldn't be careful about causing those fires, though."

"Yes, we don't want to cause a fire, because this isn't a completely wild forest and it would burn buildings as well." Brian had spent most of his life in areas that truly were wild, far from humans. Now he stopped by a circle of trees. In the center of the circle was an old blackened stump. "Can anyone tell me what happened here?"

Kiya eyed the area and the stump, not sure what else beside fire damage Brian was trying to call attention to. He waited for someone else to speak up or for Brian to explain.

"Debra?" Brian acknowledged among the couple of hands up.

"A fire killed the old tree, but the heat opened the pine cones causing a ring of new trees to grow around it," Debra answered.

Brian nodded to both. "Yes, like the myth of the phoenix, sometimes new trees grow in the ashes of the old."

"People call them fairy circles," one of the other women chimed in.

"Some do," Brian agreed, eyes twinkling. He would love to tell them why and about the magic in the trees, but that was outside the scope of the biology class. The woods thrummed with Fae magic. It was one of the reasons Brian had chosen to live here.

"That's pretty cool," Kiya murmured quietly, mostly to himself as he looked around the area once again. He breathed in deeply and let it out in a sigh, relaxed. He loved the forest. It always made him feel more at home than anywhere else.

They moved deeper along the trails, while Brian pointed out various things they had read in the books, such as plants like Poison oak and Redwood Sorrel. He stopped again. "You don't have to be an artist, but it is important to try to draw sketches of what you see. And, yes, before you ask, I know most of you have cell phones with digital cameras. You can take pictures, too, but sketching a plant can help you notice things you would miss otherwise."

Kiya walked up to Brian after they stopped again, laying his hand on the man's arm and showing Brian his drawing. Kiya didn't think he was an artist, really, but his father was and he had learned most of what he knew from him. "It's the stump over there," he explained, nodding over at the plant.

Brian tried not to step back when Kiya moved in so close to him. The touch sent a tremor of desire through Brian's entire body and he felt the wolf within stir at that, sniffing the air. And sniffing, too, at that smell-not just the soothing smell of the woods themselves, but also the musky spice of the young man. It was difficult to focus on the drawing with Kiya standing so near. Brian felt the hair on his arm tingle at the warmth of Kiya's hand, even through the fabric of his shirt sleeve.

Kiya looked up at him when he didn't get an answer, nudging him gently. "Is it that bad?" he asked, raising an eyebrow.

"Oh, um," Brian stammered, flushed. He never did that. "Yes, that's good. I like the way you captured the lichen growing on the rotting wood, and the sorrel around the base." He took another deep breath, having to work not to groan aloud at the intoxicating scent of Kiya. It was flooding his senses and provoking Saoi into wanting more. The wolf stirred within the human form, stretching as if it would break free of the disguise.

Both of Kiya's eyebrows rose in surprise at the sudden reddening of the man's cheeks, wondering what was going through his mind at that very moment. Maybe Kiya had a chance with Brian, after all. "Thank you," Kiya murmured, a slow smirk turning his lips up. "Are you okay? Do you need water?"

"F-fine," Brian insisted. He kept telling himself to move away from Kiya, but the wolf inside him was urging the opposite. The wolf wanted to press against Kiya, to take him to the ground and rub itself against him.

Kiya let go of the man's arm and reached to pull his water out of his bag, holding it out for Brian. "It's not open," he said, watching him. The change in Brian was sudden. Kiya hoped that it meant he was affecting Brian, but he wasn't certain. Maybe it wasn't even what Kiya thought. His eyes narrowed in concern as he wondered just exactly what was causing Brian's strange reaction.

Brian didn't even think as his hand closed over Kiya's on the water bottle. The touch of skin against skin sent another jolt through him and he ground his teeth to keep from growling.

Kiya looked down at their hands when they touched, noticing how warm Brian's felt over his, like his entire body was flushed now. Kiya knew he should've pulled his hand back, but the longer he held it there, the more he thought of where else Brian could be holding him ... touching him. Kiya felt his cheeks redden slightly and he looked up into Brian's eyes again.

"What is this plant?" one the other students asked, and Brian glanced up to see the boy was holding a three leaved plant in his hand -Poison Oak. He groaned, letting go of Kiya's hand and water bottle and turning his attention back to his work.

Kiya blinked when Brian stepped away, a little shaken and disappointed. He felt as though the other student had interrupted something that could've been really good. Kiya scowled. He deserved the rash, Kiya decided.

Brian had to show the student how to use a bottle of water to quickly wash his hands and gave yet another talk on how to spot and avoid Poison Oak. It helped clear his head a bit. He was chiding himself for letting himself get worked up by Kiya. He couldn't go there, he kept lecturing himself. And not just because Kiya was a student. It was too risky to get involved with a normal human. Any human.

Kiya kept closer to Brian after that, brushing against him when he could manage to without making it seem obvious. Kiya didn't care if Brian was a teacher, he still wanted him. He wished there was some way to work around that, really. It wasn't as if they would get together and tell the whole world. There didn't need to be any announcements made. It could be kept a secret. He wanted to talk to Brian about that, but he couldn't, not here.

Hiking was usually a way, whether as wolf or man, Brian worked off stress. But leading three groups of students on a hike that week had not been relaxing. Now the intoxicating scent and warmth of Kiya was driving him to distraction. By the time they made it back to the upper entrance to the woods, Brian was worked up and having a difficult time remembering who he was and what he was supposed to be doing. He dismissed the class and turned to head back to his office.

Kiya was sweaty, worked up and in need of a shower, but instead of heading back to the apartment, he followed after Brian. It wasn't just that he wanted another chance with him. He was also a little concerned about the man's strange behavior. "Hey," he said, having to hurry to catch up with Brian. "I wanted to make sure that you're okay?"

Brian frowned, barely able to remember human speech. "I hike all the time," he managed to answer tersely.

"I figured, but it seemed like something happened. Like you got overheated or something," Kiya said, looking closely again. Brian was definitely flushed and sweating.

Brian sighed. "Kiya, you have no reason to worry about me and I would prefer it if we stuck to the topic of the class rather than discuss my personal life or health." He'd meant it to come out dispassionate, but it sounded almost a snarl instead.

Kiya bit his lip, going quiet for a moment before he spoke up again, more quietly in case anyone else was around. He took a step closer to Brian. "Was it because of me? Because, you know, we could talk about that."

Brian forced himself to step back despite the urge to lean in and sniff the sweaty young man. "No, there is nothing to talk about," he answered. His voice had dropped lower, a growling sound.

Kiya wouldn't give up that easily, despite hearing the difference in the man's voice. He should've left, but something felt like it pulled him forward, toward Brian. He could feel something between them and he wanted Brian to admit it. "Are you sure?" he asked quietly, taking another step forward, fingers touching Brian's arm again. "I mean, I won't tell anyone. I promise."

Brian's hand came up, palm flat on the boy's chest. He had meant it to hold Kiya back, but the sensation was like a rush of heat up his arm as he felt the other man's heartbeat through his skin.

"Stop," Brian croaked.

"So you really... don't?" Kiya asked, resting his hand on top of Brian's unbelievably warm one. He was almost sure that Brian would give in... or maybe Kiya was reading this all wrong. Kiya felt such a strong surge of feeling that he was confused by it.

The hand didn't help. Brian was instantly aroused and he felt the wolf aspect in him pressing up into his fierce animal consciousness. He had the urge to grab Kiya's shirt and pull him close, to taste him. Instead, Brian pushed, trying to force distance between them. As a human, Brian was usually an articulate person, but the words fled him now, just as they did when he was a wolf.

Kiya stumbled back from the force of the push, managing to catch himself before he fell down. So he guessed that meant no, that he was reading everything wrong and he had invaded the man's personal space more than he should have.

"Okay... okay. Bye," he said and nodded, feeling embarrassed as he quickly turned away and fled back to his dorm. Kiya felt like he wasn't walking fast enough, so he broke into a run, not looking back. He felt the sting of tears and tried to hold them back. He didn't do well with rejection at all, and what he felt right now was overwhelming him.

"Shit," Brian swore, smacking his hand against the cinderblock wall of the building beside him. Now he had scared a student, a young man who hadn't done anything more harmful than flirt with him. "I am a fucking idiot," he whispered, resting his forehead against the cool brick. Despite it all, he was still aroused.

Brian hurried back to his office at the Earth and Marine Sciences building. He stored his laptop inside his desk, locking it. He knew he wasn't going to get any work done now, being this keyed up. A run in his wolf form was the only way he knew to burn off some of the frustration. He had to struggle to hold the human form as he took his near empty pack with him and walked out back to the forested area and down into the ravine below the building. He found the small copse of trees he usually changed in, stripped his clothes and stored them in the pack, hiding it in an alcove of the old Lime Kiln ruin. Then he just let go. That's how it felt. Changing wasn't really difficult for his kind. The magic flowed and his body with it, reshaping into the four-legged beast.

With the shift came the changes in perception. Brian was the wolf, but the wolf saw and felt the world differently than human Brian. Saoi could hear every rustle of leaves, every flap of wing, every smell and sound of the woods and the people not far away. And Saoi didn't care about classes or rules or schedules. His world was dominated by senses, urges and the need for freedom. Saoi let those senses pull him deeper into the forest, keeping off the paths and to the cover as he explored. Saoi went hunting.

❧

Kiya didn't stop running until he reached his apartment-heading up the stairs, rushing inside and heading straight for his room. He unlocked and pushed the door open, ignoring James as he set his backpack in the room and went directly to the shower. He wasn't sure how long he stayed in there, but it must have been a while because one of his roommates started knocking on the door to make him get out. He did, finally, pushing past James and getting dressed, but he couldn't bear to just sit there in his room. There was too much to think about, and he couldn't really do much of that there. So, after getting dressed again, Kiya left. He went back to the woods intending to take a long walk.

Kiya didn't feel he could think around other people, but in the woods he could calm down and figure out what to do. He wasn't exactly sure how he would face Brian after what had transpired, but he really had no choice if he wanted to pass the class. He'd just have to grit his teeth and deal with it. Kiya knew he had pushed too far. Yet, it had felt right, felt like he needed to touch

Brian and that somehow Brian had needed to be touched, too.

Stepping into the woods was always like stepping into another world. The redwoods were hushed, as if listening, and he felt safer among them than anywhere else. Kiya made sure to not go too far, not wanting to get lost. He kept to the same paths he knew, using the trees to guide him.

Kiya stopped and sat down among one of the groups of trees, leaning back against the tall straight trunk of a big one. He wished he could talk to someone, but not his friends at school or anyone else nearby. He felt around for his phone and pulled it out, looking to see if he had enough reception before he dialed. He looked through the numbers in his phone and stopped on Ted's for some reason, not even sure why he hadn't deleted it from his phone. He felt vaguely bereft, like he needed a hug or just to be held and comforted. But if he called Ted now, that would be like admitting that everything the other man had said about the break-up was right. He wasn't about to do that.

So, Kiya ended up dialing his mother's phone number, letting his head rest against the tree as he listened to the ring. His mother didn't answer though, it was his father who picked up the phone.

"*Ate?*" Kiya asked in surprise as he slipped into Lakota, his native language. "Where's mom?"

"She left her phone here," Maka replied. "Don't you have class now, *ciksi?*"

"No, I'm in between classes. Just needed someone to talk to," Kiya explained quietly. It felt good to hear his father's voice.

"Why? Is everything okay? That boy isn't bothering you anymore, is he?" Maka asked, already sounding worried.

"Everything's fine," Kiya insisted, not wanting to give his father something to actually worry about. "How's Mapiya and Tehya?"

"Mapiya and Sarah are doing good. He has a new job. Tehya is doing well. She is dancing at the next Pow Wow." His father filled him in on the news. Tehya was Kiya's baby sister, and she was

44

only four. Kiya had been about the same age when he had started dancing at Native American gatherings, too. He missed that part of his life back home.

"Oh, make sure you get pictures," he told his father.

"I will," Maka assured him. "They miss you. Along with the rest of your family. You should write more often to your grandparents." Kiya's parents always urged him to write more but they didn't have email, so it wasn't easy.

"I really have to get grandma a cell phone," Kiya murmured, smiling a little now. Juanita White Cloud refused to get one after hearing some bogus report about them causing cancer. Now she insisted that he write home all the time and, while it was nicer, it took more work.

"Yes, I know. Are you sure there is nothing bothering you, Kiya? You sound troubled," Maka said.

"I'm sure. I guess I just miss you guys," Kiya said, shrugging as if he could see him. He looked around the forest as he spoke, noticing that he'd probably have to get back before it got too dark.

"Ah, well, you were the one who decided to go so far. You're always welcome to come back here and go to school closer," his father said. He was always trying to convince Kiya to do that, too, but as much as Kiya missed his family, it wasn't enough for him to actually do it.

"I'll think about it. Look, it's getting dark and I'm in the woods, I should probably start heading back. I love you, tell Mom I called. Tell everyone I love them, too," Kiya said, moving to get up.

"I will. I love you. Get back safe."

"Bye, Ate," Kiya murmured, hanging up the phone. He felt better, if only a little.

Kiya got to his feet and began to trace his path back to the college, but it felt as though someone was watching him, so he looked around again. He couldn't see anyone or anything. He still had that feeling, though. Kiya didn't want to focus on it for too long and risk losing the daylight, so he turned back and quickly walked back the way he had come, looking up at the sky through the thick canopy of the trees. It was getting darker, and the trees brought nightfall into the forest faster than anywhere else. It was nearly dark when he spotted the lights of his apartment building. He looked back at the woods curiously and then continued on his way, heading inside. Even as he made his way up the outside stairs to his apartment, Kiya looked back into the darkness of the forest, feeling like the forest looked back.

∽

Saoi wasn't even conscious of following a scent until it became stronger. It was that same alluring musk he had found before. But now, he recognized it. It was that boy, Kiya. In his wolf form, Saoi had no qualms about knowing that he wanted him. Kiya smelled right in a way that no one else did. Saoi crouched in the brush, sniffing the air and licking his lips. He was still aware enough that he knew he could not approach the boy, but following Kiya, watching him and listening, was natural for the wolf.

When the boy began talking, many of the words were in a language Saoi didn't understand, but he found his heart thrilled at the sound of Kiya's voice. It almost felt musical, soothing to Saoi and he laid his muzzle on his forepaws, listening. Saoi almost dozed in that state of calm as he listened to the boy on the phone, but blinked alert when the cell phone snapped shut.

In human form, Brian has refused to let himself dwell on Kiya. Now, Saoi allowed himself to look at that lean body, that light brown skin and long dark hair. The boy's eyes were very green and his lashes seemed enormously long. Saoi had the urge to nuzzle him, to scent mark him and glory in the feel of him.

Saoi followed him and knew to stop at the edge of the forest, having learned to keep his wolf form hidden, of course. He waited in the dark for a while, just watching the building Kiya had disappeared into before Saoi finally decided he was hungry and would go chase down something to eat.

Kiya kept to himself the weekend after the field trip. He didn't stay in his room the entire time, though. Sometimes he sat on the balcony, just staring off into the woods. In the evening, he went out for walks, enjoying the quiet as the forest enveloped him. Kiya still felt that he was being watched during his times there, but whenever he looked, no one was there. It should have made him feel uneasy, but instead, it had an eerie feeling of safety as if the forest was watching out for him. He was thinking about calling his father about it, but decided that, with all that had happened, he was simply over-thinking things.

He didn't tell his friends about what had happened with Brian, but they probably noticed that he didn't talk about the man anymore. When they mentioned him, Kiya merely shrugged and said he was over that, and didn't go into detail when they asked why. They didn't need to know about that particular rejection. He was embarrassed enough without anyone else knowing.

Come Monday morning, Kiya told himself that he was completely over it, even though seeing Brian again in class certainly showed him that he wasn't. Yet, that didn't mean Kiya would give the man any kind of attention. He was going to treat Brian the way the man said he wanted to be treated. Like a teacher. Kiya didn't stay after class that day, leaving the moment it was over. He could feel Brian's eyes on him even when he wasn't looking up, and while he wanted to look up back at him, Kiya forced himself not to.

After class, Kiya went back out for his now daily walk in the woods, and again felt the same presence of someone or something watching him. He pretended not to notice and then looked around quickly, this time getting a glance of an animal just as it drew back into the shadows. It was big and brown. Would stray dogs be in the woods? Kiya didn't think pets were allowed on campus. He'd heard that there were occasionally mountain lions in these woods, but he was pretty sure that wasn't what he had glimpsed.

The following day he headed back into the woods again, and this time he got a better look at the animal. It looked like either a really big dog… or a wolf. And Kiya was almost sure that wolves weren't supposed to be in the area. And they most definitely weren't supposed to follow you around and watch you.

His grandfather, John, had told him of animal spirits that could watch over and protect some people, but Kiya hadn't yet actually seen one that would do such a thing. He wanted to call his father about it, but he also didn't want to jump to conclusions so quickly. The thought of having a wolf watching over him like that made Kiya feel strangely safe. A wolf was wakan, sacred. Kiya wasn't afraid of the animal. He was certain that the wolf wasn't going to hurt him and that if it had wanted to, the wolf would have already done so.

Kiya wanted to see the wolf now, to actually walk up to him so that he could see for himself if it was a spirit or not, but whenever he caught a glimpse of it, the animal turned and ran away. Kiya had to tell himself not to make any quick assumptions that this was some kind of protector. He knew that he was feeling lonely and rejected and might only be making more out of the animal's presence than he should be.

❧

Brian should let it go. He knew that. He couldn't afford to let Kiya's crush continue. It wouldn't be good for either of them. The problem he had was that he could only seem to remember that when he was in human form. The minute he transformed to wolf, it suddenly felt very clear that he needed to see Kiya, be near the boy and protect what was "his." Telling himself that Kiya wasn't "his" anything didn't help.

So, over the weekend, Brian tried not to change into a wolf. It didn't work. The wolf wasn't a separate thing, it was who he was. He changed every day and it was one of his greatest joys and best ways he knew to relieve stress. If Brian stayed in human form too long, it became more and more difficult to hold the shape. He grew edgy and began pacing. So, he let himself shift.

48

Yet, as a wolf, his mind worked differently than it did as a human. Saoi had different concerns. Usually, that was good. It had never interfered with his life as a man, as Brian. He usually did well balancing his needs as a wolf with those of a man with a career. Yet, that weekend, after following Kiya in the woods, he felt driven to do it again. Instead of finishing grading papers, Brian found himself repeatedly slipping into the woods, changing into his other form and following Kiya.

He learned more about Kiya than he should, of course. He could smell what Kiya ate, who his friends were and the rhythm of his schedule. Saoi watched with a prickling sensation, believing that if he didn't something bad would happen. Every instinct told him he couldn't afford to leave Kiya unprotected.

By Monday morning, Brian realized that Saoi's obsession was not going to go away. And he couldn't just blame the wolf. The wolf wasn't a separate thing-it was him. He wanted Kiya, but couldn't have him. So, he did his best to keep his distance as Brian, but couldn't stop himself from following Kiya as a wolf. Brian sat in class, knowing he probably had dark circles under his eyes from his sleepless nights filled with arguments with himself and the repeated erotic dreams about that dark haired young man. Even now, he tried to not look, but found his eyes straying to find Kiya.

Chapter Five

It was Wednesday, which meant it was time to meet up with Jack and Audrey at the Center. Kiya was finally beginning to feel somewhat better about what had happened with Brian. He resigned himself to the fact that he couldn't have the teacher. Now all Kiya needed was to find someone else to give his attentions to. Maybe he'd meet someone at the Queer Coffee House tonight. Rather than taking the shuttle, Kiya made his way through the path in the woods that led to the Center. He looked around, hoping he'd catch a glimpse of the wolf.

Brian had finished leading his Wednesday section and, feeling that pull that he couldn't resist, transformed, seeking out Kiya again. Brian had noticed that Kiya refused to really look at him in class now, and Brian could hardly blame him. But he couldn't resist watching Kiya. So, in the twilight of early evening, Saoi waited and felt his pulse race when he saw the boy coming into the woods.

Kiya was about halfway through the woods to the Center when he realized he felt that presence again. He stopped and looked quickly around, but didn't see anything. It was getting dark and he wondered which of the shadows hid the wolf.

"Where are you?" he whispered.

Saoi heard him but didn't move, didn't respond. He was considering whether or not he should retreat when he caught another smell in the air besides Kiya's. That wasn't unusual given how many students used these foot paths, but something about it made the hackles on his neck and back rise.

"Kiya," a voice called behind the young man.

Kiya hadn't been expecting the animal to reply. Or was that even it? No, the voice sounded much too familiar. He turned around quickly to see who was there and found Ted on the path behind him.

"There's my pretty boy," Ted greeted, smiling as he reached for Kiya.

Kiya stepped back before Ted could touch him, frowning at him. "I'm not your pretty boy, Ted. What are you doing here?" For a moment he thought it might have been Ted who had been following him around. But no, it couldn't be, he would have seen him already. Ted wasn't known for his subtlety.

Ted took his hand despite Kiya's attempt to evade. "Aww, still mad?" he asked in a voice that held a condescending tone.

Saoi could smell the desire of the intruder and it made him shake with a kind of protective anger, eyes narrowing as he tried to reign in the urge to attack the man.

"Why won't you take a hint? I don't want you. We're not together anymore," Kiya insisted as he tried to pull his hand away, wishing he could slap some sense into Ted. "That's that. Find someone else."

"No," Ted insisted, his voice no longer playful. He was more muscular than Kiya and he managed to get an arm around him, pulling Kiya against his own body. "You're mine, baby, and nothing's going to change that."

From his place under cover, Saoi growled. He shouldn't reveal himself, he knew that. But he didn't like the other man touching Kiya. And he could tell that Kiya didn't like it either.

"Ted," Kiya said, pressing his hand against Ted's chest and trying to push away. He was trying not to be scared of Ted, and wondering how he had never noticed how forceful his ex was before. Did he like it or something? Kiya shook his head, hearing something that sounded like a growl. He wasn't quite sure what it was or where it was coming from; he couldn't focus on it. "Please, let me go," he begged, really starting to get frightened.

"Kiya, you're being foolish," Ted insisted. "I told you that you ARE mine. You need to stop playing games and come with me." Then Ted was grabbing Kiya's hair with one hand and using it to hold him in place while he brought his lips to Kiya's.

Kiya gritted his teeth once he was pulled into the kiss, trying to pull away, but he couldn't with Ted's hand gripping his hair the way that it was. His heart was pounding now as he realized Ted wasn't going to stop. He had seen him like this before.

When he smelled Kiya's fear, Saoi burst from the brush, unable to think or stop the impulse that told him to tear out the throat of the stranger. He skidded to a stop only when he faced the pair, his fur standing on end and an ugly snarl emitting from behind his bared teeth.

Kiya jumped and clutched at Ted's shirt when he heard the snarl. He couldn't even look to see what it was, but he immediately hoped it was the wolf and not some other animal.

It seemed to take Ted a minute to realize that they were no longer alone. Still holding Kiya's waist and hair, he pulled back from the attempted kiss to look toward the sound. His brows furrowed when he spotted the large wolf. "What the fuck?"

Saoi snarled louder, lips curled back from teeth, preparing to attack if the man didn't let go of Kiya immediately.

Kiya wrenched his head, ignoring the pain in his scalp as he tried to look back over his shoulder so that he could see what was happening. His eyes widened when he saw the wolf. It was beautiful-large with red-brown fur and glowing amber eyes. But it was also terrifying, lips drawn back over its teeth as it snarled. It looked like it was preparing to attack them... or maybe just Ted.

"We should-I mean, you should go," Kiya mumbled.

Ted let go of Kiya and backed away. Saoi, completely still and steely-eyed with anger, read the man's full measure in his retreating posture. The man was smart enough not to challenge the wolf, but also a coward for being willing to let Kiya stand between himself and danger.

Kiya nearly sighed in relief when Ted stepped away. He was still scared of the wolf, but stayed where he was inbetween Ted and the snarling animal keeping his actions slow and deliberate. "Go," he said to Ted. Kiya was taking a big chance here, and for all he knew he'd get attacked anyway, but, for reasons he didn't understand himself, Kiya trusted the wolf more than Ted.

Ted didn't hesitate, didn't grab Kiya or try to talk him into leaving too. He just turned and ran back the way he had come.

Saoi snarled and gave chase. It was instinct. The acrid scent of the man's fear filling his nostrals as the tore after the running man.

Saoi had to control the urge to chase him down and sink his teeth into the bastard.

Kiya was startled, both by Ted's sudden flight and the wolf bounding after him. "No," he shouted after the wolf.

It took only moments before Saoi had nearly caught up to the running man-and Saoi's rational mind caught up with what he was doing. He forced himself to come to a stop, teeth bared as he stood watching the retreating man until Ted was out of sight. Then he huffed and shook himself out, trying to calm down.

Kiya hurried to catch up to the wolf, relieved when he saw that the creature hadn't attacked Ted. He couldn't believe that Ted had left him like that. Kiya knew that meant Ted didn't really care for him as he had claimed. Ted only cared about Ted.

Saoi looked back up at the beautiful boy standing there. Why hadn't Kiya, run too? Most people faced with a wolf, especially a snarling one, would have left as quickly as possible.

Kiya took a deep breath, his teeth worrying his bottom lip nervously. Instinctively, he looked down at his shoes rather than into the wolves eyes.

"You're not gonna hurt me, are you?" Kiya asked quietly.

Saoi looked up and blinked slowly with undisguised adoration for Kiya. And the smell. It was fantastic! He made a small happy noise in the back of his throat, lowered his chest and head to the ground in a playful bow, and wagged his tail like a dog.

And with that reaction, Kiya knew that this wasn't a normal wolf. It was definitely his protector. If the wolf hadn't been there, Kiya knew all too clearly what Ted would have done. "Thank you," Kiya said with a smile, kneeling down in front of the beast.

Saoi moved forward without thinking, immediately pushing his muzzle against Kiya's hands.

Kiya reached out carefully, holding his hand out to the animal. Saoi sniffed his figners and then licked his wrist. It was fantastic to finally touch Kiya.

Kiya was encouraged but that, scratching the chin of the beast. "You saved me. I owe you." He didn't even care if the wolf had no idea what he was saying. "My protector," he whispered in Lakota. He would have to tell his grandfather about this the first chance he got.

Saoi groaned in delight, shivers of pleasure from nose to tail. He nuzzled Kiya's face, licking his cheeks and reveling in the taste.

Kiya laughed softly as he leaned back, finding that the wolf's tongue tickled. "You're not a normal wolf," he murmured.

Saoi could have licked and nuzzled Kiya all night, lost in the sensations. The laugh was like music to him and he licked again.

Kiya would just have to tell Jack and Audrey later that he got caught up with homework. There was no way he could tell them about his wolf, and he wouldn't tell them about what happened with Ted, either. He did wonder, though, if Ted would go to tell some official about there being a wolf in the woods.

"You should probably go," Kiya said after the animal got a few more licks in. "I don't want you to get caught."

Saoi wasn't leaving Kiya alone in the woods, especially after what he had witnessed. He kept rubbing against him instead, practically knocking the boy over in his excitement.

Kiya laughed as he got to his feet, looked around and listening for any other footsteps. He didn't hear anything, but he was still cautious. "Go on," he said, as he pulled his shirt up to wipe at his face.

The sight of Kiya's naked belly and chest brought an immediate reaction in Saoi's body and he whimpered. Being this close to Kiya was intoxicating.

"What's wrong?" Kiya asked when he heard the sound, dropping the shirt and looking down at the wolf. "You should really go, protector. I don't know what they do with animals that aren't supposed to be in these woods, but I don't want to find out. I'll be fine, promise."

Saoi slid against Kiya's leg, rubbing him and waiting for him, looking up happily at the beautiful boy.

"You can't follow me back," Kiya said with a small frown of worry, reaching to pet the wolf again.

Saoi was content to lean against Kiya. Getting to touch what he had forced himself to ignore when he was Brian was addictive. He wanted more, wanted it badly.

Kiya sighed, wishing he could spend the rest of the night with the wolf, but he was too nervous about him getting caught. "All right, let's go," he said, looking around once more and then turning to walk back toward his college, assuming the wolf would follow him.

Saoi padded alongside Kiya, making sure to breathe deep and enjoy the young man's scent. He was disappointed when they reached the edge of the forest and he had to stop before coming out into the open.

"Goodnight then," Kiya said quietly, kneeling down again to scratch behind the animal's ears. "I'll probably go for a walk tomorrow, too, so I'll see you. Thank you again," he said, wishing there was some way for him to really talk to the wolf.

Saoi happily licked and nuzzled Kiya and then watched as the boy went back to his dorm. Saoi didn't leave until he saw Kiya safely back inside. He still marveled that Kiya hadn't been frightened of a wolf. He didn't know why, but it was a delight.

Kiya made his way to his apartment, not sure of what to think about what had just happened. He had a new protector, and for that he was glad, but he also realized that Ted wouldn't take no for an answer, no matter what Kiya did. He didn't know if Ted would give up after seeing the wolf. It wasn't as if Kiya was always in the woods, and Ted did know where he lived. Kiya didn't want to dwell on those bad thoughts. Instead he began looking around for his phone so that he could lie to Jack and Audrey about why he hadn't made it.

∿

It was Friday and Brian was waiting in the classroom for Kiya's section to show up. Brian's heart sped up the moment Kiya walked in and he couldn't help but look over, sniffing the air in the room, which was almost perfumed with Kiya's scent. Saoi had spent what free time he had in the last two days watching over Kiya. It wasn't just that the sight and the smell of the young man that drove him wild. Having seen a man attack Kiya, Brian was worried that the creep would come back. At least he managed to get the papers graded as well.

Kiya was no longer one of the first to walk into Brian's class. He didn't care about getting there early anymore, even if it meant not getting his seat in the front. That day, however, he managed to get it and he went straight to the seat, sitting down and pulling out his books. Opening the front pouch of his backpack, Kiya pulled out a hard candy and, after unwrapping it, popped it in his mouth. He had caught himself nearly sucking on his thumb during the last class with Brian and hoped the candy would put a stop to that. He knew it was somehow related to the rejection from Brian and his recent problems with Ted, but Kiya wasn't about to get caught in class sucking his thumb. That would just be too much.

Brian blinked and had to remind himself that he wasn't in wolf form; he had to try to behave. He couldn't be caught staring at Kiya. "Um, so everyone should have field notes to turn in," he began.

Kiya opened his binder to get the notes, looking them over once before he passed his paper in. He was trying very hard not to look at Brian, reminding himself that it wasn't going to happen.

Brian passed back the last week's graded papers and spent most of the hour answering questions about the readings and lectures, then going over the next field trip, which would be on

56

campus again. His gaze kept straying back to Kiya, trying not to feel disappointed that the young man was avoiding him. As ridiculous as it seemed, Brian now missed those touches that Kiya gave him as a wolf. He knew he couldn't get involved with a student. Yet, Brian's desire only seemed to be growing stronger the more he was around Kiya. And when class was over, he had to clench his fingers around the edge of the desk not to call out to Kiya, to call him back.

Kiya did look up at one point, catching Brian's eye before he could look away. Why was Brian looking at him now? If he didn't know better, Kiya would think Brian was suddenly interested in him. Kiya packed up more slowly, watching Brian for a moment longer before he stood up and left the room so that he wouldn't be the last one in there with him. He didn't want Brian thinking that Kiya was going to try again or something. He couldn't ... not again.

～

It was Monday and, over the last five days, Kiya had taken to spending more and more time in the woods with the wolf. After he finished his homework and studied for a bit, he headed outside and among the redwoods looking for his companion. He wondered if he should give the wolf a name or just keep calling him his protector.

Saoi didn't know if he would see Kiya on any given night, but sometimes he liked to sit in the woods just outside the boy's apartment and watch over him anyway. He was surprised when he saw Kiya leaving the apartment. Saoi stood, tail wagging excitedly.

"There you are," Kiya said with a smile when he saw him, reaching to pet the wolf as he led him more deeply into the forest.

Saoi leaned into that touch, delighting in the unexpected visit with Kiya. Did the boy come just to see him? It thrilled him to think that.

Kiya walked until he thought they were deep enough. He

found a redwood tree circle and sat down, leaning back against a trunk as he waved for the wolf to come closer.

"I missed you," he admitted.

Saoi licked the boy's face in response, his tail thumping the ground with his excitement.

"Yeah, I can see you did, too," Kiya chuckled. "Class today..." he trailed off, sighing. Sometimes he didn't like to think about Brian, especially after what had happened.

Saoi was captivated by being so close to Kiya and laid his head in the boy's lap, enjoying both the body warmth and musky smell. When Kiya spoke, he looked up, waiting and wondering if he would continue.

"You probably won't know what I'm talking about, but... my teacher. He's so gorgeous. Even though he wants nothing to do with me, it's hard to not look at him and stuff, but I guess it's for the best, right?" Kiya asked the wolf, looking down at him as if he could answer.

Saoi cocked his head, trying to think past the effect being near Kiya had on his wolf body and listen to what he was saying. Could Kiya actually be talking about him?

"I mean, he pushed me away and stuff, so that's a good sign that he doesn't like me," Kiya mumbled, running his fingers through the wolf's fur. "But, I ... sometimes I feel so alone. I have a bunch of friends, but I need someone closer. Not even Ted could give me that, as you saw. He was all about one thing and only one thing."

Saoi felt an intense need to make the boy happy. He knew it was the wolf emotions in control, but it was very real. He tried to remember why he had to push the boy away. It felt wrong when he was like this to even consider Kiya as anything but his. Saoi rubbed his head against Kiya's hand and thigh.

"You make me feel a little better," Kiya murmured, smiling softly as he petted the wolf with both of his hands. "But you're not a guy, so... and I realize that I'm talking to an animal, but you understand me, right?"

Should he admit that? Or let Kiya believe him to be a normal wolf. Not that wolves were normally found in this area, let alone on campus, following students. Saoi blinked and nodded.

"I knew it," Kiya said, smiling more broadly as he ran his fingers through fur again. "Wish you could tell me your name."

Saoi thought about that. He couldn't tell Kiya who he really was. He nodded, again, nuzzling Kiya's side.

"Still, I have to tell my grandpa about you," Kiya told the wolf. "Now that I'm sure you're an animal spirit that's found me. I do wonder why, though. Did I need you?"

Saoi felt drawn to Kiya. He didn't know if Kiya needed him, or if it was the other way around. He just felt better when he was with Kiya than when he wasn't.

"I think I needed you. I feel better when I'm with you," Kiya said, unable to explain that feeling he got. "It's weird ...." He leaned against the wolf, pressing his face to he fur at the creature's neck.

Saoi just relaxed against Kiya, listening. He hadn't been touched this much in years and he'd forgotten how good it felt.

Kiya was quiet for a while, looking up at the sky as he too relaxed, enjoying the quiet time with the wolf. "I used to do this a lot back home," he murmured, running a hand through his own hair and shaking it out a little. "Not with wolves, mind you. Just by myself. I remember my dad would have to go out and find me sometimes, because I'd fall asleep outside. I love the woods."

If he had been human at the moment, Saoi would have smiled. He was born a wolf, and spent most of his childhood in the forest. That was one of the main reasons he chose Santa Cruz for graduate school. It was one of several graduate schools he could have chosen for his research.

"I spent a lot of time outdoors at home, you know. On a reservation, yeah. If you didn't know already, I'm Native American," Kiya told the animal, shifting to lie down on his stomach next to him, the branches and leaves not bothering him. "Half, at least.

But it might as well be full anyway."

Saoi 's heart sped up when Kiya lay down and he scooted up beside him, pressing his body alongside the boy's.

Kiya liked that, and he moved closer, almost halfway on top of the wolf. "I like that I am. Even though it seems to surprise people when I tell them. Once a guy walked up to me speaking in Spanish! I didn't think I looked Hispanic until that day," he chuckled, nuzzling fur.

It surprised Saoi that he was still aroused by Kiya in this form. Usually, as a wolf, he only found other wolves attractive. And it was more than attraction; he was comfortable in a way that he didn't usually feel around anyone who wasn't of his own kind.

"But it's nice. I can usually get any guy I want... usually," Kiya said, frowning a little at the thought of the one man he couldn't have.

Saoi felt a surge of jealousy at that. Unreasonable, he knew, but as a wolf he was rarely reasonable about such things. Pressing up against Kiya, he didn't want to think of anyone else touching the boy but him.

Kiya wasn't sure of what else to talk to the wolf about, so he went quiet after that, trying not to think about Brian or anyone else. He wasn't exactly sure when it happened, but he fell asleep soon after, his hand gripping the wolf's fur as he drifted off.

∽

Saoi woke in the woods. This wasn't that unusual, but waking up with the scent of Kiya in every pore and then realizing that the boy was wrapped around him, that was new. And very arousing. Luckily, he hadn't shifted in his sleep and was still a wolf. But he didn't know how Kiya would feel about waking up holding a very aroused wolf.

The first thing Kiya felt when he started to wake up was that he was a little damp and cold. Then he started to feel other things. The ground was hard and crunchy when he shifted, but he was also curled around something very warm and very soft. He blinked open his eyes and looked around, not yet realizing where he was.

Saoi tried not to react to Kiya wriggling against him. He didn't want to startle him.

Kiya blinked a few more times and then slowly looked down at the wolf in his arms. "Fell asleep," he murmured quietly, not moving to get up just yet.

He couldn't help it, Saoi licked Kiya's throat. He tasted fantastic.

"Morning to you, too," Kiya mumbled, closing one eye as he yawned again.

Saoi's fur was damp from the morning fog, but one of the advantages of being a wolf was that he was still warm. And the body holding him felt really good.

Kiya slowly started to pull himself away, stretching and making a small face as he groaned quietly. "Well, I can certainly feel you are male," he teased the wolf.

Saoi rolled on to his belly, hiding his erection from the boy.

Kiya blinked a few more times and rubbed at his eyes. "Can't believe I did that again," he mumbled and then stood up, reaching for the zipper on his jeans as he turned around to face the tree. "Gotta pee ..."

As a human, Saoi might have been embarrassed, but not as a wolf. On the other hand, it didn't really help ease his erection. Instead, he moved closer.

Kiya finally got himself out of the jeans and sighed, resting his free hand on the tree as he relieved himself.

Saoi was instantly alert, sniffing excitedly as the human marked the tree the same way a wolf would. He sniffed the air again, and, like all wolves, learned more about Kiya from the scent.

"Hey," Kiya complained and shook his head at the animal crowding him. He fixed himself back up when he was done, turning around to look at the wolf again. "I guess I'll have to go now," he said with a small sigh. "Class and all ...."

Saoi hadn't even been thinking about his own responsibilities, but the reminder made him feel foolish. He nodded and stood up, nuzzling Kiya's hand again.

"I'll come look for you later, yeah?" Kiya said, leaning down to pet him and nudge his cheek against the wolf's nose so he could lick him if he wanted to.

Which Saoi happily did, tail wagging.

"Okay, see you," Kiya said, petting him one more time before he stood up and stretched again. He smiled down at the wolf and then looked around, finding out where to walk before he headed that way.

Saoi walked Kiya to the edge and then ran back through the woods to where he had stored his own clothes, changing and dashing to class. The same nine o'clock biology class in which Kiya was his student.

Chapter Six

The week after he fell asleep with the wolf, Kiya found himself spending more time in the woods than ever. And much of the time the wolf would be there, waiting for him. Even when he wasn't, Kiya enjoyed the quiet and it made him feel closer to the wolf in some way. His wolf friend made him feel like he could tell him anything, and Kiya did spend time talking about school and his family back home. The wolf listened. Other times Kiya didn't want to talk, and the wolf seemed perfectly content to just sit with him. Unlike people, there was no pressure either way, and Kiya felt more like himself around the unexpectedly gentle animal.

The following week was the second field trip in Brian's biology class. This time they went to the beach instead of the woods. Brian had arranged to borrow a van to take those who didn't have cars to meet down at the Natural Bridges State Park. He wasn't surprised to find Kiya among the students who crowded into the passenger van. Yet, he did feel a mixture of relief and sadness when Kiya sat at the other end, as far from Brian as possible. And Brian couldn't help glancing in the rear-view mirror to watch him.

Once at the ocean, Brian led his class down and around the beach, along the cliffs, to the rock area of the tide pools. It was a warm day, but the wind off the ocean was cool and whipped everyone's hair and clothing. He watched in amusement and want as Kiya struggled to tie his hair back so he could see.

Kiya had grown up in South Dakota, and he'd been to the beach only a couple of times since arriving last September. He was really surprised to realize that so many different kinds of sea life lived in the rocks along the shore. He'd known there were many different animals in the water, and had enjoyed seeing the seals and otters at the pier. Now he learned about a whole new world of kelp, algae, mussels, crabs, anemone, and star fish. They were everywhere, living on and in the rocks. He watched and listened as Brian explained it. The teacher had to shout over the wind and the students were huddling close so they could hear him. It was difficult for Kiya to keep his distance when he wanted to be so much closer, and not just for warmth. When Brian set them off for exploring and drawing, Kiya found a pool in the rocks, water still filling it as the tide had gone out. In it was a spiney creature and a crab. Kiya set about drawing it and noticed all the tiny creatures in the small area. He was startled when a shadow fell across him and looked up into Brian's eyes.

"That's very good," Brian encouraged. "You've got at least a dozen plants and animals in that two foot pool." He tried to keep his voice even. The wind gusted and the waves were loud but he still felt like he and Kiya were in some kind of bubble, the rest of the world forgotten for the moment.

"Yeah, there's a lot in there," Kiya said. Why did Brian still have to have such beautiful eyes and such a warm smile? He flushed and hunkered over his drawing again, trying to make sure to list every creature he could identify. It was hard to use the book with the wind blowing the pages.

Brian stood for another few moments and then forced himself to push away his disappointment and move on to check on the other students. One of the students got too ambitious and actually fell in the icy water when one of the waves crashed against the rocks he was climbing. Luckily, he wasn't injured. Only cold, salt encrusted and embarrassed. Brian eventually managed to round them all back up and get them loaded into the van.

Kiya was in the back again, tired and a little chilled from his day at the sea. He had learned more than he thought he would, but his thoughts now turned to the man driving the van. Even though Brian was still giving him looks, Kiya didn't dare take it as interest, since Brian had so obviously and literally pushed him away. He wished he could get over his feelings for Brian, but they didn't seem to be fading at all.

☙

By the time that they were back on campus, Kiya was worn out and feeling sticky with the sea salt, so the first thing he did after getting to his room was to go take a shower. The hot water made him feel warm and comfortable. No one was in the apartment so he walked back to his room in just a towel. Sitting down on his bed, Kiya dried his hair first before he went about getting dressed in just an old pair of shorts and a t-shirt. Once dressed, he grabbed a band and pulled his hair up and away from his face. It was much too hot to leave it down. He decided to get some studying in, laying down on his stomach across his bed with a lollipop in his mouth and putting his headphones in as he pulled out his textbook.

"Such a beautiful sight."

The sudden voice startled Kiya and then he felt a hand on his ass.

For a minute, Kiya thought that James was back and he was being a little pervert, but he realized that James would never do something like that with him, even if he were playing around. He pulled the headphones out of his ears and moved away from the hand as he looked back, frowning when he saw Ted.

"What the hell are you doing in here?" Kiya asked, his heart beating faster.

Ted sat down, blocking Kiya into the bed and reaching for his hair like he usually did.

"Come to give you what you need," the big man insisted with a strange look in his eye.

"I don't need anything from you," Kiya said, shaking his head as he tried to lean away. "Ted, seriously, you need to stop this."

But Ted ignored Kiya just as he always did. Leaning over, Ted used his body to pin Kiya to the bed, fingers tangling around his damp hair as he closed his mouth over Kiya's.

Kiya's words were muffled against Ted's lips as he twisted

65

around and pressed his hands against Ted's chest, attempting to push him away.

"I said stop!" he gasped, once he was able to turn his head away. The hand in his hair pulled sharply, causing his neck muscles to strain. "I don't want you or this!"

Ted wasn't listening, one hand still holding Kiya by his hair while the other moved down his body, fumbling to open his shorts. Ted kissed and nipped at the side of Kiya's face.

Kiya was beginning to panic. He struggled, hitting Ted in the chest and wherever else he could reach. He broke free of the kiss and yelled. "Stop it, Ted! What are you doing?"

Ted ignored his struggles, ripping open the front of Kiya's shorts. Then he pulled and pushed Kiya onto his stomach again and began yanking down Kiya's shorts and underwear.

Kiya was shaking. He couldn't let this happen. He had to fight more, no matter how much bigger and stronger Ted was. Kiya knew nobody was home to hear his cries and desperately struggled to free himself from Ted. He pushed himself up onto his hands and knees the first chance he got and kicked out as hard as he could, hoping he would hit Ted hard enough to leave him alone. But the kick glanced off Ted's leg and left Kiya even more vulnerable as Ted used the motion to strip off the shorts and maneuver between Kiya's legs.

"Ted," Kiya cried out. He felt like his heart was trying to beat its way out of his chest in his fear of what would happen next. "Please don't do this!"

"Just settle down, Kiya," Ted said in a soothing voice that didn't fit his actions. "Relax and enjoy it," he added, licking his fingers and then reaching between Kiya's legs.

"No! Dammit, I said no!" Kiya insisted, clenching his buttocks together in an attempt to stop him.

Ted caressed and squeezed Kiya's bottom as if he truly thought that if he just fondled him more, Kiya would submit and enjoy it. Kiya still couldn't believe this was happening, no matter what he did or said. It was as if Ted just didn't comprehend that he was doing this against Kiya's will. Kiya knew Ted was forceful, but he never thought that it would get this far. He didn't realize that he was crying until he tasted the salt on his lips, which only made him start to struggle more, a burst of energy helping him.

"Fuck, I've missed you," Ted moaned, fumbling to open his own jeans, his other hand still holding the back of Kiya's hair.

"You're hurting me," Kiya whimpered when Ted's grip tightened, hoping that maybe he could get through to Ted and that he would stop if he started to realize what he was doing. Kiya knew, though, from experience, that Ted had no intentions of stopping until he got what he had come for.

"Don't fight it, Kiya, I know you want me," Ted insisted, having freed his cock now and rubbing the head against Kiya's bare ass.

"I don't. I really don't. Please stop this," Kiya sobbed, his hips jerking away when he felt Ted's cock.

"What the-?" another voice gasped from the doorway.

Kiya couldn't see who was there, but he sobbed in relief. "Help me!" he managed to choke out, his voice quavering.

"Ted, what are you doing? Kiya, are you okay?" James' voice shook.

"Get him off of me!" Kiya cried, squeezing his eyes shut in embarrassment. He couldn't take care of this himself. He hated needing someone else to help him.

"Get out," Ted insisted, snarling at James.

James wasn't having any of it; he strode into the room and grabbed the back of Ted's shirt, yanking on it.

"Ted, leave Kiya the fuck alone or I swear I will break your neck!"

Ted let go of his dick and Kiya's hair, taking a swing at James and falling backwards when James dodged.

Kiya scrambled away the moment his hair was released, pressing himself back into the corner of the bed as he watched James fight. For him. Which was surprising, to say the least.

James stepped closer to Kiya, moving between him and Ted,

who was staggering to his feet. Kiya could see that James was upset and shaking but had his fists raised in front of him like he was in a boxing ring or something. He yelled, "Get the hell out of here, Ted, or I am going to have to fuck you up."

Kiya never thought he'd be so glad to see James in the room. He brought his knees up to his chest and reached for the blanket to pull up over his body, waiting for Ted to leave.

Ted glared at James, tucking his prick back into his jeans. "Kiya's my boyfriend," he declared. "You shouldn't get between us like this."

"Get! Out!" James barked, face red now.

Ted looked past him to Kiya. "I see now why you've been afraid of me," he said, the clearly unbalanced man now implying that the situation was James' fault. "This isn't over," he declared and then strode out, slamming the front door as he left the apartment.

Kiya stared after him for a moment in shock before he burst into tears again, clinging onto the blanket as if it were a lifeline.

James collapsed then, sitting on the edge of the bed and shuddering. He looked pretty shook up as he glanced over at Kiya. "Hey, are you okay? Did he hurt you? Should I call somebody?" he asked.

"I'm so stupid," Kiya mumbled in between his sobs, feeling like an idiot even though it really wasn't his fault. What could he have done to stop Ted?

James was pale as he reached a shaking hand out to touch Kiya's arm. "Key, did you hear me? Are you okay? Do you need a doctor or something?"

"I'm fine," Kiya murmured tearfully, using the blanket to wipe at his face. He just wanted to curl up under it and disappear. He looked up at James for a moment, noticing the effect the ordeal had had on him. "I-I'm sorry."

"That guy is nuts," James declared. "He still doesn't even get it." James wiped his hands on his jeans; apparently they were sweaty.

"I'm not his boyfriend," Kiya mumbled, looking down for a moment. "If it weren't for you-I-James, thank you. I know I treat you like shit half the time, but thank you." He dropped the blanket and leaned over to hug him, since really, if James hadn't walked in there and pulled Ted off, things would have been a hell of a lot worse.

James hugged him, awkwardly patting Kiya's back.

"He doesn't have the right to touch you if you don't want him to, Kiya. I'm not in this college by accident. I'm straight, but I don't confuse that with thinking gay means you have to put up with a creep like him."

Kiya nodded, remembering that they were in College Ten, the one for social justice and everything else related to it. "I don't know what to do. He just walks in here like he owns me and-ugh, I hate being scared like this," he mumbled against James' shoulder, tears still stinging his eyes.

"Well, first thing is-we are gonna start locking the front door. Do you want to call the police? I am a witness to what he-erm, was doing." James offered.

"I don't know," Kiya said quietly, and then shifted to pull the sheet around himself again without moving away from James. He had realized that he only had a shirt on that wasn't covering anything. "You saw the way he was acting? Like he's delusional or something."

"I think he's crazy all right," James added, frowning. "But that means he might not stop. You know?"

"I know. He hasn't," Kiya sighed. He knew that James probably wasn't very comfortable with Kiya clinging to him like he was, but he was feeling really vulnerable at the moment which he hated. And which gave him another reason to resent Ted.

James sat there, quiet for a few minutes. He didn't pull away from Kiya, even if he was a bit stiff. "Is there someone you want me to call?" he asked, eventually.

"No," Kiya murmured, forcing himself to pull back and move away from James. "Sorry about that."

James patted his arm. Though he looked relieved, he still said, "That's okay. Hey, that threw even me." He seemed to search Kiya's face. "You sure there isn't someone you want to be with right now, a friend or something?"

"Yeah, I think I do," Kiya said, pulling his knees up to his chest under the sheet. He wasn't actually thinking of someone. Not Jack or even Audrey. He was thinking of the wolf; he just wanted to curl up with him and cry until he felt better.

"Well, I'll help however I can," James said. "And I'll make sure everyone else in the apartment knows to lock the door and keep an eye out for Ted."

"I don't want everyone to know what happened," Kiya said immediately, not wanting to get pitying looks or anything that would make his situation worse than it already was.

James frowned. "It's not your fault, Kiya," he insisted. "But I won't tell them details if you don't want. Just that Ted is getting dangerous."

"I know it's not my fault. I just don't want people treating me like I'll break," Kiya said, sliding his arms around his legs. "But thank you. That's fine."

James got to his feet and retrieved his backpack from where he had dropped it near the door. "I'm gonna lock that door right now, just in case," he warned as he gave one last concerned look at Kiya and left the room.

Kiya nodded and watched him go, waiting a moment before he moved to get up, finding a new pair of underwear to pull on. He then went to his closet and got a pair of jeans, dressing and pushing his feet into his shoes quickly before James could get back.

He heard James in the kitchen when he was done.

Kiya knew his hair was probably a mess, but he didn't bother with it, leaving the room without even looking at it. "I'll be-I'll be back later. You'll be around?" he asked when he saw James.

James looked surprised but nodded. "You gonna be okay?"

"Yeah, just-be around," Kiya said, nodding with a small smile before he left the apartment. He headed straight outside and toward to the woods. He looked around nervously, afraid for a moment that Ted might still be nearby. Kiya then darted into the forest.

∽

There were more students arriving back in the apartments now, music blaring and people talking. But once Kiya was in the woods, all that seemed to fade to quiet. He didn't see any sign of Ted and, after moving further among the trees, he heard a soft "wuff" sound that he recognized right away as his wolf greeting him.

"There you are," Kiya whispered, his eyes already welling up as he turned, stumbling over to him. "I needed you."

Saoi sniffed and felt the fur on his back stand up as he smelled that other man on Kiya. He rushed up to the boy, struggling to control himself so that he wouldn't knock him down in his haste to rub up against him.

Kiya knelt down in front of him, sliding his arms around the wolf's body to pull him closer as he started to softly cry.

Saoi longed to shift, wanting nothing more than to be in his human form so he could wrap his arms around Kiya. He didn't dare. Instead, he moved so that he was pressing as much of his body to Kiya's as he could, licking salty tears off the boy's face gently as Kiya cried. Saoi could smell that the man who had bothered Kiya in the woods before had been touching him and growled, worried about what that could mean.

"I wish you were there," Kiya whispered after a few minutes of weeping, his fingers tight in the wolf's fur.

Saoi felt an overwhelming swell of anger at the man who would cause Kiya to be so frightened and growled without realizing he was doing so. He realized that, wolf or man, he was going to put a stop to it. All he could do at the moment was let Kiya take comfort from him. He nuzzled Kiya's face, licking away tears.

Eventually Kiya calmed down enough to say more, knowing

that the wolf was probably really worried. "I'm okay," he said softly. "Just feeling shaken up, I guess. He wouldn't stop-no matter how many times I said no, he just wouldn't stop-and it felt like before ..."

Saoi's heart sped up and, without thinking about it, he immediately began sniffing at Kiya more closely, trying to figure out just what the man had done to him. There was the scent of Kiya's fear and the smell of the other man's sweat, but no hint of blood or sex. Saoi was too concerned over unanswered questions to be relieved.

"My roommate came in just in time," Kiya continued to explain quietly. "He saved me."

Saoi wasn't going to allow this to continue and he growled again thinking about it. He was furious that anyone would hurt Kiya, and the part of him that was more wolf than man wanted to tear anyone who touched Kiya apart until there was nothing left.

"It's okay," Kiya whispered, realizing the wolf was angry. "I'm okay. I just-I need to be with someone right now." He knew the wolf was an animal, but he felt like so much more than that to Kiya.

It amazed Saoi that Kiya had chosen to come to him after that. Despite Saoi's anger at what had happened, he couldn't help the feeling of pride running through him at this affirmation that Kiya trusted him, wanted his comfort. He did his best to give it. Saoi nuzzled and licked the boy, pushing his muzzle under Kiya's hair and against his neck to be as close to his skin as he could get.

Kiya lay down on the ground and waited for his wolf to snuggle up closer, his eyes closing as he slid his arms around the furry body again. "I never thought I'd do this here. Back home, sure, but here-it's different here," he murmured after a while.

That definitely had Saoi curious. Did Kiya know wolves where he lived? He seemed so relaxed around Saoi. As he thought about this, Saoi draped himself against Kiya's body, half covering it, but careful not to crush him with his weight. He wanted to cover

Kiya and never let anyone touch him again.

This was just what Kiya needed. Who cared if it was with a wolf and not another person? He didn't have anyone else that would just hold him while he cried and listen so intently to whatever he said. Now Kiya was beginning to feel tired. Unbelievably so. It was all the fighting and the crying; it was finally getting to him. He sighed and quietly began to relax, feeling warm and safe where he was. No longer fighting the urge, Kiya found himself bringing his thumb to his mouth and closing his lips around it, sucking gently. With Saoi covering him and lost in the comfort of his thumb, Kiya's eyes began to grow heavy.

Saoi laid his head on the boy's shoulder, nose near his neck, and began to relax his own body when Kiya did. He lay there, listening to Kiya's breathing and heartbeat, reveling in the scent and the feel of the boy's body against his own. Saoi wished again that he could shift and let himself enjoy and comfort Kiya as a man.

Kiya was asleep before he knew it, feeling more relaxed than he had felt all day. Just before he drifted off, he remembered thinking that he wished the wolf was a man, because this was just the kind of man he needed.

For the rest of the weekend, Kiya tried to be around the wolf as much as possible. He slept for the rest of the night with him and woke up in the morning, only to head back to his room to tell James that he was fine. He showered and dressed and walked right back out into the forest. He didn't seem to care about schoolwork; too many other things were weighing on his mind to be able to focus on that. He figured he'd just have to work hard to catch up later.

❧

As a wolf, the passage of time signaled the rhythm of the natural to Saoi; its pull told him when to hunt, when to patrol his territory, when to seek shelter. His priority now was Kiya-he needed to be there for Kiya, to him and help him feel better. Saoi had spent the entire weekend in the woods with Kiya. Monday morning was a rude shock for Brian, shifting back into human form and nearly panicking, both about how far he'd fallen behind and also over his concerns about the man who had been harassing Kiya.

Brian managed to fake his way through the morning lecture class but found he could hardly focus with Kiya so nearby. Kiya appeared a little lost and frazzled-a bit different from the way he usually looked. Brian kept having to stamp down the urge to comfort him. It was almost painful not to be able to touch him after spending so much time curled together. Brian spent most of the class in a silent argument with himself about his involvement with Kiya. He had already crossed the line, even if no one but himself knew it. He couldn't stand to do nothing about Kiya's problems. So when class ended, he quickly moved to intercept the young man.

"Kiya," he called out to him.

Kiya was terribly behind in his course work. He had struggled through class, writing down as many notes as he could and telling himself that he had to catch up or else. He was thinking of bringing his homework with him to the woods instead of leaving it in the room. Maybe he could do it while spending time with the wolf. Sure, he wouldn't get any help, but as long as it didn't rain, he'd be fine. Kiya was hurrying out of the class like he usually did now, but stopped when he heard someone call his name. He looked back, frowning a little as he waited for Brian to walk up to him.

Brian caught up to him quickly. "Do you have another class right now, or do you have time to talk a bit?" he asked, shoving his hands in his pockets to keep from reaching out and touching Kiya.

"I don't have class after this, but I have to study," Kiya mumbled, not wanting to be near Brian any longer than he had to. Since the rebuff, Kiya felt awkward around him and was doubly embarrassed to be so behind in his course work.

"I know I don't have the right to ask, but could you talk with me for a bit?" Brian asked. Being close to Kiya was intoxicating, the smell and warmth making everything in Brian ache to touch him. It was no longer only the wolf that had fallen hopelessly for Kiya.

"Okay, but just for a bit," Kiya agreed quietly, still not looking up at him.

Brian led them away from the entrance of the building to a bench set under some trees and motioned for Kiya to sit down.

Kiya pulled his bag off and slowly sat down, resting the bag in his lap as he waited for Brian to talk.

Brian paced for a moment and then forced himself to stop and take a seat on the bench. Turning to face Kiya, he gripped the edge of the bench hard with his hand, still warring with his instincts. "I know I don't have the right to pry into your personal life," he began, feeling like he was stumbling through it. "But I am worried about you."

"What for?" Kiya asked in confusion, looking up at Brian. "I thought you didn't care about me."

Brian flushed, looking away. Shit, this was difficult. He forced himself to address the issue head on. "You were flirting with me, and if I flirted back or anything else, it would have been a violation of the university's ethics code," he explained.

"You pushed me away," Kiya said, still vividly remembering the moment. "You could've just said 'stop flirting with me' or whatever, or you could've even said what you just said. But you pushed me."

Brian winced. "Yeah, I should have tried to explain it better," he said. "I wasn't trying to upset you, but it rattled me."

"So what are you saying now?" Kiya asked guardedly, refusing to get his hopes up.

"Um," Brian stumbled again. "I noticed that you seemed upset and I wanted to offer my help if there's a problem."

"I'm fine," Kiya answered, still unsure of what Brian wanted, exactly.

Brian frowned. He knew it wasn't true but he couldn't say how. "It can be hard to be, um, different and far from home," Brian tried. "Sometimes you get in over your head and don't think people will understand. I know, my family is far away too."

"Yeah," Kiya murmured, a small frown still on his lips. "Do you think I'm going to tell you about everything that's going on now or something, just because you said that?" He knew very well that he was being overly defensive, but he couldn't help it. He could still feel the sting of Brian's earlier rejection.

Brian sighed. "I suppose not," he answered. "But I don't want you to feel like you can't if you want to. And if you don't want to talk to me, please find someone you trust."

"I kinda ... I kind of have someone," Kiya murmured, biting his lip gently. The wolf never talked back to him or anything, but he listened and he obviously gave him what he needed.

Brian realized again that he had no way to ask Kiya about the man harassing him without giving away that he was the wolf. "Okay, just-well, I hope you aren't afraid to ask for help if you need it. UCSC is strongly supportive of alternative students. And I will help if I can, too,"

"What do you mean by 'alternative'?" Kiya asked, tilting his head slightly.

Brian nodded. "Well, I assume that if you were flirting with me, you aren't straight," he explained, though he could probably have added that there were support groups for students of color as well. But since Kiya's problem was with a man, it probably wasn't about his race or heritage.

"Oh, well, so now you're assuming that I'm having troubles like that?" Kiya asked, scowling as he started to get up.

This was why Brian hadn't tried to talk to Kiya when he had been flirting. He just wasn't good at things like this. He didn't know how humans handled certain emotional issues. He groaned. "I really didn't mean to offend. I just-you seemed upset, so..."

"Okay, whatever. If I need someone to talk to, I'll find someone," Kiya said, really wishing he knew where this was all coming from. There were a million things that could be bugging him, but why would Brian jump straight to relationship problems? He didn't know about him and Ted, unless someone told? He doubted James would have.

Brian felt helpless and foolish. After spending weeks, even several nights, with Kiya, he felt very close to him as a wolf. It stung to be pushed away now, even when he knew Kiya had no reason to suspect he was the wolf. "Okay," he said quietly, resigned to the fact that he wasn't going to be able to help like this.

"Bye, Brian," Kiya murmured, and then left, walking toward his college so that he could set his things down and then go out to meet the wolf.

Chapter Seven

It was Wednesday, and Kiya was finally feeling caught up with his classes. He had spent most of the last two days reading and figuring out what was going on so he could at least regain control of that part of his life. Now he was heading out to the Coffee House to meet up with Audrey and Jack since he hadn't talked to them in a while. He still wasn't planning on telling them about Ted, though. When he arrived, Audrey and Jack were on the sofa, with a couple of other people. Audrey was smiling at a young woman sitting beside her, and, Kiya noticed, holding her hand.

"Hey, you guys," Kiya said, walking over after he got his coffee. He smiled at the new girl, holding his hand out for her to shake. "I'm Kiya. I don't think I've met you before?"

"Oh, so you're Kiya," she teased. "I'm Debra. Audrey's told me about you." She shook his hand and then gestured to the dark-haired young man sitting on a chair. "This is Jacob."

"Good things, I hope," Kiya said with a smile, turning to see Jacob. He smiled at him, holding out his hand for him to shake as well.

Jacob grinned up at him, holding Kiya's hand just a bit longer than normal and giving it a small squeeze as he let go. "Nice to meet you," he said, dark eyes shining. Jacob had near black hair and an almost coffee complexion.

"Nice to meet you, too," Kiya said with a small smirk, as he very obviously looked up and down Jacob's fit body. "Why haven't I seen you around here before?"

Jacob blushed and shrugged. "Just started coming to the Coffee House last time," he said. "And I had a Wednesday night class last quarter. Of course, if I'd known about you, I would have found a way here sooner."

"Yeah? Well, now you know what to do with your Wednesday evenings," Kiya murmured, raising one eyebrow suggestively. Flirting came naturally to him, it was nothing.

"Is he always like this?" Debra asked. Both Audrey and Jack nodded, laughing.

"I hope so," Jacob added.

"It obviously isn't a bad thing," Kiya said as he sat back in his seat, taking a small sip of his coffee. "Jacob likes it."

"So, where were you last week?" Jack asked. Jacob scooted his chair closer to Kiya's.

"Had school crap to do," Kiya said, definitely noticing Jacob's move, but pretending not to, only glancing at him for a second.

"The quarters go by so quickly," Jacob complained. "It's half over and I am behind again."

"Do you need help studying?" Kiya asked curiously.

"Oh, I'd like that," Jacob answered, grinning again.

"Yeah, like either of you will get any work done then," Audrey teased. Debra rolled her eyes and kissed her.

"We could," Kiya said, looking at Debra. "For maybe the first thirty minutes."

Jacob's eyes lit up and he seemed very eager. "Sounds good to me."

Kiya grinned at him and nodded, thinking that he needed some kind of sexual relief that didn't involve his hand. "It's a plan then, Jacob."

They laughed and talked for the next couple of hours, with Jacob getting bold enough to reach out and touch Kiya sometimes. It was fun, like it had been before Ted got so possessive and controlling.

Kiya had already made up his mind. He was going to either go back with Jacob to his place, or Jacob was coming back with him to his room. Kiya needed the sex and maybe something else would come from it, but he wasn't sure, since all Jacob seemed to be interested in was his looks. Which was fine for the time being.

When the Coffee House was over and his friends were leaving, Jacob slid his hand into Kiya's, smiling at him. "So, do you have to go home?"

"Is that your way of inviting me over to your place?" Kiya asked, smirking and squeezing Jacob's hand. "Or we could go back to mine, but my roommate wouldn't enjoy seeing two guys fucking right across from his bed."

Jacob's eyes widened at that. "My place," he said, nodding eagerly.

Kiya could tell that excited Jacob and was pleased. "Lead the way then, my friend," he said, nodding slightly.

Jacob slid his arm around Kiya's waist as they moved outside. "I have a place near campus," he said.

"Kiya, what are you doing?" Ted was leaning against a tree nearby, waiting.

"Fuck," Kiya groaned before he even saw him, his hand tightening around Jacob's. "None of your fucking business. Keep going, Jacob."

Jacob looked confused, but nodded.

"Fooling around on me, Kiya?" Ted sneered, stepping in their path.

"I'm not fooling around on you because we're not fucking together anymore!" Kiya snarled. He was really getting pissed off by Ted and his crazy behavior. "Leave me alone!"

"If he says he's not with you anymore, then you'd better believe it," Jacob warned Ted.

Ted looked like he was about to hit Jacob or do something equally nasty when several other people stepped out of the Center, including Jack.

"Ted, you bothering Kiya again?" Jack said in a voice that was both mocking and held warning.

"I suggest you go," Kiya said to Ted, thinking that the man was damn lucky he hadn't report him for attempted rape already. If he kept harassing him like this, though, Kiya would forget about his pride and do it.

Ted looked between them, still seeming like he might challenge them. Then he scowled. "This isn't done," he snapped and strode away.

"Who was that guy?" Jacob asked.

"A nut case who won't leave Kiya alone," Jack answered, and gave Kiya a friendly pat on the back.

Kiya looked after Ted, sighing and shaking his head as he tried to calm down. Kiya could only pray Ted never caught him alone again. "Sorry you had to see that," he told Jacob.

Jacob nodded. "Not your fault," he said and guided them to his car, parked nearby.

"Annoys the hell out of me, though," Kiya murmured, running a hand through his hair and shaking it out a little.

Once in the car, Jacob reaching a hand out to touch Kiya. "You look amazing," he said.

"I know. You're not so bad yourself," Kiya teased, tilting his head into the touch.

Jacob leaned over from the driver's seat, lips pressed to Kiya's, and Kiya closed his eyes leaning up into the kiss, telling himself that he needed this so badly. He really did. Jacob kissed him, a bit sloppily but certainly enthusiastically, his other hand coming to rest on Kiya's thigh. Kiya opened his mouth more for the man, his head tilting as the kiss was deepened and Jacob's hand crept up Kiya's thigh, teasing and then cupping his crotch. Kiya made a small surprised noise against Jacob's lips, pulling back to smirk at him. "Couldn't even make it back to your place?" he asked.

"Hard to keep my hands off you," Jacob agreed. "But I suppose it would be more fun if we drove to my apartment now." With that he gave Kiya's cloth-covered cock a gentle squeeze and then turned back to start the car.

"Mmmhmm. Unfortunately, I can't help but be irresistible," Kiya said, reaching to pull his seatbelt on.

◞◝

Saoi watched the scene from his hiding place in the darkness of the nearby trees. It took all his control not to leap at the man who threatened Kiya. He wasn't going to let that tall blond man anywhere near Kiya again. He didn't dare show his wolf form in front of the small crowd of people, though. Still, he was on the verge of doing just that when one of Kiya's companions intervened.

Saoi was also quite distracted and upset to see Kiya with another man. He could tell by the scents on the air though that the new one wasn't the one who had tried to hurt Kiya. He could also tell that Kiya was aroused by him. Saoi had to fight back his jealousy at the new dark haired man and his arm around Kiya's waist. Even more distressing was watching Kiya get in the car with the stranger. The wolf didn't care if Kiya was supposed to be off limits. In this form, Saoi felt deeply that Kiya was his, was supposed to be his lover. He crouched in the dark, growling low in his throat as the other man kissed Kiya.

Ironically, one of the things that helped Saoi keep control was that he wasn't the only one watching the scene with seething jealousy. Ted, as he heard the blond man was named, was also standing in the shadows, hands clenched tightly as he watched. Saoi could smell the man's anger. Saoi focused on him, trying to memorize everything about Kiya's attacker. He was alert to see if Ted would try to interfere again and thought the man was close to doing so when the kiss ended and the other man behind the wheel drove away, with Kiya beside him.

The wolf shook himself again, trying not to imagine what Kiya would be doing that night. Instead, he followed Ted as the blond bully stalked away. Saoi tracked him to his car, making sure to memorize not only the smell of the car, but the make, model, and license number as well. Ted's car had a student parking sticker, which meant that his car would be registered with the parking department. Brian was going to find Ted and let him know that Kiya was not to be touched again.

⁓

Jacob laughed. He drove them down to the Westside of town and pulled into the parking lot of an apartment complex. Once there, he led Kiya up the outside stairs. Jacob fumbled with his keys for a minute before unlocking it. "I share the apartment, but I have my own room," he whispered.

"That's cool," Kiya murmured in reply, looking around curiously as the door was unlocked. He heard the sound of music coming from one of the rooms, but the front room was empty.

"Um, want something to drink? Water, soda, beer?" Jacob offered.

"Just water is fine," Kiya said, slipping his hands into his pockets.

Jacob stepped into the small kitchen area, getting a glass and filling it with ice and water and grabbing a soda for himself.

"Thanks," Kiya said, taking a sip of the water once he got the glass. "So, going to give me a tour of your bedroom?"

Jacob nodded eagerly, taking Kiya's hand and leading him to the back. It was small, with a futon bed, a chest of drawers, a desk with a computer on it and some band posters on the wall. Jacob set his soda on a bedside table and then turned back to wrap his arms around Kiya.

Kiya leaned back against Jacob with a small smile, sipping at the water as he looked around the cramped but mostly comfortable room. "Not bad," he said, teasing again.

Jacob rubbed against Kiya and Kiya could feel Jacob's erection pressing against his ass. Jacob pulled back Kiya's hair, nibbling on his neck.

"Mm, okay, want you," Kiya mumbled once Jacob nipped at a particularly sensitive part of his neck. He leaned over to set the water down and then turned around in the man's arms, cupping Jacob's face as he kissed him again, harder. Jacob kissed and licked Kiya's mouth. One arm was still wrapped around Kiya's waist, hand at the small of his back, pulling him against his own body.

Kiya hissed softly against Jacob's lips, his chest arching as he leaned up to kiss him harder, one arm sliding around the man's neck. "Mmm...." He felt Jacob's hand move down his back to squeeze his ass and the fingers of the other hand sliding down his chest and pinching his nipple. "Bed," Kiya moaned, thrusting against him.

"Yeah," Jacob agreed, giving Kiya's ass another squeeze and stepping back. He kicked off his shoes as he stripped out of his jacket and shirt.

Kiya followed him, pulling his own shirt off and starting on his jeans. "You have condoms? I have them if you don't," he asked as he pushed his jeans down with his underwear.

"Sure, I got them," Jacob answered, stepping out of his jeans and shorts too. His cock bobbed in front of him as he stepped forward, reached into a drawer beside his bed and pulled out a couple of foil packets and a bottle of lube.

Kiya watched him, biting his lip once again as he looked Jacob over. The man's body was good, even a bit more muscle than he had thought before. "Hot," he said, beckoning Jacob closer.

Jacob eagerly reached for Kiya again. "You are so hot," he whispered.

"Mm, tell me something I don't know," Kiya murmured, looking up into the man's dark brown eyes.

"Vain too," Jacob add, pulling Kiya against him so that their cocks rubbed together.

"Nothing wrong with that," Kiya said, his eyes falling shut as he thrust against him, moaning once again. Jacob didn't answer, exactly, choosing to suck on Kiya's neck right below his ear, both hands sliding down to cup Kiya's ass. Kiya tilted his head a little more so that Jacob could bite down harder, his hips still moving against Jacob. "More," he murmured.

"I want to fuck you," Jacob whispered against the damp skin of Kiya's neck.

"Then fuck me," Kiya whispered in reply, reaching to run his fingers through Jacob's hair before he gripped it. "Bite me harder."

"Mmm," Jacob answered, sucking hard on Kiya's neck and

reaching for the bottle of lube. He slicked his fingers and reached between Kiya's cheeks, sliding along the crevice to the hole.

Kiya's eyes squeezed tightly shut, his back arching a little so that the man's fingers would move down more.

"Yes," he whispered, not sure if he could keep standing up at this rate. He felt Jacob's fingers teasing his puckered opening, then pushing a fingertip gently inside. Jacob's hips wriggled, cock sliding against Kiya's and leaving a slick trail on his belly. Kiya clenched round the fingertip, trying to press down on it even as he continued to rub against him. "Jacob... please..."

Jacob wriggled his finger. "How do you want it?" he asked, licking Kiya's neck.

"Starting on all fours," Kiya murmured, breathing in sharply when the finger started to move. He wasn't planning on staying in one position the entire time, though. He liked to move around and change every now and then. It seemed to last longer for him when he did that.

Jacob gave another nip before pulling his finger back, and letting Kiya go long enough to help maneuver him onto the bed. Kiya flipped his hair over one shoulder as he got up on his knees, his legs spreading apart for Jacob. He was reminded for a moment about Ted forcing him into this position not too long ago. But this was now. This was wanted. He wasn't going to focus on Ted anymore. Just his own pleasure.

Jacob knelt between his legs, bringing those slick fingers to his hole again and working two in this time. Kiya closed his eyes and relaxed for him, biting his lip as the fingers slid more deeply inside. "Fuck, yes," he whispered wanting more.

Jacob twisted his fingers, finding and rubbing Kiya's prostate. Kiya jerked and groaned loudly. It had been so long since someone else had done that.

"Ready?" Jacob asked after another minute.

"Yeah," Kiya replied, looking over his shoulder back at Jacob. "Should be asking if you are?"

Jacob paused, seeming unsure how to take that for a moment.

Then he nodded and slipped his fingers out to reach for a condom.

"I'm kidding, Jacob," Kiya murmured with a small smile, having noticed the pause. "Just fuck me. I can already tell you're going to be good."

Jacob smiled at that, tearing open the package and quickly unrolling it onto his prick. He added more lube and moved up. They both gasped as he pushed inside. Kiya's fingers tightened in the sheets below him. It stung a little, but that was just because it had been a while, almost two months, since he'd done this.

"Oh, fuck, that's good," Jacob gasped, hands on Kiya's hips, as he pulled back and thrust in again.

"Mmm, yes," Kiya agreed quietly, biting down on his lip as he pushed back to move along with Jacob. Jacob thrust in and out, holding on to Kiya's hips. The bed squeaked under them and Kiya could hear the man panting. It was good, really good, but it wasn't exactly what Kiya wanted just yet. "Harder," he moaned, leaning down onto his forearms.

"Okay," Jacob gasped and picked up the pace.

Jacob was thrusting faster, but it wasn't much harder. Kiya bit his lip again and moved with him still wanting more than this from Jacob, but he didn't want the man to feel bad so he didn't ask again. At least as Jacob got closer, his thrusts got harder.

"Can... you... come?" Jacob panted, clearly trying to hold back for Kiya.

"Little more," Kiya whispered, reaching underneath his body to stroke himself as the thrusts finally got nearly as hard as he wanted. Jacob's thrusting managed to hit Kiya's sweet spot more often than not. Then he shuddered, groaning as he came. It took Kiya a few more moments, stroking himself and clenching around Jacob until he came as well.

Jacob was still panting and fell forward slightly so that he was bracing an arm against the bed on one side of Kiya.

Kiya swallowed hard, shifting so that he could rest his cheek on the bed as he caught his breath. He felt the man's cock slip from him, and Jacob fumbling a bit with the condom. Then Jacob lay down beside him, smiling and still trying to catch his breath. He reached up to stroke Kiya's sweaty hair back off his face.

Kiya lay down too, trying to avoid the spot he left on the bed. "Sorry about the wet spot" he murmured, smiling a little at him. "It was good."

Jacob grinned at him. "No problem," he said. "You are amazing," he added, fingers playing over Kiya's lips.

"I know," Kiya said out of habit, shifting closer to him as he kissed his fingertips.

Jacob looked a little confused by the response, apparently not sure how to react when Kiya made his smug quips. "You want to stay over?" he asked.

"If you don't mind?" Kiya asked softly, leaning over to kiss his lips once. Jacob kissed him back, hand caressing Kiya's face as he did. "Thanks, Jacob," Kiya murmured, his eyes closing as he moved closer for warmth.

Jacob picked his own t-shirt up off the floor and laid it over the wet spot. Then he pulled up the covers and wrapped an arm around Kiya. "Good night, Kiya."

"Night," Kiya whispered, opening one eye to look at Jacob before he drifted off to sleep.

The next morning, for the first time in a long time, Kiya woke up in another man's bed. It felt good, unbelievably good. He didn't even want to get up once his eyes were open, but he knew that he'd have to get back to campus before his class started. He turned over in Jacob's arms and gently shook his shoulder, trying wake him. Jacob made a small sound of protest but didn't open his eyes.

"Wake up," Kiya murmured, leaning over to nip at Jacob's bottom lip. "I have class."

Jacob sort of grumbled and blinked open his eyes. His expression changed when he looked at Kiya, smiling and leaning up to kiss him.

Kiya smiled against his lips, but didn't let the kiss linger for too long. "Morning," he said, already shifting to get up. "Sorry I had to wake you up."

"I guess I forgot to ask when you needed to be back," Jacob conceded.

"It's okay," Kiya said, pushing the covers away and stretching his body out, groaning slightly.

Jacob rolled toward him, hand sliding down his chest. "So, do you have an early class? You could skip it?"

"I could. Are you going to give me a good reason to?" Kiya asked, raising an eyebrow. He glanced at the time, noticing that they were up pretty early, and technically, he didn't even have a morning class.

"Sure," Jacob answered, hand continuing down to fondle Kiya's cock as he leaned in for another kiss.

They sucked each other off again, in the shower. It was a lot of fun, but Kiya wasn't exactly sure how he felt about Jacob just yet. Sure, he was hot, and he could see himself finding him for sex, but for an actual relationship... he could imagine getting bored with that very quickly. He didn't tell that to Jacob, though. Luckily, nothing about a relationship came up for the rest of the morning. Jacob took him back to the school, and left him with another kiss.

Chapter Eight

Kiya was making his way up the hill to his apartment when he heard his name spoken. He froze in place just as Ted stepped out from between two cars. Kiya cursed quietly and stopped, shaking his head when he saw him. This was what he had been afraid of, Ted catching him alone. "You have got to be kidding me," he said, glancing around quickly only to feel his stomach clench when he saw the area was deserted.

"What the hell were you doing last night?" Ted demanded. "I can't believe you went home with that guy. How dare you cheat on me?"

Kiya stepped back carefully, making sure that there was a good distance between them. "It's not cheating and you don't own me. I can go home with whoever I feel like!"

"No, you can't!" Ted shouted, as he advanced on Kiya. "You're behaving like a whore! You're nothing but a filthy whore, Kiya, and that's all you ever will be!"

"How? He's the first guy I've been with since we broke up!" Kiya exclaimed loudly, making a point to say, again, that they broke up. He knew that Ted's words were a lie but they cut into Kiya's heart just as sharply as if they had been the truth. Shock caused Kiya to falter, allowing Ted to move closer.

Ted closed the distance between them and, for the first time, he seemed to realize what Kiya was saying to him. Rage began to settle over his features as his skin darkened to an angry red and his eyes fixed themselves heatedly on Kiya. "No, I don't accept that!"

"Oh fucking well, Ted, you really don't have a choice," Kiya said, finally trying to step back again. "Just leave me alone and let me live my life!" Being this close now to Ted, Kiya saw that his ex-boyfriend's eyes appeared to be unfocused and tiny muscles in his jaw twitched involuntarily. Fear washed over Kiya as he realized that he may have misjudged the depth of Ted's jealousy. Kiya began to tremble.

Ted grabbed Kiya's wrists, his large hands squeezing and twisting mercilessly. "No, I won't!"

"You will," another voice behind Kiya said, sounding firm and familiar.

"Ow, Ted!" Kiya cried out, just when the other person spoke. He thought he recognized the voice, but he wasn't sure and was too busy trying to get away from Ted to think it through. Ted didn't look up either, yanking Kiya closer.

"Let Kiya go immediately!" Brian stepped up beside the two of them. His lip curled, baring his teeth as he cocked his head, the whites of his eyes showing as he glared at Ted.

"Who the fuck are you?" Ted snapped, warily eying Brian, who was as tall and probably more muscled than him. Brian's arms were held out to his side, ready.

Kiya looked up in surprise. "Brian?" he gasped, still tugging against Ted's tight grip, trying to free himself. His hands were beginning to go numb and his shoulders ached slightly from the effort of trying to pull away, but Ted's hands were like a vice.

"Fuck off!" Ted yelled at Brian.

Brian didn't flinch. He kicked the back of Ted's knee and reached a hand out to grab Kiya as Ted fell backwards. With Brian holding on to Kiya, Ted lost his grip on the younger man and he fell, hitting the ground while bellowing in pain and rage.

To Kiya, everything seemed to happen much too quickly. One moment he was being pulled painfully closer to Ted, and then the next he was being held by Brian, of all people, as Ted lay on the ground. "Brian!" he whispered in shock, looking up at him again.

Brian allowed himself to wrap an arm around Kiya's waist, supporting the shaking young man. "Let me call for help," he said, pulling out his cell phone and dialing campus police. Ted was howling and rolling on the ground.

"How'd you-why are you here?" Kiya asked in confusion, still watching as Brian put the phone up to his ear.

Brian relayed to the campus police where they were and asked that they send an officer, then hung up. Ted was still down, cursing them both. "I heard yelling," Brian said to Kiya.

Kiya still didn't know why Brian would be around his apartment at this time and at Kiya's college, but he didn't ask, noticing that the man still had his arm around his waist. "You didn't have to call anyone," he murmured after a moment.

"He was hurting you," Brian said. "We do have anti-harassment policies on this campus, Kiya. You don't have to put up with this." He moved them back, away from Ted. After the last time, Brian had found out what the human rules were about such behavior and had been ready to follow them.

"I don't want everyone to know," Kiya said, stumbling back with him as he eyed Ted. "Did you really hurt him?"

"I didn't do any permanent damage," Brian explained. "I don't think you have any reason to be ashamed. He's the one doing something wrong, Kiya."

"I know," Kiya said quietly, looking down at the arm around his waist. "Could I go back with you?"

Brian's eyes widened. "We need to give statements to the police, but I will be right here beside you and after, if you want."

Kiya nodded, not exactly sure why he asked that, but feeling it was probably too late to take it back. He thought he should still be angry with Brian for the initial hurtful rejection, but he felt safe with him after what had just happened.

The campus police showed up then and called an ambulance for Ted. They put him in the back of their car in the meantime as a safety precaution. They asked both Kiya and Brian for their accounts of what happened.

Kiya told the police that Ted had been harassing him that day and that it wasn't the first time he had done it, but he didn't go into details about before, still feeling strange talking about that.

He wasn't sure why. The police said they would probably need follow up statements later but that Kiya and Brian were free to go for the time being. They were arresting Ted and would be taking him to the hospital to make sure he wasn't hurt badly.

Brian had let go of Kiya during the questioning but stayed nearby. "Can I walk you to your apartment?" he asked.

"Thought you were going to let me go back with you," Kiya said softly

Brian cocked his head. "Back where?" he asked. He reached out and took Kiya's hands, checking his wrists to see if they were okay. They were an angry red and looked like they might swell. "Maybe we should take you to the Student Health Center to make sure you aren't injured."

"I'm fine," Kiya said quietly, looking down at his wrists as well. They would probably bruise, knowing him. "And wherever you want to go, I'll go with you."

"Well, I think we should put ice on your wrists to keep down any swelling," Brian explained. "Don't you live near here? I don't have ice in my office."

"I just want to talk to you okay? I won't jump on you the minute the door closes," Kiya said, thinking that Brian was making up excuses now.

Brian smiled a bit sadly, having to resist the urge to cup Kiya's cheek with his fingers. "I trust you, Kiya. I just want to make sure you get the care you need."

"Fine. I'll get ice somewhere," Kiya said, rubbing at his wrists slightly.

Brian sighed, trying not to feel stung by how prickly Kiya was with him when he was human. It was ironic. Brian always thought those not like him would be afraid of him as a wolf, not as a man. "We can pick up an ice pack at the store if you like, and go somewhere... to talk."

"Please?" Kiya asked looking up at him again when he said that. "It's just-you said it would be okay to talk to you."

Brian rested a hand on the small of Kiya's back, unconsciously guiding him as they made their way to his truck in the parking lot.

"Still seems weird that you were around at just the right time, but thank you, I guess," Kiya said quietly once they reached the truck.

"Just lucky I was there, I suppose," Brian answered. It wasn't luck. He had been watching for Kiya and spotted Ted waiting for him, as well.

"Ted must've been waiting for me" Kiya said quietly.

Still worried about Kiya's wrists, Brian opened the door and helped him inside before going around to climb into the driver's side. When they were both buckled in, he eased the car out and headed off campus. There was a convenience store near the base and he hoped they carried ice packs. If not, he could just get ice. He never needed things like that himself. He was rarely injured and when he was, shifting form would usually heal most anything.

Kiya was quiet for most of the ride down the hill, his mind somewhere else as he looked out the window. He was trying not to think about where he was, in this car with Brian, the same man he'd been avoiding for weeks. Trying not to get his hopes up, because, in spite of Brian's rejection before, Kiya still wanted him.

Brian wasn't a talkative person to begin with. Like the wolf he really was, he was usually more comfortable with just being with someone he cared about and listening to them. He glanced at Kiya as he drove, wondering what to say next. Soon, they were at the store.

"I'll get the ice. You want anything else? A drink or snack?"

"Water," Kiya replied, glancing up at his rescuer for the first time since they had gotten in the truck. He was feeling a little out of it, not himself. He was still trying to make sense of what just happened. "Please."

Brian smiled and nodded. Inside, he grabbed a couple bottles of water and two ice packs that could be wrapped and secured around wrists. Once he had purchased them and got back in the truck, he opened a bottle for Kiya and then unwrapped the ice packs. They were the instant kind that had a chemical pack inside and were cold immediately once they were cracked. He reached for Kiya's hand.

"They really aren't so bad," Kiya said, holding his hands out for Brian. The skin was redder with a slight swelling and they did hurt. It wasn't even the pain that was bothering him, it was the fact that Ted had done that to him, once again showing him just how weak he was. "He always had such a tight grip without even trying."

Brian had heard enough to assume that Ted and Kiya had been involved. He didn't like thinking about it, though. He simply nodded. Without realizing it, he kissed the inside of Kiya's wrist before wrapping the pack around it and securing it with the Velcro strip to hold it in place.

Kiya's eyebrows rose at the kiss. Brian's lips were soft, a lot softer than he would have thought, but oh, they were perfect. He almost wanted to grip the man's chin and pull his lips up to a better place, but, of course, Brian had made it clear that he didn't want that. Yet, that didn't explain why he had kissed Kiya's wrist. Kiya lifted up his other wrist, hoping he'd do the same to that one.

Brian didn't disappoint him, kissing the other wrist and then pausing when he realized what he had done. He had an urge to lick, the way he would if he were in wolf form. He forced himself to focus on wrapping the wrist instead. "There, now try not to use them too much for now," he said. "Where do you want to go to talk?"

"Your place?" Kiya asked, not really sure of where else they could go. Plus, being alone with Brian would be beyond perfect. Those small kisses made him hope again, hope for a chance with the man he wanted.

Brian stilled. He had never taken anyone into his den before.

"Um, are you sure you feel comfortable with that?" he asked. Kiya had been so angry with him and Brian didn't want to push his place as a teacher too far.

"I don't know where else would be a better place to go. And I'll be fine," Kiya said, looking down at the ice packs on his wrists.

Brian nodded and started the truck. His cabin was a couple miles up Empire Grade and then down a back road into the woods. "It's not much," he explained. "And it's probably not very clean."

"I don't mind," Kiya said, smiling at him just a little for the first time in a while. He looked out the window again. Now he really wanted to see where he lived because, to him, Brian didn't seem messy or disorganized at all. "Single guy's apartments usually aren't the cleanest places."

Brian was nervous about this but he wanted to help Kiya. Among wolves, letting someone into your den was an act of trust, and maybe Kiya would be more likely to open up to him if he did that. So he pulled onto the road and began the drive up. Brian worried so much about Kiya that it scared him a little, since it was so different compared to the way Brian was before, when he had kept everyone at a distance. He was so preoccupied that he nearly missed his turnoff, only the scent of the llamas reminding him that he was close. The truck bounced down the back road as it curled out of sight from any of the neighbors.

Chapter Nine

Kiya was surprised at how far from campus Brian drove. Most students kept close to the bus lines, on the west side or downtown when they could. This was a bit remote. It felt like being alone in the wilderness even if it was only a few miles from campus. How could Brian live like this?

Brian pulled up beside his cabin, a shed-like structure nestled among the redwoods, and turned off the truck. "Let me get the door," he warned as he got out.

Kiya did as he was told, waiting for Brian to walk around the truck and open the door. Kiya really thought that he could have done it himself, but he liked being taken care of. As he waited, Kiya looked around. Brian's building looked more like a single garage than an apartment or a house. Brian opened the door and then held on to Kiya's elbow, helping him out of the truck. "Thank you," Kiya said, still quiet.

Brian was nervous now. He wondered if this was a mistake. "It's, well, a bit rustic," he admitted. "I like it because it's private and on the edge of the woods."

"Me too," Kiya agreed. He couldn't wait to see Brian's territory. "Really, I won't mind how messy it is."

The door was on the side, facing the woods, not the road, and Brian led them around to it. While Brian fumbled to find the right key, Kiya noticed that there was a large pet flap which took up most of the lower half of the door. "You have a dog?" Kiya asked.

"Um, yeah, a big one," Brian answered as he turned the key and pushed the door open. "I hope you don't mind dogs."

"I love dogs," Kiya told him, smiling a little again. Having a dog only made Brian look even better in his eyes. "I love animals in general."

Brian smiled, thinking about how well Kiya got along with him when he was in his wolf form.

The first thing Kiya noticed, was that it was dark inside, even with the light. The couple of small windows had their shades pulled and dark curtains drawn. The second was that the place smelled like dog, too. Not overwhelming in a bad way, but with that musky scent that underlies everything. It was also one big room, like a studio apartment. It was sort of loosely divided into four sections. In one corner, near the door, were the sort of items you would expect in a student room-a bookcase, desk and chair, all overflowing with books and papers. The next corner held a refrigerator, some shelves with a few dishes and a small table and chair. There was no sink, stove or microwave in sight. To the right of them, another area held a chest of drawers and what looked like a portable closet. A duffel bag sat next to it, overflowing with laundry. The last corner, furthest from the door, had a futon mattress on the floor. It wasn't made up. Instead, it was piled with pillows and blankets in what looked kind of like a nest.

Kiya figured it would be messy, but this wasn't exactly what he'd expected either. He didn't say anything for a long while, slowly turning around as he took in everything. Kiya was usually a clean freak, and his fingers tingled to start organizing and cleaning things, but he could also tell that it was kind of an organized mess, in a sense. Brian could probably find whatever he wanted, and fast, too. "Nice," he murmured after a while, turning to face Brian again.

"Um, I've never had anyone else in here," Brian said, flushing a little. He closed the door behind them and headed to the table. It had a single chair and he moved folded towels off of it and onto a nearby shelf. "Have a seat," he said, before retrieving a second chair from in front of the computer desk.

Kiya sat down, and continued to look around. It could have been just a messy dorm room, but the other major difference in the room was the walls. There were no band or other posters. The only decorations were drawings. Dozens of hand drawn, unframed sketches were stuck all over the walls with pushpins. Some were of plants, like the ones Brian had been teaching them to draw for field notes. A few were of people. More than half of them were of what looked like big dogs. Kiya noticed that there was no other door in the place. Which meant there was no bathroom? At least none in sight. He supposed he'd just ask if he needed to go.

Brian placed the other chair facing Kiya and sat down in it. Leaning forward on his elbows, he studied the young man's face.

Kiya didn't notice he was being watched. He was still looking around the area, now eyeing the drawings on the walls. Brian must really love animals to have so many drawings of them. He wondered if he'd get to meet Brian's dog.

"So, how are your wrists? Is the ice helping?" Brian asked.

Kiya looked down at him, and shrugged, nodding a little. He didn't want to talk about them again. He was trying to change the mood. "I guess so," he replied. "They feel numb."

Brian reached for one of Kiya's hands, lifting it carefully and unwrapping the ice pack. "It's best to leave them on for only a short while, then take them off and put them on again in an hour."

Kiya nodded, looking at the sorely bruised skin and wishing the color and pain would just go away so that Brian wouldn't continue looking so worried. "Okay. How do you know that?" he asked.

"I took a first aid training course," Brian answered, looking embarrassed about it. He'd done it because he hadn't had the first idea of what to do if a human got injured and he never liked not knowing things. He'd found out humans were very fragile compared to his own kind.

"Oh, cool. That's helpful," Kiya said, not sure of why Brian looked embarrassed about it.

Brian set the pack on the table and reached for the second hand, unwrapping it as well. "I like to know what to do if something goes wrong," Brian explained. "So, you going to tell me about this guy?"

Kiya shrugged slightly, looking away from him again. "I can't believe he called me a whore," he whispered after a while, because that was what was bothering him the most out of the entire altercation.

Brian felt a surge of anger at that, too. It had taken all his control not to maim Ted when he took him down. "You don't have to take that from anyone," he said, a tinge of a growl in his voice.

"I used to date Ted. He's the only one I had been with here until yesterday," Kiya went on, running his fingers through his hair as he sighed. He really felt stupid for getting together with Ted now, since it was obvious that he had never been good to him.

The desire to have been the one Kiya had gone home with the previous night instead of the other man was so strong in Brian that he had to take a deep breath, reminding himself that it wasn't his place. "So tell me how this happened. How long were you together?"

"Since last October. I broke up with him before I left for spring break," Kiya explained quietly, "Or at least, I thought I did."

"But he won't accept it. I heard that part," Brian said. "Has he been giving you trouble before today?" He knew the answer, but he needed to have Kiya tell him as Brian, too.

"Yeah," Kiya admitted, sighing. He didn't want to tell Brian everything, but it did help to talk to someone who actually could reply. He'd talked with the wolf, but no one else about everything happening with Ted.

Brian was surprised to realize that he was still holding one of Kiya's hands. Then he remembered he needed to put the ice packs in the freezer for Kiya to use again later. He didn't want to let go of Kiya's hand, though. "Want to tell me about it?" he encouraged.

"When we were together, he was always kind of forceful and

rough, but I don't know... It was just how Ted was," Kiya started to say, looking down at their hands. He couldn't say that he liked the roughness, not wanting Brian to think he was weird or something. "I dealt with it. It wasn't until he didn't want to use condoms anymore that I started to say no."

Brian nodded. He understood why condoms were important for humans to use. There were diseases they could catch without them. "He shouldn't force you to do something like that."

"I know. So I broke up with him," Kiya said, his hand moving to lace his and Brian's fingers together. It was almost as if he wanted to show Brian that he really was okay, even if he didn't look it at the moment.

In a wolf pack, Brian would have shown his concern through touch, so he did that now, giving a gentle squeeze of his hand and nodding. If he had been in wolf form, he would have licked Kiya. He missed being able to do that. "He's been bothering you," Brian prompted. He knew of at least three times before today, but could only admit to knowing about the current incident.

Kiya nodded slightly, still not wanting to tell him everything. It was too much, and Kiya didn't want Brian to think he had millions of problems. "Yeah. Most of the time it was like what you saw today," he said, shrugging again.

"He hurt you before, didn't he?" Brian said, drawing Kiya's hand closer, like he wanted to do with the rest of him.

When Kiya thought about it, he realized that there were plenty of times that he had gotten bruised and hurt by Ted, but he hadn't cared as much then. He had wanted it then. But now, he didn't, not so much. He flushed, nodding again. "Yeah, I guess so," he replied.

Brian held Kiya's hand against his chest, thumb caressing the back of it. He wanted to wrap his arms around Kiya and tell him he would never let anyone hurt him again. "I want to help," he whispered.

"How?" Kiya asked, looking confused. "How you can help

me? Besides just getting him arrested or whatever?"

Brian had to remember that human rules required he didn't hunt down and hurt Ted, despite how much he wanted to do it. "If you tell the police what he did to you, they will lock him up," he said. "But even if they don't, I will help you in any way I can."

Kiya was quiet for a long time, watching Brian as he thought. "I don't want him to go to jail. He just needs help," he told him. Kiya really and truly didn't want to say what he was about to, looking down and taking a deep breath before he continued, very quietly, "He tried to rape me before."

Brian shuddered, his anger at Ted making it difficult to think. His pack wouldn't have allowed a wolf who raped to live. He didn't know why people allowed men like that among them. And he didn't know what to say to Kiya. So he did what felt right to him. He reached for Kiya's other hand.

Kiya let Brian take his second hand, sniffling and blinking when he realized that his eyes were watery. "If it weren't for my roommate, he would've done it," he whispered. "I hate feeling weak. I hate it so much."

Brian nodded. "I understand that." Although Brian knew Kiya wasn't pack, he felt as protective of him as if he were. "Do you know anything about wolves?" he asked suddenly.

Kiya's eyebrows furrowed and he leaned back a little to look up at him. "Um, a little, why?" he asked, wondering now if Brian had seen him with the wolf in the woods.

"It's one of the areas I study," Brian said, gesturing to the drawings of wolves on the wall. They also happened to be his family members, but he didn't explain that. "Wolf packs work together to protect their members from outsiders. The strong protect the weak. It's their way."

Kiya thought that would probably explain why his wolf had acted the way he did when Ted had been bothering him that one time in the forest. "I understand that," he said with a small nod. "But what does that have to do with anything?"

"It has to do with understanding that the weak are just as

important to the pack as the strong. It's the pack as a whole that matters. Stronger wolves hunt and defend the area, but weaker wolves tend the young, provide comfort, warn of danger and help the pack survive. A lone wolf, no matter how strong, is never as good as a pack." Brian felt sad when he said that out loud. He was a lone wolf now.

"Are you saying I shouldn't be alone?" Kiya asked quietly, still unsure of where this was all coming from.

"I am saying that being physically weaker than another man doesn't make you less important. Ted should not be allowed to hurt you," Brian insisted.

"Oh." Kiya understood it now, and that made him smile a little, because he hadn't thought of it that way. "I get it."

"Good," Brian smiled. He still held both of Kiya's hands and he gently brought them together, checking the wrists again. They were red and would probably be sore for a day or so, but the swelling had gone down. He looked up again. "Humans and wolves are alike in some ways. They both live in groups because it is better for all of them if they take care of each other. Do you know what happens to a lone wolf?"

"No, what happens?" Kiya asked, He still wanted Brian, more now than ever, and he was really enjoying being touched by him. Kiya was leaning over with his hands in Brian's but he wanted more, wanted to wrap himself up in Brian.

Brian looked into Kiya's beautiful green eyes, his own expression a little sad. "It is said that they go mad from loneliness and die. The strong need the weak as much as the other way around."

"That's so sad," Kiya whispered, looking down as he thought about the wolf in the woods. He hoped that would never happen to him.

The desire to touch Kiya was powerful and Brian had to take another deep breath not to reach for him, to hold him close. And every deep breath flooded his senses with the young man's scent, stirring the wolf inside. His fingers in Kiya's squeezed gently.

Kiya was quiet again, watching Brian's face. He thought Brian was holding something back, but what it was, he didn't know. On a sudden impulse he leaned in closer and kissed Brian's lips softly, finally giving in to the urge he felt.

The shock of pleasure as Kiya's lips touched his was so intense that Brian didn't even think to resist. He gave a little growl in his throat and pressed back, tilting his head to encourage the kiss.

Kiya was surprised and delighted, because he had feared that me might be pushed away again, like before. Being kissed back was hugely preferable. He didn't think he could take being rejected again, but had risked it because he hadn't been able to think of any other way to express his gratitude to Brian for his unexpected support and concern.

Brian's lips parted, tongue hungrily moving to lick at Kiya's lips. The taste and smell of Kiya was powerful, Brian's body reacting more intensely than he could ever remember feeling before. Without conscious decision, he released one of Kiya's hands and wrapped his arm around his waist, pulling him closer.

Kiya slid out of the chair when he was pulled, his free arm moving to wrap around Brian's neck. His lips parted to touch Brian's tongue with his own, and he gasped softly.

The power Kiya had over him felt as strong as shifting, and any doubts Brian had about resisting him were gone. He pulled Kiya the rest of the way into his lap, their tongues twisting together.

Kiya was startled when he was pulled into Brian's lap, but he didn't pull away, his hand moving up and into Brian's hair to grip it gently, trying to keep up with the rapidly building intensity of the kiss.

Brian lost himself in the sensations- the slide of his lips against Kiya's, his tongue exploring his mouth, that hand gripping his hair and Kiya's bottom wriggling in his lap. Brian's heart was pounding and his skin grew hot as he growled again, nipping at Kiya's chin.

Kiya heard the growl, and for some reason it excited him, his hand tightening in Brian's hair as he kissed him again, harder.

Brian felt like he could crawl inside the other man, arm pulling him as close and tight as possible. He continued to devour Kiya's mouth, his jeans becoming tight with his arousal.

Kiya could feel Brian's excitement press against him, and as much as he wanted more with him, he hesitated. "Brian," he murmured in-between the kisses. "Wait."

It took a minute for the word to register and, when it did, Brian had to force himself to stop, closing his eyes and taking deep breaths.

"Want you, but..." Kiya kissed the corner of Brian's lips, sighing softly. "I want to wait."

Brian's body was thrumming so powerfully that he had to concentrate to make sense of the spoken language. He tried to remember who he was and what he was doing-and flushed remembering that he shouldn't be doing any of this at all. Kiya was his student. He let his head fall back. "I shouldn't."

"Forget who we are," Kiya told him, reaching to run his fingers over Brian's cheek. "Just do what you think is right."

Brian opened his eyes. That may have been a mistake, because looking at Kiya only made him want him more. "Right?" he whispered. It was like there were two rights. The rules he had been told to follow that said he couldn't have Kiya because he was his subordinate in the university hierarchy. And the right of the pack that told him the exact opposite-that the dominate had the right to a willing subordinate. Yet, that was the same pack that would never understand him using a pure, frail human for anything but the most immediate pleasure. It was maddening, and as Brian's mind raced through irreconcilable loops, his body felt on fire with the need for Kiya.

Kiya rested his head against Brian's shoulder, sighing softly and closing his eyes. "I just feel so good here in your arms," he murmured after a moment.

"Yes," Brian admitted, one hand still clutching Kiya's and the other petting his back soothingly as he tried to rein in the intensity of what he felt.

"Can I stay here with you for a while?" Kiya asked quietly, reaching to play with the hem of Brian's shirt.

Brian groaned. The touch to his belly and so close to his groin did not help him think. "Why would you want that?" he asked, voice so low it was almost a whisper.

"Why wouldn't I?" Kiya asked quietly, looking up at him. "I feel safer here than I've felt in a long time."

Brian wanted to bring Kiya to his bed, to lay him back and take him, repeatedly. The images that swirled in his mind made it difficult to know what to say. He imagined lying with Kiya in his arms, holding him, petting him. He closed his eyes and took another deep breath. "Are you afraid Ted will hurt you if you return there?"

"A little," Kiya admitted, looking down again. "He knows where I live. He knows what I do every day. The only thing he doesn't know is my current class schedule."

Brian knew he couldn't let Kiya stay with him. He could barely control himself sitting there fully clothed. There was no way he could resist him if he spent more time there. And then there was the bigger problem. Brian was a wolf, not a man. He couldn't stay in human form that long. "I can make sure he doesn't hurt you again," Brian said. He glanced around the room. "You do realize this is all there is. I don't even have a bathroom here."

"I don't need a bathroom," Kiya told him honestly.

"You hardly know me," Brian tried arguing. It was true in more ways than he could explain. He wished he could share everything with Kiya, especially after Kiya showed himself willing to accept and trust the wolf. But pack laws forbade him from telling a human anything about the Faewolves.

"If you really don't want me to stay, I won't," Kiya murmured, sighing and resting his head on Brian's shoulder again.

Brian released Kiya's hand and moved his own to Kiya's jaw, sliding his fingers along the smooth skin there and having to suppress another growl at just how good that felt. "Wanting you is my problem," he admitted.

"Why? Besides the fact that I'm your student?" Kiya asked, tilting his head back up again.

"Which isn't fair to you and can get me expelled," Brian pointed out. But his hand ignored his words, fingers sliding along the back of Kiya's neck and skull, spreading to feel the thick hair between them. Brian's cock twitched and his body gave a little tremor. His body didn't care about rules.

"But you want to fuck me, don't you?" Kiya asked suddenly, nuzzling the side of Brian's face. He needed to be sure.

Brian's breath hitched and his eyes closed again. Oh, how he wanted that. And he wanted a lot more. His fingers gripped Kiya's hair and pulled him back, turning to look into his eyes. "I could not be a one night stand," he said, voice almost a growl.

Kiya didn't want that either, if he was being honest with himself, but he was curious as to why Brian had felt the need to say that. "Why not?" he asked, mindful of the hand gripping his hair.

Brian had the urge to lick Kiya again. Instead, he kissed him once more, lips barely caressing this time, breath mingling and his body shuddering with pent up energy.

Kiya's eyes slid shut as soon as their lips touched, a small sound of need escaping him as the kiss deepened.

The second kiss was even better, Brian's grip on the back of Kiya's head and hair providing him with the ability to control the angle and moves. He gently, thoroughly, plundered Kiya's sweet mouth, the warm body squirming in his lap adding even more fuel to the fire of Brian's arousal.

Kiya gave in and let Brian control the kiss. It felt so good to be wanted, to be touched by someone who seemed to want to take care of him as well as enjoy him.

Brian felt Kiya relax into the kiss, which released whatever caution he still had, his other hand on Kiya's hip now. He pulled Kiya so that he was more firmly seated on Brian's cock, rubbing those firm cheeks against the flesh that strained at the denim of his jeans. Brian moaned into Kiya's mouth.

Kiya took advantage of the new position to press down harder as they kissed, moving his hips in a slow circle. The growl was back, Brian sucking and nipping at Kiya's lips and chin, his hips shifting to accommodate the weight of his body. Kiya heard the chair creak under their weight, and for a moment he thought it would break. It might be better just to go to the nest of pillows on the futon, but he couldn't even pull back to say that. He thought his lips would be swollen by the time Brian released him, and that only excited him further.

Brian's hand slid from Kiya's hip to between Kiya's legs, cupping the arousal he found there and rubbing the fabric covered flesh with the heel of his hand. Brian's mouth was working its way up the line of Kiya's jaw to the fragrant soft skin of the boy's throat.

"Shit," Kiya whispered, his hips jerking at the unexpected spike of pleasure. "Brian..."

"Kiya," Brian groaned against the skin of his neck, licking the spot just below the hinge of the jaw.

"Bite, please?" Kiya asked quietly, tilting his head back a little more.

The rush of heat that answered that plea was enough to startle Brian. He didn't want to hurt Kiya. Humans seemed so fragile to him. But he needed to feel that flesh between his teeth. He opened his mouth against the skin below Kiya's ear, tongue pressed to the pulse point as he gently bit down.

Kiya groaned loudly, his head falling back more as the shock of desire went through his entire system. "Harder," he whispered.

Brian's cock spasmed with the feel of flesh between his teeth and he bit down. His tongue pressed against the skin, lapping. At least his human teeth were blunt compared to his wolf ones.

Kiya's hips were moving faster now, trying to establish more friction than he was getting. Brian was biting him hard, and it felt wonderful, but he still needed more, still needed a sensation he couldn't express. "Brian," he whimpered softly, gripping his shirt.

Brian could smell and taste Kiya's arousal driving his own hard. It took effort to lift his teeth from Kiya's neck and whisper. "Yes."

"Wanna come," Kiya whispered after a few minutes, his fingers tightening in Brian's shirt.

Brian wanted this, wanted to feel Kiya's pleasure and see it in his face, but he slid his hand off Kiya's cock. "Not here," he whispered.

Chapter Ten

Brian kissed the red mark he had left on Kiya's neck and pulled back to look at him. "Not now, not here on this chair. I want to touch you," Brian admitted. He was crossing the line; he knew it and he wasn't going to allow himself to feel guilty about it. "I want to touch your skin."

Kiya whimpered, reaching to touch himself when Brian's hand moved away. Now he shifted back and got off of him, pulling his shirt quickly up and off.

Brian's eyes were drawn to the display of smooth golden-brown skin and dark sienna nipples. His mouth watered for wanting to nip and suck them.

Kiya looked up after a moment and smiled, thinking that the break was actually good for him. It gave him a chance to calm down and actually tease, like he usually did. He caught Brian's eyes and then started to unzip his jeans and push them down, as slowly as he could manage.

Brian licked his lips, eyes following the movement of Kiya's hands as he revealed the line of his hip bones and then, slowly, unveiled the swelling flesh between.

Kiya kicked away his pants and then set his hands on his hips, knowing that he looked good. "Want to get on your, um, bed?"

Brian slowly stood, eyes never straying from Kiya's. He gave the same kind of show Kiya had, slowly unbuttoning his shirt, first the cuffs and then down his front, revealing a muscled chest dusted with red brown curls.

Kiya couldn't say that he had ever been with a man Brian's age, but that wasn't about to stop him. He looked just as muscled as Kiya thought he would look, if not better.

"You want more," Brian whispered, fingers stopping at the

top of his button-down jeans. He loved the knowledge of that, that this beautiful young man was looking at him like he was starving and, at that moment, Brian was the only thing that could sate him.

"I want more," Kiya agreed, his eyes already trailing down Brian's body, letting him see just how much he did want.

Brian's body thrummed with energy as he popped open each button and pushed his jeans down his own hips. He didn't wear underwear.

Kiya's eyes did widen when the other man was completely exposed, biting down on his lip. Brian was big, that was much was for sure, but not in a scary way. Kiya's mouth watered as desire flooded his body.

Brian wasn't sure what to expect from Kiya once he was undressed. He had rarely shown his body to a human. He was pleased with Kiya's reaction. Brian smiled and sat down again, long enough to remove his boots, socks and jeans. Then he stood up and stepped close to Kiya, looking down into his eyes.

Kiya looked up, swallowing once. "Can I suck you off?" he asked quietly, stepping close enough so that they were touching.

"Not yet," Brian said, taking Kiya's hand and drawing him toward the bed. "I want to feel your body against mine." Kiya pouted slightly, but nodded, letting Brian lead him over to the bed. Brian told him to lie down on it.

Kiya got down on his knees first and then rolled over to lie back on the bed, finding that even though it wasn't a normal bed, it still felt warm and cozy.

Brian grinned down at the lean body of the beautiful young man. Kiya's dark hair fanned out around his head and his cock jutted up eagerly from the dark hair between his legs. Brian sank down, crawling up over him, his cock brushing against Kiya's. Brian straddled Kiya's hips, pressing their erections between them and leaned forward to kiss him again.

Kiya gasped when their cocks touched, his eyes closing slightly. He reached out for Brian, wrapping his arms around Brian's neck and pulling him down more closely, tilting his head and kissing him harder.

Brian rocked against Kiya, hips moving as they slid together. He nipped and sucked Kiya's mouth, growling again while Kiya moaned and thrust his hips up, wrapping his legs around Brian's waist so that he was directly against him as they moved together. Brian thrust his fingers into Kiya's long dark hair again, gripping it gently but firmly as he mapped Kiya's mouth with his tongue. He could feel the slickness of their pre-come as their cocks rubbed together. It made him feel the same kind of rush he got when running in wolf form. He'd never felt this way with anyone.

"Ngh, more, Brian..." Kiya whispered against his lips, and then hissed "yes" when he felt teeth at his neck. Kiya's arms tightened around Brian as he rocked more roughly against him, tensing.

"You taste so good," Brian whispered, licking and nipping down Kiya's neck. Then he pressed his teeth into flesh again, biting down as he rocked faster, panting and growling. He could feel Kiya's pulse against his tongue and in their erections sliding together. He wanted to taste every inch of the warm flesh against his own.

Kiya was sure that none of the men he had been with growled as much as Brian did. Yes, it was growling, not groaning or anything like that. It was surprisingly a big turn-on for Kiya. "Close," he gasped suddenly, digging his nails into the skin of Brian's back.

Brian wanted to feel Kiya writhing and crying out beneath him. He tugged on his hair, biting harder as he thrust repeatedly against him.

Kiya barely had breath to cry out Brian's name before he was coming, jerking and shuddering hard under Brian. It felt as though that last bite might have broken his skin, but he didn't care.

Slick heat coated Brian's cock and belly and he shuddered, the taste of blood in his mouth the last push to send him over the edge. He came, snarling as he lapped at Kiya's skin.

"Brian," Kiya whispered yet again, panting as he slowly came down from his high. He still hadn't realize that he was bleeding. Brian licked the small wounds on Kiya's neck, kissing and nuzzling him while Kiya kept his eyes closed, enjoying being petted, his breathing slowly returning to normal. It was only then that he realized Brian was still licking at the spot. He blushed at the idea that Brian had marked him. "I could get used to that," he murmured softly.

Brian licked and kissed his way up to Kiya's face, then lapped at those beautiful full lips. "Oh, yes," Brian whispered, looking into Kiya's eyes then. He wanted Kiya. Not just now, but over and over and ... always. Is this what love is? he wondered. He'd never been in love.

Kiya smiled brightly up at him as he was watched, reaching to slowly run his fingers through Brian's hair. "Never thought you'd actually let me do this with you. After the way you pushed me away that first time."

Kiya's smile brought Brian another wave of pleasure. "I wanted you," he whispered. "I've always wanted you."

"I know that now. You're just really good at stopping yourself," Kiya said, patting Brian's cheek.

"No. If I was, we wouldn't be here," Brian admitted, laying small kisses on Kiya's lips and nose.

"Everyone has their breaking point, I think," Kiya explained, closing his eyes a little as he was kissed.

"You are my weakness then," Brian teased, moving to lay beside Kiya, still-aroused cock rubbing against Kiya's hip.

"That feels good to know," Kiya hummed, grinning up at him. It was interesting to feel Brian hard already, or still, before Kiya even had the chance to recuperate. He figured he'd ignore that for just the moment. "So where is your dog? Do I get to meet him today?" he asked.

Brian smiled, fingers tracing down Kiya's neck and over his

chest, lightly caressing Kiya's nipples. His cock twitched when they hardened under his touch. "My... dog's a bit wild. He ranges pretty wide and is probably hunting."

Kiya sucked in a breath, glancing down at the hand on his chest. "That's cool. Maybe one day I'll catch him when he's around," he said softly, gazing back up at Brian and smiling. "Can't believe I'm here with you."

"With me," Brian agreed. He couldn't resist pinching a nipple then, delighting at the sensitive flesh.

Kiya gasped softly and blushed, shifting and getting on top of Brian, straddling him. He rested his hands on the man's chest. "So, how are we going to do this?"

Brian let Kiya climb atop of him, smiling up at the cheeky move. He smirked at the question. "Which part?" he asked, hands exploring the smooth skin of Kiya's chest, belly and hips.

"Us first," Kiya asked, thinking of the sex as well, but wanting to talk before another go.

"We can't tell anyone until after the quarter is over," Brian insisted, fingers tracing the lovely angles of Kiya's hips.

Kiya nodded in agreement, moving his hand up and brushing his fingers along Brian's cheek. "I knew you wanted me," he murmured.

"Smug about that?" Brian teased, turning his head to kiss Kiya's fingers.

"Of course," Kiya said with a smirk, running his fingers over Brian's lips now. "I've been called cocky before, and it's pretty true."

"I can see you might require a bit of taking down to handle," Brian grinned in return, fingers trailing down the boy's thighs.

"You really think so?" Kiya asked, an eyebrow rising as he bit the inside of his lip. "Are you going to do that?"

"If that's what will keep you," Brian answered, serious this time. He moved quicker than Kiya could have, hands sliding up behind him and rolling until Kiya was on his back, with Brian on top of him and between his legs.

Kiya didn't even get the chance to blink before he was on his back, his legs still curved as if he continued kneeling. "That was fast," he had to admit, looking up at Brian.

"I think I'll have to be to keep up with you," Brian teased, loving the wide-eyed breathless look on Kiya's face. "Because no one but me touches you."

"No one but you?" Kiya asked softly, wanting to hear it again.

"If you want to be with me, then no one else unless we both agree otherwise," Brian confirmed, studying Kiya's face to see if he really understood.

"No one else," Kiya agreed, nodding slightly. "I think you can handle me just like I like to be handled." He reached to touch the mark on his neck.

Brian caught the move, understanding that it meant Kiya liked the bite, liked it a bit rough. He smiled, cock still full and twitching at the idea of it. "What else will you need?"

"I think you'll figure it out," Kiya murmured, blushing again.

"I will have to be harder on you than anyone else in my class. I can't let you slide," Brian warned, hand sliding on Kiya's skin as he spoke.

"I'll just have to study harder. You can help with that, can't you?" Kiya asked, smiling a little.

"Personal lessons?" Brian teased, loving the idea. He wanted sex, of course, but the idea of exploring the woods with Kiya, teaching him things, was also very appealing.

Kiya slowly grinned. "Personal lessons, yeah. I'd like that a lot," he replied.

Brian knew, not just from class, but from all the time Kiya had been with him as a wolf, that Kiya liked the forest. He wondered what it would be like to make love to him outdoors. He slid his hand to where Kiya's cock was filling again, fingertips teasing the foreskin as he did.

Kiya bit his lip harder and arched a little, wanting more. "No teasing, though," he mumbled, since he didn't have enough patience for that.

"Teasing is offering something I won't give you," Brian whispered. "I keep my promises." He emphasized this point by wrapping his fingers around the shaft of Kiya's cock and stroking.

"Good," Kiya moaned, squeezing his eyes shut as he thrust into the circle Brian's fist made.

"Yeah, very good," Brian agreed, body shuddering with renewed want for his lover writhing under him. "I want to be inside you," he said, voice grown hoarse with the sudden tension in his body.

"Yeah... yeah, me too," Kiya managed to whisper, his legs opening a little wider on their own as if in agreement.

Brian nodded, trying to think how humans did this. He moved back a little, letting go of Kiya's cock. "Turn over, on all fours."

Kiya quickly did as he was told, pushing himself up onto his hands and knees for Brian, and the sight was almost more than Brian could take-the urge to mount him and thrust immediately into Kiya was overwhelming. Human, Brian reminded himself, and reached his hands to squeeze and part those beautiful buttocks, revealing the darker skin between. He shuddered in anticipation, licking his lips.

Kiya could feel his cheeks reddening as he was exposed, not exactly sure why, since he had done this just last night. But it was already different with Brian.

The scent of Kiya alone was nearly enough to send Brian over the edge. He leaned over and ran his tongue down the crevice, from the top all the way down, lightly over the puckered hole and down to the soft sac that hung between Kiya's legs.

Kiya wasn't expecting that. A finger or two, but not tongue. He breathed in sharply and felt himself tense up slightly, his face reddening even more.

Brian couldn't believe how good Kiya tasted. He lapped at the young man's balls, licking and sucking them, letting himself revel in scent and taste and texture.

Kiya bit down on his lip hard, his hands clenching the pillows beneath him. "Brian," he whispered, beginning to moan.

Brian smiled as he worked his tongue up to that tight pink little hole again, teasing it. He could feel Kiya's flesh fluttering in pleasure with every lick. He buried his face in between those sweet cheeks and lapped harder and faster. He wished he could do this as a wolf when he had a bigger tongue, because it was fantastic.

Kiya fell forward with a groan, his hips jerking with the pleasure of the act. Why hadn't he gotten anyone else to do this for him before? It felt good, better than good, especially once he just let go.

Brian thrust the tip of his tongue into the center of the fluttering opening, unaware that he was making little growling noises as he did so.

Kiya couldn't do much more than whine softly, his hands clenching and unclenching in the pillows. He heard the growls, and they only made his hips move, trying to press back onto Brian's tongue.

Brian could feel Kiya's body quivering around his tongue, hips lifting, begging for more with every move. And that's what he gave him, using his tongue to fuck his lover, delighted by how responsive Kiya was.

Kiya reached in between his legs, wrapping his fingers around his cock so that he could stroke himself as he tried to fuck himself on that wonderful tongue.

Brian delighted in this, but he wanted more- wanted his cock sunk into the intoxicating heat of Kiya's body. He thrust his tongue a few more times and then rose up, moving closer. "Do you want my cock?" he asked, voice deep with desire.

"Yes!" Kiya cried out almost immediately, his hips still wriggling for more.

The eager response was exciting and Brian could smell how much true it was. He used one hand to hold Kiya's buttocks open and began to rub the head of his cock against the hole.

Kiya honestly didn't think that Brian had any kind of disease or anything like that, but he couldn't help but lean away when bare tip touched him. He'd broken up with Ted over this, after all. Kiya had promised his mother not to take chances. "Condom?" he asked, praying Brian had one.

Brian stilled, remembering that Kiya had already told him about this, how important it was. Problem was that he had never used a condom. He had never needed one before. "I ... I don't have one. Do you?"

"Uh ... uh, shit," Kiya cursed, thinking hard. "I might have one in my pocket." But Kiya did not want to get up to find it, he just wanted to be fucked, and fucked hard. Getting up would just mess up the rhythm they had going.

"Don't move," Brian insisted, making a sound of frustration as he moved to get Kiya's jeans, tossing them on the bed in front of him. "Get it."

Kiya reached for the jeans without shifting in his position, reaching into the pocket and thankfully pulling out a condom. He held it out for Brian.

Brian looked at the small foil square. He had no idea what to do with it. "Put it on me," he said, moving to kneel in front of Kiya instead and handing it back.

Kiya also pulled a small tube of lubricant out of his jeans, setting it on the bed. Now that they had stopped, he wouldn't be as relaxed as he was a few minutes ago. He opened the foil package and pulled the condom out, leaning up on his knees. He hesitated just before he leaned down to take Brian's cock into his mouth, sucking hard as his eyes slid shut.

"Ohhh," Brian gasped, shuddering as that wet mouth enveloped the head of his prick. Kiya's lovely plump lips looked good, too, long hair falling around his face as he took Brian in his mouth.

Kiya couldn't pull all of Brian into his mouth, but he sucked and licked what he could, wrapping his fingers around the base and stroking. He felt the need to do this for him, especially after what Brian had just done to him, which had felt incredible.

Brian braced one hand on the wall, the other coming to rest on the top of Kiya's head. "Good, yes, Kiya," he gasped, fingers stroking that silky hair.

Kiya could do this until Brian came, which would defeat the purpose of rushing to get the condom in the first place, he supposed. He pulled back to shake the hair out of his face and look up at Brian, smiling as he swirled his tongue around the very tip. Kiya reached for the condom, carefully rolling it down over Brian's cock. "Here," he said, holding out the lube for him as well. "Just to make it easier."

Brian watched the way Kiya did it, making sure he could put it on himself next time. The latex was very tight on his cock, a little uncomfortable. He wondered if they came in larger sizes. Taking the tube and nodding, Brian leaned in to give Kiya a quick kiss before moving back behind him.

Kiya got back onto his hands and knees for Brian, tilting his hips up for him again. "Can't wait," he whispered.

Brian opened the tube and squeezed some lube out onto his fingers, coating the outside of the condom and then reaching to push a finger into Kiya. "It's going to feel so good inside you."

"I know," Kiya said, clenching around the finger before he relaxed, shifting back to press down more.

His finger felt good there, and Brian's cock was twitching in anticipation. "I'm kind of big, so I'll go slow," he warned, sliding in another finger. "You tell me if it is too much."

"Okay," Kiya agreed, nodding a few times. "I can take it, Brian."

"Take only what pleases you," Brian warned, smiling as he withdrew his fingers and pushed the head of his cock against the slick opening. He rubbed it in a circle, pressing gently and feeling the skin ease around the head.

Kiya's eyes slid shut as he concentrated on relaxing, his hands clutching a pillow. The head slipped past the tight muscles, stretching him. Kiya shuddered as well, breathing in deeply and letting it out in a small groan, working to relax for Brian.

"Yes, good," Brian encouraged, shuddering at the amazing feeling of Kiya's body swallowing him. Brian squeezed and petted Kiya's ass, letting his body adjust. He could feel the tightness ease a bit and shifted, pushing inside a little more. "Keep touching yourself, it will help," he explained.

"It's fine," Kiya managed to gasp, his voice sounding strained.

Trusting the boy to tell him if he needed to stop, Brian began to work his cock back and forth, each time a little deeper. It felt fantastic. Brian had never fucked a human. But then he had never wanted anyone like he wanted Kiya. "So good," he whispered, still caressing.

Kiya tried moving with him, his back arching slightly to make his movements smoother. After a while, he reached in between his legs and started to stroke himself slowly, having noticed that his erection had started to soften.

"Yes, Kiya," Brian managed. He worked most of his length inside him now. He didn't know if it was a good idea to try for all of it the first time. Even in human form, Brian's prick was longer than the length of his hand. He kept his thrusts shallow. Even so, the pleasure was intense.

"God," Kiya whispered once the pleasure started to override the discomfort he felt. Every thrust was nudging against his spot, his moans increasing in volume. "More... please, more."

Kiya's begging for more raised the excitement for Brian. He held Kiya's cheeks, spreading them wide as he worked his prick deeper, growling when he felt his hips pressed to the swell of Kiya's ass.

Kiya had to admit that he had never had anyone as big as Brian, and he felt unbelievably full because of it. And it was so good. "Brian," he started to chant softly over and over, shaking.

Brian was reaching that place where words were difficult, growling as he began to rut faster, hips rotating as he worked in and out of that tight hole. Kiya was perfect-his body, his smell, his reactions-all reaching inside Brian and setting him on fire. He was draped over Kiya, covering him with his own body and his own scent. He licked and nipped Kiya's back and shoulders.

Kiya didn't even need to touch himself anymore as Brian sped up, each thrust making him cry out in pleasure. He was close already, which was different because it usually took him longer, especially when he wasn't stroking himself off.

Brian was frustrated by the condom, its constriction and barrier making the sensations less than they should have been. He wanted to feel Kiya's flesh, that wet channel. He growled, pumping faster, harder.

Kiya thought that if there was anyone that he would have liked to devote the rest of his school year and more to, it was Brian. He honestly hoped this wasn't a dream, and if it was, he didn't ever want to wake up. He tensed and came quite unexpectedly, a cry of shocked ecstasy escaping him at the same time.

Kiya's pleasure, his sounds and the feeling of his tight hole pulsing around Brian's prick sent the wolf into a frenzy, Brian fucking hard and fast. Cock buried deep into Kiya's body, Brian came with a howl.

Kiya fell forward with the force of Brian's last thrust, turning his head so that his cheek was pressed against the pillows allowing him to breathe. He was panting raggedly.

Brian slumped forward, his face pressed against the damp skin between Kiya's shoulder blades and his prick still sputtering deep inside him. Brian's hands against the mattress on either side barely held his weight from crushing Kiya.

"Fuck," Kiya whispered when he could catch his breath, feeling a mixture of so many things that he didn't even know what else to say.

"More?" Brian teased, his cock twitching in spite of just coming.

"Let me recuperate first," Kiya laughed, smiling and opening his eyes.

Brian kissed the soft skin of Kiya's back and then nuzzled the back of his hair. If they were wolves, they would stay joined for a long time. Brian knew enough of human biology to know that wasn't the way it worked with them. "Do you need me to move?" he asked, not withdrawing yet.

"Maybe a little to the side, but I don't want you to pull out just yet," Kiya murmured, liking this fullness more than he probably should have. The feeling was nearly addictive.

Brian made a contented sound, sliding an arm under Kiya to hold them together as he pulled sideways. Now they lay on their sides, Brian's cock still throbbing inside as he spooned up around Kiya. Brian sighed happily.

"I don't know about you, but I think I'm going to take a nap," Kiya whispered, his eyes already closing as he got comfortable.

Brian kissed the back of the Kiya's head, petting him and listening to his breathing as it evened out. It took a while for Brian's cock to subside and slip from between those plump cheeks. The condom came half off him too and Brian had to remove and dispose of the sticky thing. Kiya was soundly asleep, curled into the nest of Brian's bed.

After watching for a while, Brian got up and went outside to relieve himself. He had an outhouse, but preferred to mark specific trees as he would in wolf form. He thought about rinsing off in the outdoor shower he had rigged up but decided he liked the smell of sex on his skin.

Brian checked again to make sure Kiya was still asleep and then decided to go for a run. He shifted form and took off into the woods.

Chapter Eleven

When Kiya woke up, he realized three things-that he was cold, he was alone, and he was sore. Very sore. He shifted and slowly sat up, yawning and stretching as he looked around. "Brian?" he asked, pushing his messy hair away from his face. When he didn't get any answer, he moved to get up. He wondered where Brian had gotten off to, but he figured he would be back soon enough.

Kiya picked up Brian's shirt and pulled it on, buttoning up a few of the buttons. It was big enough to cover him, but if he bent over, he'd be exposed. He continued to walk around, looking at the drawings on the wall. They really were beautiful wolves, he thought, and he wished that he could see them in real life. Maybe Brian would take him to see some one day. That meant he'd have to show Brian the wolf in the woods by his college. Kiya continued to explore the room. In the kitchen area, he pulled open the door to the refrigerator to see if there was anything to drink.

All he saw was beer. And meat. Raw steak. Nothing was cooked at all. He found that strange, because Brian didn't have an oven or stove. How did he cook the meat? Kiya shrugged and pulled out a bottle of beer, looking around for an opener.

Unable to find an opener, Kiya pouted, wrapping his hand around the top so that he could carefully twist it open while he started to walk around again. He stopped by the door and looked out, wondering how long Brian would be gone. The door faced the woods and he thought he saw a familiar shape among the trees, so Kiya leaned out and narrowed his eyes as he tried to get a better look. Was that the wolf he was seeing?

Saoi was coming back from a run and saw Kiya in the doorway. He forgot himself and bounded up to the him, eager to smell and taste and touch.

"Hey!" Kiya said excitedly, kneeling down to pet the wolf. "How'd you know I was here? Did you follow me or something?"

Saoi nuzzled and lapped his lover's face, inhaling the scent of Kiya and sex. It was exciting and made him want to rub against him.

"I missed you, too," Kiya murmured as he was licked, his eyes closing as he continued to pet him.

Saoi made a happy growl, licking every inch of Kiya's face, nipping gently on his chin, and then starting on his neck.

"You're giving me a bath here," Kiya started to laugh, opening one eye as he ran his hand down the wolf's back. "You'll never guess what happened, though."

Saoi could taste Kiya's come on the skin under the shirt. He pushed his muzzle under the hem, trying to get to more of it.

"Hey, hey," Kiya mumbled, trying to keep the shirt down. "I'm trying to tell you a story here!"

Saoi heard him but wanted to taste, so he kept pushing and nuzzling, accidentally nudging Kiya until the boy landed on his ass on the ground.

"Oww. What's up with you today?" Kiya asked, smiling, trying to take most of the weight off of his sore backside. "I don't need a bath now, you know."

Saoi wanted to lick all of Kiya's skin. He wanted to mount him again. Then he remembered that in wolf form, he couldn't have that. He gave a big sigh and lay his face against Kiya's neck, trying to calm down.

"There we go, deep breaths," Kiya murmured, realizing that the wolf was trying to calm himself. He honestly couldn't say that he had ever had someone get so worked up over seeing him like that before.

Saoi wanted to change form and kiss Kiya, make love to him again. But that was impossible at that moment without being found out, so he nuzzled Kiya and waited for him to talk.

"Now that you've calmed down, I was saying that I finally got Brian. Remember him? He pushed me away but now I've got him for myself," Kiya said, sounding proud of himself.

Saoi licked his lover's face, laughing. He was delighted with Kiya's bragging.

Kiya had never heard an animal laugh, but he was almost sure that's what the wolf was doing. It made him laugh too, turning to nuzzle the wolf's face. "And the sex is... well, unbelievable," He sighed softly, just the thought of it making him smile.

Saoi rubbed back, happily enjoying both the touch and the words.

Kiya lay there for a few more minutes, sliding his arm around the wolf. After a while he moved to sit up, feeling a chill since he was only in a shirt. "I'm gonna go back inside," he told the wolf, getting up and turning to walk back into the house.

Saoi padded in after him and then stuck his head under the table, finding a large bone he had left there. He lay down contentedly and began chewing on it.

Kiya glanced back when the wolf followed him inside; an eyebrow rose when he saw that the animal was chewing on a bone. The wolf seemed to know where to get it and everything. "Hey, wait a minute," Kiya murmured, looking at the door and then back at him. "Are you Brian's dog?"

Saoi's eyes widened and he realized that he had forgotten to hide that he was at home. He looked down at the bone for a minute and then resumed chewing on it. He was hungry.

It made sense when Kiya thought of it. That's why the wolf would have been there, and it would also explain all the meat in the refrigerator. "Hungry?" Kiya asked as he watched the wolf gnaw on the bone. He went back to the kitchen and opened the refrigerator, reaching to pull out some of the meat.

The wolf's ears swiveled forward as Saoi raised his head and looked curiously at Kiya. Was the boy offering him his own food? Saoi worried for a moment that Kiya had figured everything out, but then realized he was just assuming that the wolf was a pet.

When Kiya lifted the package of steak from the refrigerator, Saoi nudged a pan on the floor with his nose.

"I knew you lived here," Kiya said with a grin, taking the steak out of the package and kneeling down to put it in the pan. "Eat up, then."

Saoi had never had a human watch him eat and, in a strange way, it felt as intimate as what they had done before. At first, he shyly licked the meat, eyes on Kiya.

Kiya smiled and patted his head, settling on the floor and reaching for the beer bottle he had set down, taking a sip. It wasn't so bad. He was a little hungry, too, though.

Saoi relaxed, sharp teeth tearing into the meat as he gulped it down. Red meat after great sex. It was perfect.

Kiya watched him as he sipped at the beer, wondering when Brian was going to come back. Just watching the wolf made him hungrier. "You know, I should probably tell you how wonderful your owner is," he said, looking up at the ceiling with a sigh. "At first, I thought I just wanted to fuck him. I mean, he really is even more beautiful naked... but now, I feel like there's so much more. I think I might be falling for him or something."

Saoi nearly choked on his meat. He gulped it down and licked his lips, thinking not just of the meal but of Kiya.

"And, you know, I think I might have finally found the right guy for me. I mean,that's probably me being way too optimistic, but I have a good feeling about it." Kiya was aware that Saoi wasn't able to answer him, but that didn't matter. "I'm really happy."

Saoi finished his meat, set both bones back in the pan for later, and nudged it back under the table. Then his attention was once again solely on Kiya. He pushed his head against him, licking at a bared collarbone. He was excited that Kiya wanted him, though confused about how to have a human lover and keep his secret.

Kiya slid his arm around the wolf, tugging him closer. "And did I mention how fucking awesome he is in bed?" he said, feeling his skin flush as he thought about it.

Saoi shuddered in happy reaction to both being held and to the praise. He lapped at Kiya's mouth.

"Eww," Kiya laughed, letting him lick a couple more times before he turned his head so that the wolf was licking his cheek. "You just ate a raw steak."

Saoi huffed, something close to a laugh as he licked cheek and then neck. Kiya tasted good no matter what form he was in.

"Now I have the both of you to myself, right?" Kiya said happily, nuzzling him.

Saoi wanted more of Kiya, wanted to take him back to bed. Which meant he would have to change shape again. He gave him another lick before heading to the pet door.

"Goodbye, then," Kiya said, watching him go. "I'll talk to you later." Maybe he'd talk to them both at the same time one day.

Saoi dived through the pet door and out into the woods. It didn't take long, He transformed and Brian walked back to his door, only pausing when he realized he hadn't brought any clothes with him. There was nothing he could do about that, so he sighed and stepped inside.

Kiya looked up when he saw Brian, raising both eyebrows. "So, you walk around the woods naked?" he asked, slowly beginning to smile.

Brian flushed and shrugged. "Just to the outhouse," he explained.

"Uh huh," Kiya said, not sounding very convinced. "I saw your dog!"

Brian smiled down at Kiya sitting on his floor. "You met Saoi," he acknowledged, getting a beer from the refrigerator for himself.

Kiya smirked again. "But you lied to me," he said.

Brian's movements stilled and his heart sped up. "Did I?" he asked, worried.

"That's not a dog. He's a wolf."

Brian chuckled, relieved. "Yeah, but it isn't legal to keep a wolf as a pet."

"I won't tell anyone. I really like him," Kiya promised.

"Good, I wouldn't want him to get sent away," Brian answered, dropping to the floor beside Kiya.

"Saoi is his name? What's it mean?" Kiya asked, smiling once Brian settled down next to him.

"Gaelic for someone who reads, a scholar," Brian answered, rolling his eyes.

"He is smart," Kiya laughed softly, resting his head on Brian's shoulder.

With one hand holding his beer, Brian wrapped his other arm around Kiya, inhaling his scent and smiling at the fact that Kiya was wearing his shirt. "Within my family, it's not really a compliment," Brian explained with a snort. It was the name his family had given him as a child and it had not been a compliment. Faewolves valued wolf skills more than human.

"Why not?" Kiya asked curiously, wanting to know more about Brian's family.

"My..." Brian almost said pack, "...kin really don't live that way. We don't even speak English with each other and what matters the most is taking care of each other. They think reading books is a waste of time."

"You speak another language? Gaelic?" Kiya asked, looking up at Brian again.

Brian bent his head to give Kiya a soft kiss, smiling. "Well, technically, Gaelic is my first language. English was what we learned to talk to outsiders." He let his accent fill the sound as he spoke, watching Kiya's reaction.

Kiya could hear the accent. It sounded Irish. He grinned, finding that he liked it. "I speak another language at home, too."

"Native American, right?" Brian asked, then took another swig of his beer.

"You can tell?" Kiya asked, nodding a bit.

"I grew up in areas with several different tribes," Brian acknowledged. "My clan gets along better with Native Americans than with most outsiders."

127

"Probably why I like you so much," Kiya said with a smirk, nudging him. "But yeah, we used to live on the Pine Ridge Reservation. My grandparents still do. It's different from other people, I guess, but I love it."

"Which tribe?" Brian asked.

"The Sioux tribe. I speak Lakota," Kiya told him.

"That's South Dakota, right?" Brian asked, fingers playing with Kiya's hair.

"Correct," Kiya said, liking that Brian knew so much already. He usually had to explain everything to the people he met.

"I've been to the Black Hills," Brian acknowledged. "Beautiful place." His pack hadn't stayed long though, because the protection for wolves was still very limited in the United States.

"Paha Sapa," Kiya grinned. "Really is beautiful. And I picked the best guy here to like, haven't I?"

Brian didn't know if Kiya would be as pleased if he knew the truth of it. But they were a lot more alike than most people. He leaned in and captured Kiya's mouth again, tasting the beer and the way it combined with the taste of Kiya.

Kiya lazily kissed him back, his eyes closing as he breathed in through his nose and let it out with a sigh.

The bottle clinked as Brian set it down, using his hand to cup Kiya's face as they kissed. Finally, he pulled back to look into those green eyes again. He had never felt so comfortable with anyone, not even his pack.

Kiya smiled softly up at him, reaching to touch Brian's cheek. He never thought that he'd feel so deeply about Brian so quickly. It was exciting, though. "So, I'm pretty hungry," he murmured after a few minutes of silence.

"Oh," Brian said, realizing he had eaten but had forgotten to feed Kiya. He felt some dismay at not providing for him. Problem was that he didn't really keep human food at home. "Well, I suppose we had better get cleaned up and dressed then."

"If you had a stove, I'd be able to cook some of that meat you've got," Kiya said as he moved to stand up. "Or is that only for Saoi?"

Brian grinned. "Yeah, I feed him sometimes. He hunts too, but I don't want him getting in too much trouble. For myself, I eat out." He kissed Kiya's forehead and got to his feet, holding his hands out to help Kiya up too.

Kiya pulled himself up and stretched again, still feeling pretty sore. "I'll be feeling you for days, just so you know," he murmured.

Watching the muscles of Kiya's body and the way the shirt rode up to reveal his ass, Brian wanted him to be feeling him right then. He wanted to drag him back over to the bed and take him over and over again. Brian swallowed hard, unable to form coherent words.

"So where do you shower?" Kiya asked, glancing back. He saw that Brian had gotten excited again, and he wondered what he had done.

"I have a shower outside, but it only has cold water," Brian answered, and realized it might take a cold shower to get him back into his jeans.

"Ouch, but okay," Kiya said, guessing, after looking around, that he didn't have another choice.

Brian had to force down the idea of licking his lover clean, and the thought certainly wasn't helping him with the now very rampant erection. He grabbed a couple of towels, tossing one to Kiya.

Kiya caught it, still eyeing Brian. "I could take care of that in the shower, if you want," he said, smiling at him.

The cold wouldn't affect Brian much but he didn't think Kiya would be very comfortable. But Brian wouldn't turn down anything Kiya wanted. He leaned forward and nipped at his lovely lips and then drew him out the door to the shower area. "Not much privacy out here," he warned, turning on the shower head that was rigged to the outside wall at the back of the cabin.

"There aren't a lot of people out here anyway, right?" Kiya asked, unbuttoning the shirt and taking it off once they were outside.

Brian's eyes were on Kiya's beautiful body, which didn't do anything to calm his arousal. "No one out here," he agreed.

Kiya nodded, eyeing the shower now. "Alright, I should just jump in," he mumbled, but didn't move to do so.

Brian turned it on and stepped into the cold spray, grinning at him.

"Isn't it cold?" Kiya asked, edging closer to the water.

"It is," Brian confirmed, holding a hand out to him.

"Oh, alright then," Kiya said, taking Brian's hand and stepping under the water with him. He immediately winced and started to jump back. "Too cold!"

Brian pulled Kiya back under the water with him, laughing as he held him against his own body, nipping his chin.

Kiya groaned and pressed his face against Brian's chest, trying to gather some warmth from him. The water felt like tiny daggers of ice chilling him to the bone.

Brian held them both together, his still hard cock pressed against Kiya as the water flowed down their skin.

Kiya eventually started to warm up, and it wasn't the water, but Brian's body, that was helping him do that. He sighed and slowly started to relax.

Brian turned them until they were thoroughly rinsed and then shut off the water.

"My hair is going to get frizzy," Kiya mumbled through chattering teeth as he continued to shiver, his arms tight around Brian's body.

Brian was unaffected by the cold, but very affected by the smooth body moving against him. He reached for a towel, wrapping it around Kiya's backside.

"Mm, thank you," Kiya said softly, taking a small step back and reaching to wrap the towel around more of his body.

The shower hadn't done anything to quell Brian's erection, not with Kiya against him the entire time. He dried himself off and hung the towel up on a pipe near the shower.

Kiya shook his hair as well, watching Brian at the same time.

"Still want me to take care of that?"

Brian glanced down at his cock and then back at Kiya. He took his hand again and led them back inside before pulling Kiya close, kissing him.

Kiya forgot about his hair and slid his arms around Brian's neck, kissing him back a little harder.

"I'm crazy about you," Brian admitted, whispering against Kiya's lips, body thrumming at the sheer power of his feelings for him.

"I'm that awesome, I know," Kiya chuckled in reply, running his fingers through Brian's damp hair. "So, how are we going to do this?"

Several different possible positions came to mind immediately and Brian's hands slid down Kiya's back to his buttocks. "How do you want to do it?" he nearly growled.

Kiya wanted it any way he could have it, but he didn't have any more condoms. That made him hesitant, even though he still didn't think Brian had anything bad that he could give Kiya, and if he did, he would've known already. "Uhm... well ..." he trailed off.

Brian wondered if he was presuming too much. "We don't have to do anything you don't want," he reminded Kiya.

"Oh, no, no! I want everything, all the time every day, every hour," Kiya said, looking up at Brian as he nodded.

Brian couldn't help but be amused and aroused by the enthusiasm. "But?"

"I don't have any more condoms with me," Kiya told him, pouting slightly. "I mean... you don't have anything, do you? You'd tell me, right?" This was probably the only thing he was overly cautious about when it came to sex.

Brian was glad that Kiya didn't take those kinds of risks. Brian himself was immune to HIV and any of the other diseases that affected humans. "I'm safe, but I am sure Ted said that too," he answered carefully. "So, we will get you food and buy some condoms."

"Thank you, Brian," Kiya said gratefully, leaning up to softly kiss Brian's cheek. "It doesn't mean I don't trust you or anything."

"I want you to take care of yourself," Brian agreed and stepped away from the temptation, looking for where he'd thrown his jeans.

Kiya nodded and watched him walk away, biting his lip gently. "Hey, wait, let me at least suck you off... that's gotta be uncomfortable," he said. He knew, he'd had to pull his jeans on over an erection on more than one occasion.

Brian paused with his jeans in hand, and looked back over at Kiya. His cock twitched eagerly at the idea of those lips around him. "That's safe?"

"Yeah, mostly," Kiya told him, wondering if Brian was a virgin before this. He had seemed very comfortable with the sex but didn't seem to know anything about protection.

Brian reached down, stroking himself and smiling. "If you want to suck me, I certainly won't object."

Kiya grinned and nodded towards his makeshift bed. "Lay down then? So my knees don't ache along with other things," he said.

Brian couldn't help but smile at the reminder, wanting to offer to lick the places that hurt. Later, he told himself. He lay down on the messy bed, opening his legs in invitation as Kiya crawled up between them, licking a line up the middle of Brian's cock slowly, looking up at him the entire time. Brian groaned, the soft wetness making his prick jerk. His eyes were riveted to the sight of Kiya, hair streaming around his naked body, pooling on either side of Brian's thighs as he knelt there.

Kiya continued to lick up and down for a few minutes, teasing Brian until his own mouth was watering. "Tell me how much you want it," he prompted, sliding his fingers around his lover's shaft.

Brian wasn't used to talking during sex. Most Faewolves didn't talk during, even in human form. But now he found it excited him to hear Kiya talk to him like this. "I've thought about your mouth on me like this since I met you," he admitted.

"You're good at hiding things," Kiya murmured, purposely rubbing his lips against the crown as he spoke. He kind of wanted Brian to be demanding about this, like he was before. "What do you want?" he prompted.

Brian pushed himself up on his elbows, watching Kiya. "I want to see those beautiful lips around my cock, sucking me," Brian said, voice hoarse.

It was a good start. Kiya nodded slightly and finally pulled the tip into his mouth, his eyes closing as he swirled his tongue around first and then started to take more of that thick flesh into his mouth.

"Yes, like that," Brian encouraged.

Kiya couldn't take as much as he wanted to into his mouth, but he made up for that by stroking where he couldn't reach, his head beginning to bob.

"Oh, yes, use your tongue," Brian gasped, shuddering. And Kiya did as he was told and, swirling his tongue, made sure to lick around the edge of the head. "Oh, sweet *leannan*, yes, lick me," Brian groaned.

Kiya built up a good rhythm of sucking and stroking, his head and hand moving together. He figured Brian would warn him when he was about to come, so there were no worries there. Brian growled, hands twisting in the blankets. He was still speaking but in words Kiya didn't know now. Babbling instructions in Gaelic instead of English. Kiya would have smirked if he could, definitely enjoying the fact that he had reduced Brian to mumbling a mess of words he didn't know.

Brian's hand reached for Kiya, plunging fingers into his thick hair. "Ah, *leannan*!"

Kiya pulled his mouth off Brian's cock then, but didn't remove his hand, still stroking him. He took that as a sign that Brian was close, since it was the loudest he had gotten. Words disappeared into growls as Brian's cock spasmed, come spurting over Kiya's hand and hitting his chin. Kiya watched with wide eyes, wanting to taste, but still too cautious to do so.

Brian pushed up, and drew Kiya to him, licking his come off the boy's chin. Kiya smiled, murmuring a small "thank you" and tilting his head up a little more for him. Brian licked and kissed Kiya until the rush settled. "I suppose I had better feed you now," he teased.

"That would be a great idea," Kiya said with a grin, kissing Brian's lips once more. "And fill your house with condoms so we'll never have to stop!"

Brian knew they had classes and other responsibilities, but he nodded. He would spend as much time with Kiya as he could. And summer was only weeks away.

Chapter Twelve

They ate dinner together at a local steak house Brian liked. He couldn't believe he was with Kiya. He wanted to never let Kiya out of his sight, but knew he couldn't keep him at his place. There were just too many risks involved, particularly since Brian couldn't remain in human form while he slept. So he told Kiya he would take him home, make sure he was safe and pick him up for class in the morning.

When they reached his college, Kiya made a small pouting face. He wasn't ready to go back yet. He wanted to stay with Brian, but he knew it was best, for now, that he went back. He needed a warm shower and some clothes. And he needed to study. After recent events, Kiya had already fallen behind in his work once and didn't want that to happen again. He sighed, glancing over at Brian. "All right ...."

Brian parked his truck and reached a hand to Kiya, wanting to touch him again. His hand slid up Kiya's thigh as he leaned over for another kiss. He thought he would never tire of kissing those full lips.

Kiya kissed him back for a long moment, since he wouldn't be able to do so again until tomorrow after all his classes were over. He didn't ever want to stop kissing Brian.

Brian's body was definitely arguing with his mind that he should take Kiya back to his den, and his bed. He tried to quell his arousal and pull back. "I'll walk you to your apartment."

Kiya nodded and looked down at his wrists, touching the bruises idly. "Will you let me open the door this time?"

"Do they hurt?" Brian asked, frowning at the reminder of what Ted had done.

"Feels weird, but nothing debilitating," Kiya said, shrugging.

He shook his head and went ahead to open the truck door, not wanting to be stopped by something so stupid. Kiya hopped out and looked around to see if anyone was watching; particularly worried about Ted.

Brian huffed but got out, coming around to the passenger side of the truck. He took Kiya's hand and nodded for him to lead the way.

Kiya didn't let go, walking them both up the hill and then stopping at the base of the stairs on the side of his apartment building. He paused for a minute and then started up the stairs and, relieved when Brian followed, walking him all the way to the front door of the apartment.

Sniffing the air as they went, Brian was satisfied that Ted wasn't anywhere nearby. He had gone easy on the man the first time but he wouldn't if Ted tried anything again. Now that Kiya was his lover, Brian felt even more fiercely protective than before. He barely wanted to let go of Kiya's hand so that he could unlock the apartment door.

"Thanks for bringing me back," Kiya said to him once the door was open, not sure if he could take Brian back to his room or not. He never knew whether or not James would be there.

Brian could smell other men in the apartment. He tried to remind himself that it wasn't a reason to worry, that Kiya would be safer surrounded by others. "I will be back for you in the morning," he whispered, fingers coming up to trace along Kiya's jaw.

"And I'll see you in class," Kiya said, wanting to kiss Brian, but he was too afraid of someone catching them. Instead he pressed his lips against two of his own fingers then pressed them against Brian's cheek, smiling.

Brian tried to remind himself that on campus he needed to be more careful. He nodded, and stepped back. That was more difficult to carry out than it sounded. "Lock the door and call me if you need me," he reminded him.

"Will do," Kiya said with a small nod. "Good night."

Brian didn't leave until Kiya had closed and locked the door behind him. Walking back to his truck and heading out to his place, he knew he would need to try to catch up on the homework he had been neglecting while with his lover. His lover. It had been less than a day and it already sounded just the way it should be.

Kiya took a deep breath and walked back to his room. Exhaustion was setting in and all he wanted to do was sleep.

Joey stuck his head out of the other room just as Kiya opened the bedroom door. "Kiya! Hey, we've been worried about you," he insisted.

"You have?" Kiya asked, stopping to look back at him. "Sorry about that. I'm alright."

"Someone said they saw Ted and the cops, and you've been gone since Wednesday," Joey said, stepping into the hall, wearing only his pajama bottoms.

"Yeah, he's been bugging me. The cops got called," Kiya explained quietly, shrugging slightly as he pushed his hands into his pockets, in case the bruises were showing.

"So are you okay? Did they arrest him?" Joey asked.

"I'm fine. And yeah, they arrested him. I don't know what happened after that," Kiya told him. "Have you seen him around?"

"Not today," Joey answered, stepping closer and really looking at Kiya. "You have a bruise on your neck."

"He's been around before, then?" Kiya asked, reaching to touch the mark that Brian had left.

"I saw him Wednesday night, but not after," Joey answered, still looking at Kiya's neck. "You okay or is that... I mean... " He flushed.

Kiya blushed, continuing to finger the mark. "It's fine, Joey, really. I, uh, consented?"

"New boyfriend?" Joey asked, seeming happier.

"Er, yeah," Kiya admitted, blushing harder. "Or, at least, I'm not sure yet." He was lying, but he didn't want Joey asking for a million details.

Both of Joey's eyebrows rose. "Well, if you need me to tell the cops about Ted, I will," he offered. "And I know James would, too. Oh, he told me to tell you he's over at his new girl's place tonight."

"That would be great, thanks. And all right, I've got the room to myself!" Kiya grinned, turning to walk back into his room. "Night, Joey."

"Good night, Kiya," Joey answered.

Kiya walked into the room and closed the door behind him, locking it. He then undressed and pulled his pajamas on, brushing his hair out before he lay down in bed. He wished he could be with Brian, but he'd rather be alone than get Brian in trouble. He fell asleep thinking about what had happened over the past day, reliving it in his mind, especially the parts where they made love. He touched himself as he thought of Brian. It felt good to know that he had someone of his own again, someone that would keep him safe.

❧

It was lucky for Brian that he didn't need as much sleep as humans. He managed to get papers graded to pass back to the students. When he did sleep, his dreams were full of erotic images of Kiya. He managed to get a run in before it was time to dress and meet Kiya in the morning before the section, even arriving a little early.

When Kiya woke up the next morning, he was hot and sweaty, his pajama pants sticky. He couldn't even remember the last time he'd had a dream like that, and luckily he remembered most of it. It was mainly all about Brian, what they did before, and what Kiya still wanted him to do. He sat there for a few minutes before he hopped out of bed and went for a shower, remembering that he was going to meet Brian before section. Finishing his shower and dressing, Kiya then pulled his hair up into a ponytail so that it was out of his face. He packed his bag quickly and was out, locking his dorm door behind him.

Brian's heart beat faster the moment he saw Kiya. He had to curl his fingers into fists to stop from grabbing and kissing him right there. He smiled instead, although anyone near would probably be able to see right through him.

Kiya spotted him and smiled as well, heading over to him. "Good morning," he said, not standing too close, but close enough for him to feel Brian's warmth.

The sight was only eclipsed by the smell of Kiya, and Brian nearly growled with desire. He needed better control than this. He had to teach with Kiya in the class! "Morning," he answered, his own eyes locked on Kiya's green ones.

"Wanna go somewhere private?" Kiya asked, his voice lowering a little.

Brian trembled. They had some time before class but not enough to go back to his place. "Where?" he asked hopefully.

"Woods?" Kiya asked, not sure of where else they could go. "Or we could go back to my room," he went on, suddenly remembering that James wasn't home.

Brian nodded, looking around but willing to risk it given that he was going to have to try to control himself after. It would be a difficult morning unless Brian had at least a few moments to hold Kiya and touch him, and definitely more, if they had enough time.

"Come on," Kiya said and turned, walking back to his dorm without looking back at Brian.

Brian followed, eyes happily watching Kiya's ass and imagining what they would be doing soon.

Kiya unlocked his door and slipped inside, waiting for Brian to join him inside before he locked it again. He was sure Brian could easily tell which side of the room was his. James' side was a little more messy and Kiya's was very well kept. Pictures of Kiya and his family when he was younger adorned his desk. On the wall behind his bed, there was a dream catcher. Kiya's father had given it to him when he was very young.

Brian took it in quickly, deciding to ask questions later,

because right now he wanted Kiya. He barely gave him time to lock the door before he pulled Kiya's slim frame against his body and brought his lips to his lover's.

Kiya hummed in surprise, but quickly caught up, kissing him back as he slid his arms around Brian's neck, almost pulling himself up his body.

Brian didn't even think about it-he scooped Kiya into his arms and carried him the few steps to the bed, laying him down on it and pressing his own body atop him.

That was when Kiya knew he was going to be sore for the upcoming field trip, more so than he already was. "Brian, you have them, right?" he asked, a little breathless already.

"The condoms we bought?" Brian whispered, nipping at Kiya's neck, already hard as he rubbed their bodies together.

"Yeah," Kiya replied, barely able to keep his eyes open when Brian started to move against him. Even if Brian didn't have any, Kiya had some of the special bigger condoms they had bought.

"Yes," Brian answered and lapped at the spot he had marked the night before, fingers already tugging at Kiya's shirt.

Kiya raised his arms above his head so that Brian could pull the shirt off more easily. "Faster," he said, not sure how much time they had to do this together.

Brian nodded and scooted back, nearly ripping his own shirt buttons off in the effort to strip quickly.

Kiya reached to undo his jeans when he moved back, kicking his shoes off as quickly as he could before pushing the jeans down and off. He reached under his pillow for the lubricant he kept there, holding it out for Brian.

Brian was just dropping his jeans over the side of the bed and took the bottle from Kiya, opening it and coating his fingers.

Kiya spread his legs and pulled his knees up to his chest, his arms sliding behind them. He glanced at the door nervously, hoping James stayed over at the girl's place for a long time. "Maybe you should get under the covers with me?" he asked, thinking that in case someone walked in, he could pull the covers over Brian's head. He couldn't help but think that far ahead.

"I want to see you," Brian answered, shaking his head and reaching fingers to press inside Kiya.

Kiya bit his lip, but nodded, his eyes starting to close when he felt Brian's fingers. He felt sore from yesterday but breathed into it, the pleasure quickly overcoming the stretch.

Brian's prick shuddered at just the feel of a couple of his fingers sinking into the heat of Kiya's body. He growled and fumbled for one of the little packages with his other hand.

Kiya clenched around the fingers and pressed down a little on them, groaning loudly. He could only hope no one heard them, or worse, heard them and decided to investigate.

Brian wasn't sure how to open the package with one hand, so he ripped it open with his teeth and the small disk fell to the bed. He was still sliding fingers in and out of Kiya while trying to put the condom on. Only he seemed to get it backwards and it wouldn't unroll at first. He growled in frustration, turning it around.

"Brian," Kiya moaned, his eyes still closed as he was fucked with just the man's fingers, wanting more.

Brian flushed, not sure how to admit that he'd never put a condom on before. And it was stuck again. He had managed to unroll it over the head but it seemed to have gotten snarled up after.

"What's wrong?" Kiya asked softly when he felt Brian pause, blinking open his eyes and leaning up a little. "Need help?"

Brian didn't want to admit it but he nodded. "Stuck," he said.

Kiya sat halfway up and reached to help him, pulling it off again, and then rolling it back on, slower and more carefully this time.

Brian groaned, the touch of Kiya's fingers making him even more eager. He withdrew his own from inside Kiya and added lube to the outside of the condom, fingers sliding over Kiya's as he did.

"Fuck me, Brian," Kiya said, leaning back again and pulling

his knees up for Brian once more.

The words were thrilling but not as much as that beautiful young man spread open for him. Brian quickly moved into place and then pressed the head of his cock against the slick ring. He wanted to plunge in, but after only a day since their first time, he knew Kiya's body wouldn't be ready for that yet. "Yes, inside you," he agreed, sinking into him.

Kiya bit down on his lip and squeezed his eyes shut when Brian really started to push inside, his fingernails digging into the skin of his legs.

"Kiya?" Brian asked, pausing with the head of his cock just inside of his lover.

"Don't stop," Kiya said groaned, his legs wrapping around Brian's hips.

Brian cupped Kiya's ass, squeezing and spreading as he slowly pushed further into him. "Yes, so beautiful, so good," he gasped.

Kiya was panting, and Brian wasn't even completely inside of him yet. "Just don't stop," he whispered, reaching to pull the band out of his hair so that he could tilt his head back as much as he wanted to without it digging into his neck.

"I don't have to be all the way inside to enjoy it," Brian told him, not wanting to hurt Kiya.

"I'll tell you if it hurts too much," Kiya said, reaching to cup Brian's face as his eyes opened.

Brian smiled. It felt fantastic and the trust Kiya had shown him was beautiful. He was about halfway inside now and could feel the warm tight flesh squeezing his cock.

Kiya already felt full, but he knew that Brian still wasn't all of the way inside of him. He reached to grip his arms, taking deep breaths to relax himself more.

Brian didn't try to push further inside yet, but pulled back instead and then in again, moaning at the feeling.

"It's good," Kiya groaned, his back arching when the tip of Brian's cock nudged against his spot. And he wasn't even working to do it.

That was the reaction Brian was looking for, enjoying Kiya's shudder. He angled more then, trying to make sure to give his lover everything. "Yes, very good," he growled as Kiya's body spasmed around him.

"More?" Kiya asked, his legs tightening around Brian as he braced himself, his cock hard and bobbing between them.

"Ah, leannan," Brian gasped, pushing a little deeper with each thrust now, breathing in their combined scents of sweat and sex.

The pet name made Kiya feel proud that he had already gotten Brian to that point. He'd have to definitely come up with something to call him in return. He moved with Brian, lifting his hips with each thrust, moaning softly.

"I want to see you come," Brian told him, having worked most of his length inside Kiya now.

"Harder then," Kiya told him, opening his eyes a little to look up at him.

"Stroke yourself, leannan," Brian growled, eyes half closed in delight as he began to thrust faster and deeper, finally feeling his balls slap against Kiya's ass.

Kiya reached between them and wrapped his fingers around his own shaft with a moan. "Oh, Brian," he whispered, stroking himself.

Everything about Kiya made Brian feel intoxicated-the feel of him writhing beneath him, the sound of his pleasure, the smell of his desire, the look on his face. "Yes, come for me," Brian growled.

Kiya wasn't exactly sure how or when he had reached the point he was at, but it didn't matter because in the next moment he was coming, his mouth dropping open to cry out Brian's name.

Brian could only growl with his own orgasm riding him as he thrust into his Kiya, pulling him tight against his own body as he did.

"Brian," Kiya moaned, arms and legs gripping him. "So good," He didn't know what else to say to him.

Brian held him-Kiya's legs still wrapped around his hips, cock buried inside him and his own arms around Kiya too. Brian licked and nuzzled the soft damp skin of his lover's neck.

Kiya loved the way they were entwined, feeling connected with Brian in a way that he couldn't describe with words, because he really wasn't sure if any words existed that could convey the strength of his emotions.

Brian had to teach a class, but he didn't want to let go of Kiya for a moment. "We have to go soon," he whispered, then sucked lightly again on Kiya's neck.

"I know," Kiya whispered in reply, really wanting to just lay around for the rest of the day with Brian, exactly how they were.

Brian sighed, breath against Kiya's, then drew back, giving him another kiss before slowly withdrawing from his body. It was difficult to do while he was still hard. The condom slipped a bit, but he caught it.

Kiya shifted and lay back on the bed, his legs loosening and then dropping from around Brian's waist.

It was difficult to let his arousal subside with Kiya lying there looking delicious and smelling of the two of them. Brian swallowed. This wasn't going to be easy, pretending. "We'd better get dressed," he reminded him.

"I know." Kiya nodded, but didn't move, instead reaching in between his legs to gently touch his entrance, his eyes closing slightly. It was a little sore, but twinged in a way that happily reminded him of what they had just done.

Brian had picked up his jeans but stood transfixed, watching and wanting. His cock hadn't softened much at all and now it grew even harder. "You okay?" he asked, voice low with desire.

"Yes," Kiya whispered, nodding slightly and pulling his hand away. "I'll be feeling this the entire hike."

That brought a grin to Brian and he licked his lips. Of course, he would be smelling his lover the entire time, too. "Better get cleaned up so we aren't late."

"You leave first?" Kiya asked, finally sitting up to look for his things.

"Sure," Brian answered, having to force himself to look away. He grabbed his pack and moved to the front of the apartment, waiting for Kiya outside.

Kiya got dressed a little more slowly than before, brushed his hair to fix it, hefted his bag over his shoulder again and left, definitely walking a little awkwardly as he stepped outside.

❧

Brian tried not to grin as they made their way down to the shuttle that would take them to the Field House, where the class was gathering. They sat beside each other and the warmth of Kiya's arm, when it brushed his, made Brian shiver. He sat as still as possible, fingers tightly curled around a metal support as the shuttle made its way around the campus.

Kiya gave him sly smiles and rubbed his knee against Brian's whenever the vehicle shifted. It was fun teasing him and he was almost disappointed when they reached their stop and made their way to the back of the Field House. Kiya wanted to stay near Brian, but he knew that would look too suspicious. So he stayed with the rest of his classmates once they reached them.

Class went well, despite Brian being distracted. It was a long warm hike through the large meadow while they talked about the ecology of grasslands, taking time to draw specific plants. He smiled sometimes, remembering hunting elk with his pack, running across plains much larger than this one. He missed it so much his heart ached some days, but when he looked up and caught Kiya's eyes, he realized there was even more reason now for him to stay in the human world.

Kiya almost wished it was cold enough for him to be able to wear a turtleneck. There were at least two marks on his neck now, and by the time the class was halfway over, he had gotten more than a few questioning and embarrassed looks from others, a couple of students even asked about them. It was difficult not to look over at Brian when he told them that they were nothing. "Bug bites," he said, but he knew they didn't believe him. He walked over to Brian when he got the chance to show him his drawings, brushing purposely against him.

Brian shuddered at the touch, having to fight the urge to growl at the smell and heat of him when Kiya was near. No one else seemed to notice though and Brian was again amazed at how unobservant humans were. Any wolf would have smelled their desire and their mingled scents.

Kiya wanted to pull Brian into a kiss right there in front of all of them. He knew that there were a few girls and at least one other boy who all thought Brian was good looking. Knowing that Brian was now his made Kiya feel a mixture of lucky, proud, and possessive sensations running through him. "That's good, right?" he asked Brian, knowing it was, but he needed more of an excuse to be near him. He idly wondered if anyone would notice their change in attitudes.

"Very good," Brian answered, surprised at how much his voice gave away and feeling slightly worried when one girl gave him a strange flushed look as if the very sound had aroused her.

Kiya looked up when Brian did, noticing the girl as well. He narrowed his eyes at her, but didn't say anything, turning towards Brian again. "Brian."

Brian moved away from Kiya, giving him a warning look as he reached for one of the other student's notebooks instead.

Kiya bit his lip and glanced quickly down at his book when he got the look, knowing that he was being stupid. He had reacted without thinking and those exact actions were the kind that could get Brian in trouble.

Most of the students were hot and tired by the time the hike was over, the scent of their sweat getting on Brian's nerves. Of course, Kiya's scent was the hardest to ignore, but they made it back to the Field House before Brian broke and reached for him. "Here are your papers back from last week," he told the students, handing them out. "Make sure I have this week's field notes by next section. After that, you need to work on your research papers and prepare for the final exam."

Kiya was ready to just go to sleep, his body exhausted. He

sighed and put his things back into his bag and went to the front to get his paper. He found it after a moment or two and eyed the grade on it, glancing worriedly up at Brian who was busy trying to answer questions from several students at once. Kiya was upset that he had only gotten a "B." Sure, it was a good grade, but it wasn't the best. Kiya figured he wouldn't get a chance to talk to Brian about it with the other students around, so he walked over to a bench near the shuttle stop, carefully sitting down and shifting as his body reminded him again what he had spent the last day and early morning doing.

Brian tried to patiently answer everyone, despite his urge to just run off with Kiya. He noticed one young woman was touching his arm a lot and seeming to ask more than was necessary. He wasn't surprised to smell that she was aroused by him. He ignored it and eventually all the questions were answered and he was able to turn and look for Kiya. Spotting him on a bench, he walked over and stood staring down at his lover. He wanted to kiss him right there but knew he couldn't. "You look tired," he said softly.

"I am," Kiya told him, holding a hand out so that Brian could pull him up.

Brian pulled but had to step back rather than draw Kiya against him. He held his hand for a moment, squeezing it before letting go.

"Your place?" Kiya asked quietly, so that only Brian could hear him.

Brian's heart sped up. He had thought Kiya would rather go home to sleep. "My truck is over by your apartment. You can pick up what you need there," he answered, nodding and guiding them over to wait for the shuttle up to College Ten.

Kiya nodded back in reply and followed him, rolling his shoulders and looking down at the paper still in his hands. "And what's up with this grade?" he asked.

"Are you asking me as your teacher or as your lover?" Brian whispered.

"As my teacher first, then my lover," Kiya answered, just as quiet.

"You were sloppy. You could have done better," Brian answered honestly.

Kiya frowned a little. He hated being criticized. "I know I can," he mumbled.

Brian could tell that Kiya was unhappy but he didn't know what to do about it. He couldn't go easy on him just because they were involved with each other. They sat in silence while the shuttle made its way up the hill to College Ten and then Brian followed Kiya up to his apartment.

"Now tell me as my lover?" Kiya asked.

"When we are alone," Brian whispered. His hearing was better than any human, so he was aware that someone was home in Kiya's apartment. As Kiya went to open the door, Brian stepped back.

"Meet you out here," Kiya said, nodding at him before unlocking the door and going inside to his dorm. He set his bag down, emptied it and then went to find another outfit and his pajamas. Something told him he wouldn't need anything to sleep in, but he packed them anyway.

James came out of the bathroom. "Hey, Kiya, where ya been?"

"Hey, James," Kiya replied, looking up at his dorm mate. "I've been around."

"You doin' okay? I heard Ted was messing with you again," James said, looking worried.

"I'm doing alright, yeah," Kiya said, stepping over to sit down on his bed as he zipped his bag up. "I haven't seen Ted since yesterday, so..."

"Where you going?" James asked, gesturing at the way Kiya was packing.

"My friend's place, I'll be back," Kiya told him, smiling a little. "I heard you were at your new girl's place."

James grinned. "Gonna spend the weekend there, so it looks like neither of us will be home."

"Yeah, guess so. I hoped I'd see you before I left so that you wouldn't worry," Kiya said.

James seemed almost embarrassed at that but managed to nod and shrug at the same time. "Have fun," he said as Kiya moved toward the door.

"You too," Kiya said and left, heading outside to see Brian.

Brian was leaning against an outer wall, arms crossed over his chest and watching the trees. He'd been human all day. It got uncomfortable after a while.

"Hi, again," Kiya told him as he walked over.

A smile changed Brian's face, lighting it up as he looked at Kiya. He thrust his hands into his pockets to stop from reaching to take Kiya's hand as he led the way to the truck.

Kiya did the same after he slung his pack on to his back, waiting for Brian to open the door for him once they reached the truck. He had already proven the evening before that he was capable of opening his own door if he wanted to. Kiya was content now to let Brian do it for him.

After Brian unlocked it, he guided Kiya inside before coming around and getting into the driver's seat, turning to look at Kiya. "You still want to go back to my place?"

"Where else would we go?" Kiya asked, slightly smug as he glanced over at him.

Brian put the truck in gear and drove down the hill, and then turned to head back up Empire Grade to the cabin.

Kiya watched him as the man drove, his eyelids growing heavy. He wasn't sure of when it happened, but he started to doze off, his eyes falling shut.

Chapter Thirteen

Brian pulled up into the little gravel drive that led to his cabin, trees sheltering it from view. Kiya had fallen asleep, so Brian just sat there watching him for a bit. He was still amazed by how good it felt just to do that. When it was clear that Kiya was not going to wake up quickly, Brian got out and strode up to the small building, unlocking his door before coming back for Kiya.

He opened Kiya's side of the truck and then gently unlatched the seatbelt, sliding his arms under his lover's knees and behind him, easily lifting him. Kiya's head fell against his shoulder and his hair tickled Brian's neck. He kissed Kiya's forehead as he carried him inside, laying him in the bed. Kiya shifted once he was set down and made a small sound before he quieted again, bringing his thumb up to his mouth and gently beginning to suck on it in his sleep.

Brian had thought he would just let Kiya get some rest, maybe go for a run while he did. But he couldn't resist touching him. He smoothed the hair back from Kiya's face, smiling at the soft noises he made and watching those beautiful lips suck at his own thumb. Kiya hummed and leaned up into Brian's small touch against his hair. He sucked the thumb harder and his eyes fluttered, but he didn't open them. It made Brian hard again. Everything about Kiya seemed to do that, and Brian was rubbing the front of his own jeans before he realized it.

Brian pulled himself away and then quickly went back out to the truck and brought their things inside, making sure to have the condoms nearby for when they were needed. Then he stripped his own clothes off and gently removed Kiya's shoes. He would have rather felt skin against skin, but crawling in beside Kiya, he was delighted just to be holding him. It was difficult living alone, missing the warmth and closeness of a pack. Holding Kiya, Brian felt that sense of belonging he hadn't had as his own in a long time.

Kiya turned around in Brian's arms and easily settled down, mumbling something incoherent around his thumb before he quieted again. Wolf pups didn't suck thumbs, not really having any, so Brian had never watched anyone do it before. And the sight of Kiya's full lips sucking anything was rather suggestive. Brian reached down to stroke his own cock, eyes focused on Kiya's mouth. He remembered how good those lips and that tongue felt on him. He gently worked his fingers up and down his own flesh, moving the foreskin and rubbing the head with his thumb. After several minutes he found himself unable to resist bringing that now slick thumb up and rubbing it against the outside of Kiya's mouth, wondering what his sleeping lover would do.

Kiya opened his mouth, his thumb slipping out as he blinked open his eyes. It took him a few moments to focus on Brian and what he was doing, but when he did, he smiled a little and beckoned him closer, opening his mouth more for him.

Brian moved up so that his cock was near Kiya's face and rubbed the slick head against his lips.

Kiya licked his lips, eyeing Brian as he leaned in closer to wrap his lips around the head, starting to suck. Kiya wasn't even completely awake, but he wasn't complaining. He liked doing this.

Brian moaned, shivering in pleasure, his hand coming to rest on the back of Kiya's head, while Kiya sucked harder, breathing in and out through his nose. Brian knelt low beside Kiya, fingers caressing his hair and watching in rapt pleasure as those lips held the crown between them. "Lap it, use your tongue," he said, voice a hoarse whisper.

Kiya closed his eyes and started to move his tongue around the tip, pulling a little more of Brian's cock into his mouth.

Brian reached down, wrapping his fingers around the base of his own shaft, stroking himself. The movements made the head move back and forth just inside Kiya's mouth.

Kiya shifted his balance when Brian started to move, his teeth nicking at Brian's cock a little. Brian nearly came at the touch of teeth to his sensitive flesh and he groaned, fingers sliding into and curling around the silky strands of Kiya's hair. His hand sped up, pumping his shaft.

Kiya's eyebrows furrowed a little when he felt a hand tighten in his hair, his eyes fluttering open again. He smirked around his lover's cock and sucked harder, wanting him to come.

Brian was gasping now, trying to hold back his release but becoming even more aroused as Kiya looked up.

"Your tongue, yes," Brian growled, shaking with the effort it took not to thrust into the warmth of Kiya's mouth.

Kiya moved his tongue more, teasing the crown and relaxing back on the bed once again to let Brian have his way.

"I'm going to come soon," Brian told him, feeling the tension in his balls, his thighs trembling with the effort of holding back.

Kiya was still sleepy and wasn't even thinking about safe sex. He nodded slightly as if encouraging Brian.

Brian growled, fingers tightening in Kiya's hair as he began to shake, cock spasming as the hot slick liquid shot from him.

Kiya closed his eyes when he first felt it, his nose scrunching up a little. It took him a moment to realize that Brian was coming, and it was in his mouth, without any protection or anything. His eyes flew open as he turned his head quickly to the side. Come splattered on Kiya's cheek, and Brian groaned, the head sliding against the soft skin as his seed pumped from his cock, dripping down Kiya's face. Kiya let what had gathered in his mouth leak out, his eyes closing again as he panted softly. His heart was beating unbelievably fast in his chest, and he told himself to calm down, that he wouldn't get anything.

Brian was unaware of Kiya's fears. He didn't know what was safe or not safe for humans. Instead, he was rubbing the head of his cock against the slick on Kiya's chin. "So good," he whispered.

Kiya took a deep breath and let it out slowly, still too afraid to even swallow. He couldn't help the fears he had about it, he was too aware of the potential dangers.

That's when Brian noticed the frown, and the smell of fear mingled with the scents of sex. "Kiya?" he whispered. "Did I hurt you?"

"I'm fine," Kiya answered, looking nervously back up at Brian.

Brian moved, lying down beside his lover and pulling him close. The look and smell of his come marking Kiya's face assured that he remained aroused. He was still worried that he had made some type of mistake but he still didn't resist the urge to lick Kiya's chin.

"You started to come in my mouth," Kiya told him, shivering a little at the feel of Brian's tongue.

"Is that good or bad?" Brian asked, arm sliding around Kiya's waist as he continued to lap at his skin, cleaning his own seed from Kiya's cheek.

Kiya's eyes closed a little, his head tilting a little more so that Brian could lick better. "Well, no one's ever done that. Either because they were wearing a condom or they pulled out."

It made Brian want to do it again, to really come inside him now, to watch him swallow it. Yet, he was smart enough, even distracted like this, to realize he was still missing something. "Why?" he asked, tongue working on the drips that had slid down Kiya's neck.

"Why what?" Kiya asked, not sure of what he was supposed to be explaining.

"Why didn't they... or you?" Brian asked, stopping his licks so he could pull back enough to look into Kiya's eyes.

"Do you know about sexually transmitted diseases?" Kiya asked suddenly, because now he was almost sure that Brian didn't know about them. Why else would he be asking all of these questions?

Brian flushed then. He knew about diseases; he did teach biology. Yet, he didn't know about the specifics of human sexual diseases. "I don't know what the rules are on how not to catch them," he admitted.

"People can get diseases from stuff like this," Kiya explained looking up into Brian's eyes. It surprised him that this man, who was several years older than him, wouldn't know this stuff. It did reassure him that if Brian was that inexperienced, he probably didn't have anything, and that made Kiya just a little more calm. "So, if you were to have something, coming in my mouth or inside of me could give me whatever you have."

There was no reason for Kiya to trust him, especially after Ted, but Brian wanted to assure him anyway. "I have no diseases," he said. "Yet, I can respect any safety rules you have. So, I am not to come inside your body. But on the skin is safe?"

"Yeah, on my skin is fine," Kiya told him, biting his lip gently. "Unless there is a cut or something. You tell me you don't have anything and I believe that you don't. I'm just overly scared about those things. Maybe sometime... soon, we won't use condoms." He smiled, nodding.

Brian didn't like condoms. They were confusing and distracting. And he wanted to feel Kiya without something between them. Yet, he was proud of Kiya's resolve to take care of himself. It was also a new concept for him to realize that humans didn't lick each other's come because it was dangerous. It was one of Brian's favorite things, and part of his wolf instinct. "I can still taste you, can't I?"

"Of course," Kiya said, blushing a little now. "I'm clean. I've even been tested."

Getting dirty was more of what Brian had in mind. "You taste fantastic," he assured his lover, licking and nipping Kiya's chin again to emphasize it.

"I'm sure I do," Kiya murmured, smirking a little. "And, by the way, that's the first time I've woken up and given a blow job before I even had a chance to stretch."

"Did you like it?" Brian asked, nibbling Kiya.

"Yeah, I like when you're like that, actually," Kiya said, blushing. Then he realized Brian must have seen him sucking his thumb. Was that the reason why he got hard? "You got hard just from watching me doing that."

"I love your lips," Brian admitted, sucking on the bottom one then.

"I love when you kiss me," Kiya said softly, his eyes closing a bit.

That sounded like an invitation, which Brian eagerly accepted. Brian's mouth closed over Kiya's, lips pressed together and tongue sliding inside his mouth. He pulled Kiya, still dressed, against his own very naked body.

Kiya kissed him back slowly and thoroughly; sometimes it was nice to just enjoy kissing rather than going straight to sex.

Holding Kiya made Brian feel a sense of peace that he hadn't felt since he was small and curled up with his family. He petted, kissed and nuzzled him. "I woke you," he whispered. "You can go back to sleep."

Kiya was still a little sleepy, but he didn't want to sleep just yet. "I dunno," he mumbled, biting into the tip of his thumb as he thought.

Brian settled back, fingers still playing with Kiya's hair, as he waited for him to talk about what was bothering him.

Kiya didn't say anything, quiet as the minutes went by. Then he got up and started to undress, feeling constricted in his clothes. When he only had his shorts on, he crawled back into the bed and curled up next to Brian, reaching for his hand.

Brian waited for cues from Kiya. He'd never been intimately involved with a human before. He accepted Kiya's hand, his long fingers curling around the smaller ones as he watched him closely.

"It's your fault that I'm so sleepy," Kiya said after a while, playing with Brian's fingers as he looked up at him with a small smile. "How are you not?"

There would be other questions like this, and Brian knew he was going to have to come up with explanations. It had been easy to lie to most people. No one was close enough to him to matter. Yet, Brian wanted to give Kiya the truth. "I don't sleep much," he admitted. "Only a few hours a day, actually."

"How do you manage to do that?" Kiya asked, his eyebrows rising in surprise. "I could never... I love sleep way too much."

"I like sleeping too," Brian tried to explain. "I just don't seem to be able to do it for very long." Brian wondered if that was an evolutionary response for wolves since they, his kind in particular, had been hunted by humans for generations.

"Oh, okay," Kiya said, idly bringing Brian's hand up to his mouth without thinking about it. "Well, as long as you're comfortable."

Brian decided this might actually help keep his secret, so he added, "So when I can't sleep, I tend to go for runs in the woods. Don't worry if you wake up and I'm not here."

"You should take me with you sometimes," Kiya said, rubbing Brian's thumb against his bottom lip. "I need to go running like I used to."

"Yes," Brian responded, but he couldn't have said whether it was due to the running or to the sensation sparking through his body at the touch of Kiya's mouth on him.

"Remind me sometime," Kiya said, nipping the tip of Brian's thumb.

Kiya affected Brian like no-one else, human or wolf, had ever done before. His whole body felt drawn to Kiya, and one small nip was more than enough to have Brian's cock twitching eagerly against his hip.

Kiya licked and then pulled the thumb into his mouth, sucking softly as he sighed, his eyes closing a little again.

That sucking went straight to Brian's cock and he moaned, body shuddering.

Kiya's eyes closed completely, sucking lightly as he relaxed, enjoying Brian's response.

"I guess," Brian gasped, "it's a good thing I don't need much sleep."

Kiya nodded in agreement, his head resting on Brian's chest

as he continued to suck, feeling drowsy again.

Brian would have easily and happily rolled over and had another round with Kiya. He was certainly aroused enough. Yet, he saw that Kiya's eyes were closed and that his lover wasn't as aroused. Brian smiled adoringly at the sleepy young man and held him.

Kiya was falling asleep again within minutes, his lips tight around Brian's thumb. He couldn't say that he had ever felt this way before, and he loved it already. They had only been lovers for a few days, but Kiya felt cared for and safe.

Brian lay beside Kiya, just enjoying him. Eventually, Kiya's mouth slackened and released Brian's thumb. So Brian slipped out of the bed, then the room. He needed to run. To be a wolf for a while. Shifting effortlessly, he loped off into the trees.

∽

When he got back, Kiya was still asleep, so Brian got dressed, grabbed his wallet and keys and drove down to Mission Street to one of the fast food places. He didn't know what Kiya favored, so he bought some burgers, fries and sodas from a drive through.

Kiya wasn't sure just how long he slept, but when he woke up, Brian wasn't there. He rubbed at his eyes as he stretched his back with a groan. He figured Brian had gone off for another one of his runs, and he'd be back soon. For now he'd just wait. He didn't bother with checking the refrigerator for food, because he knew what he'd find in there.

Brian preferred to eat as a wolf, but he did occasionally enjoy burgers and other cooked food. And the smell of the meat had his stomach growling. He stepped inside his cabin and smiled when he saw Kiya's green eyes looking back at him. Brian held up a bag. "Food."

Kiya smiled brightly and waved him over. "Thank goodness," he answered, his stomach grumbling at just the thought.

Brian dropped the bag on the bed and then sat on the edge, pulling off his boots. "I had to guess what you would want," he explained. "I got one with and one without cheese. Just take the one you like best."

"Thank you, Brian," Kiya said with a smile, leaning over to kiss Brian's cheek before he reached for the bag. "I'll take the one with the cheese."

Brian opened the bag first and pulled out the paper wrapped packages, handing the cheeseburger over and setting a carton of fries beside him too. He pulled the vegetables off the other burger and started in on it.

Kiya picked up the discarded lettuce and tomato and put it in his own burger, taking a bite out of it. "Mmm," he hummed as he chewed.

Brian paused, eyes on Kiya's mouth. His mouth fascinated Brian. He blinked, licking his own lips and then returned to eating.

Kiya didn't talk until he was about halfway through his cheeseburger. "So, now that I'm fully awake, you and I are going to discuss that 'B,'" he said, reaching for one of the sodas.

Brian kept chewing, nearly done with his. He arched an eyebrow and waited.

"I don't see how it was messy," Kiya went on after he took a good drink, setting the cup down. "I stated the points, and I explained them carefully."

Brian swallowed. "I said it was sloppy. You did the bare minimum. You're smarter than that."

"Sloppy, messy, the same thing. And it wasn't either," Kiya said. "It was worth at least an A minus. I know there were a few points I could've gone into more detail about, but...."

"I said if we did this you had to do your best in my class," Brian insisted. "That wasn't even close to your best. You're better than that."

"Alright, yes, it wasn't my best, but it was not my worst," Kiya admitted, frowning now.

"An 'A' is for excellence, not just what you can get away with," Brian said with a sigh, throwing the empty wrapper back into the bag and ignoring his fries.

"Still think it's bullshit," Kiya said, setting down the rest of his cheeseburger.

Both of Brian's eyebrows rose at that. "You're saying you can't do better?" he challenged.

"Of course I'm not saying that," Kiya huffed, tucking a bit of his hair behind his ear when he looked down. He'd always managed to get high marks in his classes without having to work too hard.

"You earn the 'A' and you will get it," Brian assured him, shoving the wrappers off the bed and reaching to cup Kiya's chin. Fingers caressing that fine tawny skin, Brian smiled. He wondered how often Kiya thought that what people valued in him was how pretty he was, not how smart. Brian wasn't fooled.

"I'll do better on the next one," Kiya told him finally, sighing and looking over at him.

"I know you will," Brian agreed, leaning in to kiss him.

Kiya kissed back and then pulled away to finish eating his cheeseburger, resting his head on Brian's shoulder. "Thanks for not going easy on me, I guess."

Smirking at the ways in which Kiya pushed his limits, Brian nodded. "You are more than capable, *leannan*."

"I know," Kiya replied, smiling again as he took another bite of his burger. He was beginning to get full already, so he offered the rest to Brian as he reached for the fries. "What does that mean anyway?"

Brian took the burger and leaned back against the wall, legs spread out in front of him. He actually blushed then, pulling the meat out and popping it into his mouth.

Kiya caught the blush and arched an eyebrow, moving up in between Brian's legs as he munched on the fries. "What's it mean?" he asked again, really curious now.

Brian chewed for a minute, then swallowed, finally lifting his eyes to Kiya's. "It's Gaelic," he whispered. "It means lover."

"Oh," It was Kiya's turn to blush hard. "Lover... in Lakota, tehila means lover. Should I call you that now?"

Brian's heart sped up, and he felt open and exposed, like Kiya saw something no one else did. "If you want," he whispered.

"Tehila," Kiya said softly, trying it out. "Imagine me screaming that in pleasure."

Imagining Kiya screaming anything in pleasure sent a shiver through Brian and his jeans seemed too hot and too tight. "Yes," he whispered.

"Good," Kiya said, setting his fries down and moving further up so that he was against Brian's chest now.

Brian's hands automatically rose, fingers splayed on either side of Kiya, clutching his waist. He didn't know if lover meant more than sex partner in English or Lakota, but it did in Gaelic. Had he really only known Kiya for just over a month? It wasn't uncommon for his kind to mate for years, or even life, with another wolf they just met. But that was among wolf kind.

Kiya turned his head and tilted it up to kiss Brian's chin. "This is nice," he murmured softly. "Nice just sitting here."

Brian would call it a lot more than that. "Very nice," he agreed, heart speeding up and fingers pressing gently against Kiya.

Kiya wasn't tired anymore, so he wasn't about to fall asleep again. He was feeling comfortable and relaxed. "So," he murmured, thinking of what they could do next.

Brian didn't know what humans did together for fun. He spent most of his time as a wolf. It was Friday night and that meant they had several days before they had class again. If he could hide what he was, he wanted to keep Kiya with him. "Tell me what you like to do," he said.

"Like, with my friends?" Kiya asked, looking up at him again. "Sometimes we go out. Usually we meet up at the Coffee House or whatever."

Brian realized he couldn't really take Kiya out, not until after the quarter ended and he had turned grades in to the department. Then he would no longer be Kiya's TA. Which brought up another question for him. "Will you be going back to your people for the summer?"

"Yeah," Kiya answered with a small nod. "I miss them too much to stay here."

Brian frowned. He didn't want Kiya to leave, to be away from him, for very long. But he didn't have the right to interfere. He missed his own pack, too. He hadn't seen any of them in five years. And he could hardly offer for Kiya to stay with him over the summer. He might be able to hide what he was for a couple days, but not months. "We could go for a hike tomorrow if you want," he suggested.

"That sounds like fun," Kiya told him with a smile, but then he noticed the frown. "Maybe you could come back home with me and meet my parents?"

"Meet your parents?" Brian asked. "They wouldn't be... angry, my being a man and not tribe?"

"Well," Kiya paused, trying to think about how to explain that. "First, my mom isn't Native American. Tribe isn't just about blood anyway. Maybe that makes them more open about who I date and all."

"And they know about you and men?" Brian asked.

"I've always known I was gay, and well, they probably knew before I really knew, you know?" Kiya asked.

Brian nodded. He was actually attracted to both males and females, but his reaction to Kiya specifically was more intense than anything he had felt before. Pair bonding among wolves was geared toward mating, toward producing pups. He didn't know if it meant the same for two males. "So they accept it?"

"Yes," Kiya answered, shifting around so that he was facing Brian. He tapped his chin thoughtfully, nodding.

Brian considered the implications. "So you only like sex with men?"

"Yeah, only with men," Kiya said, smiling at Brian again. "Basically, I'm just really gay. And I love it."

Brian smiled, hands sliding down to cup and squeeze Kiya's ass. "Well, I am glad of it, since it means you want to be with me," he admitted.

"With you," Kiya murmured, nuzzling the side of his face. "So what about your family? Are they as traditional and stuff?"

Brian blinked. He tried to think of what he would be allowed to tell about his family. "They don't live like most people," he said cautiously. "They really don't approve of me even being here."

"Why not?" Kiya asked, his turn to be surprised.

"They think I read too much, and they don't understand why I would leave my ... family and want to be with others, to attend college or do the work I do," Brian explained.

"Oh, they wouldn't like me then?" Kiya asked, frowning a little.

"They don't like any outsiders," Brian confirmed. "But they don't really like me most the time, either, so I don't care what they think of you."

"Oh," Kiya wouldn't know what he'd do if his family treated him like that. "I'm sorry anyway."

Brian leaned forward, giving his lover a gentle kiss. "I care deeply for family, but their way of life isn't enough for me."

Kiya nodded, thinking that Brian was old enough to live on his own anyway. "As long as you're happy."

Brian couldn't say that he was happy, at least not before Kiya had shown up. He was doing work he enjoyed, but he was lonely. He hadn't even allowed himself to think about how lonely he was. "I am now," he whispered.

"Me too," Kiya said, grinning now. "More happy than I've been in a long time."

They kissed again, and soon, were stripping and touching each other. Brian managed the condom without mishap and lost himself in the bliss of Kiya's willing body. Lying in a sticky, happy tangle of limbs afterward, he watched him drift off to sleep again. Brian had never felt as comfortable as he did at that moment.

Chapter Fourteen

Eventually, Brian dragged himself out of the bed and outside, shifting to his wolf form. He could see and smell the night so much more clearly then. After running for a bit, he stopped to renew his boundary markers and then made his way in a circle back to his den. It was a delight to come back and find a beautiful boy in his bed. Kiya made the place smell more like home than it ever had. Saoi hopped into the bed and curled up outside the covers against Kiya's legs.

Kiya normally never slept so much in one day, but he felt he needed it, especially after he and Brian had sex. He was just so exhausted. Satisfied, but exhausted. He shifted and opened his eyes a little when he felt warm fur against his legs. Curled up beside him was the wolf, the one he had first met in the woods and then here before.

"Hey, you," Kiya said sleepily, smiling and moving closer to him. "Haven't seen you in a bit." He slid his fingers into the thick fur and petted the wolf.

Brian loved being a man with Kiya, but being a wolf was so much a part of who he was; he had really missed this too. Saoi eagerly rubbed his head against his lover's hand.

"Yeah, come closer," Kiya said, snuggled up agianst the wolf, getting as close as possible.

Saoi eagerly pressed his wolf body to his lover's skin and shuddering in delight at the feeling. In the pack, they usually slept together in warm happy piles of furry bodies. He had lost that when he left home.

"You're like a big fluffy pillow," Kiya murmured, resting his head against the wolf's body.

Saoi happily licked Kiya's chin, rubbing his muzzle against

him.

"Hey, where's Brian? It'd be nice to cuddle both of you but I still haven't seen you two at the same time," Kiya said.

Saoi wondered if that meant that Kiya suspected something. Yet, who would guess their boyfriend was a wolf? He sighed and nuzzled his lover's neck, enjoying the scent of sex from their earlier coupling.

Kiya snuggled him until he fell asleep once again, hoping that the next time he woke up, Brian would be there too.

Saoi woke early, as was usual for him. Kiya had wrapped both arms and a leg around the big furry wolf and his face was buried against Saoi's neck. It was wonderful and arousing. Saoi had to find a way to get out of the bed, though. He moved slowly, scooting further from his lover until Kiya made an unhappy little sound and rolled over. The boy's backside didn't help Saoi control his response. He sighed and padded out of the room to change form. Then he took a shower and dressed. Kiya was still sleeping, so Brian went to get something for the young man's breakfast.

~

Kiya was screaming for help, struggling his hardest to get away from Ted who was holding him down. No one seemed to hear him, and Brian wasn't in sight. He tried pleading with Ted again. "Stop!" he yelled-and then he woke in a cold sweat, sitting up sharply in the bed. He looked around and recognized where he was, taking a few deep breaths to calm himself down.

Brian had purchased coffee and breakfast from a local drive-through. He was climbing out of his truck when he heard Kiya cry out. Abandoning the food, he left the door of his truck open and ran to the cabin, ready to shift and rip apart whoever was hurting his lover.

Kiya's head snapped up when the door slammed opened, letting out a sigh of relief when he saw who it was. "Brian," he sobbed.

Brian couldn't smell anyone else nearby but looked around

just in case. Then he strode anxiously to the bed. "Kiya, what's wrong?"

"I had a bad dream, that's all," Kiya said softly, realizing that Brian must have thought something was actually happening.

Brian dropped to his knees on the bed and took Kiya into his arms. Touch was important to him, important to the pack, and he hoped Kiya understood it.

Kiya met him halfway, moving to wrap his arms around Brian. "Sorry I scared you," he murmured against the man's chest.

Brian's heart had sped up in fear, but now remained pounding from the rush of adrenaline and the feel of his naked lover in his arms. He petted Kiya's hair. "It's okay," he told him.

"You smell like coffee," Kiya muttered after another few minutes.

"I bought some and food," Brian admitted, smiling.

"Really?" Kiya leaned back to kiss Brian's lips softly. "Thanks. Sorry I'm sleeping so much, too. Must be boring for you."

Brian returned the kiss and his smile broadened. "I like watching you sleep," he admitted. "But you're probably hungry," he added, moving to go back for the abandoned food.

"Yeah," Kiya said, watching him go. He got up after a moment because his bladder decided to make itself known. He remembered that Brian didn't have a bathroom, and went right outside, looking around for the outhouse.

Brian came up behind him while he was scanning the area. He had a bag in one hand and was balancing a paper tray with two coffees in the other. "It's behind those trees," he said, gesturing with the bag toward a clump where the small shack-like structure was hidden.

"Thanks," Kiya said, and headed off into that direction, hoping no one was around because he didn't want anyone to see him just walking around naked. He found the outhouse and quickly emptied his bladder. Sighing in relief when he was finished, he went back to the house.

Brian was sitting on the bed, unpacking the food and sipping his coffee. He smiled at the beautiful young man when he returned. He didn't think he would ever get tired of looking at, smelling or touching Kiya.

Kiya climbed back onto the bed and reached for his cup of coffee, taking a long sip.

Brian was nibbling on an egg and sausage sandwich when he heard a strange trilling noise. It took him a moment to realize it was coming from Kiya's backpack.

Kiya looked up when he heard it, frowning for a moment. "Oh!" He got up and went to his bag, finding his cell phone and answering it without even looking at who it was. "Hello?"

"Kiya, I've been trying to find you," Ted said.

Kiya mentally cursed when he heard Ted's voice, feeling stupid for not having looked at caller ID first. "Why?" he asked.

"I'm worried about you," Ted insisted. "This was all just a misunderstanding. You have to know I never meant to hurt you."

The hair on the back of Brian's neck prickled. With his sensitive hearing, he recognized that voice.

"A little too late for that, you know," Kiya said, biting his lip as he walked around the room. "You did hurt me."

"Who was that man who attacked me? Is he bothering you, Kiya? Is he the reason you stopped seeing me?" Ted continued.

Brian growled tensely, fingers partially crushing the paper cup holding his coffee. He didn't even flinch when the hot liquid spilled down his hand and onto his denim-clad thigh.

"I stopped seeing you way before he saved me," Kiya explained, feeling as though this was the hundredth time he said so. "Ted, you're the only person who has been bothering me and hurting me, constantly."

"Hang up," Brian said, voice cold with his anger. He wanted to take the phone from Kiya and tell Ted that he would kill him if he ever came near Kiya again.

Kiya nearly jumped when he heard Brian's voice, turning around to face him.

Brian dropped the remains of his food back into the paper bag and set the mangled cup down. He held a hand out for the phone. "I'll tell him if you want," he growled.

Kiya shook his head and hung up the phone before Brian could reach him.

Brian dropped his hand, his anger feeling like a pressure inside his chest. "I don't want him near you."

"I know," Kiya finally answered, still a little cautious. Brian's voice had really scared him.

Brian took several breaths and opened his mouth to speak when the cell phone rang again.

Kiya snapped it open. "Hello?" he answered, still staring at Brian.

"Don't hang up. Meet me, so we can talk," Ted insisted.

"What part of 'no' don't you understand?" Kiya asked in reply.

Brian couldn't help another growl, hands tightening into fists.

"You can't mean that, Kiya, not after everything," Ted insisted.

"I do mean it, Ted, honestly. I don't love you and I never will, so just leave me the fuck alone!" Kiya hung up the phone again before Ted could answer.

"He won't listen," Brian warned. He had the urge to go hunt down Ted-and rip his throat out. He could practically taste it.

"I'm such an idiot," Kiya mumbled.

Brian moved to Kiya, taking his hand. "I won't let him hurt you."

The phone rang again.

"What!" Kiya yelled into the phone when he answered it.

"Kiya White Cloud?" a new voice asked.

"Oh, uh, yes?" Kiya asked, frowning slightly.

"This is Officer Turner with the Santa Cruz Police Department," a woman's voice continued.

"Oh, hello, sorry about the way I answered," Kiya said, feeling stupid now. "Is there something you wanted to tell me?"

"I'm following up on a complaint lodged by you Thursday," she explained. "We will need to have you come to the station to file formal charges."

"Oh, when do I have to come down?" Kiya asked.

"Well, it's Saturday, and the accused has been released on bail," Officer Turner explained. "Monday would work unless you want to come in sooner."

"Earlier might be best, I guess. Is there any way I could add more to my story?" Kiya asked softly.

"If there is more than you reported, we can include it," she confirmed. "Has there been more than one incident?"

Brian sat listening, able to hear both sides of the conversation. He wished he could report everything he had seen to the police.

"Yes, there has, I'm sorry I didn't tell you before," Kiya told her, his voice lowering as if he didn't want Brian to hear.

"I understand Mr. White Cloud. Did you want to come in today?" the police officer asked.

"Yes, that would be good," Kiya answered, thinking that it would probably be best to get this done before he changed his mind. "Will I be talking to you?"

"If you come in while I am on shift, you can ask for me," she explained.

"What's your name so I know?" Kiya asked.

"Officer Turner," she repeated.

"Right, okay, I'll be there soon. Thank you, Officer Turner," Kiya said, then hung up. He stood there for a moment, staring at the phone in his hand.

"Finish your breakfast and then I'll take you," Brian said.

"Thanks." Kiya sighed and returned back to the bed. "I'm sorry about all of that."

Brian didn't know why Kiya kept apologizing when he had done nothing wrong. "I want to protect you."

"You are," Kiya said, reaching for his sandwich to eat.

Brian sat back, watching his lover eat and waiting. He was working on clamping down on the fierce emotions of the wolf, who wanted nothing more than to destroy the threat to his … to what was his.

Kiya finished and then pulled out clean clothes from his bag.

"I honestly don't know why he's acting like this. Things were different in the beginning."

Brian didn't know if he wanted to even think about Kiya with the other man, but he nodded. He needed to understand more about Kiya. "What was he like?"

"He was nice. He used to always compliment me, and buy me things," Kiya said as he pulled on a fresh pair of underwear. "When he got possessive, I liked it."

Brian cocked his head. "Why?"

"I dunno. I like things like that," Kiya admitted, blushing. "Isn't that obvious?"

Brian got to his feet and stepped closer, looking down at the young man. "You want to be protected."

"I want someone who can be rough with me, tell me what to do, but only when I want them to do that. If I say no, it means no," Kiya murmured. "And they have to be able to love me at the same time."

Among wolves, that meant Kiya wanted to be part of a pack, to follow a dominant male. Brian smiled. It suited him fine, since Brian was a dominant. "To give up power to another, you have to choose someone you trust."

"I know. I made a bad choice," Kiya said, sighing as he went to put on his jeans. It wasn't his only bad choice, either. His first boyfriend had been worse than Ted in some ways. Certainly he had been abusive.

Brian wanted to declare that he was the one to take care of Kiya. The urge, the desire to be that, was so overwhelming he shook with it. "We will make sure he leaves you alone," he said.

Once Kiya managed to get the jeans on, he smiled and pulled Brian into a hug. "Thank you, again. Maybe I made the best choice this time around."

It hurt to think that Kiya probably wouldn't want him if he knew the truth, if he knew Brain wasn't human. Brian wanted him very much. "I'll do my best," he whispered and kissed him.

"I know you will," Kiya murmured, kissing him once more

before he pulled away to finish dressing.

⤳

Brian drove them down to the central police station. He stood beside Kiya while someone behind the desk went to get Officer Turner. Kiya had sat fidgeting nervously on the way there. He had never had to talk to the police before and still felt uncomfortable about doing it.

Turner turned out to be a black woman in her thirties with a nice smile and an easygoing attitude. She introduced herself to both of them. "Oh, Mr. Fenwick, I read the report that says you helped Kiya," she acknowledged. Her eyes seemed to add the question as to what their relationship was and Brian didn't know what to say to that so he just nodded.

Kiya smiled at her, knowing that he'd like her just from the sound of her voice. She seemed like someone who really wanted to help and it made it easier. "So, do I talk to you now or...?"

"Yes, come into my office," she invited and then, gesturing at chairs, asked if they wanted coffee or something to drink.

"I'm okay, thank you," Kiya said, taking his seat but perching a bit on the edge of the chair.

Brian shook his head. "Nothing, thank you," he answered, sitting in the chair next to Kiya's while the officer closed the door and sat down behind the desk. "Mr. White Cloud, can I call you Kiya?"

"Yes, that's fine with me," Kiya told her, nodding again. He smiled nervously. It was always odd to him when someone called him "Mr. White Cloud." It was the "Mr." more than anything that got to him.

"On the phone, you said you had more to add to what you told the officers on the scene Thursday," she began, picking up a pen and writing something out on a pad of paper on the desk.

"Yeah, he, uh, well," Kiya paused, clearing his throat and looking down. He plucked at his jeans for a moment, trying to pull his thoughts together. Telling a stranger about this was going to be difficult when he had trouble even facing it himself.

Brian watched Kiya, worried about him. He wanted to reach for his hand but worried that would only lead to trouble if people found out about them.

Turner looked between the two of them. "Do you need more privacy to talk about this?" she asked, eyes glancing worriedly at Brian.

"No, it's okay," Kiya said, since he figured Brian would hear anyway, and he found his presence comforting. He really did feel safer with Brian around. He took a deep breath and swallowed, his voice low when he spoke again, "Ted tried to rape me."

The shudder of anger that ran through Brian escaped in a small noise at the back of his throat and his jaw clenched hard. He had a sudden image of ripping out Ted's throat with his teeth.

Turner gave him a concerned glance but focused her attention on Kiya. "When did this happen?"

"A few days before the last time he bothered me, I think," Kiya answered quietly. Actually, he knew the exact day and time, but the whole thing seemed more like a nightmare now. He forced himself to take a deep breath and tell the story, explaining what had happened. As the words haltingly fell from his lips, Kiya felt almost disconnected from the memory of what had happened, speaking in a monotone voice and avoiding any eye contact. It was easier to relate it as a story rather than a memory.

Brian listened while Kiya told the police officer about that day. Brian remembered the young man running into the woods, remembered how scared he had been, the smell of fear on Kiya practically assaulting his own wolf senses. He also remembered the time he had confronted Ted harassing Kiya in the woods. He couldn't testify to that incident since he had been a wolf at the time.

"I can tell my roommate to come here if you need a witness or whatever," Kiya finished, since he was the only other person that knew what had happened. Besides the wolf.

"I really want to encourage you to press charges for both the attempted rape and the later assault, Kiya," Turner agreed and took down the names and phone numbers of Kiya's housemates, since they could talk about other incidents of harassment.

"I will now," Kiya said, nodding again. "Will it be kept quiet and how long will he go to jail for if he's convicted?"

"We try to keep names of victims out of the press," she explained. "How long Roark serves depends on a lot of different issues. The district attorney's office will have to review the case. I would also suggest you go to court and have a restraining order placed on your attacker. It would make it illegal for Roark to call you or come near you." She handed him a piece of paper. "This is a group that helps with situations like yours and also has counseling services. Your school has them, as well."

Brian had sat quietly through all of this but his heart was still pounding and he was angry. What she described didn't sound like enough to him. "Why isn't he in jail?" he demanded.

She looked at him, frowning. "I understand you are concerned for Kiya's welfare," she began. "But Ted Roark is out on bail. This will add to the charges against him, but the law does consider him innocent until proven guilty. It takes time, but we will do our best to put him away."

Brian growled, eyes narrowed. "And if he comes after Kiya again?"

Kiya looked down at the floor as they talked about the situation, hating that he had got himself into this in the first place. There was no way he could not tell his parents now. It wasn't just embarrassing. He also didn't want to upset them. He knew that his mother would be very worried and his father probably angry with the man who had done this. They had been so proud of Kiya getting a scholarship and he didn't want them to feel he couldn't be trusted on his own. Kiya cared a great deal about the feelings and concerns of his family.

"Kiya," Turner said, "Get the restraining order. Then you can call the police if he even comes near you again."

"All right," Kiya murmured, taking the paper from the woman and looking it over. He felt overwhelmed just looking at it, knowing he would have to explain in front of a judge what

Ted had done. That would mean more eyes watching him as he stumbled over his words, worrying that he would somehow be blamed for what happened.

As she walked them back out, she assured Kiya, with careful glances at Brian, that they would do everything possible to make sure that Ted was locked up.

"Thank you," Kiya told her again as they walked out. He was thinking about going to the counseling, but then, at the same time, he didn't want to because then he'd have to talk about the incident and tell people his name. He wasn't sure he could explain about Ted, that people wouldn't think him crazy for being with him in the first place. How do you explain liking someone to be forceful but still wanting them to listen to you? Would that sound odd or weird? He sighed, unsure of what to do next.

Brian was quiet as they returned to the truck and sat for a minute without turning on the engine. "You do what she says, but I also want to be there to make sure Ted doesn't try anything," he said.

"Okay," Kiya said, looking out the window instead of at Brian when he spoke. Did Brian think him weak for having let this happen? He hoped not.

Brian started the truck and drove. "Are you hungry?" he asked, when he realized, once again, that he didn't have food for Kiya at his place.

"A little, yeah," Kiya replied, glancing over at him finally. "I'm gonna get huge at this rate, though."

Brian frowned, not getting the reference. "Huge?"

Kiya smiled a little, shaking his head. "Fat."

Brian rolled his eyes. "If that worries you, I can think of ways to help you exercise," he assured him with a mischievous look.

"That's probably my only way of exercising," Kiya said, laughing.

"That and running in the woods with me," Brian insisted.

"Hopefully I can keep up with you," Kiya said, poking him

gently. Brian still wanted him and it went a long way toward making Kiya feel better.

Chapter Fifteen

They stopped at the grocery store on their way home and stocked up on snacks Kiya liked, drinks and a few things with which to make sandwiches. Brian also bought more meat for "his dog." Once they got back to Brian's home, Kiya went about making a few sandwiches for them. They sat on the bed again, and Brian leaned against one wall, watching Kiya as he ate. "You should call that number she gave you," he said.

"What number?" Kiya asked in between bites, glancing over at Brian.

Brian reached over and picked up the paper Turner had given Kiya and handed it to him.

Kiya looked it over, nodding slightly and setting it down. "I don't know about the counseling, but I'll call about the restraining order."

Brian could accept that. He didn't know anything about counseling and he wouldn't want to talk to a stranger, even about things that he could discuss.

When Kiya called, the volunteer said they could meet him at the courthouse on Monday to go before a judge and get the order. Brian wasn't happy that it would take so long, but he was at least confident that he could watch over Kiya that weekend. Kiya still seemed agitated and Brian didn't know what to say or do for him. He decided a change of scenery might help Kiya. Brian remembered how much time Kiya had spent with him in the woods as a wolf. "Want to go for a walk with me?"

"In the woods?" Kiya asked, sitting up and nodding. When Brian nodded back and held out his hand, Kiya took it. Outside, he paused, breathing in the fresh air and letting it out with a sigh.

There were numerous deer trails, widened by Brian's use as a wolf over the year and a half he had lived there. Brian unconsciously stepped into teacher mode as they walked, pointing out plants and animals, explaining the ecology again.

It was like his own private lecture and Kiya was loving it. It was just what he needed, a nice walk through nature to forget about all the problems he was having with Ted.

Brian found Kiya's excitement exhilarating. Kiya asked questions and added observations of his own. It made Brian grin, almost smugly, knowing he'd been right about how much more capable Kiya was. They paused in one of the redwood circles, surrounded by the towering tress. Brian's eyes twinkled mischievously again. "Did you know these are called Faerie circles?"

"Why?" Kiya asked curiously, looking around at the area.

"It's said they concentrate the Fae magic, that they can be gateways from this world to the other," Brian explained, leaning against one tree. It wasn't just legend, of course. The Fae heritage of his own people meant he could feel the magic vibrating around him. It was intoxicating.

"Cool," Kiya said, not sure if he actually believed it or not. It was still nice to think about.

"Come here," Brian whispered, holding out both hands to his lover. Kiya walked the short distance and took Brian's hands in his, smiling up at him. Brian pulled him against his body, placing Kiya's hands on his chest. "Close your eyes and breathe slowly," he whispered.

When Kiya did as he was told, Brian let his eyes unfocus and his second sight take over. He used the Fae magic that allowed him to remain human, calling now to the energy in the ground and trees. He wasn't a shaman, he couldn't do spells or the like. But Brian could let the hum of it vibrate his body in a way that was more than a little pleasurable, and he hoped that Kiya could feel it, too.

Kiya breathed in sharply when he felt the strange vibration go through him, trying to figure out where it was coming from.

Whatever it was, it felt good... really good. It reminded him of how he felt when he was in a Sun Dance or a Sweat Lodge.

Brian bent down slightly, forehead against Kiya's as he let it swirl through their bodies. It was difficult to hold his form but it felt wonderful. "Magic is in everything," he whispered. "Every tree, every rock, every animal."

Kiya believed him, because there was no other way to explain what was going on in between them. "Magic," he whispered, opening his eyes to look up at Brian. He leaned up to kiss him, feeling the need to connect with Brian even more.

Kissing Kiya was always magical, but letting the energy flow between them made Brian's entire body feel like it was in the kiss and he moaned into Kiya's mouth, greedily sucking and licking his lips. And Kiya responded, arms tightening around Brian's neck as if he was trying to pull himself up further. Brian's hands slid down Kiya's body and cupped his ass, pulling Kiya not just against his own body but lifting him up, holding him.

Kiya gasped and clung to Brian, wrapping his arms around his lover's shoulders and his legs around Brian's waist. "Brian," he whispered against his lips.

"Trust me, Kiya," Brian implored, lifting him more.

"I do," Kiya murmured, nodding quickly, "I do, Brian," It wasn't fear that made him tighten his legs. Kiya felt a surge of desire to be as close as possible.

With Kiya's legs wrapped around him, Brian could feel Kiya's arousal rubbing against his own through their jeans. Brian shuddered in pleasure and need, kissing and nipping along Kiya's jaw to his neck. Kiya already bore several of his marks but Brian had the urge to add more.

Kiya tilted his head back so that Brian could do what he really wanted to do. "Come on," he whispered, not even wanting to go back to the house first.

Brian's fingers dug into the firm rounded cheeks of Kiya's ass while his mouth closed on his neck, sucking the pulse point below Kiya's ear. He could feel Kiya's heartbeat in his mouth.

"Yes," Kiya gasped softly, his eyes falling shut as he moaned for more.

Brian wanted more, too. He wanted Kiya bare and open and pressed skin to skin. One hand still holding his lover's bottom to support him, he used the other to push and then pull Kiya's shirt up and over his head, releasing his mouth on Kiya's neck only long enough to remove the shirt.

Kiya shivered slightly, but pressed his chest against Brian's still clothed one, feeling the warmth radiate through him.

"Get mine," Brian growled, licking and nipping at Kiya's shoulder.

Kiya reached to pull Brian's shirt up and over his head, dropping it somewhere over his shoulder. "Jeans?" he asked, wanting to go faster.

Brian bit Kiya's shoulder, grinding their bodies together. He wanted them naked, but he didn't want to have to let go to do it. With a frustrated growl, he set Kiya down and began tearing off his own jeans. "Yes," he managed.

Kiya undid his own jeans and worked as quickly as he could to push them down and off. They both managed to reach for each other at the same time and Kiya was smiling as he was pulled into Brian's arms.

Brian leaned back against the trunk of the tree again, using it to brace himself as he lifted his lover back up against his body. "That's better," he gasped as Kiya's cock slid up his hip and then pressed against his own.

"Yeah, better," Kiya whispered, sliding his arms around Brian's neck and rocking against him again.

Brian returned to nipping and sucking on Kiya's shoulder and down along the line of his collarbone. His fingers dug into flesh now, squeezing the cheeks of Kiya's ass as he held him up while Kiya writhed against him, thighs tight against Brian's sides.

"More?" Kiya asked after another few minutes, kissing along Brian's chin and then whispering in his ear. "Please?"

"I want to be inside you," Brian groaned, his cock dripping

pre-come as it slid against Kiya's.

"Want you inside me," Kiya agreed, needing it before he came just like this.

That's when Brian remembered he needed to get a condom. Human sex was getting very frustrating. "Condom?" he asked, hoping Kiya had one with them.

"I don't care," Kiya panted in reply, nodding his head. "I trust you."

Brian thought it was probably wrong of him to let Kiya drop his rules but he also knew he wasn't able to pass on a disease to a human. And he wanted, felt like he needed, to feel every part of Kiya. He brought his fingers up to Kiya's mouth. "Wet them," he told him.

There was still that part of Kiya that was scared of catching something, but he simply kept telling himself that Brian was being honest, completely honest about everything. He sucked three of Brian's fingers into his mouth at once and swirled his tongue around them, making sure to get them wet enough, because he figured this would be his only lubricant. He didn't care if he was sore for days, all that mattered was Brian getting inside of him as quickly as possible.

Kiya's mouth and tongue around his fingers made Brian shudder, cock twitching eagerly. When he withdrew them, they shone in the light that filtered through the trees. He reached behind Kiya, pressing two against his lover's entrance. He watched Kiya's face as he did.

Kiya's eyes fell shut as he bit down on his lip, his head falling back with a small groan. He worked to relax around the fingers as they started to press inside, his back arching a little.

Kiya's wriggling was exciting, even if it did make it more difficult for Brian to hold him up. "You want to ride me?"

"Okay," Kiya whispered, pressing back onto the fingers already. "Need a little more."

"Hold tighter," Brian warned, shifting Kiya's weight up more so he could push three fingers in and work them deeper.

Kiya nodded and whimpered, his arms tightening around Brian as the fingers worked inside him. "Lay down on the ground," Kiya whispered after the fingers were sliding in and out easier.

Brian didn't want to hurt Kiya. He was big and didn't know if the spit would be enough to ease the way. It felt amazing being under the trees, in the Fae circle. Brian withdrew his fingers, both hands holding Kiya as he stepped into the center of the circle and sank to his knees, then fell back into the thick carpet of redwood duff. It was scratchy but he didn't care. It was an amazing view then, Kiya on top of him and the trees disappearing into the sky above him. "Beautiful," he whispered.

Kiya moved down Brian's body and leaned down to suck Brian's cock into his mouth first, getting him wet enough to make it easier.

Brian growled, eyes half closed in pleasure and his cock seeming harder than possible. His body was thrumming with magic as well as desire.

Kiya didn't spend very long sucking, wanting to get to the next part more than anything. He moved back up when he thought he was wet enough and straddled Brian, reaching back to position himself.

Brian's hands slid up Kiya's thighs, petting and squeezing. He could feel the leaves and sticks below him digging into his skin, the contrast with Kiya's warm smooth skin just seeming to further excite Brian. "Yes, take me inside, leannan," he encouraged, eyes on Kiya's face.

Kiya nodded and swallowed, taking another deep breath before he started to slowly press down, his head falling back. First thing he felt was the usual burning sensation he got whenever he wasn't prepared long enough with proper lubrication. He stopped for a moment to adjust to that and then continued on, still taking deep breaths.

Brian moaned in delight as he felt Kiya's body clench around his prick. He had to force himself not to thrust, but to lie there and let Kiya set the pace. Instead, he wrapped his hand around Kiya's cock, squeezing and stroking gently.

Kiya whimpered as he continued to move down, shaking his head and stopping when he couldn't take anymore at that moment.

One hand still caressing Kiya's cock, Brian reached his other up to cup his lover's cheek. "I can feel you. Feel the wet heat of you," he whispered. "Even this much is enough. Just lean forward onto my chest."

Kiya wanted to take more of Brian inside, but he nodded and rested his forehead on Brian's chest. "You feel so good," he whispered against his skin, swallowing hard.

That tight opening was spasming around the upper half of Brian's cock, while Kiya's body was pressed against him, hair flowing down like a silky blanket around them. Brian kissed the top of Kiya's head and stroked down his back, fingers caressing hair and skin both. "Very good," he echoed.

Kiya wasn't sure how much longer he stayed like that, but soon he felt like he could handle more. He started to move slowly, pulling himself up and then pressing down again.

Sparks of pleasure rippling through him with each of Kiya's movements, Brian gasped and his hand on Kiya's cock trembled. Despite the cool of the forest, he felt his skin heating up.

Kiya felt the chill on his back as well, but Brian's warmth was countering it and making him even more excited. He flipped his hair over one shoulder and buried his face in Brian's neck, beginning to build up a slow rhythm. He tried pressing down a little more with each rocking movement, moaning as the pleasure built.

"Oh, yes, *leannan*, it feels so right with you," Brian gasped, heart pounding as his Kiya rode him. He rubbed his cheek against the part of Kiya's face he could reach and shivered at the breath on his neck. "Never felt this way before," he admitted.

"Me neither," Kiya managed to whisper in reply, beginning to move faster, almost all of Brian inside now.

They were both moaning and moving together. Brian felt the magic swirling in his blood and sparking in every point of contact with Kiya. "*Leannan*, yes, ride me," Brian gasped. "I want to fill you up, become part of you, Kiya."

Kiya couldn't even explain how he was feeling. There was the obvious pleasure that was coursing through his body, but there was also that humming that Brian had told him was magic, adding even more feeling. "Want that," he gasped, pushing himself so that he was sitting up again, the weight of his body taking him down the rest of Brian's shaft. "Want to be a part of you."

Brian's gaze was on Kiya, looking into those startling green eyes. He knew he'd never seen anything more beautiful in his life. "Yes, together," he gasped.

Kiya nodded in agreement, gasping with each thrust now, his eyes squeezing shut once again. "Together!"

"Come for me, *leannan*," Brian encouraged, hand sliding up and down Kiya's prick, thumb rubbing the slick head on each stroke.

Kiya had already started to tense up, reaching to grip Brian's free hand, lacing their fingers together first. He came in a cry, clenching tightly around Brian.

"I want to come, inside you!" Brian gasped, body tensing. He couldn't hold back much longer but knew Kiya had worried about doing this before.

"Come then," Kiya told him, his eyes opening to look down at him. He no longer cared that Brian wasn't wearing a condom.

Brian arched his back as his cock spasmed, releasing his seed inside his lover's body. The wolf in him growled, feeling the thrill of marking Kiya as his.

Kiya watched him, his eyes widening when he actually saw Brian's eyes change color, a shining yellow-gold. Kiya blinked and shook his head, collapsing on top of Brian again who was panting beneath him. Kiya thought what he saw must have had something to do with the light. For a moment, Brian's eyes had looked just like the wolf's.

Brian wrapped his arms around Kiya, panting in the aftermath of his orgasm and shuddering with the pleasure of being so close. "Leannan," he breathed, burying his face in Kiya's hair.

"Brian," Kiya whispered, relaxing on top of him as he breathed in and out slowly. He felt fine, better than fine, actually. "Thank you."

Brian's cock didn't soften immediately, but his come made it slicker so that it slid more easily as Kiya wriggled a bit on top of him. Brian had never enjoyed his human form more than he did right then, sweaty body pressed to Kiya's satiny smooth skin. He wanted Kiya, not just for this, but for his own. He wrapped his arms around him, holding tight.

Kiya loved this. Even though he was in the middle of the woods, naked for all to see with Brian still inside of him, he didn't care about any of that. "Ah, tehila," he whispered, nuzzling the side of Brian's face.

The word shivered down Brian's spine, making his cock twitch with desire. "Yes, your lover," he whispered.

"My lover," Kiya whispered, kissing his skin.

Brian might have sensed something, but he was so caught up in the sensation of Kiya that he was surprised to look up and see Ted standing over them. Before he could react, Ted had grabbed Kiya by the hair at the back of his head and yanked. As Kiya was being dragged back, Ted's other hand brought a gun up and fired into Brian's chest.

It all happened so fast. One minute, everything was good, better than good. Kiya was happy and even contemplating living the rest of his life with Brian. The next he was being pulled up harshly, a whimper of pain escaping him. Then out of nowhere he heard the gunshot, his ears ringing with the pain. He saw the blood and Kiya screamed, reaching back for Brian. Brian was shot, shot in his chest and there was so much blood! "Brian!" he wailed. Kiya didn't even know who was pulling him back, all he could concentrate on was the horrifying sight of his lover dying in front of him.

Kiya was dragged backward off Brian, off his cock and off his body. Blood had splattered on the front of Kiya, dripping down his chest and belly. "Fucking whore," Ted screamed, pulling Kiya across the ground, letting his legs drag through the dirt, twigs and leaves.

"Brian!" Kiya continued to sob, tears running down his face as he was pulled farther and farther away from him. Various items of debris were digging into his skin as he was dragged, and he felt that his hair was being ripped from his head completely. But all that mattered was that he had to get back to Brian, to help him. He looked up into the mad face of Ted. Ted's face was screwed up with rage and splattered in blood. Brian's blood.

"Let go of me!" Kiya screamed, thrashing. He tried clawing at the hand that was gripping his hair as he struggled to get his feet under himself. Kiya eventually managed to stumble to his feet but Ted didn't let him go, pulling him along the path, away from Brian.

"Screwing around with that asshole," Ted was yelling. "I can't let you do that."

"You're so fucking stupid!" Kiya yelled through his tears, turning and trying his best to strike out at Ted wherever he could reach while struggling not to fall again. "You're going to jail forever for that! You shot him!"

Ted didn't seem to hear or understand what Kiya was saying. Kiya couldn't see Brian anymore. Ted slowed and then shoved Kiya against a tree, holding him by the throat with one hand and waving the gun around with the other as he continued to shout. "I should kill you for fucking around on me!"

Kiya groaned when he was slammed against the tree, his eyes widening when he saw the gun. He shook his head, crying out of fear now. "I wasn't! We're not together anymore, Ted," he said, his lips trembling. "Don't kill me."

"Cunt!" Ted screamed. He pressed the barrel of the gun under

Kiya's chin. "It ends when I say it does!" He looked like he was about to shout more when a sound pierced the forest. It was howling, a wolf howling.

Kiya could only cry harder when he felt the gun against his skin, pleading with Ted. When he heard the howl, he prayed that it was Saoi, that the wolf would come to help them.

Ted was at least sane enough to look frightened. The wolf howled again and Ted looked around wildly. There was a crashing sound as something tore through the underbrush and Ted fired the gun wildly as the wolf leapt. He fell under it as it landed on top of him, snarling. Ted didn't even have a chance to shoot the wolf. He screamed in terror and pain, bringing his gun arm up to cover his face. The wolf latched onto it, tearing flesh.

Kiya fell to his knees, shaking. Brian was most likely dead and it was completely his fault. Kiya looked up when he heard Ted's screams. "Stop! Don't kill him," he yelled, not sure why he was helping the man.

Ted's arm was bloody and the wolf was growling as he tried to hold it off.

"Ted, drop the gun or that wolf is gonna rip you apart," a man's voice said behind Kiya.

Kiya quickly looked around when he heard the new voice. Still on the ground, Kiya peered up to see a middle-aged man with a rifle pointed at the two on the ground. Behind him was a slightly younger man with another rifle. "Drop it, Ted," the older man barked, eyes still focused on the struggle.

Kiya wasn't exactly sure if they were trying to save him or not. They were pointing the guns at Ted, so he assumed they were helping him. But there was something strange about it.

"Get it the fuck off me!" Ted yelled, dropping the gun. The other two men chuckled.

"Call your wolf off, boy," the older man said, glancing down at Kiya now.

"Saoi, I said stop," Kiya said to the wolf, moving closer again. "Look, I'm fine. We need to help Brian."

Saoi growled again and, after a pause, released Ted's arm. Ted slumped, eyes rolling back into his head. Saoi's teeth had barely left the man's skin when Kiya heard a snap and a thunk. Saoi yelped, jaws snapping at something on his back. Kiya saw some kind of dart had hit him. The wolf looked him in the eyes. Eyes that reminded Kiya of the way Brian had looked when he came. Then the wolf fell.

Kiya's eyes widened and he scrambled over to the wolf, his fingers grabbing on to Saoi's fur, thinking he had been shot as well. "Why'd you do that?" he screamed, looking back at the two men. Another man had also stepped out from behind a tree, holding another rifle. He cocked it, and Kiya realized he had been the one to shoot the wolf.

"The wolf's owner-he-Ted shot him. Is there any way you could check on him or call someone to help him?" Kiya asked, watching as they bound Saoi. Kiya felt helpless. Brian was probably dead. Ted had blown a hole in the man's chest. But Kiya needed to try, just in case.

All three men laughed then and the leader shook his head. "Jackson, see how messed up Ted is," he ordered.

"But you can't just leave him back there! Brian might still be alive," Kiya pleaded.

The three men ignored Kiya. Jackson moved up, picking up Ted's gun and checking the prone man. Kiya saw him check for a pulse. "He's alive," he said with a tone that sounded disappointed. Ted woke with a sob, clutching his savaged arm to his chest.

Kiya knew now that they weren't there to help. He didn't know what they wanted,. He gripped Saoi's fur and buried his face in it, wishing the wolf would wake up. "Please be okay," he whispered. He could feel Saoi was breathing but otherwise the wolf didn't move.

"Rick, take care of the wolf, just in case," the older man ordered and the third man nodded, picking up a metal device. He ignored Kiya as he knelt down and pushed Saoi off Ted. The device was black iron and rattled as he worked it over the wolf's head.

"Why are you doing this?" Kiya asked, looking between the men. He felt dizzy, but he struggled to get to his feet.

Rick didn't answer, working what looked like a muzzle and collar into place and then bolting locks to hold it on. "He's what we're hunting," the older man answered.

"That has to be illegal," Kiya said immediately, shaking his head as his eyes leapt from one to the other, fearful of their intentions. "You can't do this! He belongs to someone," He trailed off, knowing that Brian was probably dead now. Kiya swallowed the lump in his throat as more tears welled up in his eyes at the thought.

"Not much of what I do isn't illegal," the older man laughed.

Rick pulled out duct tape and began wrapping the wolf's front paws together with it.

Kiya didn't want to leave Saoi with these men, but he needed to get to Brian. He started to back away and the leader turned, aiming his rifle at Kiya again.

"Stand still and put your hands behind you," the man ordered.

Kiya did as he was told, knowing that these men would shoot him. He looked down and closed his eyes, hoping that he'd wake up and this would all be some kind of really horrible nightmare. Kiya was still naked, dripping with Brian's come and blood, and now he felt the man who had been tying up the wolf wrapping duct tape around his wrists. It was tight, digging into his skin. When he looked down at Saoi, he could see that the wolf's front and back paws had all been bound.

"I'm sorry," Kiya quietly whispered to Saoi, wishing he could touch him. The tape around his wrists was too tight for him to even try and get out of.

The man with the tape, Rick, stood up and gestured at the others. "Get the pole, Jackson," he said, gesturing toward a tree.

Jackson nodded and reached for a long metal pole they had

187

apparently brought with them. They used it to hoist the wolf up, so that the creature's body hung by his bound feet. "Fucking heavy monster," Jackson complained.

"Be careful, don't hurt him," Kiya mumbled, looking up when they lifted him.

The leader laughed again, gun still pointed at Kiya. "Not much can hurt a thing like him. I even have to use special knives to cut them."

"No," Kiya insisted, more fear spiking through him. He didn't think he could take this. First Brian, now Saoi?

"What about Ted?" Rick asked.

The leader grunted and walked over to look down at Ted, who was still moaning. "Ted, seeing as you did us a favor showing us where to find the wolf, we're gonna let you live. But you got the cops looking for you and now you've gone and shot somebody. So, you better get the fuck out of this town and don't come back. Got it?" He was pointing his rifle at Ted during his little speech.

Ted shuddered, wide eyes. "But I'm bleeding, my arm."

"Frankly, it would save me a lot of trouble if you bleed to death, but I'm gonna give you a chance, boy. Take it or I might lose my patience."

Ted nodded. "I will, I swear."

Kiya couldn't even stand to look at Ted. He hoped Ted did bled to death He had killed Brian and brought these men here. Men who would probably kill Saoi and maybe even Kiya.

The leader motioned and the other two men nodded, and began along the path back toward the house, apparently struggling under the swaying weight of the wolf's body. The man grabbed hold of Kiya's arm and shoved him along behind the others and pointing his rifle at his back

Kiya kept his eyes on Saoi as they walked away. Saoi hung limply from the pole, mouth open. Kiya shuddered, frightened. He didn't want to go with the strange men even if that meant being with the wolf. The leader prodded him and Kiya stumbled behind the others.

Chapter Sixteen

The only sound for several minutes was the crunching of the redwood duff underfoot and the men panting under their burden. Kiya saw Brian's cabin ahead and a large dark blue van parked beside Brian's truck. Kiya was terrified. He had no idea what would happen next or what he could do about it. He wished he at least had clothes on but thought better than to ask.

The leader stood with his gun still ready while the men opened the back of the van. There was a black metal cage in it and they hefted the wolf inside and locked it.

"Let's see his den," the leader said and gestured for Kiya to go forward into Brian's cabin.

Kiya stepped inside and looked around, his eyes stopping on the papers on Brian's bed. It was the form about requesting a restraining order. It all seemed pointless now. Ted had killed Brian. They'd never even had a chance to call the police.

The older man clucked his tongue and Kiya saw he was looking at the walls. He stepped forward and ripped down several of Brian's drawings of wolves, shaking his head as he looked at them.

Kiya turned to watch him, unsure of why the man was doing that. "Those were Brian's," he told him, wishing he could take them and keep them for himself. "This is his house. Why are you here? Why don't you go and help Brian? Why are you taking Saoi away? Why aren't you answering me?!" He couldn't help that he was crying again and it made him feel weak and frustrated at his helplessness.

"They call me Hunter. It's not just a name," the man said, ripping down and collecting more of Brian's drawings. He took every one that had a wolf or a person in it and then folded them, stuffing them in his jacket pocket. "I hunt creatures like your wolf."

"And what for?" Kiya asked again. "You never answered me."

"Sometimes there's a bounty on them," Hunter said, knocking over a small trash can next to the bed and spilling out the condoms and wrappers they had used before. "You didn't use condoms back there. Lucky for you, it ain't contagious." He gave Kiya a look up and down which seemed part disgust and part arousal.

It made Kiya's skin crawl, and he frowned, unconsciously taking a step backward when the man looked at him. "I didn't-I didn't have sex with the wolf," he told him.

Hunter laughed at that. It had a nasty sound. He grabbed one of Brian's shirts and then shoved Kiya toward the door. "Let's go. We need to get going before he wakes up." He walked Kiya back out and shoved him into the back of the van with Jackson. Rick was behind the wheel already and, after slamming the door, Hunter got into the passenger side.

"Fuck," Kiya mumbled when he fell to the metal floor of the van, struggling to sit up and look around again. It was a cargo van, stripped down to nothing but metal, no seats or carpeting. There were things, tools of some kind, tied to the sides and then the cage in the back. The van started up and Kiya nearly hit his head falling back again when it pulled out into the road. Kiya cursed, wincing in pain. He had no idea where they were going, or what they were going to do with him. It scared him more than having a gun held up to his head.

Jackson was grinning at him in a way that was very frightening. He made sure to glance first at Kiya's naked body and then the sleeping wolf. "Quite the pervert, aren't you?" he sneered.

"I didn't sleep with a wolf," Kiya repeated, once he realized what the man was implying. He was still trying to figure out why they thought he had.

All of them laughed again. "Sleep's not what I would call that either," Rick added and the laughter got louder again.

Hunter turned around, looking back over the seat. "It's possible the boy don't know," he said and the other two looked at him.

"Still a pervert," Jackson insisted.

"Don't know what?" Kiya asked when he could, feeling a mixture of confusion and fear. Did Brian really have something and now he had it? But Hunter had said that he wasn't contagious but Hunter hadn't been talking about Brian when he said that. The men didn't answer him this time.

They had pulled out onto the main road heading up the mountain for a while and then turned again, going down a narrow track that was bumpy. Naked and tied, Kiya kept falling against the metal sides. He was aching, terrified and longed to have his thumb in his mouth for some small comfort, but it was impossible with his hands bound behind his back. The van lurched to a stop and the men got out, opening doors. Hunter grabbed Kiya by the upper arm and hauled him out. The other two were struggling to move the wolf again. They were parked in front of a metal building. It looked like some kind of old warehouse or garage. Hunter released Kiya and drew out keys, unlocking the door.

Kiya shivered, looking around quickly to see where they were. It looked like the middle of nowhere to him, especially since he didn't know the area all that well.

Hunter rolled back the large metal door. Inside was a concrete floor and a larger metal cage, like the one in the van, but about ten square feet. Rick and Jackson were struggling to carry the wolf inside.

"Shit!" Jackson yelled. "He's moving."

"Well, get him in before he gets loose on you!" Hunter yelled back.

The two men hurried forward, dropped the wolf, pole and all, in the cage and ran out again. They slammed the cage door closed just as they all heard the sound of duct tape ripping. Saoi lunged to his feet but swayed, apparently still drugged by whatever was in the dart.

"Saoi," Kiya whispered, gladdened to see that the wolf was awake. Even though the wolf was locked in a cage now, Kiya was relieved that Saoi was alive and, hopefully, strong enough to fight back.

Hunter pushed Kiya forward, into the building, and then closed the door with a slam, locking it again. He flipped the switch and overhead lights came on. Flipping open a knife, Hunter cut the tape holding Kiya's wrists together. "Your boyfriend's awake now," he sneered.

Saoi was swaying, but his eyes focused on Kiya and then the other men. There were strips of duct tape still sticking to the fur of his feet. He tried to use his mouth to pull one off but found the metal strips around his head kept him muzzled. He growled.

"Shh," Kiya murmured, ignoring Hunter as he walked closer to the cage. "I'm still here."

Saoi walked up to the bars, trying to push his muzzle through them but the device stopped him. He whimpered.

Rick and Jackson pulled up old metal folding chairs and sat down at a beat up wooden table, laying their guns on it. Hunter leaned against the wall and set his rifle down within reach. "So you really don't know what you've been fucking?" he asked.

"Are you planning on telling me anytime soon?" Kiya snapped. He pulled the duct tape from his wrists, wincing at the pain when his arm hair came with it. Then he reached through the bars to run his fingers through Saoi's fur, trying to soothe him. Saoi managed to lick Kiya's arm as he did.

"That thing in front of you is your boyfriend. There's never been a Brian Fenwick," Hunter announced, laughing again.

Kiya frowned and looked back at Saoi, blinking in confusion. "What do you mean?" he asked quietly, staring at the wolf as he waited for an answer. Those amber eyes looked up at him, seeming almost pleading, and then down at the floor.

"See, I used to hunt big game. But then I found out there are real monsters in the world. Much more exciting to hunt and profitable too." Hunter walked over to an old refrigerator, pulling out a beer.

Jackson grunted and came over to collect a few too. "Black magic market pays well for their parts," he added and winced when Hunter gave him an annoyed looked at being interrupted.

"Monsters?" Kiya asked in a whisper, not looking back at the men as he bit into his lip. He couldn't believe that, mainly because he didn't think that Saoi was a monster, not at all. The wolf was his protector. But that part about Brian—"Brian is a wolf? Like... a werewolf?"

Hunter grinned in approval, then took a big swig of his beer. "Exactly, you're catching on. See there're sorta three kinds of werewolves. Really only one is a werewolf, but the other two do change between man and wolf, or other animals, too," he explained. "Your basic lycanthrope is like you see in the movies, mostly. He, or sometimes she, has been bitten by one and got kind of infected. Like a disease, though really it's a curse. They've got no control over it. They change shape at the full moon, usually kill people when they do. Some do get control over it or learn to lock themselves up at least. Nasty curse, usually spreads because of it."

Kiya went quiet, thinking over the meaning of this. He was having sex with a man who turned into a wolf. It explained so much. Why there was raw meat in the fridge, why Saoi knew where Brian lived. Why the two were never in the same room together. But to him, that only meant that Brian was alive. "He's alive," he said, his eyes welling up in tears as he reached for the wolf again. That probably wasn't the reaction the men were waiting for, but he didn't care.

Hunter laughed at that. "He still thinks you're Brian," he taunted the wolf. "So let me explain about the other two kinds. The second is a Skinwalker. They get called that because lots of them use the skin of the animal for the magic, though not all. They are shamans, witchdoctors or the like, who use spells or invoke demons to change into animals. They have to have part of the animal that they turn into to do it. Wearing a pelt of a wolf, for example, makes it a lot easier than just wearing its claw or tooth. They actually pay big money for the parts you see." Hunter seemed to be enjoyed his lecture and laughed particularly hard when Saoi growled in response to this part.

Kiya shook his head, not wanting that to happen to Saoi. But how could he stop it? "Can I go in the cage with him?" he asked after a moment, sniffling.

"He's a monster," Hunter insisted, shaking his head. "You really are a twisted kid. I still ain't told you what this one is."

"I don't care!" Kiya yelled, just wanting Brian back. He didn't care if Brian was a monster that killed other people. He cared about him, and wanted to protect him. He missed him. He... loved him.

Hunter moved up and grabbed Kiya by the hair, pulling him back and against his own body. Saoi snarled and threw himself against the bars. There was a sound like a sizzle and the smell of burnt fur.

"Careful there, wolf, that's iron," Hunter teased, laughing. "And that is the big key to what he is, isn't it boys?" Rick and Jackson nodded. "Get the camera," Hunter ordered and Rick pulled a digital video camera out of his pocket, moving around to film the snarling wolf. "See, iron burns this kind," Hunter said.

"You're hurting him," Kiya yelled, ignoring the pain in his scalp. "Stay away from the bars, Brian."

"Told you, boy, there ain't no Brian," Hunter sneered. "That thing was born a wolf, he just uses the shape of a man as a disguise. Kind of a were-human rather than a were-wolf. They're really called Fae-wolves. A race of wolf, some say mated with a Fae long ago and now they have magic and can pretend to be people. That's why they can't stand iron, they have Fae blood in them. But make no mistake, it's still an animal."

"He's still Brian to me," Kiya said quietly, trying to understand that new bit of information. So Brian was a wolf disguised as human. It didn't change the way Kiya felt about him.

Hunter shook Kiya, pulling painfully on his hair again. "So you don't mind that you've been fucking an animal?" he challenged.

Kiya winced hard, his eyes watering. "No," he answered, shaking his head as much as he could. Saoi was barking and snarling at Hunter, hackles raised.

"Seems your wolf doesn't like me touching you," Hunter drawled. "Fucking crazy thing seems to have decided you belong to him. They ain't even supposed to like humans."

The other two laughed again. Rick got a little closer, filming the angry wolf as Saoi launched at the bars. Frightened, Rick stumbled back and nearly fell. The smell of singed fur once again filled the air.

"He can't get through iron, can't change either with that iron around his neck," Hunter reminded Rick. "Just get the shots. We're gonna make money off of the footage and the carcass."

"Please don't kill him," Kiya begged, starting to struggle to get away from Hunter. He looked around to see if there was anyway he could get them out, any kind of tools or weapons.

Hunter pulled out the knife he'd used to cut the tape earlier and pressed it to Kiya's throat. "Settle down or your wolf will outlive you," he threatened.

Kiya went still and nodded slightly, even though he wasn't sure if it was better to live and watch Brian be killed right in front of him.

"Ted seemed to think you were worth killing for and this one seems to agree," Hunter began, voice dropping even lower in a way that made Kiya's skin crawl. "Maybe I should find out for myself if your ass is really that good."

Kiya immediately started to shake his head, understanding the implications of that all too readily. "No, don't, please," he said, his heart beating faster.

Saoi howled and threw himself at the bars again, the smell of burnt fur worsening.

Hunter laughed again. "Calm down wolf or I might slip," he

warned, knife edge pressing against Kiya's skin.

"Stop," Kiya said to Brian, unable to stand the thought that the wolf, that Brian, was hurting himself.

Saoi crouched low, still snarling. His amber eyes were glowing and he certainly looked capable of ripping Hunter apart.

"So let me make an offer," Hunter drawled again, seeming amused rather than frightened by Saoi's response. "I can bend you over that table right now and see what the fuss is about. And maybe even my boys will want a turn. I know your wolf there ain't gonna like it, but it would be fun to watch him kill himself trying to get to us. Or..."

"Or what?" Kiya asked, his eyes squeezing tightly shut at the thought of being forced again-of being raped by these men, while Brian was forced to watch.

"...Or you go in there and do it with your wolf, while we watch," Hunter finished, grinning.

Kiya swallowed and opened his eyes a little, chewing on his lip. "Brian," he said after a moment, knowing that Brian was an animal now, but also knowing that he would prefer it with him than the other men.

"Do it and we'll let you walk out of here alive," Hunter added. He looked at the wolf then. "You want us to let the boy go, don't you, wolf?"

Saoi growled menacingly in response.

"What about Brian?" Kiya asked.

"You keep forgetting, Brian doesn't exist," Hunter insisted. "And the wolf is mine."

"No," Kiya insisted, not wanting to give him up just like that. "That's not fair."

"Fair ain't an issue here, boy," Hunter laughed again. "We're giving you a choice of being used by us and then dying or taking it from the wolf and living. Those are the only options you got here. I think I can tell you which your wolf would take right now."

"I'll go to him," Kiya murmured quietly, resigned that he

would have to do something and this might give him time to consider possible options for getting them both safely out of there.

"I thought so," Hunter responded smugly, but didn't let Kiya go. He looked at Saoi instead. "You back up to the other side and we'll send the boy in," he told him. "But I know you think that you can protect him once we do that. You remember the dart that took you down? We got more. Tranquilizer strong enough to take down an elephant with a mix of Wolf's Bane and a few other secrets ingredients. You do anything I don't like or refuse to cooperate and the next time you wake up, you'll get to watch us take your boy here and rip him apart."

Kiya was quiet, looking down at the floor instead of anyone else in the room. It was still Brian, but it didn't stop him from being nervous.

Saoi backed up as told and Jackson held the tranquilizer rifle up, aimed at the wolf while Rick kept filming. Hunter took the blade down from Kiya's neck and pulled him forward, opening the door of the cage just wide enough to push him through. Then he picked up a wooden crate and tossed it in as well.

Kiya stumbled inside and stood there awkwardly for a moment, watching Saoi. "You won't hurt me," he said softly, walking closer. The iron bars clanged shut behind him, Hunter bolting the lock again.

Saoi moved to Kiya, looking up at him as if he was afraid that Kiya blamed him for their predicament.

"I missed you," Kiya said, kneeling down in front of him and wrapping his arms around the wolf. He had to ignore the fact that the men were not only watching but video taping as well.

"Ain't that cute," Hunter laughed. "You can take his muzzle off, but leave the iron collar."

Kiya worked to pull the muzzle off Saoi's face, dropping it to the floor and pulling him closer. Saoi lapped and nipped gently at Kiya's face, nuzzling him, and Kiya closed his eyes and gripped his fur lightly, nuzzling the side of his face in return.

After several minutes of holding the wolf, Kiya heard the men outside muttering. "Get on with it," Hunter finally snapped.

Kiya pulled back and sat down in front of Saoi, not sure of how to start. "Tehila..."

Saoi glanced over at Hunter but then turned back, eyes meeting Kiya's.

"You can do it," Kiya said, biting his lip again. "Should I get on my knees or...?"

Saoi licked Kiya's face again and then nodded.

"Okay, just get it over with," Kiya said, then turned to get on his hands and knees, trying not to look at the men who were watching.

Hunter walked to the edge of the cage and shoved the wooden crate toward the pair. "Use this. The wolf will be heavy enough you'd collapse and we want a good shot," he insisted.

Kiya pushed himself up and went over to the crate, kneeling and bending over it for Saoi. Kiya still refused to look up at Hunter or the others. He closed his eyes and tried to relax, thinking that it was just Brian and that they had done this only hours ago.

Saoi followed him, rubbing his furry body along Kiya's and sniffing him. There was still blood and come dried on Kiya's skin from earlier and the wolf licked at the blood on Kiya's hip.

Kiya wanted to look back when he was licked, but decided not to, wishing Brian would just get it over with. But then he realized that this would be the last time Kiya would be with him if they did kill Brian afterward. He looked back then, wishing his lover could change back into Brian one more time. He longed to feel Brian's arms around him again.

And Brian was looking back, amber eyes on Kiya as he licked his way back, tongue now sliding over the cheeks of Kiya's rounded ass.

Kiya could see it now, he could see Brian in the wolf and he wondered how he had managed to miss it before. "Brian, yes," he murmured, nodding for more. That seemed to encourage the wolf, because he began licking more enthusiastically, tongue now lapping its way down the cleft of Kiya's ass. Kiya bit his lip to stop the moan when he felt his tongue swipe over his entrance, his back arching a little.

"Fuck, that's hot," Jackson gasped from his place outside the cage.

"He's licking his own come from before," Rick added and Kiya could hear a mixture of disgust and excitement in his voice.

Saoi growled but didn't stop, his nose pushed between Kiya's cheeks as he licked harder. Kiya gripped the edge of the crate and moaned, unable to stop himself this time. With his eyes closed he tried to focus only on the sensations.

"Spread your ass, boy," Hunter snapped. "I want to get a good shot of this!"

"Hell, that's sick," Jackson declared.

"Yeah, but video of it is worth a fortune," Hunter answered.

Kiya jumped at the order and hesitantly reached back to expose himself, spreading his cheeks a little. The wolf began lapping down, licking the come that dripped down over Kiya's balls. Saoi then lapped at the soft sac, making excited sounds.

Kiya was hard almost instantly then, whimpering softly with each lick. He didn't want to do this in front of the awful men, and he most definitely didn't want to be videotaped doing it. He hated being forced with no choice and no way to help himself or Brian. Still, Saoi's tongue sent shivers of desire racing down his spine.

"Boy's a real pervert, ain't he? Look how hard he is," Rick sneered.

"Hell with the boy's dick, look at the size of the wolf's!" Jackson responded.

Hunter laughed. "Yeah, make sure you get a close up of that."

Saoi had laved Kiya's balls till they were shining wet and then worked his tongue up again, pressing it harder against Kiya's hole. Kiya spread himself open wider, realizing that Brian was trying to push his tongue inside of him. And when that thick tongue pressed harder, Kiya's body opened to it. It was probably good that they had done it earlier that day, since he was still stretched and slick. Kiya rested his forehead on the crate, lifting his hips and then moving back a little, wanting to press down on the tongue.

"Dogs will eat anything," Jackson sneered.

"Yeah, but that ain't it," Hunter said, sounding surprised. "He's preparing him."

"I'm good," Kiya murmured after a few more minutes, thinking that if Brian continued, he'd come just from the feel of his tongue, in front of the other men.

The wolf huffed, giving Kiya's hole another lick before moving forward, front paws on either side of the Kiya's hips. Kiya could feel the slick cock sliding between his cheeks. It felt bigger than Brian's in human form. Now, Kiya began to second guess himself as fear ignited within him, but there was no turning back. His grip on the crate tightened as he felt the wolf shifting, trying to find the angle to press that thick shaft inside him. Kiya felt the wolf's breath on his back, and then the animal's muzzle at his neck.

Kiya was trying his best to relax, but it wasn't easy. He tilted his head a little more to the side when he felt the muzzle there, swallowing hard. The angle allowed Brian to lap at Kiya's cheek, rubbing his nose against his face. Then he felt the head of the wolf's cock slide into place, catching on the rim of his hole as Saoi began to push inside.

"It'll rip him open," Jackson declared.

"He took one almost as big in the forest," Hunter argued.

Kiya's eyes squeezed tightly shut and he breathed in sharply, tensing up slightly. Despite the preparation, the entry burned and Kiya did fear that he wasn't going to be able to take it. Saoi whimpered, pressing his face against Kiya's. Kiya turned his head so that he could press his cheek against the side of Saoi's muzzle. "I'm-I'm okay. Don't stop," he whispered.

It must have encouraged Saoi, because the wolf kept pressing slowly forward, thick cock stretching Kiya uncomfortably. Now Kiya wasn't even thinking about the men watching and recording him. He couldn't even if he wanted to. "Brian," he murmured. The shaft worked further into him, Kiya's body giving slowly around it. Saoi growled again, apparently not willing to push faster and risk hurting Kiya.

"Yeah, give it to him, wolf," Hunter added.

It was moving too slowly and now Kiya wanted to move, to get past this point. "Brian, it's okay. Just do it," he whined softly, resting his forehead on the crate again.

Saoi relented, letting both Kiya's encouragement and his own body's urging push him forward, cock pressing deeper into Kiya. A growl of pleasure reverberated through him.

Kiya gripped the crate's edge so tightly that his fingernails dug into the wood. He couldn't even make a sound, his body was so tense. He could feel the soft fur on the wolf's hips and legs, pressing against the back of his ass and thighs. He was stretched beyond what he thought he could take, burning, but not as bad as he had feared.

"He did it," Rick said, awe in his voice.

"Oh, that's just the beginning," Hunter assured him. "Right now that boy's tight ass is squeezing the base of the wolf's prick. That's going to make the knot at the base swell inside him."

Despite not wanting to, Kiya couldn't help but hear what Hunter said. Kiya didn't think he could take anymore than this. Brian began to rotate his hips, the prick inside Kiya moving in circles with it. And despite the painful stretching, it began to rub against Kiya's prostate. Kiya gasped and moaned softly, his back arching slightly in pleasure, because he wanted more already, but felt ashamed to ask for it.

Kiya could feel the swelling inside him but was surprised to realize it didn't hurt the way Hunter suggested. It increased the pressure on that place inside him while his lover kept rocking and moving. Saoi's growls of pleasure grew too, and Kiya now recognized that it was very similar to the sounds Brian made when he was human. Kiya felt soothed by those sounds and found himself moaning louder, leaning up so that Saoi could move a little more. "Harder?" he asked very quietly, hoping the men didn't hear him.

"Yeah, fuck that boy," Rick exclaimed, camera still focused on them.

Saoi was rocking and panting. With his knot swollen, he couldn't pull out, but he could push in more and he did.

Kiya still had his eyes closed, and for that he was happy, able to enjoy what would be his last time with Brian, who was nuzzling and licking the side of his neck, teeth grazing his skin as he worked his hips faster.

"Bite?" Kiya asked after a while, rocking with each of Saoi's thrusts.

Saoi growled and his teeth closed on the muscle where Kiya's neck and shoulder met. His teeth pressed into flesh, not ripping but tasting blood anyway. The taste was enough to push him over the edge, growling as he came inside Kiya.

"Fucking hell!" Rick exclaimed.

Kiya jerked and came a moment later, crying out softly and shuddering hard. He heard one of the men's words, but he barely paid attention to him.

"Shit, he really came from that!" Jackson exclaimed.

"You'd better have gotten that, Rick," Hunter added.

"Oh, yeah," Rick answered.

Saoi released his lover's skin, licking at the small cuts and shuddering as his prick continued to twitch inside Kiya.

"Brian," Kiya whispered, slumping against the crate with a small groan.

Chapter Seventeen

"Keep filming," Hunter said, and Kiya heard the metal scrape as the man opened the door to the cage.

Still atop Kiya, Saoi turned his head, snarling at Hunter.

"What the hell are you doing?" Jackson asked.

Kiya blinked open his eyes and turned his head to look at the door, eying Hunter warily. Even dazed as he was, Kiya didn't want that man anywhere near him or Brian. Hunter was grinning and the look he gave them made Kiya's skin crawl.

"See, the wolf's stuck now, tied to the boy under him. He can't pull out without not just hurting himself, but probably ripping the boy open," Hunter explained, reaching down and picking up the metal muzzle Kiya had removed earlier.

Kiya winced at that thought, but realized the man was probably right. Brian's cock was still tight and full inside him.

"Keep that dart gun aimed, Jackson," Hunter warned and then held out the muzzle. "You're gonna let me put this back on you, wolf, or I will blow the boy's brains out."

Saoi snarled at him but, as Hunter had predicted, didn't move. In fact, his paws seemed to hold tighter to Kiya. Usually Kiya felt safe around Saoi, and he trusted him now, but he knew the men had the upper hand in this situation. Safety, even in the presence of Saoi, was only an illusion.

Hunter held the device out and slid it over the wolf's face, buckling it into place. "There, just in case you decide your own skin means more than the boy's," Hunter said.

Kiya wasn't exactly sure what Hunter meant by that, but he didn't ask, shaking his head and resting his cheek against the crate. He felt a mixture of exhausted, anxious and terrified, and it was beginning to take a toll on him.

Hunter walked all the way around them and then crouched down in front of the two locked together. He reached a hand out and touched the cut on Kiya's shoulder. "So you always bottom?" he asked. "I bet your wolf's not taken it up the ass."

Kiya frowned and shook his head, looking away and shrugging his shoulder to dislodge the man's hand.

Hunter took hold of Kiya's chin, fingers digging into him. Saoi growled and Kiya could feel him trembling in anger.

"I got about twenty minutes with your wolf tied this way," Hunter said. "There are some illegal porn sites that will pay big money for what we just recorded. I don't think anyone's ever taped someone getting it from a wolf," Hunter said.

"But you can't do that without my permission," Kiya told him, his eyes glancing up at the camera for a second.

Hunter laughed. "Illegal sites don't give a shit about your permission," he explained. He grinned up at Saoi, meeting his eyes. "I've killed a hundred wolves over the years, but never taken one of your kind alive before. I wonder how much they will pay for a wolf being fucked by a man?"

Kiya immediately started to shake his head. "No, I can't do that," he said quietly, knowing what the man was thinking now. "I don't want to"

Saoi snarled and Hunter laughed. "Oh, I'm not asking you. That's something I intend to enjoy myself. And you've trapped the wolf in a very awkward position. He can't resist me without hurting, maybe even killing, you."

"Oh." Kiya suddenly understood and he hated that they were using him to hurt Brian. His heart sped up and he began to shake uncontrollably. He realized that Hunter was about to rape his boyfriend

Hunter was grinning, eyes once again focusing on the wolf above Kiya. "You're a dominant wolf, aren't you? Bet you've never taken it up the ass. Not even from one of your own kind. Wonder how tight you'll be. Bet it'll hurt a lot."

Saoi didn't respond but Kiya could feel Saoi's heart hammering. Kiya bit his lip, tears welling up in his eyes. "I'm sorry, Brian," he said quietly, his lips trembling. "This is all my fault."

"It is," Hunter agreed, chuckling. "I never even knew he was here until Ted got drunk in the bar and starting ranting about a wolf in the woods." Hunter stood and began unbuttoning his jeans.

That didn't make Kiya feel any better. He sniffled and wiped at his eyes, but that didn't help as the tears continued to fall. Ted had been Kiya's mistake, but it was a lapse in judgment that would now bring pain to Brian and, probably, cost both of them their lives.

Hunter seemed pleased with the tears, grinning down at Kiya as he pulled out his already half-hard cock and began stroking it. "Yeah, gonna fuck your wolf and then skin him alive."

"And you deserve to die the worst death possible," Kiya hissed, looking up at him, suddenly feeling so angry he shook with it. "Someone should rip you apart." Kiya felt a spike of something within himself, a powerful anger that seemed to make him tingle inside.

"It ain't gonna be you, little boy," Hunter taunted. He gave his cock several more strokes, pre-come dripping from the tip.

"If not me, someone else will. And if not now, one day soon," Kiya said as if he were completely sure of it. As if he were delivering some kind of curse. Above him he heard a noise. There was a flap of wings and Kiya looked up to see a large black raven in the girders of the building. He realized, absently, that there must be a hole up there where it came through.

Hunter shook his head and circled around behind them and Kiya could feel the wolf trembling. Saoi was frightened. Kiya closed his eyes as a sudden rush of feeling went through him, causing him to shudder in surprise. He wasn't sure of what it was, but the only way he could describe it was that it felt like the magic he had experienced in the woods with Brian.

There was a loud cawing noise and when Kiya opened his eyes again, looking up, he saw that several more ravens and at least a dozen crows had come in through the hole in the roof and were sitting in the metal struts.

"Hunter, don't you want a condom? You might catch something," Jackson called to him.

"Nah, his kind are immune to everything like that; safest fuck you'll ever have," Hunter laughed.

Kiya felt Saoi shudder again as the man grabbed his tail. Kiya stared up at the birds, his eyes widening when he saw that they were staring back. The first raven flew down, landing atop the cage. It was almost as big as a medium-sized dog. The glossy black bird looked Kiya in the eyes. Kiya was suddenly unafraid. He was angry. He focused his attention on the raven. "Help us," he asked in Lakota. He wasn't sure why, but it just felt right. The large raven gave a caw as if in response to Kiya and more of the birds poured in through the hole, coming down to land on top of the cage.

"Shit," Kiya cursed quietly, his eyes wide. He nodded quickly, knowing that he didn't have much time before Saoi was badly hurt. Kiya knew that Saoi would prefer to suffer before he would allow Kiya to be harmed while Hunter fucked him. "Help now!"

Several of the small birds swooped down, flying past Hunter's face. "What the hell?" Hunter complained, pausing just as he positioned himself. He looked up. "How'd those birds get in here?"

Saoi whimpered and Kiya felt a surge of fear and anger. Kiya wanted the birds to deliver exactly what he said Hunter deserved before, the worst death possible. He imagined it vividly in his mind. "Kill them," he said in Lakota.

The crows screamed in response and dived at Hunter, who fell back batting at them with wildly flailing hands. When Kiya looked up, he was able to see blood dripping down from several wounds on Hunter's cheeks. Rick and Jackson started yelling too and when Kiya looked over, he saw birds diving at them as well.

Kiya had a feeling the birds wouldn't hurt him or Brian, but he didn't think it was safe to stay where they were. He turned to reach back and take the muzzle off of Brian's face as quickly as he could. The angle was difficult but he did it, and threw that off to the side before working on the collar too.

There was more flapping and the crows began screeching, Hunter cursing and screaming. Blood splattered as one of the ravens went for his face again. Jackson fired a gun, the sharp crack causing Kiya to jump and fumble as he desperately worked at the collar. The birds went for Jackson then, taking him to the ground in a mass of feathers and blood.

Once Kiya had gotten the collar off, he threw that to the side as well, running his fingers through Saoi's fur. "Can you change?" he shouted over the screeching and screaming. The wolf's amber eyes were wide with fright and looked between Kiya and the birds. Saoi nodded.

Kiya felt a surge of that energy again and a rush of heat. Then the fur had turned to flesh and he felt Brian's arms around him. Brian was gasping and Kiya felt his cock, now human again, slip from inside him. Kiya spun around the minute he could, sliding his arms around Brian's neck. "Brian," he whispered, burying his face against Brian's neck.

Brian's chest had a large pink splotch where the gunshot would have been and his neck was reddened, too. Holding Kiya, he looked to the other men and found all three of them were trying to fight off the birds but losing. There were small bodies of crows on the floor of the cage where Hunter had managed to take some out, but Hunter's face, hands and arms were streaming red rivulets of sticky fluid and coldly glittering eyes were now nothing but a blackened mess of blood and gore. Jackson had dropped his rifle and was curled up on the floor and covered with birds. Rick had dropped the camera and raced to the door where he banged on it, but seemed unable to get the lock open.

"We should get out of here," Kiya said shuddering at the carnage. He couldn't believe he had somehow caused it, and yet knew instinctively that he had.

Brian growled, but gave Kiya a squeeze. "Wait here," he told him and strode over to where Hunter had fallen to his knees. He hesitated, clearly worried about the birds, but then he reached in past the birds and drew the knife out of the man's pocket, flipped it open and thrust it into Hunter's chest. Crows screeched as if in approval and Hunter's hands tried to claw at Brian. Then Hunter fell backwards, knife sticking out of his chest. He was immediately covered in birds, ripping and shredding at yielding flesh as they tore him apart.

Kiya didn't stay where he was, instead scrambling over to the entrance of the cage and, reaching through it, managing to get the camera. He found out how to take the memory card out and broke it in two. Then Kiya picked up the camera and started slamming it against the bars of the cage. He felt that surge of rage again as he screamed, breaking the camera into bits against the metal.

Brian was shaking with anger too and the realization of what had happened to them. Hunter had fallen, and birds were feasting on the now silent, still body. Brian forced himself to search Hunter's pockets and found a set of keys. He looked up to see the birds had taken down both of the other men, too. He didn't know why the birds had attacked, nor why they only attacked the other men. It was a horrifying sight. Brian got up again and went to Kiya, gently stilling his movements and wrapping his arms around him. "We have to go," he said.

"The cage is locked, I think," Kiya said with a small nod, finally dropping the destroyed remains of the camera. No one would ever see that video. He looked around at the birds, able to spot the raven that he had first talked to. "Thank you," he said, speaking in Lakota again. The creature cawed in response.

Brian pulled his lover with him and searched the keys for one that fit. It burned his fingers when he touched the metal of the cage, trying to get it open.

"Let me do it!" Kiya said the moment he saw it was burning Brian's fingers. He gently pushed him away and took over, taking the keys and trying them. He found the right one and unlocked the cage, pushing the door open wide enough so that Brian wouldn't brush against it.

They had to step over Rick's body to get to the front door. They couldn't see anything but dark red carnage and black flapping wings. The sharp smell of blood and death filled the hot metal building. Kiya still had the keys, so Brian waited for him to unlock it. "We don't have clothes," Brian said, realizing they would have to get away.

Kiya had forgotten about that, but he would have probably realized it once they stepped outside. "We can't take theirs," he murmured as he unlocked the door and pulled it open. "We can just drive straight back to your house?"

Brian nodded, still feeling numb after everything that had just happened. He pulled Kiya out of the building and over to the van, holding his hand out for the keys.

Kiya handed them to Brian as he slumped down in the passenger seat, finally allowing himself to take a deep breath. He looked himself over and surveyed the damage. He still had Brian's dried blood on his stomach and chest and there were various other scratch marks and bruises. His scalp felt sore and tender from all the tugging, and he wasn't even going to think about the way his ass felt. As a matter of fact, it felt like he was leaking. Which was more than a little embarrassing.

Brian started up the van, not even bothering with a seatbelt. Being naked would probably be more of an issue if he were stopped. He'd been unconscious when he'd been brought to the building, so he didn't know where they were. But the driveway only went one way, so he quickly pulled out and drove.

Kiya was quiet, watching Brian drive. He couldn't believe what had just happened, and there was no way he could even tell anyone about it. Who would believe them? There was no longer any video of it, either. He cautiously ran a hand through his hair, rubbing his throbbing scalp and shifting in the seat so that all the weight wasn't on his sore behind. He went back to staring at the man next to him. "I-I thought I'd never see you again," he whispered.

Brian flushed, looking sideways at Kiya. Even after everything they had just been through, even filthy and bruised, Kiya was the most beautiful sight he'd ever seen. Maybe because of all that. Because it meant they were alive. Brian didn't know what to say or do, except that he wanted to be with and take care of Kiya. Brian was still cursing himself for having put them in danger. He hadn't protected Kiya from Ted, either before or when the man had shown up with a gun. Brian had been so lost in his pleasure, he hadn't heard or smelled the man coming up upon them in the woods. He shouldn't have let his guard down like that and not only had the bullet come close to killing him, he had let Ted get his hands on Kiya again, despite his promises of protection. It had been stupid and arrogant not to realize Ted would find them. "I'm sorry," Brian whispered and then was distracted as they reached the main road. "Which way?"

"I don't know," Kiya answered, peering out at the road. "They kept me in the back. There were no windows or anything."

They sat at the stop sign, engine running while Brian tried to figure out which way to go. He took a few deep breaths and then pulled on the wolf part of himself, feeling its instincts. He turned left and followed the winding road, relieved when it began to slope down. Brian tried to think ahead, to what they would have to do. He'd killed a man back there and left three bodies behind. And Ted. He didn't know if he had killed Ted or not. Either way, he didn't know how safe his own home would be anymore. "I'm sorry," he repeated, not knowing what to say to Kiya.

"I should be the one saying sorry," Kiya said, shaking his head. "Did you hear what he said? He wouldn't even have found you if it weren't for Ted. You would've never gotten shot or hurt in anyway, if it weren't for me."

Brian wanted to pull over, to talk with Kiya, but didn't want to risk being found like this. Brian knew it was his own fault, first as Brian, but also as a Saoi. When Ted had shot him, Brian had nearly died and had shifted so quickly he scarred himself. Then he had let his rage and terror override his natural instincts to pay attention to his surroundings. He had been so intent on stopping Ted, Saoi had missed the greater threat of the three men with guns. His own blood had masked the scents and Brian figured the men had also used either chemicals or magic to do the rest. However they did it, Saoi had been caught by the very thing his family had warned him about for years-wolf hunters who knew what he was and how to trap him. And this was his own fault because he had also revealed himself to Ted, who had been the one to lead the hunters to him. "He was a sick fuck who said that to hurt you," Brian growled. "Nothing was your fault."

"I don't know, Brian," Kiya murmured. It was difficult to get the idea out of his head because it made so much sense. Everything just had to be his fault.

"You were hurt because he hunts monsters and wanted to hurt me. That makes it my fault, Kiya," Brian insisted. He swallowed hard. "And he used me to hurt you." Brian shuddered again at the memories, both the horror of the situation they had endured and at his own guilt at how much he had enjoyed mounting Kiya. Sex as a wolf was so much more intense, more primal, more natural, that he couldn't help but desire it. He would never have presumed that any human would want that from him, but it didn't change the fact that even in that horrible setting, Saoi had enjoyed it. Now that he had had Kiya like that, it would be even more difficult not to want it again. Brian knew that he should leave and never see Kiya again. It would be safer for both of them. And he would not be surprised if Kiya ran from him now.

Kiya shook his head, looking over at Brian again. "Let's just-I just want to get home so I can get clean and not think about it," he said.

Brian was so rattled by everything that he nearly missed the turn, but managed to get them back to his cabin. Brian's truck was where he had left it and Ted's car wasn't anywhere to be seen. "Stay in the van and lock the doors, while I check it out," he insisted.

Kiya nodded a little nervously, reaching over to engage the locks when Brian stepped out. He hoped Ted finally understood and stayed as far away as possible. If he didn't, he didn't know what would stop him.

Brian looked around, sniffing the air. It smelled of blood. He glanced at Kiya, making sure he was secure before shifting form, Brian's body melting into the wolf.

Kiya's eyes widened and he leaned over closer, blinking a few times. Hearing it was one thing. But he had just watched Brian change into a wolf. He changed so easily, like it was nothing, and Kiya finally understood what Hunter had told him. It was Brian's true form, and he just changed into a human to fit into society, to pass as human.

Saoi looked up into Kiya's green eyes, wondering if this shocked him. Would Kiya leave him now that he knew? He forced himself not to think about it yet. The smell of blood was stronger now that he was a wolf. He lowered his muzzle, seeing the drops on the ground and under the sharp sweet smell of blood was the scent of Ted. Saoi followed it first into his own cabin. The door was open and there was a hand smear of blood on the frame, more on the floor. A blood soaked towel was tossed to one side. Ted wasn't there, but he had been. And he had been bleeding from the wounds Saoi had left.

Saoi turned and followed the blood trail out, past the van and his own truck to where Ted must have parked the car he had driven there in. The trail ended abruptly there. Ted had left. Yet, to be sure, Saoi backtracked into the forest. The scent was less there until he reached the place where they had fought. The scent of Hunter, the other men, and Kiya also lingered there. Satisfied that the immediate danger was past, Saoi returned to where Kiya waited in the van.

Chapter Eighteen

Kiya hated waiting. He found himself worrying, thinking that Ted might be waiting for them, if not in the cabin, then in the woods. What if Ted came back and found Kiya sitting there? What if he shot Brian again? Kiya couldn't help but imagine worse and worse scenarios. He was so relieved when he saw Saoi walking back, Kiya unlocked and pushed the door open, jumping out of the van.

Saoi sat down, waiting. He wondered if he should change back but, for the moment, wanted to see how Kiya would react to him in wolf form, especially after what had happened.

"What's wrong?" Kiya asked as he knelt beside Saoi, reaching over to run his fingers through the wolf's fur. "Is everything okay?"

Brian licked Kiya's hand and then pulled the magic to him, shifting to his human form. "Ted's gone," he answered.

"That's good, right?" Kiya asked. "I want to get out of here, okay?"

Brian nodded but held back from doing what he wanted, forcing himself not to wrap his arms around Kiya. "I need to get a few things," he said. "I can come back and clean everything up after I have you somewhere safe."

"Alright," Kiya said, disappointed that Brian was being so distant. Kiya pulled his hand back from where it rested on Brian's bare shoulder.

Brian felt awkward for the first time since he and Kiya had become lovers. There was so much that had happened and he didn't know how he felt, let alone how Kiya felt about it. "We could go to a hotel, get cleaned up and figure out what happens next from there," he suggested.

"Okay, could I borrow some clothes from you?" Kiya asked, crossing his arms in front of his chest. Thinking about it now, his clothes were somewhere in those woods.

Brian had to fight the urge to touch Kiya, to hold him. He wasn't sure if it was to comfort Kiya or himself. Yet, Kiya didn't reach for him and Brian didn't know if Kiya was disgusted by the fact that he was a wolf and what he had done to him. "Sure," he said, standing up and heading back into the cabin.

Kiya walked inside behind him, noticing the blood soaked towel as they walked inside. "Was someone else in here?" he asked.

"Ted," Brian answered, grabbing his backpack and pulling clothes out of his drawers. "He's alive." Brian wasn't happy about that. Ted had shot him and that meant he would know something was wrong when he found out Brian wasn't dead.

"I didn't want you to kill him," Kiya said, feeling the need to explain himself. "I wanted him to go to jail for the rest of his life so that he could think about what he did to you." He sat down on the bed with a tired sigh, waiting for clothes.

Brian's clothes were too big for Kiya, but he found a pair of sweat pants and a t-shirt that would work and laid them on the bed. "You'll probably want a real shower at the hotel," he said, "but you might want to rinse the blood and..." He stopped, not wanting to say the rest.

Kiya blushed and nodded slightly, looking up at Brian when he stopped talking. There was something wrong with him. It upset Kiya but he didn't know what to do about it. Brian walked him back to the shower and waited with him while Kiya rinsed off and dried himself. When Kiya asked if he would shower, Brian told him that he would do it after he took care of things. The sun was setting when they walked back into the cabin. Kiya glanced nervously at the very quiet man. "Brian?" he asked, walking over to him. "Will you be honest with me?"

Brian winced. Kiya doubted him now. He supposed that was inevitable given the secrets he had kept. "Yes," he answered, looking down into green eyes that still made him shake with want.

"Tell me what's wrong then?" Kiya asked, taking Brian's hands in his. "You still want me, right?"

Brian's eyes widened, his heart racing and his hands holding tight to Kiya's. "You... still want me?"

"Why wouldn't I?" Kiya asked, frowning.

Brian blinked in surprise, mouth opening to speak but no words coming out for a minute. "You heard what he told you, about me, and you've seen that it's true."

"And? You know I love Saoi," Kiya said softly. "It's like the best of both worlds now."

"You do get that I'm not human, right?" Brian asked. He couldn't help it, he didn't believe anyone could accept such a dramatic truth so quickly.

"You're a wolf," Kiya said simply. "I understand, Brian."

Brian had been taught all his life that if humans knew what they were, his kind would be hunted down and slaughtered. All Faewolves were literally oath-bound never to tell an outsider, and men like Hunter were exactly what he expected. Kiya's acceptance shocked him. Brian searched Kiya's eyes to see if it was true and found his gaze not only accepting but adoring. "Kiya," he whispered.

"Brian," Kiya said in reply, sliding his arms around the man's neck and leaning up. "Wolf or human, I'm staying with you."

It was like the magic before it had all gone bad in the forest. Kiya's touch made Brian's body tremble with a kind of warm energy. They were naked and dirty and their skin still felt perfect. "With me," Brian echoed, hands sliding around Kiya's waist and then lips pressing to his lover's.

Kiya surrendered to Brian's kiss and pulled him as close as possible, ignoring the fact that neither of them were as clean as he would have liked. Kiya was simply relieved that the nightmare was over, that they had survived.

Wolves like touch. It's an important part of who they are and how they communicate. And Brian felt that now more than ever, wanting to touch every part of Kiya, assure himself that he was still there. And that he still wanted to be with him. He kissed Kiya for several minutes, hands sliding up and down his back. Then Brian forced himself to draw back. "You continue to surprise me," he whispered.

"Of course I do," Kiya said, smirking slightly up at him. "But really wouldn't want you getting bored of me. Even though that's not possible."

Brian's eyebrows rose. "Not bored, that's certain," he smiled. "Now get dressed so we can get you somewhere safe." He gave a light slap to Kiya's left buttock as punctuation.

"Yes, master," Kiya said sarcastically, stepping around him and picking up the sweatpants Brian had given him to pull on. "You'll stay there with me, right?"

Brian smiled and began pulling on jeans and a shirt. "I will meet you there and we can figure out what to do next. Can you drive my truck?"

Kiya nodded, having learned to drive in his father's pick-up back at Pine Ridge. These days, he hardly ever drove. "Are you gonna get rid of the van?"

"Yes, and clean up the mess in the woods," Brian said. "I can't leave evidence of what happened up there or that Ted shot me."

"He probably thinks you're dead," Kiya realized. He pulled on Brian's shirt.

"Yes, and if he finds out I am alive and not in the hospital?" Brian asked.

"I don't know what we'll do about that," Kiya said, frowning as he went to his bag to pull out his brush and fixed his hair.

"He'll know I am not... what I seem to be," Brian answered. "Ted's insane, which makes him difficult to predict."

"Yeah, not everyone recovers from that so easily," Kiya said as he brushed his hair gently, wincing as it tugged on sore spots. He turned around, biting his lip gently as he remembered seeing Brian shot and bleeding. "How did you manage to do that, anyway?"

Brian was looking for a plastic bag to put the bloody clothes in. He looked over his shoulder and saw the expression on his lover's face. So he stopped and went to crouch in front of where Kiya sat on the bed. "I am hard to kill," he assured his lover. "The bullet wasn't pure iron, it didn't hit my heart directly and it went all the way through. I was still alive, so I shifted. When we shift, it heals most wounds."

"Oh. I hated that most out of everything that happened," Kiya murmured, setting his brush down. "Just the look on your face and all the blood. I wanted to get back to you so badly."

Brian reached out, running his fingers through the silk of Kiya's long hair. "I saw your face," he whispered. "I came for you as quickly as I could. Changing with that much damage was harder than it usually is."

"But you came for me," Kiya whispered, smiling at him. "Just in time, actually." He touched the area where the gun had been pressed up under his chin.

Brian couldn't resist leaning forward to kiss Kiya again, leaving small kisses from that spot up to his lips. But he was still sad when he pulled back to look into Kiya's eyes again. "I was trying to protect you but I made it worse instead. The things those men threatened to do to you... because of me."

"I don't wanna think about that," Kiya said softly, shaking his head and sighing. "Only glad they didn't do it... to either of us."

Brian wanted to ask about that, about how they were saved. Crows, a lot of them. And they normally wouldn't attack people. "The crows," he whispered.

Kiya started to shake his head, not sure of how to explain that either. "I don't know. I just remember needing to help you so badly. And I felt this... well, magic-like we felt in the circle?" he asked.

Brian's eyes widened and he nodded. "You called them?"

"I think I did," Kiya said. "They understood me."

Brian felt a shiver down his spine. "I am glad you did," he said, both awed and a bit frightened of that kind of power.

"So that was some kind of magic?" Kiya asked. "It's never happened before."

"You saved my life," Brian said. More than his life, but he didn't want to talk about that. He cupped Kiya's chin, thumb caressing his lips.

"It's only fair, right?" Kiya asked, smiling again. "You saved me more than once."

Brian rubbed his nose against Kiya's and then kissed him again. But he needed to get them moving, so he sighed and pulled back, handing Kiya the keys to his truck. "There is a place called Sunset Hotel on Mission Street. Go there. Is your wallet here or in the woods?"

"Here, luckily," Kiya said, nodding over at his bag.

"Do you need money?" Brian asked.

"Uhmm, yeah," Kiya answered with a nod. "I'll pay for the night?"

"Yeah, we can figure out what happens next after that," Brian confirmed, getting to his feet and retrieving some money he had stashed in a drawer and handing it to Kiya. "Be careful. Lock the door and don't let anyone but me in. I'll call your cell when I am done."

"Alright," Kiya said, reaching to run his fingers through Brian's hair. "You realize we've known each other for only about a month?"

Brian shivered in pleasure at the touch, smiling. "Too fast, I know," Brian said. But it felt like it was the way it should be.

"But at the same time, it's not too fast. Actually it feels like it's been so much longer," Kiya said softly. "But that's okay. It feels right."

"Yes, you feel perfect," Brian admitted. He wanted to pull Kiya into the bed and never let go. "I will be with you as soon as I can."

"Okay, let's go then," Kiya said, leaning over to give him a quick kiss before he stood up. He brushed his hands down over the clothes, not used to going out in just sweatpants and a shirt. "I don't look too bad, right?"

"You are beautiful, and you know it," Brian answered, gaze

lingering hungrily.

"I know," Kiya said, blushing slightly as he continued looking down at himself. "I just like hearing it."

Brian walked him out to the truck, still sniffing the air to make sure no one else was near.

Kiya took Brian's keys and unlocked the doors, walking around to the driver's side.

Brian watched Kiya get in and had to stamp down the fear of letting him out of his sight.

"I'll see you," Kiya said once he got inside, leaving the door open so that Brian could give him another kiss goodbye.

Getting the hint, Brian moved up, bending to kiss Kiya. It wasn't a gentle kiss. It held too much need and fear in it and he didn't want it to end.

Kiya's eyes fell shut as he kissed Brian back, his head tilting to the side. He hadn't realized how much he needed the reassurance of physical contact.

One of Brian's hands clutched the top edge of the door opening, but the other came up to slide into Kiya's hair, cupping the back of his head as he deepened the possessive kiss.

Kiya made a soft sound and clung to him, wishing Brian was going to the hotel with him so that they could kiss for the rest of the night. He had come so close to losing Brian and was still nervous about being separated from him.

Brian nipped and nuzzled Kiya's chin. He was aroused again by the time he made himself stop, forehead pressed to Kiya's and eyes closed for a moment. "I will be there as soon as I can," he assured them both.

"You better be," Kiya said softly, nudging his nose and then forcing himself to pull back. "I should go then."

"Yes," Brian answered, forcing himself to let go and step back. He closed the door for Kiya.

Kiya pulled the seatbelt on and started the truck, waving at Brian. He blew him a kiss and then put the truck in reverse, looking back as he pulled out of the driveway.

Brian's entire body was rigid with effort, holding himself in place as he watched Kiya drive away without him. The wolf part of him wanted to howl and chase the truck, furious and terrified at sending Kiya out of his sight, away from his protection. Only Brian didn't feel he had been much of a protector that day. He had failed at every turn to keep Kiya safe.

Hunter, whatever his real name had been, and his men had come prepared, knowing the weaknesses of a Faewolf and exploiting them. Iron was poison to any of Fae heritage, and Wolfsbane to any werewolf or Faewolf. If it hadn't been for Kiya, they would have already butchered Saoi and sold his body parts to collectors and those who would use them for their magical properties. Hunter was the kind of human that had almost led to the genocide not only of Faewolves, but of all wolves. Sadistic, greedy and full of hate, Hunter had forced Saoi to hurt Kiya. Saoi had known that Hunter had been lying, that he had no intention of letting either of them live. It was Saoi's fear of having to watch Kiya taken by the other men that had worked to manipulate him into mounting Kiya in front of the men and their camera. Saoi had known, even when Kiya hadn't, that they would be tied together, helpless, after coupling like that. The surprise for Saoi was that the act itself hadn't injured the young man, let alone disgusted Kiya. Most humans were pretty horrified by what they called bestiality.

Brian thought about this, wrestling with himself as he turned back to his cabin, searching until he found a couple of plastic bags and made his way back into the woods to collect the clothing left there. Since both of them had been naked when Ted attacked, their clothes weren't really damaged, just extremely dirty including blood splatters on his shirt. Brian found his cell phone still in the pocket of his jeans.

There was a large amount of blood soaked into the ground, both where he had been shot and where he had mauled Ted. Brian wasn't sure how to handle that. He ended up hauling water out to the spot and diluting it so that it all soaked in to the dark earth. It was messy, but he also managed to dig the slug from the gun out of the ground. Then he worked on cleaning up the blood outside and inside his cabin, bagging up the bloody towels to dispose of somewhere. He changed clothes again, realizing he was running out of clean ones since he hadn't done laundry in a while.

Then he stood again, staring at the van for a long time. How was he supposed to dispose of a vehicle? And what about the bodies up in the warehouse? What would the human authorities make of the men torn apart by birds? Would they be able to tell he had stabbed one? Brian knew about DNA and forensics, so he figured he couldn't just walk away from the situation. His and Kiya's fingerprints, blood and even semen, were at the scene. He couldn't risk leaving them.

His stomach felt like it wanted to curdle at the idea of what he would have to do, but he got back in the van and drove up to the warehouse. It was full dark by the time he arrived, but as a wolf, that didn't hinder him as much as it would a human. He stood for probably longer than he should have, staring at that building, having to force himself to look inside again. He wasn't afraid of blood or bodies. He was a wolf, a hunter. Blood excited him. The problem was that in the context he found himself in, he didn't want to feel that excitement, much less the memories the scene would bring up.

As he knew they would be, the remains of the three men were grisly. The crows hadn't just killed them, they had literally torn them apart, devouring them. The clothing and bones remained, blood soaked and with bits of flesh and organ matter sticking to them and splattering over the concrete floor. The smell threatened to overwhelm him and it was a struggle not to shift into wolf. Blood could cause him to lose control, to revert to his natural form. But he needed hands for this task.

He retrieved the knife he had used on Hunter first. Then he began to search out every place that either he or Kiya had touched, wiping fingerprints. By the time he finished using a cloth to wipe them from the cage, collar and muzzle, Brian's fingers were red, blistered and scorched.

He had brought cleaning solution, ammonia. He used that to clean the blood and semen from the floor where he had mounted Kiya. On hands and knees scrubbing, the smell of sex and blood nearly sent him back to wolf as his mind also replayed the scene that had occurred there. His body trembled in memory of how good it had felt to be on top of and inside Kiya, the taste and scent making Brian's heart race and his cock twitch. He actually sniffed the ammonia then, using it to try to counter his lust. It burned and kept him on task.

When he had managed to wipe down everything that he thought might trace back to himself or Kiya, he looked around until he found a generator out back. He used the fuel line to fill empty beer bottles on the site and then set about soaking the remains of the men's bodies. In their pockets, he had found driver's licenses, cash and other items. Brian memorized the facts about the men and took the cash. He then made sure to soak the wallets and their contents in gasoline as well, before setting fire to the bodies. He repeated the entire procedure on the van as well, adding the bloody clothing and cleaning rags as he set them afire too.

Brian retreated to the trees, watching the flames and the black billowing smoke, waiting until he was sure that the fire would destroy what it needed to without spreading to the surrounding forest. While he waited, he buried the camera and the knife in the woods. It was late in the night when the work was finally done. Brian tossed the clothes he had worn while cleaning onto the last of the fire and then shifted to his true form, disappearing into the trees.

∽

Kiya stood in the shower of the Sunset Hotel, letting the water flow over him. He was bruised and sore and the water was as hot as he could stand it. He stood there for a long time, until his skin was wrinkled and red. He almost couldn't let himself think about what he had been through in the last couple of days. The highs and lows were so extreme that even flashes in his mind made him tremble.

Eventually, he turned off the shower, wrapped his hair in a towel and began drying himself off. He felt nearly numb. He found himself holding Brian's sweat pants and t-shirt in a tight grip, shaking as he put them back on. The room had a King size bed and it seemed immense next to his dorm one or Brian's futon. Kiya climbed onto it and sat in the middle, braiding his hair into one long plait. His scalp was still tender and a reminder of the way both Ted and Hunter had yanked it. His mind flashed to blood again, to Brian lying in the middle of the redwood circle, a gaping wound in his chest. Kiya realized that, for him, that had been the worst moment of the entire day. He had thought Brian was dead. He had almost lost both Brian and Saoi, before he had even learned that they were the same. Kiya loved Brian. And he loved the wolf, Saoi. And now he knew that his protector and confidant in the woods was also the man he had been lusting after since they had met. It didn't scare Kiya, even if it should have. It made sense to him, made all of the little things add up in way that was whole and comforting.

At every twist and turn of the very long day, Kiya had worried not just for himself, but for Brian. And now they were both alive. He couldn't wait to be together again. Unfortunately, waiting was precisely what he had to do. He pulled out his cell phone and made sure he hadn't missed a call from Brian. There weren't any new messages, not even from Ted. Ted was alive, Brian said. But what would Ted do now? Would he finally leave Kiya alone? Would he tell people what had happened, especially when he had shot Brian? Ted was crazy enough that Kiya realized he had no way to predict what his former boyfriend would do.

Kiya set the cell phone on the bed and lay down beside it, staring at it as if he could will it to ring, will Brian to call and say he was right outside. He thought about calling Brian but didn't know if that would interfere with the task he had set out to complete. So Kiya waited. And waited. He tried to distract himself with a movie on the television, but that quickly lost his attention. He ended up standing by the window and looking out into the night, watching cars drive by on Mission Street.

Then Kiya discovered a mini-bar in the room, equipped with vodka, bourbon, whiskey, rum, and a variety of sodas. After a moment of thought, he picked up a few bottles, sat on the massive bed and began drinking. Soon there was a good amount of small empty bottles scattered on the bed. Kiya blinked at the time, and shook his head. Brian still wasn't back and Kiya was tired, scared and feeling slightly drunk. What if something else had happened to Brian? How long did he have to wait?

Kiya yelped when the phone finally did ring, and stumbled, knocking empty liquor bottles to the floor, as he scrambled to open the cell. "Hello?"

"Kiya, are you safe?" Brian asked immediately.

Relief was so overwhelming that Kiya almost sobbed. "Yeah, where are you? Are you okay?" Kiya blurted out, words slurring with both his excitement and intoxication.

"It's taken care of and I am fine," Brian said.

"Good," Kiya said, smiling a little. "So you'll be here soon."

There was a pause. "Soon, no. I'm walking. I can't carry things in my other form, so I am walking it on two legs. It's at least three miles from my cabin to the motel, so it will take me a while."

"M'kay," Kiya hummed and then told Brian the room number.

"You rest and I will be there as soon as I can," Brian told him.

"Okay," Kiya murmured, nodding even though Brian couldn't see it. "I'll see you." He hung up the phone and lay back on the bed, pushing the bottles out of the way to make some space. He was feeling a little drowsy, but that was just because of all that he drank. He curled around one of the pillows and drifted to sleep imagining being held in Brian's arms.

Chapter Nineteen

Saoi often ran in the woods at night. And he knew the forest above the university better than he knew the roads, so it wasn't difficult to find his way back to his cabin. He stopped frequently, sniffing the air both to orient himself and to make sure there was no one following him. He knew with certainty that he was nearly back when he scented the llamas. His cabin was near a llama ranch which was a fact he found amusing in both forms, especially since the llamas were probably the only creatures who had figured out there was a wolf in their woods. They often cried out plaintively and went skittish as he passed them. He could smell their fear. But unlike other wolves, his kind was usually very careful not to prey upon the herds of human-kept animals. Still, the smell did remind him that he hadn't eaten that day.

He approached his own cabin cautiously, sniffing the air for the scent of visitors or anything out of the ordinary. Saoi could still smell the hint of blood and ammonia. Watching from the cover of darkness for a while, he was assured that no one was there or had been there since he had left. He entered his own den.

He had done all he could think of to clean up the mess. Now he had to figure out what to do about Kiya. And Ted. His urge to kill Ted was stronger than ever. He was certain now that he should have done so when he had the chance, but he didn't know if that meant he should hunt the man down now or not.

He shifted back into human form, and began packing his things. After he had clothes, books and other things he thought he would need over the next few days, Brian pulled out the last steak he had in his refrigerator and put it in the pan. He shifted form and gulped it down quickly. Finally, he shifted back, got dressed and left his cabin. Brian stood for several minutes, just breathing in the scents of the forest on the night air.

It didn't take long for Brian's thoughts to return to Kiya. Not that Kiya had ever really been out of his thoughts, only that he had forced himself to focus to get through the last hours. He literally felt an ache in his chest, a longing for Kiya that was worse than hunger or pain. It was probably a justification, but he told himself that he could not walk away, because Kiya might still be in danger from Ted. He needed to see Kiya safe first. So he pulled out his phone and called Kiya's cell.

The sound of Kiya's voice alone made Brian's heart beat speed up. Kiya tried to assure Brian that he was okay, but his voice betrayed how tired he was. When he hung up, Brian began walking as fast as he could, grateful that from where he was, the road was all downhill. He wished he could say the same of his other problems.

∾

Kiya was startled awake by the sound of knocking at the door. He had a momentary fear that it would be Ted, but then realized that Ted wouldn't know where he was. Kiya blinked and stumbled over to the door, nearly tripping on the empty bottles scattered on the floor. He pulled it open to find Brian standing there.

Brian felt the rush of relief again as he saw Kiya and reached for him immediately, stepping into the room and pulling Kiya into his arms, lapping and nipping his chin.

"Mmm, hi," Kiya murmured against his chest, breathing in Brian's scent.

Brian held him tight, one arm around his shoulders while reaching to shut and lock the door. He could smell the alcohol immediately. "Did you even check to make sure it was me before you opened the door?"

"I knew it was you," Kiya said, smiling up at him.

Brian decided not to push that, holding Kiya in his arms and nuzzling him. Under the alcohol and the smell of soap was a scent that was all Kiya. Brian growled in pleasure, burying his

226

face in his hair.

Kiya sighed happily and wrapped his arms around Brian in return, his eyes falling shut. He felt like everything would be all right as long as he had Brian.

After several minutes of standing still, holding each other, Brian looked around the room. There was a big bed and it looked very appealing. He was more tired after everything that had happened than he had realized on his way over. He wanted to hold Kiya, touch him, and then rest. He drew them both over to the bed, managing to avoid the bottles.

"Sorry about the mess," Kiya murmured softly.

Brian shoved the rest of the bottles off the bed and laid Kiya back, lying half atop him as he brought his mouth over Kiya's. Kiya's eyes closed and his return kiss was a little more sloppy than usual. "You're drunk," Brian whispered, nose wrinkling at the strong taste. His hands worked to remove his clothes from Kiya's body.

"Am not," Kiya mumbled, letting Brian pull the clothes off without moving to help him.

"Anyone help you drink all those little bottles of booze?" Brian asked as he stood to tug the sweat pants off Kiya's legs and then worked to remove his own clothes.

"No. Okay, maybe a little drunk," Kiya chuckled, trying to lift his hips to help but only falling sideways as he did so.

Throwing all the clothes on the floor, Brian stood for a moment, looking and marveling at Kiya. There were bruises on Kiya's arms and neck, a reminder of the events of the last couple of days. Brian felt a surge of guilt again and anger. "Turn over," he told him.

Kiya hummed as he rolled over onto his stomach, reaching to pull one of the pillows close.

The sight was arousing, but it wasn't why Brian had instructed Kiya to turn over. He saw the bruises and red marks from the wolf teeth on Kiya's shoulder and winced. "Tell me if this hurts," he said, reaching to part his lover's beautiful ass cheeks. He wanted to see if he had hurt Kiya there, as well. He didn't know what they would say if he had to take Kiya to the hospital, but he wasn't going to risk tears or infection.

Kiya nodded, shifting and lifting his hips a little for him. "Just sore."

The skin looked a bit red, but not torn or bruised. Brian was relieved. They hadn't talked about the wolf or what they had both felt when he had mounted him. "Did it hurt?" he asked quietly.

"Not as much as I thought it would," Kiya admitted. "You're much bigger as a wolf." Surprisingly, or maybe not, Kiya felt a shiver of arousal when he thought about it.

Brian didn't mention how wonderful it had felt to be inside Kiya in his true form like that. Kiya had only done it because he had been coerced. "I would never have done that to you," he whispered, fingers petting Kiya's rounded cheeks.

"Why not?" Kiya asked softly, his cheek pressed against the pillow. His body was still humming at the pleasure of Brian's touch.

Even more disturbing was that Brian wanted Kiya again now, wanted to soothe that redness with his tongue. He forced himself to stop caressing him and moved up beside Kiya on the bed. Head propped up on one hand and elbow, he reached to smooth Kiya's hair back from his face. "I wouldn't want to force something on you."

"Who said you would be forcing it on me?" Kiya asked, looking a little confused. It hadn't been that Brian was a wolf that had bothered him, but that those men and their camera were watching.

"They forced you," Brian whispered, fingers tracing the edge of the bruise on Kiya's shoulder.

"That doesn't mean I wouldn't want you like that again," Kiya said, reaching to run a finger down Brian's arm.

Brian shuddered, not sure if it was the touch or the words. His heart sped up as the meaning hit home. "You would... touch a wolf like that?"

"I would touch you like that," Kiya explained, smiling a little again. "Wolf or not."

Brian was lost in wonder at the idea of a human who wasn't afraid or even put off by what he really was, let alone who would want to touch him in both forms. He searched Kiya's green eyes as if he'd find proof that Kiya was only saying that to please him or because he was drunk. Kiya looked like he believed it. And that made Brian's entire body react with a strong surge of want.

Kiya moved closer to him, resting his forehead against Brian's. He closed his eyes for a long moment and then opened them again, leaning in to kiss him softly. "I want you, but ... I don't want to fall asleep during it," he admitted.

Brian chuckled, reaching over to pull the covers and top sheet of the bed down. "So, I should tuck you in and let you sleep," he suggested. Then he scooped Kiya up and moved him into place between those soft sheets.

"We can still do it," Kiya murmured as he settled back into the bed, reaching for him.

Brian couldn't help smile at that. He was aroused, of course, but it was the idea that Kiya wanted him so strongly that made it so much more. "Lay back and let me show you how much I enjoy you," he whispered as he snuggled under the covers and took his lover into his arms.

"Okay," Kiya murmured, laying back as told. He closed his eyes and breathed in deeply , letting it out with a happy sigh.

Brian began with a kiss, gentle but firm, his tongue sliding into Kiya's mouth. He inhaled Kiya's scent and taste and felt his own body tremble in response, cock already half hard and swelling fast.

Kiya lazily kissed him back, eyes remaining closed. Even though he was very tired, he still enjoyed Brian's touch. He felt like he needed it. Needed Brian to kiss away the fear and pain.

They lay kissing, slowly and gently. Brian felt a surge of protective pride in Kiya that still managed to surprise him. "I want you to be mine," he whispered against those full soft lips, fingers of one hand coming up to caress Kiya's cheek.

"Aren't I already?" Kiya asked softly, still kissing his lips. He felt like he floated in the warm touch of Brian's arms.

"Good," Brian answered, body pressed alongside Kiya's, arousal sliding against his hip. He licked and nipped down Kiya's throat, the feel of the pulse beneath his lips making his own heart speed up.

"I'm yours ... you're mine," Kiya mumbled, tilting his head back a little more so that Brian could kiss all the little marks he had left.

"Yes. Mine, yours," Brian echoed, voice deepening as he moved down Kiya's throat, leaving new marks in his wake. His fingers moved in advance of his mouth, finding and pinching one dark coral nipple.

Kiya made a soft pleading sound and arched his chest a little, opening his eyes to look down at Brian.

Brian's eyes met Kiya's as he lapped his way down Kiya's chest, fingers holding the nipple taut as he did so. He used just the very tip of his tongue to tease the bud.

Kiya slowly sank his teeth into his bottom lip, moaning for more. "Brian," he sighed, reaching to run his fingers through the light brown hair.

Brian tongued the point a few times before releasing it with his fingers. He pressed his mouth over the circle of flesh, sucking hard as his hand moved to the other nipple.

Kiya groaned, his hand tightening in Brian's hair as he arched once again, biting his lip harder.

Brian's eyes closed as he sucked and bit at that soft flesh, tasting the blood just under the surface but not breaking the skin that swelled against his tongue.

Kiya's hand tightened until he was tugging at Brian's hair, breathing in small pants. He almost wanted Brian to bite into his skin, even though he knew it would leave him sore for days, along with everything else.

Brian could feel Kiya's trembling and hear his ragged gasps.

And, more importantly, he could smell that wonderfully distinct Kiya-smell that so aroused him. He chuckled against Kiya's skin and lapped his way over to the other nipple, leaving the first one swollen and wet.

"More, Brian," Kiya groaned.

Brian growled and attacked the second nipple, sucking and biting a little harder.

"Fuck," Kiya hissed quietly, shuddering hard as Brian continued. "Please," He pushed Brian's head downward to tell him what he wanted.

Brian slid a hand down that smooth skin, over Kiya's waist. He traced the sharp edge of his hip. The way Kiya was squirming, Brian was pretty sure he wasn't sleepy anymore.

Kiya spread his legs when he felt Brian's hand moving down further, hoping he'd touch him where he wanted it.

Brian lapped and nuzzled down Kiya's body, rubbing his face against the smooth skin of his belly, his hand stroking Kiya's thigh.

"Please," Kiya whispered again, lifting his hips for him.

Brian smiled, climbing into the inviting V of Kiya's spread legs. He sat back and admired the sight for a moment, watching the way Kiya's cock jutted up from between those narrow hips. The hair around the base and sprinkling over Kiya's balls was dark brown and slightly curled. The shaft itself was a darker red-brown than Kiya's skin in other areas, the foreskin drawn back enough that the glistening crown peaked out of its folds. Brian licked his lips appreciatively and reached to trail fingers slowly up the length.

Kiya breathed in sharply, his eyes falling shut again as his hips jerked slightly.

The foreskin moved with Brian's touch, and he took a moment to enjoy the softness of it, the way it curled protectively over the hardened flesh beneath. Then he drew it back, exposing that bright red flesh with its slit leaking pre-come. "I am going to taste you," he whispered, using his fingers to angle it upwards more as he bent over and licked that drop.

"Taste more," Kiya found himself gasping before he could stop himself, his face flushing.

"Oh, I intend to devour you," Brian promised, smirking up at his impatient lover. He swirled his tongue around the soft slick crown, fingers curling around the shaft.

"Oh, thank you," Kiya whispered, one hand reaching to grip the sheets while the other tightened in Brian's hair yet again.

The taste was delightful and Brian savored it. It would taste even better if he were in wolf form, but he wouldn't be able to do what he wanted next then. He slid his lips down over Kiya's cock, tongue flat against the underside as he sucked him in.

Kiya let out a loud moan, not holding back. And, with the way he felt, he didn't think he could have held it back anyway.

Brian sucked and lapped, loving the slide of that flesh as he bobbed his head up and down, fingers working in time with his mouth and his other hand resting on Kiya's hip. Kiya whimpered and started to rock his hips up to meet him. Brian felt those restless hips under his hand and had no trouble giving Kiya what he wanted. He pulled more of his lover's prick into his mouth, swallowing around it when it nudged the back of his throat.

Kiya shuddered and cursed, unconsciously pressing Brian's head down more as he arched. Brian didn't mind the rougher treatment. He was used to playing around with other wolves. He groaned around Kiya's cock, sucking harder.

Kiya was going to come this way if Brian kept it up, pulling at Brian's hair as he continued to writhe. "God, Brian," he moaned.

Brian could feel the tightening in his lover's body and knew Kiya was close. He slid a hand between Kiya's legs and cupped his balls, rolling them as he sucked.

Kiya tugged at Brian's hair a few times before he was coming, crying out Brian's name as loudly as he could.

Kiya tasted as good as Brian thought he would and he loved the feel of that flesh spasming in his mouth, shooting hot liquid down his throat. He swallowed, humming happily as he did.

"Brian," Kiya whispered, falling back onto the bed with a tired sigh, his hand finally slipping out of Brian's hair.

Brian allowed Kiya's cock to slip from his mouth, licking his lips and smiling up at him. "I like the taste of you."

"Good, I guess," Kiya murmured, his eyes closing once again. He felt blissfully tired now.

Brian laughed softly and crawled up beside Kiya, kissing his lips when he reached them.

Kiya puckered his lips and let Brian kiss him, feeling the drowsiness start to come back.

"Kiya, before you sleep," Brian whispered.

"Mm?" Kiya hummed, opening one eye a little.

"I can't stay human when I sleep," Brian warned him. "Just thought you should know when you find yourself with a face full of fur."

"Awesome," Kiya murmured, turning on his side to snuggle closer. "Can you change now? I'm a little cold."

"Let me get myself off first," Brian said, pulling the blankets up over Kiya.

"Oh, how?" Kiya mumbled, opening his eyes again.

Brian lay back on the bed and wrapped a hand around his cock. "One of the advantages of the human form is hands," he teased.

"I'm sorry," Kiya said softly, feeling a little guilty but too tired to do anything more.

"Hey, I've been doing this all my life. I'm not bad at it," Brian teased, fingers working his own cock, squeezing and pulling.

"Still, you've got me now, I should be helping you with that," Kiya murmured, his eyes closing as he spoke.

"Sleep," Brian assured him, smiling at he watched Kiya. He'd certainly done this thinking about Kiya before and it was much better lying beside him, the taste of him still in Brian's mouth.

"Mm, okay. Goodnight," Kiya mumbled. He wanted to watch Brian come, but his eyes felt too heavy, his body like he was floating. He closed them again.

It didn't take much longer for Brian, one hand resting on Kiya's arm and the other making slapping noises as he fisted his cock hard and quick. His mind flashed to the feeling of himself atop Kiya, in wolf form, cock swollen inside the tight human ass. He groaned as he shuddered, coating his own stomach with slick white spurts.

Kiya's only response was to make a cute little face when he groaned. Brian smiled and slid out of bed, going to the bathroom to clean up. Then he turned out the lights and lay back down beside Kiya. He gave him a soft kiss on the lips before lying back and letting his form shift back to wolf. Saoi spent a minute inhaling the more pungent scent of Kiya and sex before wriggling up against him.

Kiya turned and wrapped his arms around Saoi in his sleep, fingers curling into soft thick fur as he breathed in deeply and lett it out in a sigh. His thumb slid into his mouth just as he drifted asleep, his lips tight around the digit.

Chapter Twenty

Kiya jerked awake, his face wet with sweat and his heart beating what felt like a mile a minute. The nightmare was fresh in his mind. He could hear the three men again, hear the words Hunter and his men had said to him and Brian over and over. Then the image in his mind flashed and he saw those same men being ripped apart by the crows that he had set on them. Kiya's stomach lurched and he suddenly felt sick, really sick.

Saoi felt him move, heard the pounding of Kiya's heart and smelled the fear. He was instantly alert, scanning the room for danger. He didn't see or smell anyone but them, so he made a little whining sound, pressing his nose to Kiya's neck.

Kiya closed his eyes and tried to calm down, but his stomach didn't seem to care. He groaned and pulled the covers back and got out of the bed as quickly as he could, running into the bathroom. Kiya fell to his knees in front of the toilet and threw up, mostly just the drinks from the night before since he hadn't had much else.

Saoi hopped out of the bed and then shifted, stretching up into his human form before following Kiya. Brian stood behind him and gathered his long hair back, out of Kiya's way. He could smell the alcohol in what was coming up.

Kiya threw-up until nothing else came out, coughing a few times and groaning softly. "Disgusting," he mumbled, reaching to flush the toilet.

When Kiya sat back, Brian let the hair fall and then reached to unwrap one of the glasses in the room, filling it with water and holding it out.

Kiya accepted it, taking a drink and swishing it around in his mouth, getting up to spit it out in the sink. He looked up at himself in the mirror and frowned at how pale he seemed to be. "Suppose that was my fault," he mumbled, looking over at Brian through the mirror.

"The booze probably was rough on the stomach," Brian agreed, but sensed there was more. He laid his hands on Kiya's upper arms, stroking them. "I smelled fear."

"I had a nightmare," Kiya said softly, realizing he probably wouldn't be able to hide those kind of things from Brian.

Brian pulled Kiya back against him, kissing the top of his head and still looking at his face in the mirror. "Even wolves have nightmares."

"Yeah? It was everything that happened. I don't know why I have such vivid dreams," Kiya murmured. "Like it was really happening all over."

Brian nodded, rubbing his cheek against Kiya's hair. "Some say those who have vivid dreams have more of the Fae in them."

"Is that possible with me?" Kiya asked, his eyebrows furrowing in thought. "What does that mean anyway?"

"You drew down crows," Brian whispered, still a bit awed by that. "I know your people have stories about them, that they are symbols of ancient power."

Kiya nodded in agreement, having heard many such stories from his grandparents when he was younger. "I guess that means I'm... magical or something," he murmured, still not sure of what to call it.

Brian smiled and turned Kiya around so he could look directly into his face. "I believe it does," he whispered.

"Me? Magical? I wonder if I can only work with birds," Kiya mused, smiling a little.

"Birds can be very powerful, as you just found out," Brian answered.

"I know. Crows in particular are important to us. There's a legend about them helping us," Kiya explained, looking up at him. "Wolves are important to us as well. Wolves and crows are wakan, sacred."

Brian nodded, taking Kiya's hand and pulling him out of the bathroom and back into the room. "Talking wolves," he answered with a smirk.

"Yes, talking wolves are the best ones," Kiya laughed as he followed Brian. "But you ... so you're a wolf, right? But a Faewolf? I still don't think I understand exactly."

Brian sat down on the bed, propping up pillows along the headboard to lean against and holding his hands to Kiya to invite his lover to join him. "Yes, not a werewolf. My people are a race of wolves with the magic of the Fae."

"Well what exactly is a Fae?" Kiya asked, taking Brian's hands and moving up on the bed with him.

The feel of Kiya's skin was like warm silk and Brian was distracted for a moment, sliding hands over him. He grinned. "Faeries."

Kiya's eyebrows rose. "Faeries? So you're... a fairy wolf."

Brian laughed. "They're not the cute little winged creatures some people think they are, you know," he warned. "They are creatures so magical that they are close to gods. It's said that that's where a lot of magic comes from. That the Fae brought it into our world."

"Wow," Kiya murmured, thinking that over. "So you must be really powerful."

Brian smiled again. "Um, not as much as that sounds really. The ancestor who lay with a wolf was probably thousands of years ago," he explained. "No one knows just how long ago. My kind don't keep written records."

"Ohhh. A Fae had sex with a wolf," Kiya said, nodding as though everything made complete sense now. "You're just mixed! I see now."

Brian laughed then, actually blushing a bit. "That's the story we are told," he admitted. "And ever since, my clan have been different than other wolves, though we have never completely separated from them."

Kiya nodded, understanding because it reminded him of the

Lakota stories about animals, magic and the ancestors. "I get it," he said with a nod.

"Most of my clan consider it more odd for one of us to be with a human than with one of the non-Fae wolves," Brian continued.

"Why? Are you born as babies or like puppies?" Kiya asked curiously.

Brian laughed, grinning. "I didn't learn to shift into a human form until I was an adolescent," he admitted. "So, puppy."

"Aww," Kiya said, turning around to look at him. "You were a little puppy. That's so adorable."

Brian kissed his lover's nose. "Very cute puppy with two litter mates. Lots of fun being a puppy."

"I bet," Kiya said, laughing softly. "Did you ever want any of your own?"

Brian grew more serious. "Yes, very much," he said. "All wolves love puppies, Kiya." He felt a pang of regret about the loss and sighed. "But I thought it was more important to do the work I am doing."

"What work?" Kiya asked, tilting his head. "School, you mean? Or something else?"

Brian's fingers slid through Kiya's hair again. "I don't know how much you know about wolves, but we have been hunted to near extinction. And there are fewer and fewer places for us to live."

"Oh." Kiya frowned, thinking about Hunter's plan to kill Brian. "Where's your family now?"

"I haven't seen them in several years. They are probably in Canada or Alaska. It's safer there."

"I'm sorry," Kiya murmured, thinking that he would have hated being away from his own family for so long.

"By leaving, they think I have abandoned them, become more human than wolf," Brian said sadly. "But I am doing it to find out what I can do to ensure my pack, my family, has a future. That's why I am in environmental studies." Brian was counting on his research with wolves to help him solve the population problem with his own kind. In some ways, it was a long shot. Brian couldn't be sure science would give him an answer to the Faewolf problem. Yet, he had gambled his own happiness that it would.

"Oh, it's good that you're trying to do something then," Kiya said, nodding as he smiled up at him. "You're so awesome."

"They don't see it that way at all," Brian explained. It hurt to be scorned by his own kind. He leaned over and kissed Kiya again, the touch easing the ache inside.

Kiya didn't let the kiss last too long, because his mouth still tasted bad. "Maybe one day they will. After you give them puppies!" he said, grinning.

Brian thought Kiya's eagerness about puppies was very cute. Unfortunately, puppies didn't seem likely in Brian's immediate future, if ever. He was in love, not just with a human, but a man.

"I'll help you with your work sometime," Kiya went on to say, pushing Brian's hair back from his forehead. "If you want me to."

Brian couldn't begin to count the ways he wanted Kiya and it made him feel even better that Kiya seemed to feel it, too. "I would really like that," he whispered.

"Great. You'll have to tell me a little more about what you do another time," Kiya said, kissing Brian's cheek.

They were quiet for a few minutes, Brian just enjoying the warmth of Kiya in his arms. He saw that it was light outside. And he was hungry. He didn't need as much sleep as humans but he usually needed a lot more food. "You want to go back to sleep or are you hungry?" he asked.

"I'm hungry, yeah," Kiya answered, remembering how empty his stomach was after what happened earlier.

Brian knew restaurants probably wouldn't serve raw meat, but he could order a steak rare. "I don't think this place has room service. I could go get something or we could eat out at a diner somewhere."

"Going out sounds good to me," Kiya agreed. He went to his bag and pulled out the last clean shirt he had, deciding that he'd have to wear Brian's sweatpants with it. "Kind of don't want to go back to school tomorrow," he said as he dressed.

Brian groaned, pulling on his own clothes. They had Biology class at nine in the morning. "I have to," he said, even though he agreed. "It's my job."

"You could call in sick," Kiya suggested after he pulled his shirt on and then went about fixing his hair.

"I have forty-seven students, including you, who are my responsibility. And that doesn't even count the classes where I am the student." Brian sighed and sat down to put shoes on. It was more than a career choice for him, of course. If he lost his position as a graduate student, he wouldn't have access to the training and other resources available to human scientists.

"I know," Kiya said from where he stood, brushing out his hair. Once he was finished, he turned and started to braid it, using a hair band to hold it together at the end.

Kiya's hair looked good that way, but it still made Brian's fingers itch to unwrap it. He smiled and held out his hand. "My truck keys?"

"Here," Kiya said, picking the keys off the dresser and handing them over to Brian.

Brian tossed them up and caught them, smirking. "So I assume my truck is still in one piece?"

"Of course it is," Kiya said with a smile, sitting down to pull his shoes on. "I'm an excellent driver."

"Good," Brian said, still smiling at him.

Kiya went though his bag and pulled out a pair of sunglasses, but didn't put them on. "Alright, ready," he said, looking at himself in the mirror one more time.

"Come on, beautiful," Brian teased, holding out his hand. "It's not good to keep the wolf hungry."

"What, you might eat me?" Kiya asked, taking Brian's hand and letting him lead him outside.

Brian scoffed, the suggestion arousing other hungers, but he kept focused on the task at hand and led the way outside. He spotted the beat-up white Ford truck in the parking lot and moved to it. Kiya pushed the sunglasses on once they stepped outside, walking alongside Brian.

∽

Once in the truck, Brian had to re-adjust his seat and the mirrors, then drove them to a restaurant he knew he liked.

"Hope they serve steak this early in the day," Kiya said, knowing that was probably what Brian was craving.

"It's practically all I eat," Brian admitted. They certainly had no trouble getting a table. Brian ordered coffee immediately.

"Coffee for me, too," Kiya told the waitress, smiling at her and then looking over the menu.

Brian didn't even look at the menu, asking immediately for two of the largest steaks they had served as rare as possible. The waitress made a face but wrote it down.

Kiya asked for a more simple breakfast of eggs and toast, smiling at the woman's expression when Brian told her what he wanted. She looked relieved by Kiya's order and went to turn it in.

Brian noticed her reaction. "She would really be shocked it she knew what I preferred." He waggled his eyebrows to make it a joke within a joke as he looked intensely at Kiya.

Kiya laughed softly and then blushed when he thought about it more and got the implication. They got their coffee and the waitress scurried away again. Brian drank his black, not waiting for it to cool before taking his first sip. Kiya winced, pouring a lot of cream and sugar into his coffee. "Didn't that hurt?" he asked.

Brian arched an eyebrow. "Did what hurt?" The last couple days had had more physical pain than he'd endured in a long time. But it was also balanced by his growing closeness with Kiya.

"Never mind," Kiya snickered, taking a sip of his coffee. They sat watching the traffic and listening to the clinking of dishes for a while. Brian finished his first cup of coffee just as their meals came.

"Did you want steak sauce with that?" the waitress asked, as she set two plates in front of him.

"No, thanks, but more coffee would be good," Brian answered.

"He likes coffee," Kiya said, chuckling as he shook his head.

Brian gulped more of the scalding liquid and began cutting into the meat. It was still too well done, but at least it bled when he cut it.

Kiya started on his food at the same time, glancing up at Brian as he chewed. He wasn't bothered by what Brian liked to eat, because now he knew why he did. Now it just seemed right.

Brian had gone through the first steak pretty quickly and was slowing down a bit for the second. "We also have to decide what to do about Ted."

Kiya frowned at the mere mention of Ted, glancing up at Brian again. "What can we do?"

Brian didn't like bringing it up either. "Depends on how he reacts now, doesn't it? He tried to kill me. Probably thinks I am dead. If he comes after you again, I won't let him walk away this time."

Kiya nodded. "But then again, how does he know those guys wouldn't have killed me?" he asked. "That's what I don't get about him."

"They would have killed you," Brian said, anger making his voice almost a growl.

"Yeah, and Ted didn't care. He wants me so bad, but wouldn't care if someone was going to kill me," Kiya murmured. "He was even going to kill me."

Brian reached across the table, fingers curling around Kiya's hand. "I won't let him. If he's smart, he has run. If not, then I will take him out."

"I should've let you kill him," Kiya said quietly, looking down at his food.

"You did what you thought was right," Brian assured him, squeezing his hand. "Wolves have different rules about these things than people."

Kiya nodded, taking a small bite out of his toast. He wasn't feeling so hungry anymore.

Brian didn't like upsetting Kiya but he knew they needed to figure out what to do next. "So I don't think the restraining order will help since I don't intend to call the police if he shows up again."

"So forget that," Kiya said, setting down the bread and sitting back in his seat. "But he does need to go to jail."

"Those hunters found out about me because of him," Brian explained. "If Ted tells people that he shot me and I am still alive, it will cause even more problems." There were things Hunter had said that worried Brian, too. Hunter's knowledge of Faewolves had surprised Brian and meant that there were other humans who not only knew about them but were willing to kill Faewolves.

"I know," Kiya said. "I know all of that." He felt a wave of guilt over the idea that he had put Brian in so much danger.

Brian's thumb caressed Kiya's knuckles. "So, we see out this quarter, if we can. And find out what happened to Ted after he left my place. I don't know how you feel about staying with me instead of going back to your dorm."

Kiya sighed and nodded. "I want to stay with you. but I can't just leave the dorms now, can I?"

"Why not?" Brian asked, releasing Kiya's hand so he could cut more of his steak.

"I kind of paid for it," Kiya said with a shrug, poking at the rest of his eggs. "I'll just move some of my stuff over to your place."

Brian smiled, chewing another large piece of meat. "Good," he answered around it, then swallowed. "When the quarter is over, you will be leaving until the end of September?"

"Usually," Kiya said cautiously, picking up his coffee. "But now I've got a reason to stick around. My mom might be mad, though. So, I'm thinking you should just come with me."

"To South Dakota, to meet your folks?" Brian asked, the corners of his mouth twisting up at that. Even knowing what he was, Kiya wanted him around his family.

"Yep," Kiya replied after he took a sip, smiling at Brian. "I think they'll like you."

"Your wolf boyfriend?" Brian teased. "Where will I sleep?"

"With me?" Kiya asked, grinning now. "My ate might want you in another room, though."

"Ate?" Brian asked, not imagining most people would want their son's boyfriend in the house at all.

"Dad," Kiya explained, forgetting, as usual, that most people didn't know what it meant.

"And he isn't going to be angry that you brought home a man, let alone an older one?" Brian asked. Being a wolf wasn't the only problem he expected.

"Well, hmm ... I don't know, actually," Kiya said, looking thoughtful for a moment. "He won't kill you, though."

Brian has finished the second steak and had to resist the urge to lick the plate. People generally didn't like that. He finished off the cup of coffee and signaled the waitress for another. "How would I hide what I am?" he asked, amazed that he was seriously considering this. Was he? Crazy? Considering this? He sighed. He knew he was not going to be able to resist Kiya.

"You're not allowed to tell anyone, right?" Kiya asked, thinking that over. "My grandparents would love to know."

"No, we don't tell anyone," Brian confirmed, starting on his third cup. "I think the reasons are pretty clear. It puts us all in danger if someone knows. I won't risk my clan."

Kiya nodded understanding. "Well, it won't be so hard to hide. You change when you're sleeping so you'll sleep in my bedroom for most of the time and when you need to go and run, that's fine, too."

"There are places to run were I won't be noticed?" Brian asked. He didn't like the idea of not being in the same room with Kiya. But in the same house was better than different parts of the country.

"My favorite forest," Kiya told him, smiling again.

"You'll show me all your favorite places?" Brian asked, returning the smile.

"Every single one of them. So you'll really do it?" Kiya asked softly.

"Maybe. For a visit," Brian nodded. "If they don't mind. But I can't stay all summer, I have to spend part of the summer in Yellowstone for my research project." It was a pilot project that he hoped would lead to more advanced research into wolf genetics. Yet, it meant spending a month in the wildlife preserve at Yellowstone. Brian didn't want to be away from Kiya that long. He smiled and cocked his head. "Maybe you could come with me there."

Kiya was already thinking of that. "I'd love that. Hopefully I won't get in your way and distract you too much."

"Thinking about you all summer would be distracting as it is," Brian insisted. "But having you with me is what I want."

"Great, now I can't wait. This will be the best summer ever," Kiya said, sounding excited.

❧

Kiya rested his forehead against the window of the shuttle bus, looking out at the passing scenery, at the trees that he used to hike in. He was used to the bus by then, having started to take it in favor of walking through the woods, which was almost torture now. Even though Brian was fine, and everything was good between the two of them, Kiya still couldn't set foot into the woods without thinking about what had happened there. How he thought he had lost Brian, and how he was almost killed himself. It was horrible, and as much as he loved the forest before, he hated it now and never wanted to be alone in there.

He sat up when the bus reached the stop for the Coffee House, getting up and making his way off. He trudged up the hill to the LGBT Center, headed inside and pulled his sunglasses off so he could look around for Audrey and Jack.

The Wednesday night Queer Coffee House was smaller than usual the week before finals, with only about a dozen people in the room. Most students were too busy with last minute papers or studying for exams. But it was also the last gathering before the end of the school year, so Kiya wanted to spend time with his friends. Audrey had already grabbed their favorite spots on the sofas and Jack was getting something off the snack table. Audrey waved at Kiya.

Kiya smiled when he spotted Audrey, getting his usual cup of coffee before he headed over to take the seat next to her, leaning over to kiss her cheek. "Hey, you."

She set her own drink down and gave him a hug. "Well, don't you look good," she teased.

Kiya's smile widened, and he ran a hand through his hair. "I haven't done anything new," he told her. He was happy, though. Maybe that had something to do with it.

Jack took a seat in the chair. "But have you been doing someone new?" he teased.

Kiya blushed. "How'd you know?" he asked.

"Oh, it's not like you haven't hinted. Even with all the shit with Ted and him disappearing, you have been incredibly bouncy," Audrey insisted.

Jack grinned, nodding emphatically. "You aren't going to leave us hanging all summer about this are you?"

It was the end of the school year, and Brian was still Kiya's teacher, but he wouldn't be once grades were turned in within the next couple of weeks, so Kiya thought he could tell them. And it wasn't like they'd tell anyone else. "Well, no, I'm not that mean," Kiya answered, smiling and taking a sip of his coffee. His voice lowered, and he beckoned them closer. "I trust you guys."

Both of them leaned closer grinning. "Why so secretive?" Jack whispered.

"You both remember Brian right?" Kiya asked first, looking at them.

"The Teaching Assistant?" Audrey asked, sounding scandalized, but grinning too.

"Yeah," Kiya said, smiling. He sounded proud when he continued, "I got him."

"You're screwing your T.A.?" Jack asked, looking worried.

"He won't be my T.A. next semester," Kiya replied smugly.

"Kiya, but you are sleeping with him now, right?" Jack continued. "You'll get the man fired."

Which was why Kiya didn't want anyone to know about their relationship, but he knew that Jack and Audrey would keep it to themselves. Audrey was looking at Kiya with a strange expression. "It's more than sex, isn't it?" she whispered.

Kiya blushed harder, looking down for a moment before he looked up at them again. "It's definitely more than sex," he replied softly.

Audrey beamed, eyes sparkling. "You're in love, Kiya?"

"I know it's only been a short while, but yeah, I think I am," Kiya admitted, having realized earlier that that was probably the only way to explain how he felt.

"Well, you better tell us about him," Jack said. Kiya could tell that he was still worried, especially after what had happened with Ted.

"Where to start," Kiya said, sitting back with a sigh. "There's probably millions of things I like about him. Besides being perfect in bed, he's caring, protective, rough when I want him to be," Audrey blushed and Jack nodded understandingly. "So yeah, I'm really happy with him," Kiya sighed. "You guys know to keep it to yourselves."

"I can imagine," Jack said, shaking his head but smiling. "I just hope he's a lot better than Ted. The police haven't found him yet, have they?"

Kiya's face fell and he shook his head, obviously not liking the change in subject. "No, not yet." Brian and the police had searched for Ted, and there was an outstanding warrant for the man's arrest for attempted rape and assault. But he had disappeared-no longer to be found at his apartment or taking classes. He was just gone, and no one knew where.

"Hope the scumbag fell in the ocean and drowned," Jack snarled. He was angry and still didn't even know about Ted shooting Brian.

Audrey patted Kiya's arm reassuringly. "So you going home for the summer?"

Kiya hoped Ted was gone forever, too. "Yeah, of course," he replied, smiling brightly again. "I miss home. And he's coming with me, which makes it even better."

"Your new boyfriend is going to meet your family?" Audrey asked. "Wow, it sounds serious!"

"It is! I probably wouldn't be able to go a whole summer without him," Kiya admitted, blushing again.

They spent the rest of the time talking about their summer plans and letting Kiya brag about Brian. He told them about Jacob and how he had liked the guy but not near as much as Brian. And even how Kiya planned to accompany Brian on his wolf research project in Yellowstone. They were just saying their good-byes, with Audrey hugging him, when he glanced up and saw that Brian was standing in the doorway of the center.

Kiya grinned when he saw him, pulling back from the hug and kissing Audrey on the cheek. "See you guys," he said, turning to hug Jack goodbye next, knowing that he wouldn't see them for a while.

Jack hugged him but arched an eyebrow when he saw where Kiya had looked. "Hot," he said, checking Brian out.

"Isn't he?" Kiya laughed happily. He took a step back and waved at them both, glancing back at Brian. "Well, I've gotta go. I'll call you both, 'kay? Keep in touch."

Audrey and Jack both laughed, watching as he went to Brian, who immediately reached for Kiya's hand despite his supposed rule about not doing so on campus. Kiya was pleased, squeezing

Brian's hand as they walked out.

Brian had parked his truck nearby-ironically, in the same spot Jacob had been parked in that night over a month before. He grinned at his lover. "How'd it go?"

"Good!" Kiya replied, smiling up at him. "Really good. How was your day?"

"Lots of work," Brian admitted. "Last sections before the test means lots of review." Kiya's last section would be Friday, and there was a paper due. "I am going to be grading papers all weekend."

"I finished that paper, basically," Kiya said, feeling a lot less stressed because of it. "Just reading it over and fixing a few things."

"Good," Brian said encouragingly as they got into the truck. "Am I taking you back to your apartment or home with me?" he asked as he buckled his seat belt.

"Home with you?" Kiya asked. "I don't want to distract you, though."

Brian hadn't yet started the truck, so he reached over, hand sliding up Kiya's thigh. "Oh, but I want you to distract me," he teased, smirking.

Of course Kiya wouldn't stop him. "But how will you finish your work?"

"After you fall asleep," Brian assured him and leaned over. "Kiss me."

"Okay," Kiya murmured, leaning over to press his lips against Brian's, unable to resist an opportunity to receive kisses.

They sat in the truck, kissing for several minutes, Brian's hand cupping Kiya's face. He swore he would never get enough of Kiya.

Chapter Twenty-One

Kiya was finally done with his first year of college. He had finished all his exams. He stood outside his apartment, backpack slung over his shoulder, and took a deep breath. Kiya thought he had done well on the Native Law class exam. He was pretty sure he had aced the Biology one, of course. And his other classes had gone well too. Now he was waiting for Brian to pick him up so they could go celebrate. With his finals over, he was looking forward to some serious alone time with Brian.

Brian had prepared a special surprise for Kiya. He had noticed that his lover had been avoiding going into the forest since the attack. Whenever Brian asked him to go for a walk or a run, Kiya made excuses, saying he was too tired or had homework to do. Brian worried that Kiya had lost something important. He knew Kiya had always loved the outdoors, especially the forest. So, Brian planned a picnic. Now he pulled up in his truck, looking for Kiya.

Kiya spotted him after a moment and smiled, heading over and pulling open the passenger's door, getting inside. "Hey," he said, leaning over to give Brian a quick kiss.

Brian wanted a lot more than a quick kiss, but he didn't push it. It was still daylight and Kiya didn't stop being his student until Brian turned in final grades. He smiled at him and gave Kiya's thigh a gentle squeeze. "Ready to celebrate?"

"Yes, yes, of course," Kiya replied, smirking and reaching to pull on his seatbelt. "Are you going to tell me what we're going to do?"

"No," Brian said with a smirk, driving off campus and up Empire Grade toward his cabin.

Kiya pouted slightly, wanting to know what on earth Brian had in mind.

Brian changed the topic, getting Kiya to talk about the last test and tell how well he did. It always made Kiya happy to tell all the things he knew he'd aced. Brian enjoyed how smart his lover was and liked to encourage him.

"So, that Biology test wasn't as hard as I thought it would be," Kiya said smugly, sinking down in his seat as he looked out the window.

"Oh, you think you did that well, do you?" Brian teased back. He hadn't finished grading papers and refused to tell Kiya if he had gotten to his yet.

"Yeah, I studied enough. I got at least an A," Kiya said proudly, glancing over at him. "So how did I do on the paper?"

"I suppose you will have to wait to find out when grades are posted," Brian said, rolling his eyes. They had made it to the gravel road that led to his cabin and he pulled into the space beside it.

"Or you could just tell me," Kiya said. "Because you're my boyfriend, and well, I want to know."

"The only special treatment you are getting has nothing to do with the class, though it may involve biology," Brian teased as he got out of the truck.

Kiya laughed, opening the door to get out as well. "That's more anatomy than biology," he said.

Brian pulled Kiya into his arms, holding him close as nipped lovingly at his chin and nose. "It's magic," he whispered.

"Magic," Kiya repeated, tilting his head up to kiss Brian's lips, smiling.

"Let's drop your bag in the cabin and pick up our supplies," Brian said.

"Supplies?" Kiya asked, turning to walk into Brian's home.

"I am taking you somewhere special to celebrate. Wear your hiking shoes," Brian warned. He had a backpack all ready with food, a couple of sleeping bags and other things they would need.

Kiya frowned slightly, looking up at Brian. He had already told

Brian that he didn't want to go into the woods to hike or do anything like that again. It was too much. "Why would I need those boots?"

"Because we are going to a place I want to show you," Brian repeated.

"What place, Brian?" Kiya asked slowly, his heart beginning to pound harder as he searched Brian's face for answers.

Brian reached to cup Kiya's face with both hands, nuzzling his cheek and then looking him in the eyes. "Do you trust me?"

"Yes, but I don't want to go there, I told you already," Kiya insisted, biting his lip and trying to shake his head, which was held firmly between Brian's hands.

"I'm a wolf, Kiya," Brian reminded him. "And we will be spending part of the summer in the forest at Yellowstone. But even more important, you love the woods. I don't want you to lose that."

"But," Kiya bit his lip harder, thinking about the last time he had been in the woods. The blood, the fury and the terror. He closed his eyes and shook his head, making an uncomfortable sound.

Brian sighed, feeling Kiya's heartbeat speed up and smelling his fear. "I won't let him take it away from us," he whispered, a hint of forcefulness in his voice. "Come with me, leannan."

Kiya really didn't want to go, but he finally gave a tiny nod, looking down.

Brian held him for another minute, kissing the top of his head and rubbing his cheek against Kiya's hair. Then he stepped back and handed Kiya the hiking shoes. Kiya took them and sat down on the bed with a small huff, bending over to untie his sneakers and kick them off, pushing his feet in the boots. Brian hefted the backpack and settled the straps over his shoulders.

When he was done, Kiya pulled his hair back into a ponytail and stood up, reaching for Brian's hand. He figured he should just get it over with, but he was also wishing he could convince Brian to give up on it. The determination in Brian's eyes told him that arguing to stay would be useless.

Brian took Kiya's hand, pulling it against his chest. "I promise to protect you," he reminded him.

Kiya knew Brian would do exactly that. "I know," he said softly, looking up at him again. "I just ... I'm scared."

"I understand," Brian answered, gently pulling Kiya out the door.

Kiya just sighed and let Brian lead him out, feeling his breathing speed up once again.

Brian deliberately took a different path than the one they had taken that day, still holding Kiya's hand, feeling that pulse quick against his fingers. Brian had to practically pull Kiya, since he most definitely wasn't willing. He kept his head down most of the way, idly biting down on the tip of his thumb nervously. His focus was on the ground but the smell of fear was coming off of him in waves.

Brian felt bad about upsetting Kiya but he also felt strongly that they needed to get past this, to find a way to reclaim what they had lost that day. He took them further into the woods than before, looking for a particularly beautiful spot he knew about from exploring. It was a large redwood circle on a hill. They had to climb a bit to get to it, but he knew Kiya would find it beautiful.

Kiya began shaking uncontrollably. He was so scared, he clung to Brian as if something-or someone-would jump out at them any moment. He looked up when they started up a hill, struggling to take deep breaths to keep himself calm.

Brian didn't know what to say, so he didn't speak, arm wrapped around his lover, helping him as they climbed. They reached the circle and Brian turned Kiya to face him, rubbing his face against Kiya's.

Kiya slid his arms around Brian's neck and held on tightly, burying his face in Brian's neck. His legs felt weak and it took every bit of trust within him not to bolt. "We're okay?" he whispered after a moment.

"Yes, we're fine and together," Brian assured him. "Now look around, see where you are.'"

Kiya waited another moment before he slowly turned around, keeping his back pressed firmly against Brian's chest as he opened his eyes. They could probably barely touch hands if the two of them stood and on either side of one of the majestic redwoods. And the ancient trees towered above them, probably at least ten stories in the air. He and Brian stood in the middle of a ring of these giants. The glen had a hushed atmosphere, the sun trickling down from the canopy to give a dappled effect. The trees were larger than on most other parts of the campus. There weren't any words that he could think of to describe what he saw. "Wow, it's beautiful," Kiya whispered, not wanting to break the silence as he reached for Brian's hands to grip them.

Brian kissed the side of Kiya's head, sliding arms around his waist. "Yes," he whispered.

"Thank you," Kiya sighed, resting his head back against Brian's shoulder. He was still scared, but Brian was obviously trying to make him remember the real beauty of the forest, something Kiya had nearly forgotten.

"I got food from your favorite deli," Brian told him. "And chocolate cake for dessert."

"So, you wanted to take me out on a date in the woods," Kiya said, slowly beginning to grin. He turned around in Brian's arms again. "I'll forgive you because you're a wolf."

"You'll forgive me because I adore you," Brian teased back, leaning in to kiss and nip again.

Kiya ran the tip of his tongue over Brian's bottom lip, pulling back before the kiss deepened any further. "You adore me?" he asked.

Brian kissed him, tongues sliding together as he held him tight, breathing in the intoxicating combination of Kiya's scent and the woods. Then he pulled back enough to whisper against his lips. "Yes, can't you tell?"

Kiya wasn't sure of exactly what Brian meant, though. To him there were a lot of meanings to the word adore. "I... adore you, too," he said softly.

Brian grinned and slid the backpack down to the ground, unfastening the sleeping bags tied to the bottom. "We can sit on these now and sleep in them later," he explained. Actually, he didn't really need them, but he knew Kiya would get cold without them.

"Are you going to change?" Kiya asked, kneeling down on the ground to help him.

They zipped the two bags together into one big one and then laid it out. "Whenever you want me to," Brian told him, pulling out the bag from the deli, a couple of sodas, and a bottle of wine for later.

"If it gets cold," Kiya said, getting onto the sleeping bags and spreading out his legs with a sigh. His panic was beginning to subside a little as he drank in the beauty of the forest around him.

"Oh, I think I will keep you warm enough," Brian said with a smirk, holding out a paper wrapped sandwich to Kiya.

Kiya smiled and patted the spot next to him, needing Brian closer. "Thank you," he said, accepting the sandwich and going about unwrapping it. Brian had gotten himself a meatball sandwich, and was happily devouring it, scooting closer to Kiya as he did. Kiya started on his ham and cheese sandwich as well, reaching for one of the sodas and then looking over at Brian. "I never realized that you do eat like an animal," he teased, taking another bite.

Brian arched an eyebrow. "Is that a bad thing?" he asked, curious. Humans were very confusing about such things. Some comparisons to animals were compliments while others were insults. Brian couldn't really follow the logic of it most of the time.

"No, just an observation," Kiya said, reaching over to wipe a bit of sauce away with his thumb. He licked it off and then continued to eat, opening his soda. "It's cute."

Brian smirked. He had finished his sandwich and Kiya was

only halfway through his own. Popping the seal on his soda, he drank half the can in one long series of gulps.

Kiya just watched him, not even trying to keep up with him. He sipped at his soda and munched on the sandwich, resting his head on Brian's shoulder after a while.

It felt comfortable, and Brian was happy that Kiya seemed to be relaxing. The sky was darkening to orange, the sun slowly setting as Brian sat holding him.

"Can't believe you got me out here," Kiya mumbled after he finished the sandwich, crumbling the wrapper.

Brian stuffed all the papers down into the pack and then lay back on the blanket, smiling up at Kiya. His lover was beautiful and framed against the trees and sunset, he looked even more startling than usual. "Come here," he whispered.

Kiya turned and crawled over to Brian, straddling his hips and sitting down. The position he was in was similar to the one they were in the last time they were in the woods, but Kiya wasn't going to stop and think on that. He wanted to create new memories. "Brian?"

Brian reached his hands up, cupping Kiya's face. "Yes, *leannan?*"

"I-I love you," Kiya said quietly, needing to admit it, needing to have the words spoken out loud after hearing them only in his heart.

Brian smiled, one thumb caressing along Kiya's jaw. "I know. I can see it in the way you touch me, smell it on your skin, *leannan,*" he answered.

Kiya didn't even know it was possible to be that obvious, but then again, Brian did notice more than anyone he had ever known. "And you love me," he whispered, leaning down closer to nudge Brian's nose with his own.

"Very much," Brian whispered, nuzzling back. He reached back and pulled Kiya's hair tie out, so that the long dark hair fell in sheets around them. Brian ran his fingers through those long dark strands, kissing and sucking on Kiya's lips and humming happily.

Kiya didn't care that they hadn't been together for very long, only a couple months. Actually, he knew that they had been through a lot more than most couples ever had to go through already. And none of that mattered when they were together. "Brian," he whispered again, his eyes closing as he kissed the man once more, his fingers sliding into Brian's hair. Kiya kept it slow, his head tilting to deepen the kisses, trying to show Brian how much he loved him, even though it was apparently more than obvious to him already.

Brian had never felt happier in his life. Kiya was his. They could love and protect each other; they were their own pack. He belonged again. His chest made a rumbling noise of contentment as he devoured Kiya's mouth. Brian slid his hands down his lover's back and gripped the hem of Kiya's shirt, then pulled up, drawing it over his head.

Kiya had to pull his lips away so that he could pull the shirt off completely, moving in to kiss him again the moment the shirt was gone. Kiya was suddenly sure that they were going to do more than have a picnic, kissing Brian harder as he started to move against him.

Brian growled as his fingers slid over Kiya's warm smooth skin, mapping his spine and the muscles of the his back. Kiya was thrusting against him now, hardening in his jeans.

Kiya knew that Brian probably wanted to make the experience as romantic as possible, and maybe moving so fast was not what he had in mind, but Kiya couldn't help it. He wanted Brian with a need that made him feel almost feverish.

Brian was very aroused as well, his large cock making his own denims bulge and rubbing against Kiya's through the layers of fabric. He moved his hands between them, working at the button and zipper of Kiya's jeans.

Kiya couldn't keep moving against him if he wanted to get his clothes off. So he leaned back again, reaching to help Brian unzip his own jeans. And Brian nearly broke the zipper on Kiya's in his eagerness to get them off, pushing the fabric down those slim hips. Kiya shoved his underwear down with them as well, not even getting up so that the jeans could be pushed all the way down and off. The air on his cock made him hiss softly, his hips lifting up. "Your turn," he whispered.

"Yes," Brian agreed, rolling so that Kiya was on his back now and then kneeling up to pull off his own shirt first.

Kiya looked up at him with a smile, running his hands over Brian's chest when his lover finally pulled his own shirt off.

Brian gasped a little as Kiya's fingers slid over his nipples, which quickly pebbled. Brian pushed his own jeans down then, and kicked them off. He was kneeling between his lover's legs, both of them wonderfully naked. "I want to make love to you all night," he told him.

"Make love to me," Kiya said softly, realizing that it was probably the first time he had ever used those words. Kiya had had sex, but never made love before. And he meant it now, meant it with all of his heart.

Brian leaned forward, kneeling over Kiya to kiss again. His breath caught at the feeling of their bodies pressed together while Kiya gasped softly and lifted his hips up a little more, wrapping his legs around Brian's waist. Brian kissed and licked, even nipping at Kiya's chin and neck. "I love the way you taste," Brian whispered and then drew his tongue up Kiya's neck to his ear, nibbling there, too.

"Mm, more," Kiya hummed, his eyes closing. He forgot where he was, focusing on nothing but Brian above him. Brian was giving Kiya exactly what he had wanted for the longest time. He had someone who truly saw him and loved him. Someone who knew what he needed even when Kiya himself didn't.

Brian rocked against his lover, their cocks sliding together, as he sucked and bit harder on Kiya's neck, making little growling noises while his body shivered with desire and the intensity of his emotions.

Kiya wrapped his arms around Brian and hugged him tightly, his moans increasing in volume as Brian bit down. "Harder," he whimpered, his legs tightening while Brian left a series of marks down Kiya's throat, even licking and nipping down his chest. Kiya moaned. "Yes, yes," he gasped, his hands sliding back into Brian's hair to grip it again.

When he reached Kiya's nipples, Brian sucked hard, nipping at them until they were swelling and red. He loved the taste, the way Kiya's skin felt against his tongue, under his hands, against his body. Kiya's scent and taste filled him, making Brian's body hum with energy.

"Fuck," Kiya whimpered, his chest arching as he panted, his cock harder than ever and his body trembling with need. "Brian, please," he mumbled, lifting his hips up for more when Brian nuzzled the soft skin of Kiya's belly. "Suck me."

Brian had moved down far enough to press his face into the soft curls around Kiya's prick, rubbing his cheek against the warm shaft. "Yes, going to taste all of you," he responded, his voice deep with desire.

"Now," Kiya insisted, rubbing his cock against Brian's cheek more. Brian was so hot when he was like this, Kiya almost couldn't handle it.

Brian pressed the flat of his tongue against his lover's cock, lapping up the shaft, then wrapping one hand around the base as he angled the crown to him, swirling around the soft flesh. Kiya moaned loudly, his head falling back onto the sleeping bag, trying to thrust up into Brian's mouth as Brian happily obliged him, sucking him into his mouth. Kiya bit down on his lip, reaching to grip Brian's hair as he started to slowly move in and out of his mouth, his legs opening wider. Brian loved doing this, especially for Kiya. He sucked and hummed around the thick flesh, his other hand moving to softly cup and fondle Kiya's balls.

It wasn't much longer before Kiya was pulling at Brian's hair, wanting and needing more before he came. "Please," he begged.

Brian lifted his head, letting Kiya's cock slip from his mouth. "I want you," he whispered.

"Want you, too," Kiya replied softly, lifting his hips again.

"Make love to me."

Brian pressed a kiss to Kiya's cock and then scooted back, lifting Kiya's legs. "Hold yourself and spread for me," he told him.

Kiya reached to grip his legs, opening them wide for Brian, knowing and wanting what was going to happen next.

Brian admired the sight, then lowered his face, lapping at Kiya's balls and then moving toward that puckered hole. Kiya jumped at the first touch of his tongue there, breathing in sharply. The scent and smell was so good that Brian moaned, lapping over and over again.

Kiya groaned and started to press himself down onto Brian's tongue, his hips rocking for more and more. He knew he had to get prepared first, but he sometimes just wanted to get to the sex, even though this was good, too. It felt like a lot of teasing, and it was only getting him more worked up.

Brian pushed his tongue into his lover's hole, loving the noises Kiya made as he shuddered and clenched around the tongue, trying to fuck himself on it. Brian lost himself in the taste and pleasure of doing this to Kiya, making growling sounds deep in his throat as he did.

After a while, Kiya thought he would come, so he started to pull away to make sure that didn't happen just yet. "Please, more, want you," Kiya encouraged.

Brian reached for the bottle of lube he had put in the side pocket of his pack. He coated his fingers and pressed inside. Brian enjoyed the feeling of Kiya's body shuddering and relaxing as he pressed two and then three fingers inside.

"I'm ready," Kiya gasped, lifting his legs up higher, resting them on Brian's shoulders. He looked up, taking a deep breath, relaxing himself.

They'd stopped using condoms since Kiya had found out diseases weren't a risk with Brian, so Brian didn't have to find one, using more of the lube to slick his own cock and then positioning himself. He growled as he pressed the thick head against that slick hole. Brian looked down at Kiya, his adoration showing in his expression, as he pushed into the young man, groaning at the feeling of that tight ring giving way around the thick knob of his prick.

Kiya tried to keep his eyes open, biting down on his lip as Brian slowly pushed inside. Even with all the stretching it still ached, but it was more pleasant than painful. Kiya's eyes finally slid shut and he moaned softly, reaching to grip the sleeping bag as tightly as he could.

Brian's cock sunk slowly into Kiya's body, and he worked his hips back and forth to ease it inside, Kiya's warmth tight around him. Brian held both of Kiya's legs, kneading the thigh muscles as he pressed forward. Kiya was nearly bent in half by the time Brian was completely inside. Brian shuddered, nearly losing control over his shape with the intensity of the feelings, his cock buried in and balls against the other man's ass.

Kiya felt full, almost too full, and yet it was all good, perfect even. "Brian," he whispered, blinking open his eyes to look up at him.

Brian could no longer speak in words, eyes gone golden as his magic flared. He let Kiya see it, see how much the young man affected him.

It still surprised Kiya when Brian's eyes would change, even though it happened almost every time they had sex now. Kiya thought it was amazing, that reminder of what his lover was, and now he really felt the magic spark from Brian and into him. "Beautiful," Kiya whispered.

Gasping, Brian began to move again, his cock sliding partially out. He felt Kiya's body pulsing around him. He felt the shudder of their combined magic, as well.

Kiya breathed in sharply when Brian started to pull back, knowing that Brian was going slow to make sure he adjusted, but really, he didn't want Brian to have to be slow. "I'm okay," he whispered, lifting his hips. Brian grinned at that, looking almost feral in the near dark, as he thrust into Kiya, who cried out, his head falling back again as a shudder went through him. He loved it even more when Brian was like this. Bracing his arms on either side of Kiya, Brian began to pump in and out of his body, snarling with pleasure as he did. The snarls reminded Kiya of Saoi, and that made him moan louder, reaching to grip Brian's shoulders, his nails digging into the skin.

Brian's magic flared stronger. He could feel the Fae magic in the woods resonating with his own energy. He growled, moving faster now, delighting in the way Kiya writhed in pleasure under him.

Kiya wasn't even sure of where his feelings were coming from. All he knew was that one moment he was having the time of his life and then the next moment everything was paused. His eyes were blinked open a few seconds later when one specific thought went through his mind. "Wolf," he gasped quietly. "Change."

Brian wasn't sure he'd heard him right. "You... want me... as a wolf?"

"Please?" Kiya moaned, his grip tightening. "Please."

They had been together nearly every day for the last month, but Brian hadn't mentioned how much he had enjoyed being in true form with Kiya, not wanting to bring up that night. Now, his cock gave a powerful twitch, body shuddering and magic flaring with the memory. He looked into Kiya's eyes and saw that it really was what Kiya wanted, as well. So he let go, let the magic take him back to his true self. Already on all fours, the change kept him in the same position, as bones, muscles and fur shifted. His already swollen cock expanded inside Kiya, stretching his lover even more.

Kiya watched, never tiring of this, of watching the magic work. And he could feel the change, the shift in Brian's body and then the swelling inside of him that made him groan, his body jerking. "Oh, yes, Saoi!"

Saoi groaned, the tight circle of Kiya's flesh around his shaft already beginning to trigger that knot of flesh swelling. And Kiya's scent was so much stronger, too. Saoi nuzzled his face, licking his lover's chin and throat.

Kiya tilted his head back a little more for the wolf, whimpering when even just a slight movement made him feel the knot that grew inside of him. He hadn't said it before, but he actually liked the feeling, he liked being able to feel connected to his lover until his erection went down again.

Saoi kept licking Kiya's throat as he rocked his hips, his swollen prick rubbing inside while Kiya's arms tightened around Saoi again, hugging him closer as his fingers slid through the wolf's soft fur, gripping fistfuls of it. Saoi liked that, enjoyed having Kiya under him and wrapped around him. He nipped gently at Kiya's shoulder, growling in pleasure.

Kiya didn't realize just how close he was until that nip, which made him moan, his cock jerking between them. "Harder," he gasped, wanting to come. It didn't take much more for Kiya to start coming, groaning and arching his back slightly.

Saoi worked his hips harder, rutting as he continued to nip and lick Kiya's shoulder. He whined and growled as he came, cock spasming inside the tight channel. Saoi's growls grew louder with the intensity of Kiya's body spasming and tightening around him. Saoi's own cock was pumping his seed into his lover's body.

Kiya continued to run his fingers through the thick fur as Saoi came. Kiya opened his eyes a little. "Love you," he said, nuzzling the wolf.

Saoi pressed his muzzle against Kiya's face. His cock was still hard and swollen inside Kiya, and would be that way for a while unless he shifted. He didn't know if Kiya would want him to shift back to human form or let them remain tied together.

Kiya didn't say anything for a bit, his legs unwrapping and resting, feet on the sleeping bag and knees still bent and pressed to the wolf's furry sides, his arms still wrapped around the wolf's neck. "Roll onto our sides?" he suggested.

Saoi was heavier than Kiya, so he didn't want to rest his weight on him. And Kiya seemed to want him to stay in wolf form, clutching tightly to his fur as he shifted to his side, Kiya rolling with him, so that one of his legs straightened while the other draped around Saoi's body.

"I like this," Kiya murmured, his eyes closing when they settled down again. "I never told you, but feeling you inside me like this. Us being tied together this way-I love it. Makes me feel like we're one. I feel whole like this."

Saoi gave a rumble of contentment, licking Kiya's face again and rubbing his muzzle against his chin. It did feel good, amazingly good to be like this. He would never have imagined a human could give him this, could make him feel like a wolf again. Whole, right. Kiya loved all of him.

Kiya was quiet for a few minutes, relaxing, and enjoying their closeness. "So was this your date? Lead me into the woods, feed me, and then make love to me?" he asked softly, not complaining at all.

Saoi nodded, rumbling again and hugging his lover.

Kiya forgot that Saoi couldn't talk, which made him go quiet again, feeling drowsy enough to sleep, but not wanting to let go of the moment.

They lay there for some time, Saoi enjoying the warmth of Kiya's body where he was held tight. When he began to soften, slipping from inside Kiya, Saoi gathered his magic and shifted again.

Kiya was almost asleep when he felt it, his eyes blinking open again and turning over in Brian's arms. "Hey, you," he murmured.

Brian grinned, pulling Kiya close again. "You are amazing," he whispered.

"How amazing?" Kiya said teasingly, feeling a little colder now that Brian had changed back.

Brian huffed but didn't stop smiling. "I can't imagine most humans would even consider what we just did," he answered.

"We're not like most humans, remember?" Kiya asked, nudging Brian's nose.

"I'm not human at all," Brian pointed out.

"Which only proves my point," Kiya said with a smile, "I don't care if we're different, all that matters is that we have each other."

Brian was pretty sure that him not being human would matter, a lot, to most people. He smiled mischievously. "You sleepy?" he asked.

Kiya was, but he noticed the look. "Why?" he asked.

Kiya smelled like sex and Brian licked his lips at the idea of what the man would taste like. "I want to lick you," he said.

Kiya laughed. "I love how straight to the point you are," he said, grinning.

"Wolf," Brian said by way of explanation, and then rolled his lover onto his back again to begin lapping the come still stuck to Kiya's belly.

As Brian moved down his body, Kiya let his head fall back, a smile stretching across his lips. He was in love with the best man, or wolf, that he could ever find, and life was finally looking good again. Good and, most definitely, interesting. Kiya knew he would love every moment of the adventures yet to come.

About the Authors

D.M. Atkins is an author of both non-fiction and fiction. anthropologist, Atkins has edited several anthologies on LGBT top including *Looking Queer*, *Lesbian Sex Scandals and Bisexual Women in the 2 Century* and is the former editor of both *Locus* and *Shadows Of...* ma zines. In recent years, Atkins has been a popular fan fiction auth under a pseudonym, and has won awards for online erotic ficti Atkins lives in the Bay Area with two husbands, a girlfriend, th son, Atkins' mother, three cats and a dog.

Chris Taylor has been writing for years but this is Taylor's f original fiction novel. Taylor is a New Yorker, attending college. Alc with Atkins, Taylor has been writing fan fiction and won awards erotic fiction in online communities.

Notes from Author D. M. Atkins

Chris and I hope you have enjoyed our story. We certainly enjoyed writing it. I thought I would share with you a little bit about our process. I always enjoy reading about the thoughts and experiences behind the stories I read.

Chris and I have been writing together for two and a half years. We have spent hundreds of hours together, but we have yet to meet each other in person. Chris lives in New York and I live in California. We met in an online role playing game and found we really enjoyed writing together. Since then we have written over a dozen novels together.

We would like to thank Cecilia Tan for inviting us to send her something from our backlog of stories. Ironically, most the stories we had completed were not science fiction or fantasy, but "real world" BDSM gay romance. So we sent Cecilia a list of story ideas and she picked this as one she would like to see us complete and then helped us develop it.

We also want to thank our two volunteer editors on this book. Laurena Baum has edited every novel we have finished and was just as fantastic as always in helping us rework and then polish this one. Devin Grayson stepped in to give it another shine. Devin brought not only her skill as a writer and editor, but her knowledge of wolf behavior and body language.

The other crew who does a lot of work on all of my writing is my "long suffering" family. I am married to two amazing men. Yes, two. We are polyamorous, having lived in a triad for years. Troy and I have been together for almost twenty-three years and we have been with Lon for fifteen. These two men whole-heartedly support my writing. Troy not only provides the computer systems that I use in my work, he often does tech support for my co-authors. Lon does my laundry, refills my tea and makes sure I remember to eat. Both often contribute ideas to the stories themselves. They make it possible for me to spend most of my time telling stories.

The experience of co-authoring isn't something a lot of people try, let alone successfully manage. I have tried it with others, but my work with Chris is something that has become a central part of my life. It's a process that takes a special kind of cooperation and trust. We spend not only hours a day using "instant message" and shared files to write, to discuss plot and character, but also to share our lives. It still amazes me the way we are able to use technologies to write together in ways that would not have been possible only a few years ago.

We are often asked how it works and I thought I would share a little of that here. We have developed a style of writing which can be considered controversial-a way of using "point of view" which differs from how it is taught. We use what is called "third person limited point of view." Yet, in standard approaches, limited point of view usually means limiting to one character. In our case, it means limiting to two primary characters, one for each co-author. That means that the reader gets to know the thoughts and feelings of the two primary characters but no one else. This is particularly visible in situations where both characters are in the scene together. It can take some getting used to but we feel it creates stories that allow both authors, as well as both characters, to have a voice in the story.

Our stories are character driven. We begin by each deciding upon a character, then find a way to bring them together. Chris had already been developing a young Lakota man-reading up on the culture and language and creating a background for him. I wanted to make a "werewolf" character.

I often do a lot of research when creating new characters. I read everything I can that I think might help the story. And the more I read about wolves, the more I decided it would be more interesting to create a wolf who changed into a human, not the other way around. I also have done a great deal of reading on Celtic myths and tales of "fairy." Thus, instead of a werewolf, we have the Faewolves.

During my research on wolves, I was particularly struck, and horrified, by people who hate wolves. The character of "Hunter" is actually inspired by a real life man who hunts wolves in Alaska. I knew about ranchers who killed wolves to protect livestock, but I had never heard of people who go out of their way to actually destroy animals as beautiful as wolves out of actual hatred of them. I found people like that a sad and frightening thing, so I modeled the primary villain in this story after a real life killer.

We chose Santa Cruz because it is one of my favorite places; I know it well and could easily revisit it during the research phase of the book. I earned my undergraduate degrees in Professional Writing and Anthropology at the University of California, Santa Cruz. My partners and I were also able to day-trip there to trace the steps of the characters and take photographs to draw from during the writing. For example, readers might find it amusing to know that the llama ranch near Brian's cabin is a real place.

Kiya's background is inspired by reading both about the stories and beliefs of the Lakota people and about the people who currently live on the Pine Ridge Reservation. Lakota tales about talking wolves and ravens helped inspire the magic of this story.

I have read dozens of books on wolves and another dozen on Lakota traditions. I have included a shorter reading list here that I thought might be most interesting to readers.

An important theme in this story is that of what is usually termed "domestic violence." Kiya's boyfriend Ted is abusive, both during their relationship and then continuing to stalk him even after Kiya has broken it off. Kiya's back story includes a first boyfriend who was also abusive. Kiya is attracted to stronger more dominant men, but he has yet to learn to distinguish between one whose strength is used to love and protect versus one who will use and hurt him. We hoped to show that as part of Kiya's journey of self discovery.

We wrote back story scenes with two of Kiya's ex-boyfriends, Ricky and Ted, so that we would know as much as we could about Kiya before he met Brian. I have also written a couple short stories about Saoi's background. It's exciting that the ebook format allows us to include extras for readers. So in this book we have included the "missing scenes" with Ted. The other back story scenes will probably show up in, or with, the next books.

This is the first of what we hope will be a series of adventures with Kiya White Cloud and Brian Fenwick. They have a long way to go before they discover where their love and magic can take them. Will Kiya learn to handle the magic he can call? Will Brian discover how to save the Faewolves? What challenges will the two of them face in trying to build a life together? We hope to find out and share those stories with you.

If you would like to write us and tell us what you enjoyed or ask us questions, please feel free to do so. We love interacting with readers.

D.M. Atkins
www.dmatkins.net

Saving Wolves

In the story, Brian Fenwick's research focuses on wolves and he is very aware of the dangers affecting real wolves in our world. Wolves have been hunted to near extinction in the United States. Despite increased awareness of the importance of this species, they are still in danger, especially in the United States where, on March 6th, 2009, U.S. Interior Secretary Ken Salazar approved the Bush Administration's discredited plan to eliminate Endangered Species Act protections for wolves in Idaho and Montana-a decision that could lead to the deaths of more than 1,000 wolves.

Chris and I would like to urge readers to support organizations that fight to promote common sense wolf management, working with federal and state officials and private land-owners to ensure that science, not politics, guides decision-making about the future of these American icons.

For more information and to find out how you can help, go to: http://www.savewolves.org

Suggested Reading

On wolves:

The Company of Wolves, by Peter Steinhart (New York: Vintage Boc 1996).

Wolves: A Legend Returns to Yellowstone. Video produced by the Natio Geographic Society; produced by Bob Landis; written by Elea► Grant; a co-production of National Geographic Television ₐ Partridge Films. (Washington, D.C.: NGHT, Inc.; Burbank, (Distributed by Warner Home Video. 2007).

Wolves: Behavior, Ecology, and Conservation, edited by L. David Mech ₐ Luigi Boitani. (Chicago: University of Chicago Press. 2003).

Wolf: Legend, Enemy, Icon, by Rebecca L. Grambo; photographs Daniel J. Cox (Ontario, Canada: Firefly Books. 2005).

On Lakota beliefs:

Lakota Belief and Ritual, by James R. Walker ; edited by Raymonᴄ DeMallie and Elaine A. Jahner. (Lincoln: University of Nebraska Prᴇ Published in cooperation with the Colorado Historical Society. 19٤ 1991).

Lakota Myth, by James R. Walker; edited by Elaine A. Jahr. (Lincoln: University of Nebraska Press in cooperation with ◖ Colorado Historical Society. 1983. Second edition. Bison Boᴏ 2006).

The Lakota Way: Stories and Lessons for Living, by Joseph M. Marshall (New York: Viking Compass. 2001).

Backstory Deleted Scenes
Kiya and Ted

Kiya had never been to a party before where everyone was queer. He'd received an invitation to the campus LGBT Center's party for new students. And it wasn't even far from his apartment on campus. The wooden, cabin-like building was lit up and looked pretty nestled between the trees on the side of a hill.

Inside it looked like someone's apartment with a little living room area and kitchen area. There was a table with cheese, crackers, fruit, cookies, and cakes. Sodas and bottled water sat in an ice chest. Kiya had arrived a bit early and there were already a dozen people inside. He didn't know anyone yet, but he did hope to meet a few people. Especially since this was party full of people like him. He got a bottle of water and leaned back against a wall as he opened it, taking a sip as he looked around. Well, mostly looking at the men. It had been a while since Kiya and his last boyfriend had broken up.

The party had both women and men; some were older than him. And while he watched more came in. One guy was tall and blond, maybe a few years older than Kiya, and hot. He caught Kiya's eye and grinned, heading toward him.

Kiya smiled back and waited, tucking his hair behind one ear. "Hey," he said, when the man reached him.

"Hi, I'm Ted," the man said, stepping close and smiling down at Kiya. "You a new student?"

"Yes, I'm Kiya," he replied, looking him over slowly. "I'll assume you aren't new?"

"Third year," Ted said, leaning one hand on the wall beside Kiya. "Physics major."

"Pre-law," Kiya said, glancing at the arm that nearly trapped him in place.

"Where're you from?" Ted asked, sipping his soda. Kiya could feel Ted's gaze wander down his body and back up again to look him in the eyes. Ted's eyes were light blue. His gaze was frankly appraising and he seemed to like what he saw.

"South Dakota," Kiya told him, feeling his cheeks redden under Ted's gaze.

"You've come a long way," Ted said. "Know anyone here yet?"

"I might now," Kiya replied with a small smirk.

The man's hand moved down from the wall, fingers playing with Kiya's hair. "Well, I'd like a chance to get to know you."

"I think I'd like the chance to get to know you, too," Kiya said, reaching to touch the front of Ted's shirt.

There were other people coming and going from the party, but Ted didn't seem to notice. "So, you live on campus?"

"Yeah, you?" Kiya asked, happy that he had found someone he was interested in so quickly.

Ted smiled and shook his head. "I have my own place off campus."

"Oh, cool. I was thinking that I'd eventually get my own place around here," Kiya said with a grin. "Not until my third or fourth year though. Maybe."

"I lived on campus at first, but I like the privacy of my own apartment," Ted answered, giving Kiya an openly seductive look.

"I'm sure it's better, yeah," Kiya replied, catching the look and blushing again. "So, uh, do you have company over a lot?"

"I'd like to have company tonight." Ted grinned.

"Really," Kiya said. He didn't think that this would happen so quickly, but he wasn't about to complain. "Well ...."

Ted had moved so close that his leg was brushing against

Kiya's. "Want to go?"

"Sure," Kiya replied, feeling his heart speed up at just the thought.

Ted took his hand, leading him outside.

"Were you just looking for someone to take home tonight?" Kiya asked curiously.

"I would never have expected to find anyone as hot as you," Ted answered, leading him to his car and then, pushing Kiya back against it, brought his mouth over Kiya's, who slid his arms around Ted.

Ted pressed his body against Kiya's as he kissed him. Kiya's arms tightened around him as they kissed, pulling back after a few minutes so that he could whisper against Ted's lips, "Your place?" he asked, breathless. "Now?"

"Yes," Ted smiled and unlocked the car.

Kiya grinned as well and got inside once the door was open, "Can't wait," he said.

Ted drove them to a place on the East side of town. Kiya hadn't seen enough of Santa Cruz to know his way around. "Nice place," Kiya told him as he walked inside. "I'm sure your bedroom looks even better."

Ted didn't even wait that long; he closed the door and pushed Kiya against it, thigh pressed between his legs.

"You really aren't wasting time," Kiya gasped softly, his legs opening a little wider.

"You are so hot," Ted whispered, kissing and biting his way down Kiya's neck as he rocked his hips against him.

"Yeah," Kiya agreed, tilting his head to the side a little more for Ted. "I know."

Ted's hands were on him too, sliding down Kiya's body as he sucked on his neck and Kiya wound his arms around Ted's neck, trying to pull himself up. Pushing Kiya's shirt up, Ted's hands slid up his sides and over his chest.

"Ted," Kiya whispered, lifting his hands above his head so that Ted could pull the shirt off completely. "Come on ... bedroom?"

Ted pulled him into the other room, stripping his own shirt off, as well, and kicking off his shoes. Kiya worked to undress quickly, undoing his jeans while he kicked his shoes off. "Condoms?" he asked, just in case.

Ted pulled him against his body, his cock already hard and sliding along Kiya's skin. "You sure you want that?"

Kiya was hard too, and he nodded, looking up at him. Even though he had just met Ted, he wanted him. It could have been because he hadn't had sex in a long time. "Yeah, I'm sure."

Ted tugged Kiya over to the bed, pushing him onto his back on the mattress and climbing on top of him.

Kiya hadn't seen Ted pull one out so he asked again, "You do have one, right? If not, I've got one in my jeans pocket."

"I have some beside the bed," Ted told him, then kissed him again.

"Good," Kiya mumbled into the kiss, sliding his hands into Ted's hair and gripping it, kissing him harder.

The man began to rock his body against Kiya's, their cocks rubbing together as he did and Kiya's eyes slid shut as his thighs spread open a little wider, moving to wrap his legs around Ted's waist. Ted reached beside the bed and came back with a bottle of lube, squeezing some onto his fingers. Then he began nipping and sucking Kiya's neck again as he reached between Kiya's legs.

Kiya hissed softly when he was first touched with the cold lube, but it warmed up soon enough. It certainly felt like Ted knew what he was doing as the man rubbed his fingertips against Kiya's hole and mouthed the pebbling nipple. It was good that he knew, because this was just what Kiya needed. He moaned and arched his back for Ted, trying to push down on the finger and Ted quickly obliged him, pressing inside and groaning.

Kiya groaned along with him, lifting his hips a little for Ted. It had been a while, but it wouldn't be too hard. A second finger joined the first and Ted sucked on his nipple harder, nipping. Kiya clenched around the fingers, his hand tightening in Ted's hair. "More...."

"Yeah, you ready for me to fuck you?" Ted gasped.

"Yeah," Kiya replied, his face flushed as he fucked himself on Ted's fingers.

Ted reached for the condom then, unwrapping one and rolling it down his shaft. "Tell me you want it," he ordered.

"I want it," Kiya immediately said, opening his legs wider for him.

Ted sat back, moving Kiya's legs up on to his shoulders as he positioned himself.

Kiya reached in between them to wrap his fingers around his cock. "Fuck me."

"Hell, yes," Ted groaned and pushed inside him, not pausing but thrusting deep in one go.

Kiya couldn't help but cry out, his head falling back as he squeezed his eyes tightly shut.

"Oh, fucking hot," Ted gasped, fingers tight where they held Kiya's legs on his shoulders.

Kiya started to stroke himself even before Ted began to move, slowly adjusting to the man inside of him. Ted was watching him as he pulled back slowly and then thrust in again and Kiya groaned. He bit his lip, his fingers tightening around himself as his hand moved. "It's good...."

"Such a tight little ass you have," Ted told him, beginning to thrust harder now, the bed rocking as he fucked Kiya, who moaned and cried out with the particularly hard thrusts, one hand gripping the sheets.

"Yes," Kiya gasped.

"I'm going to fuck you all night," Ted insisted, the sounds of his body slapping against Kiya's ass loud in the room.

"Yeah, please," Kiya mumbled, already sounding incoherent.

"Yeah, stroke yourself," Ted gasped, skin wet with sweat as he slammed into Kiya. "Want to see you fucking come with my dick inside you!"

Kiya continued to stroke himself, thinking that this was the best choice he could have ever made tonight; he had needed something like this. "A little more," he gasped, his hand moving as fast as it could.

Ted was moaning and thrusting, hard. "Yes, fuck, yes!"

Kiya came quite suddenly after the thrusts sped up, his back arching up off the bed as he shuddered, tightening around Ted.

"Oh, hell, yes!' Ted shouted, bending Kiya near double as he continued to pound into him. It was probably another minute before he groaned, coming hard.

"God," Kiya whispered, small shudders continuing to go through him when Ted came, his knees pressed against his chest.

Ted didn't pull out, but leaned in, kissing Kiya with tongue and teeth while Kiya lazily kissed him back, idly thinking that his lips would be swollen after this. Eventually, Ted pulled out and fell back on the bed, tossing the condom into the trash after tying it off. He smiled.

Kiya smiled as well, shifting next to him. "That was nice," he murmured, resting his head on Ted's chest.

Ted put his arm around Kiya's shoulder. "Hope you aren't tired yet."

"No. Hope you aren't, because I want you to keep your promise," Kiya said, smirking up at him.

"Good," Ted answer, reaching down to stroke himself. "'Cause I want you to suck me."

"Oh, you're ready for more already," Kiya said, running a hand down Ted's stomach.

"I will be when you wrap those lips around my dick," Ted assured him.

"Say please?" Kiya asked, already moving down his body.

"No, that's your line," Ted quipped, hand wrapping in Kiya's hair and tugging him down.

Kiya's eyes narrowed slightly, but he went along with it, kissing the line down Ted's stomach.

Ted arched up toward Kiya's face. "Yeah, use that mouth."

Kiya kissed the spot right above his cock and then moved further down, kissing the very tip of him before he pulled him into his mouth and started to suck gently, tasting him.

"Pretty, and even prettier doing that," Ted told him.

Kiya blushed slightly and pulled his mouth off as Ted started to harden, stroking him.

"Don't stop," Ted told him. Fingers curled around the back of Kiya's head, urging him. The hand in his hair reminded him of something his first boyfriend used to do, but he refused to think about him. He pulled Ted back into his mouth and sucked, slowly taking more of him into his mouth.

"Yes, suck me," Ted gasped, stroking Kiya's hair as he did.

Kiya started to bob his head, stroking what his mouth couldn't reach. He closed his eyes and hummed softly along with his movements, knowing the vibrations would feel good.

"Good, yes," Ted told him, and Kiya could feel his body tremble with pleasure, the cock in his mouth growing even harder. Kiya enjoyed doing this now, since it was probably the only time that he ever had some kind of control during sex.

"Turn around, so I can touch your dick too," Ted told him.

Kiya turned his body and moved over Ted so that he was straddling his chest, looking back at the man before he went back to sucking. Ted's hands reached up, sliding up Kiya's thighs and then holding his ass as he leaned up enough to suck Kiya's balls. Kiya moaned around Ted's cock again, pausing for a moment to lift his hips up a little more for him and Ted pulled him closer, licking and sucking harder.

"Shit," Kiya gasped, pulling his mouth off as he moaned more loudly.

"Don't stop," Ted warned and licked along Kiya's shaft.

Kiya nodded slightly and took him into his mouth again, sucking slowly because he couldn't concentrate with the man pleasuring him at the same time. Ted licked and nibbled along Kiya's prick until he came to the slick head and swirled his tongue around it. Kiya moaned in approval and sucked harder, while Ted tongued and then sucked Kiya's cock into his mouth. Kiya stopped moving once again, a small shudder going through his body as he forced himself not to thrust into Ted's mouth. Ted didn't slow down, sucking harder and fondling Kiya's balls as he did.

Kiya pulled off again and rested his cheek on Ted's thigh, his hand still stroking him as his hips started to rock a little. Ted seemed intent on it, not seeming to mind. His fingers and mouth worked well together. After a while, Kiya's hand stopped moving and his eyes drifted shut. No one had ever sucked him off this well before. Ricky didn't do it at all, and his last boyfriend wasn't nearly as good at it as Ted was.

One of Ted's hands was wrapped around the base of Kiya's cock, squeezing and angling it better while his mouth bobbed along it. His other hand moved below Kiya's balls and pressed fingers to his perineum. Kiya's eyes rolled back as he shuddered again, reaching to grip Ted's leg gently. "Ted," he whispered, taking a deep breath to calm himself down.

Ted pulled back, making a slurping sound when he did. "What?"

"Don't stop..." Kiya whined softly.

Ted's mouth enveloped Kiya's cock again, sucking harder. His fingers slid down and began teasing Kiya's still slick hole as he did.

"Inside?" Kiya gasped, already beginning to feel his balls tense up. Two fingers slid inside Kiya and he groaned and came almost instantly, his body shuddering hard. He hoped it was okay to come in Ted's mouth. Ted didn't pull away, but swallowed him down. It was the first time anyone had done that, too. "God," Kiya whispered, biting his lip and pressing his face against Ted's skin.

Ted kept up sucking for a few more minutes, his fingers still inside Kiya and then he drew back. "You going to do me or ready to fuck again?" he asked.

Kiya didn't answer immediately, small shudders still going through him. After a moment though, he shifted and got up, lying down on top of Ted, his back to the man's chest. "That was probably the best blowjob I ever had," he murmured, purposely rubbing his ass over Ted's erection.

Ted grinned. "Good," he said, gasping as his strong hands came up to grip Kiya's hips.

Kiya rested his head against Ted's shoulder and lifted his hips up a little, positioning himself over the man's cock. "Condom," he whispered, opening his legs a little more.

Ted reached out, fumbling for a condom and then handing it to him. Kiya ripped it open with his teeth and sat up a little, reaching to roll it down Ted's cock. He lay back down and positioned himself once again.

"Yes, I want you," Ted groaned.

"Push inside," Kiya murmured, his hips rising and falling again.

Ted guided Kiya back, watching as his cock slid into Kiya, who sighed as he slowly pressed down onto Ted's cock, moving his hair so that it wasn't in the man's face.

"Oh, yes, so hot," Ted gasped, arching up into him.

Kiya moaned softly in reply, but didn't really start to move, only rocking his hips a little as Ted pressed up into him. "Move!"

Kiya was feeling lazy, and he had hoped Ted would do the work again, even from below him, but he still opened his legs wider so that his feet were pressed against the bed to give him better leverage.

Ted took the opportunity and, fingers curled around Kiya's hips, began thrusting up into him. "Oh, yeah!"

"Fuck," Kiya mumbled along with him, not sure where to put his hands at first.

"Yes, fuck, this is good," Ted exclaimed, feet digging into the bed as he slammed up into Kiya.

"It's perfect," Kiya corrected, reaching to stroke himself while one hand gripped the sheets of the bed. "God, it's perfect...."

"Hell, yes, stroke that pretty cock," Ted gasped, as he kept up the pace.

Kiya whimpered as he stroked himself, shifting up a little so that he could reach back further and touch Ted as he moved in and out of him.

"Fuck, you're hot!" Ted groaned, and Kiya could feel his muscles trembling as he got closer.

"Yeah .. come with me," Kiya started to moan, moving with him now as they both worked to reach the end.

Ted was thrusting so hard that Kiya shuddered each time. Ted's hands were the only thing that kept him from falling. Kiya squeezed himself once more and came with a loud cry, his back arching as his hips shook.

"Yes, fuck, yes!" Ted was groaning, still thrusting.

Kiya cried out with each thrust after that, still shuddering. He was beginning to get over-sensitive, but he still didn't want Ted to stop. Ted kept slamming up, only grunts escaping his throat now as he worked at it and then finally arched so hard his back was off the bed as he came. Kiya could actually feel Ted spasm inside of him, the orgasm that intense. "Mm," he whispered.

Ted still held Kiya's hips as he collapsed back down again, panting. Kiya could already feel himself throbbing, and he knew he'd be sore for days. But this was completely worth it. "Want me to move?" he asked after a few minutes.

Ted was still trying to catch his breath. He nodded though and Kiya carefully shifted off of him, settling down on the bed. He reached to take the condom off of Ted, and tied the top before he threw it away in the wastepaper basket.

Ted turned on his side, smiling at him. "You are the hottest guy I've ever met," he said.

Kiya couldn't help but smile at the compliment, looking over at him. "And have you been with a lot of guys?" he asked.

Ted shrugged, stretching. "I've had fun," he said.

❦

Kiya was at Ted's place, lying on the bed with two books in front of him, concentrating as he tapped his pen against his cheek. It was finals week of the Winter quarter and he was trying his best to study for a test he had the next day. He had his hair up and in a messy bun so that it wouldn't get in his way, dressed in a pair of Ted's sweatpants and a shirt. They had been dating for six months.

He heard the front door open and close in the front room, signaling that Ted was back. Kiya looked up for a moment, but didn't get up, looking back down at his books. He heard Ted drop his own bookbag on the table in the front room and then walk down the hall.

"Now that's what I need," Ted said from the doorway of the bedroom.

Kiya looked up with a smile. "Not now, though, I'm studying," he said.

Ted moved to the bed, hands immediately going to Kiya's ass, squeezing through the sweatpants he was wearing. "Time to take a break," he announced.

Kiya bit his lip, trying not to arch his back. "I've taken way too many breaks already," he said. "Just let me finish this chapter?"

Instead of backing off, Ted pulled Kiya's shirt up and leaned over licking up his spine.

"Ted," Kiya whispered, arching his back this time. "I don't want to fail...."

"Oh, you always do fine," Ted dismissed, nibbling him.

"Because I study," Kiya said, pouting and shifting to move away from him. Only Ted rolled Kiya over, straddling him and grabbing his wrists. "Ted," Kiya gasped, trying to pull his hands away. He usually loved when Ted did this, but he was getting annoyed.

Ted pinned Kiya's hands above his head and began rubbing his cock against Kiya through both their pants. Kiya whimpered quietly, hating when Ted ignored what he said. And it wasn't just then, it was all the time. This wasn't the first time he was studying when Ted came in and proceeded to pull him away from his work to fuck him, despite the protests. Ted shifted his grip so that he was holding Kiya's wrists with one hand, his other reaching down to cup Kiya's crotch.

"Why don't you listen?" Kiya moaned, his hips rising automatically.

"I know you want it," Ted said smugly, squeezing Kiya's already hardening cock.

"Doesn't matter." Kiya bit his lip harder, his hips jerking when Ted curled his fingers around the elastic waistband of Kiya's pants and yanked them down over his hips, exposing him. Kiya tried to close his legs and tug harder, to pull his wrists away. "Ted, you should just stop when I say so, no matter how hard I get," he said.

Ted didn't let go, but stripped the sweatpants off Kiya. "Don't give me that," he insisted, fingers wrapping around Kiya's erection.

Kiya was about to reply, but it turned into a shudder, and he began moaning softly. Ted smiled, stroking him as he pressed a knee between Kiya's legs. Kiya tried his best to keep them closed, not wanting to give in.

"Come on, baby," Ted said, leaning in to kiss Kiya as he continued to stroke him.

"Don't 'baby' me," Kiya whispered, but his legs slowly started to open as the other man continued to stroke him and Ted kept kissing him, nudging open Kiya's thighs with his knee.

"Don't like you sometimes," Kiya felt the need to mumble, his legs completely open now.

"Mmm," Ted hummed, sounding unconvinced. He released Kiya's wrists and drew his fingertips down the underside of his arm. Kiya didn't move away, aroused and figuring it would be quicker to just give in than fight now.

Ted licked and sucked his way down Kiya's jaw to his neck, nipping, and then moved his hand below, trailing down the boy's shaft, over his balls and between his buttocks. "Bring your legs up."

Kiya pulled his legs up to his chest, sliding his hands behind his knees to keep them up. Ted's fingers were already a little slick from Kiya's pre-come and he rubbed them against Kiya's opening as he sucked hard on his neck.

"Fuck," Kiya gasped, his head falling to the side as he tried to press down on the fingers, his own fingers digging into his skin.

"Yes," Ted groaned against him as he pressed a finger inside Kiya.

Kiya clenched around the finger and pressed down on it further. wanting more already. He tried not to think about how easily he gave in, blaming it on how good Ted was at this. Ted did know how to touch him, how to move his fingers until he found that spot and made Kiya moan for more. It wasn't long until he had stretched him. Then Ted withdrew his fingers, positioning his cock head against that quivering hole.

Kiya had waited for Ted to lean over the side of the bed for a condom, but when it didn't happen, he leaned up slightly. "Ted, condom," he said, giving him a strange look. The man really should have known that by now. But Ted rubbed the slick blunt head against Kiya, not even acknowledging him as he began to push inside.

"Ted!" Kiya hissed, trying to shift back off his cock. His folded position gave him little leverage; Kiya could only wriggle slightly and stare at Ted in shock.

"Relax," Ted told him, holding on to Kiya's shoulder as he pressed again.

"You need a condom," Kiya said, clenching as tightly as he could to try and force him out. He hadn't done it without a condom since he had left Ricky. He had promised his mother that he would never do it without one again. Even though Kiya had known Ted for a while now, who knew what he was hiding. He had never claimed to have a clean past and Kiya had no way of knowing if Ted had even had himself tested.

"Shhh, Kiya, you're mine now, it's not a problem," Ted insisted, then pressed his lips over Kiya's, one hand gripping Kiya's hip as he pushed in more.

"But ..." The rest of Kiya's words were muffled when he was

kissed. He squeezed his eyes shut against the tears that were welling up, feeling his heart beat faster at just the thought of getting something from this. He would never forgive himself if that happened. Ted's tongue thrust into Kiya's mouth even as he thrust his cock the rest of the way inside Kiya.

"Ted," Kiya whimpered against his lips, feeling the spark of pleasure, but he still felt the underlying guilt of what he was letting happen. He never imagined he would find himself experiencing this again; it reminded Kiya of the helplessness he felt with Ricky.

"Kiya," Ted whispered back, "you feel so good." He began to move then, pulling back a few inches and then thrusting inside again.

Kiya wanted to say the same, too. He had figured that someday they'd do it without a condom, but he wanted that to be special. He didn't want it to happen because Ted basically forced him to without talking about it first. Instead of replying, he blinked away tears, trying to enjoy it.

"Yes, baby," Ted encouraged, seemingly oblivious to Kiya's distress, despite his tears.

Kiya had to take deep breaths so that he wouldn't panic like he wanted to, his body shuddering each time Ted pressed inside of him again. "Come outside of me?" he asked after a moment, hoping that would lessen the risk.

"You're mine and you'll never belong to anyone else, Kiya," Ted answered, kissing Kiya's chin as he rocked in and out of him.

Kiya eventually started to relax and just let Ted do what he wanted, moving with him as his moans increased in volume again. The pleasurable feelings had Kiya hating himself more each time he arched into the thrusts while the reality of what was happening slowly destroyed any feelings he had for Ted. It wasn't until he started to get closer that he started to panic again, thinking of Ted coming inside of him. Kiya wished he trusted Ted enough, but he just didn't. He couldn't. Which made him wonder why he was even in this relationship. Kiya was sure he could have just about anyone he wanted, and yet here he was with someone who did what they pleased with him and didn't even listen. Why?

He could tell Ted was getting closer, the man's fingers on Kiya's hip and shoulder grew tighter and his thrusts more erratic. Kiya shuddered and came quite suddenly after a particularly hard thrust. He bit his lip and refused to say Ted's name. That would have been the final humiliation.

Ted was groaning as Kiya moved under him, thrusting hard and fast, holding tighter. "Yes, baby!" he moaned as he came.

Kiya had hoped he'd pull out, but he felt the rush of warmth inside of him and it only made his eyes well up with tears again. Ted half collapsed atop of him, face against Kiya's neck, breath tickling his neck as Ted panted.

"I told you not to," Kiya whimpered, his bottom lip trembling.

"You worry too much," Ted huffed, one hand trailing up Kiya's body.

"Shut up and get off of me," Kiya huffed in reply, pushing at Ted's shoulders.

Ted didn't move off though, lifting his head to looked at Kiya. "Don't be that way, pretty boy," he chided.

Kiya liked when he used pet names like that, but he didn't want to forgive him just because he did that. "Ted, get off of me!"

Ted sighed and rolled, lying on his back beside him and Kiya got up as quickly as he could and ran to Ted's bathroom, going to start the shower. Ted didn't follow. Kiya stood in the harsh light, feeling Ted's betrayal slowly trickle down the inside of his thighs as he looked at his reflection. Large eyes haunted by fear stared back at him as Kiya tried to understand how he had managed to go down the same road again. Shaking fingers traced lightly over his own features and Kiya wondered what it was about him that deafened others to his pleas to stop. He had no answers and, finally, after what seemed like days, Kiya turned away and ran the water as hot as he dared while steam filled the room, slowly letting him disappear into the fog.

Kiya showered for a long time, trying his best to clean out everything inside of him. He couldn't help but cry while he was in there, feeling as weak as he did years ago when Ricky had used him. He swore to himself he would never be a victim again, but apparently he couldn't even keep that promise. He finally stepped out close to forty-five minutes later, wrapping a towel around his waist and heading back into the room.

Ted had climbed under the covers and looked to be asleep. Kiya wanted to hit him. Instead, he found his own clothes and got dressed, packing up his things when he was done. He was just going to walk out, but instead he stopped, shaking Ted's shoulder to wake him up.

"Mmm, come to bed," Ted said, voice slow and sleepy, one hand gripping Kiya's arm and tugging.

"No," Kiya said, pulling his arm back. "Wake up, I want you to hear this."

"And I want you to come to bed," Ted insisted, blue eyes blinking up at him. He reached for Kiya again.

Kiya took a step back, shaking his head. "I'm leaving."

Ted rolled his eyes. "Now what's got you pouting?" he asked with irritation in his voice.

"I'm leaving; we're through," Kiya said simply, shaking his head. "I've had enough of your shit."

"You're just tense because of finals," Ted huffed, and lay back again.

"Whatever. Just don't expect me to be back here tomorrow," Kiya said, wanting him to take him seriously for once.

"I know. You have a test," Ted answered, unconcerned.

"Ugh, just stop it!" Kiya yelled, stomping his feet. "Stop assuming that everything I say is a lie or wrong. You never listen to what I have to say! You're not my boyfriend anymore, and that's final. I don't ever want to see you again, and... you know, I don't care anymore if you don't believe me." He turned to leave after that, already dreading the long bus ride back to campus.

On the way, Kiya couldn't stop thinking. He liked Ted, he really did, but he had to admit their relationship was based on sex, and sex alone. And it was great, but he couldn't actually see himself falling in love with Ted at the pace they were going. And love was what he really wanted to find—someone who would love him for who he was and not how he fucked or how good he happened to look. He was glad he had finally figured out that Ted couldn't give him that, but he didn't like that it took him six whole months to pull himself away. Kiya took a deep breath and knew everything would be fine; he was only a freshman, he had time to find someone who might care about him more than they cared about themselves. Kiya blinked back tears as he made a wish for love.

Made in the USA
Lexington, KY
03 February 2011